PRAISE FOR REBECCA ZANETTI'S NOVELS

TOTAL SURRENDER

"Top Pick! 4½ stars! Bravo and thanks to Zanetti for providing stellar entertainment!" —RT Book Reviews

"*Total Surrender* is action packed, thrilling, and heart-stopping romantic suspense at its best." —HarlequinJunkie.com

"*Total Surrender* is in a word…WOW!" —Fresh Fiction

"Brava on a book (and a series) beautifully imagined and artfully delivered!" —GraveTells.com

BLIND FAITH

"Fast paced, suspenseful…an action-packed journey!…This is a unique, intriguing series, and *Blind Faith* is another book you won't be able to put down." —HarlequinJunkie.com

"I loved the writing. I loved the plot…Zanetti is one hell of a writer." —Melimel.Booklikes.com

"Top Pick! 4½ stars! Hang on as Zanetti whisks you into a world of danger, passion, and treachery!" —RT Book Reviews

"A great installment in the series. Everything was upped; the tension, the stakes, the angst, the romance, and of course the shrinking timeline for the Dean brothers' chance at survival…I give *Blind Faith* an A." —TheBookPushers.com

"This book totally rocked. It had me at the edge of my seat and I was totally engrossed in it from beginning to end."

—GuiltyPleasuresBookReviews.com

SWEET REVENGE

"4½ stars! Top Pick! Intense and thrilling...Filled with twists and turns and a heaping dose of adrenaline, Zanetti takes readers on a ride they won't soon forget!" —*RT Book Reviews*

"Kudos to Ms. Zanetti on another fine Sins Brothers installment, definitely a series to watch!" —GraveTells.com

"If you love action-packed, steamy romantic suspense with sexy alpha heroes, definitely give this series a try—it's one of my new favorites and has gone on my auto-buy list."

—RamblingsfromthisChick.blogspot.com

"*Sweet Revenge* is like a locomotive barreling at you at full throttle! With amazingly well-developed characters, the romantic tension, and a plot so full of subplots, this escape from reality is one of those books that you keep saying just one more page...just one more page...until it's 3 a.m. and there are no more pages left!"

—TomeTender.blogspot.com

"The magic Zanetti creates when she puts pen to paper results in my kinda romance. The basis of the Sins Brothers series is one that captivates the reader; it's fresh, unique, and I absolutely love it!"

—KTBookReviews.blogspot.com

FORGOTTEN SINS

"4½ stars! Top Pick! The rich world of romantic suspense gets even better with the first in Zanetti's tremendous new paranormal-edged series…[A] rapidly paced, clever thriller…Zanetti pulls together a heady mix of sexy sizzle, emotional punch, and high-stakes danger in this truly outstanding tale. Brava!"
                                              —*RT Book Reviews*

"[Zanetti is] an auto-buy author for me…Her world and characters captivated me, and she has maintained her grasp across three different romance subgenres. *Forgotten Sins* was no exception."
                                              —TheBookPushers.com

"Lord, I loved this book. From the first page to the last, this one left me trying to catch my breath after each action-packed page…Zanetti will always be a fixture on this reader's bookshelf!"
                                              —Ramblings from a Chaotic Mind
                                              (nikkibrandyberry.wordpress.com)

ALSO BY REBECCA ZANETTI

SIN BROTHERS SERIES

Forgotten Sins

Sweet Revenge

Blind Faith

Total Surrender

DEADLY SILENCE

REBECCA ZANETTI

FOREVER

New York   Boston

Copyright © 2016 by Rebecca Zanetti
Excerpt from *Lethal Lies* copyright © 2016 by Rebecca Zanetti

Cover design by Brian Lemus. Royalty Free Images from Getty Images.
Cover copyright © 2016 by Hachette Book Group, Inc.

Forever
Hachette Book Group
1290 Avenue of the Americas, New York, NY 10104
forever-romance.com
twitter.com/foreverromance

First Edition: October 2016

Forever is an imprint of Grand Central Publishing. The Forever name and logo are trademarks of Hachette Book Group, Inc.

The publisher is not responsible for websites (or their content) that are not owned by the publisher.

The Hachette Speakers Bureau provides a wide range of authors for speaking events. To find out more, go to www.hachettespeakersbureau.com or call (866) 376-6591.

Library of Congress Control Number: 2016943215

ISBNs: 978-1-4555-9425-2 (paperback), 978-1-4555-9426-9 (ebook)

Printed in the United States of America

RRD-C

10 9 8 7 6 5 4 3 2 1

This one is for my editor, Michele Bidelspach, who finds a way with each book to bring out the good stuff, probably by writing "more emotion here" three billion times during edits. Thank you for the hard work and insights! I'm a much better writer because I have the good fortune to work with you, and I'm very thankful you're in my life.

Acknowledgments

I'm delighted we are writing a spin-off series for those Sin Brothers, and I hope readers enjoy this new band of lost and wounded men. This series found a wonderful home with Grand Central Forever, and I'm grateful for the opportunity to work with so many wonderful, talented, and hardworking people.

Thanks to Michele Bidelspach, Beth de Guzman, Amy Pierpont, Leah Hultenschmidt, Jodi Rosoff, Michelle Cashman, Elizabeth Turner, and Kallie Shimek from Grand Central Forever for the hard work, and thanks to Dianna Stirpe for the awesome copy edits.

A big thank you to my agent, Caitlin Blasdell, who does an amazing job across the board. Thanks also to Liza Dawson and the Dawson gang for the hard work and support.

Thanks to Jillian Stein, Minga Portillo, Marquina Lliev, Rebecca's Rebels, Writerspace, and Fresh Fiction for getting the word out about the books.

Thanks also to my constant support system: Gail and Jim English, Debbie and Travis Smith, Stephanie and Don West, Brandie and Mike Chapman, Jessica and Jonah Namson, and Kathy and Herb Zanetti.

Finally, thank you to Big Tone for being Big Tone. I love you. Also, thanks to Gabe and Karlina for being such great kids. I love you both!

DEADLY
SILENCE

PROLOGUE

Twenty years ago

Ryker never figured he'd find sunshine in hell. He looked up at the shining ball in the too-blue sky. How could it be warm and sunny here? At twelve years old, after spending most of his life in a series of orphanages with a few foster homes thrown in, he knew hell was more of an abstract idea than an actual place.

Some people just ended up there and stayed.

Sure, some of the foster homes had been nice, but he'd been ripped out of those quickly. He'd escaped from the other ones and ended up back in orphanages.

But this place. Oh, this place was something special. Whatever he'd done in a past life to deserve this must've been really bad. A dark need to fight back, to hurt the adults running his life, slithered inside him, and it wasn't the first time, so he probably deserved hell.

But something told him the younger kid fighting the three bullies on the edge of the dirt field didn't deserve this beat down. Or maybe Ryker was just tired of the wrong guys winning every time. North Carolina sun shone down, pretty but not strong, illuminating the scene as the new kid fought hard and fast. And dirty.

"It's time to step in," Heath said, picking a scab on his chin, his wiry body on full alert.

"He's giving a good fight, and those guys need to know he won't roll over if we're not around," Ryker said, his own hands clenching into fists. "We can't always cover his back."

The second Heath had caught sight of the little guy—another wounded animal for him to save—he'd tried to jump into the fray. Ryker had stopped him with a hand on his arm, promising to save the kid when it was time, trying to see the entire picture at once. His heart raced and the injustice of it all clawed through him, but he had to tamp down raw emotions to survive.

It was a lesson he'd learned early and Heath had yet to figure out.

Ryker and Heath had been best friends for the six months they'd spent in the boys home, facing off against too many bullies to count—kids and adults both. Ryker had been at the home for a month when Heath arrived. The kid instantly tried to save a lost kitten he'd found on the outskirts of the ranch. Seeing Heath take a beating for hiding the kitten made Ryker approach him the next day. He'd never approached anybody, but Heath had needed a friend. Maybe Ryker had, too.

Having Heath at his back kept him from going crazy, and he had to adapt and think things through for them both, so they didn't run on emotion and totally screw up. "Let the kid get in one more good shot."

The new kid—a gangly, dark-haired boy—bit into the neck of one of his older attackers, an asshole named Larry. Larry and his buddies were around sixteen and ruled the boys home when the jerk of an owner wasn't telling everyone what to do. They'd be kicked out soon to go be adults.

The kid dug in, slashing deep with his teeth.

"Jesus." Ryker ran forward and yanked the kid away from the bully. If the kid hurt anybody bad enough to need stitches, Ned Cobb, the owner of the boys home, would beat him to death. Stitches cost money.

Blood poured down Larry's cheek, and he slapped a hand to it. "You're gonna die for that, prick."

Ryker got into his face. Even though he was four years younger, they were the same height, and Ryker filled out his shirt better. Fury threatened to eat him whole. "Leave him alone."

Larry snarled. "You taking on another pet, shit-for-brains?"

Ryker stepped closer, and his hands closed into fists. In a couple of seconds, he wouldn't be able to control his temper, so he let it show in his bluish green eyes. "I really wanna hurt you, Larry."

Sometimes the truth just worked.

Larry blinked twice and then backed away. "You are *so* not worth my time." He turned and headed for the older kids dormitory, and his lackeys followed.

"Denver? You okay?" Ryker asked the kid, noting a bruised lip and swelling black eye. He tried to make his voice gentle, but he really didn't know how.

The kid pivoted and faced him squarely, his shoulders bunched.

Ryker held up a hand. "I don't want to hurt you." Too many people had clearly already hurt the boy, and his tortured eyes probably didn't give the whole story. A part of Ryker, the part he didn't like, wanted to walk away and not look back. Not take responsibility for one more person. Not care about one more person since their chances of surviving stunk. He could barely keep Heath from going off the deep end. What if he couldn't help both Heath and Denver? What if he wasn't smart enough or lost his own temper and things went to shit?

The kid whimpered, barely, and it was that sound that gave Ryker no choice.

Ryker straightened. Heath was right. This kid needed help. They could protect him in a way nobody had ever protected Ryker before he'd met Heath. "I broke into the main office and read your file after you got here yesterday." The kid had been abandoned in Denver as an infant and then had been claimed by a so-called uncle who had problems with booze and anger. However, considering the asshole hadn't even known Denver's real name, if he'd had one, there was some doubt there. That was how Denver earned his name, which seemed to fit him anyway. "Your life has sucked so far."

The boy drew back and then snorted.

Ryker grinned. "Your file says you don't really talk." The file didn't say why Denver didn't talk, and Ryker wasn't sure he wanted to know.

Denver didn't answer.

Fair enough. Talking just got kids hit, anyway. Ryker jerked his head toward their dorm. If they could get Denver there, he could take care of the cut bleeding down his chin. "It's gonna be okay. Oh, it's gonna suck for a while, and that's the truth. But in the end, I promise it'll be okay." He'd save this kid when he and Heath made a break for it. From day one, Ryker was all in or all out, and he didn't know how to be another way. If he gave Denver his friendship, his loyalty, it was forever. Heath had been Ryker's only friend, and if Heath needed to save this kid, then so did Ryker.

A car roared up the dirt driveway.

Ryker's gut clenched as he noticed it was the sheriff's dusty brown car.

"Shit," Heath muttered, kicking the dirt. He pushed back his dirty hair. "We don't have time to run."

"No." Ryker settled his stance, his knees wobbling. The owner of the boys home and the sheriff were brothers, which explained why they both liked to hit so much. "Denver? If the sheriff gets out and starts swinging, get behind me, okay?" The kid had already taken one beating, and the sheriff was known to use his nightstick on rib cages.

Denver didn't answer.

The car came to a stop, and Sheriff Cobb jumped out. The sheriff was in his midtwenties with way-too-light blond hair and blue eyes colder than a glacier. Probably. Ryker hadn't ever seen a glacier, but it was the coldest thing he could imagine.

The passenger door opened. "Dr. Daniels," Ryker said, watching the woman carefully, his sides cramping. The urge to run away was overwhelming, but he kept his body visually relaxed. "Here for more tests, ma'am?" He'd been impolite to her once by refusing to take one more damn written test after a long day, and the sheriff had made sure he couldn't walk for about a week without puking up blood. Ned Cobb had watched the beat down with a smile on his face, interjecting only once to remind his brother not to break anything because medical doctors kept records.

The woman stepped out, her fancy designer dress looking as out of place in the dismal home's terrain as a wild peacock would. She smoothed her long dark hair, and her bright red lips pursed. "Ryker. You've grown three inches, and it's been only a few months."

Her voice purred in a way that made him shuffle his feet. It was like she was seeing him differently somehow, and he didn't understand his reaction, but he knew he didn't like it.

Why was she always making Heath and him take written and physical tests? She paid no attention to the other kids at the home.

Then her gaze, a dark blue one, turned to Denver. "I'm here to welcome Denver to the boys home as well as study him a little. Denver, your file says you have a case of selective mutism."

Ah shit. Another test subject? Why them? Ryker glanced at the kid, who'd sidled closer to him. The kid had good instincts to be wary of the calculating woman. "What's that?" Ryker asked.

"He doesn't talk," Heath whispered.

Ryker bit his tongue. No shit. But they had to hide their brains around the lady who had them take so many tests. Why, he didn't know. But his instincts were usually good, too.

"I can make him talk," Sheriff Cobb said, striding around the car and flexing his chest muscles.

Denver swallowed audibly.

"Oh, Elton, that won't be necessary," Sylvia Daniels said, clasping her hands together. "I'm sure I can get Denver to speak. Right, boy?"

Ryker eyed the gun at the sheriff's hip.

Sheriff Cobb's lips peeled back. "Try it, kid. Please."

Ryker didn't answer, but he met the cop's stare evenly. Cobb was just another bully in a world full of them, and someday they were gonna meet on even ground.

When that day came, only one of them would walk away.

Ryker glanced at Heath and then at Denver. His chest heated and cooled. The only way they'd survive this was if he remained calm and used his head, never letting his temper take over. When he stopped thinking, he was as bad as the sheriff, and now with Heath and Denver counting on him, he had more to lose than Sheriff Cobb did. That had to count for something, right?

CHAPTER 1

Present day

Zara Remington brushed a stray tendril of her thick hair back from her face before checking on the lasagna. The cheese bubbled up through the noodles while the scent of the garlic bread in the oven warmer filled the country-style kitchen. Perfect. She shut the oven door and glanced at the clock. Five minutes.

He'd be there in *five minutes*.

It had been weeks since she'd seen him, and her body was ready and primed for a tussle. *Just a tussle*. Shaking herself, she repeated the mantra she'd coined since meeting him two months ago: Temporary. They were temporary and just for fun. This was her reward for working so hard: a walk on the wild side. Even if she was the type to settle down and devote herself to one man, it wouldn't be this one.

Ryker Jones kept one foot out the door, even while naked in her bed doing things to her that were illegal in the Southern states. Good damn thing she lived in Cisco. Wyoming didn't care what folks did behind closed doors. Thank God.

She hummed and eyed the red high heels waiting by the entry to the living room. They probably wouldn't last on her feet for long, but she'd greet him wearing them. While she still wore the black pencil skirt and gray silk shirt she'd donned for work, upon reading his text that he was back in town, she'd rushed to change into a scarlet bra and G-string set that matched the shoes before putting her clothes back into place.

If she was living out a fantasy, he should get one, too. The guy didn't have to know she'd worn granny-style Spanx panties and a thin cotton bra all day.

A roar of motorcycle pipes echoed down her quiet street. Tingles exploded in her abdomen. Hurrying for the shoes, she bit back a wince upon slipping her feet in. The little kitten heels she'd worn to work had been much more comfortable.

A minute passed and the pipes silenced.

She drew air in through her nose, counted to five, and exhaled. Calm down. Geez. She really needed to relax. The sharp rap on her front door sent her system into overdrive again.

Straightening her shoulders, she tried to balance in the heels as she passed her comfortable sofa set, the shoes clicking on the polished hardwood floor. She had to wipe her hands down her skirt before twisting the nob and opening the door. "Ryker," she breathed.

He didn't smile. Instead, his bluish green eyes darkened as his gaze raked her from head to toe…and back up. "I've missed you." The low rumble of his voice, just as dangerous as the motorcycle pipes, licked right where his gaze had been.

She nodded, her throat closing. He was every vision of a badass bad boy she'd ever fantasized about. His thick black hair curled over the collar of a battered leather jacket that covered a broad, well-muscled chest. Long legs, encased in faded jeans, led to motorcycle boots. His face had been shaped with strong lines and powerful strokes, and a shadow lined his cut jaw. But those eyes. Greenish blue and fierce, they changed shades with his mood.

As she watched, those odd eyes narrowed. "What the fuck?"

She self-consciously fingered the slash of a bruise across her right cheekbone. Cover-up had concealed it well enough all day, but leave it to Ryker to notice. He didn't miss anything. God, that intrigued her. His vision was oddly sharp, and once he'd mentioned hearing an argument several doors down. She hadn't heard a thing. "It's nothing." She stepped back to allow him entrance. "I have a lasagna cooking."

He moved into her, heat and his scent of forest and leather brushing across her skin. One knuckle gently ran across the bruise. "Who hit you?" The tone held an edge of something dark.

She shut the door and moved away from his touch. "What? Who says somebody hit me?" Turning on the heels and barely keeping from landing on her butt, she walked toward the kitchen, remembering to sway her hips before making it past the couch. "I have to get dinner out or it'll burn." She kept several frozen dishes ready to go, not knowing when he'd be back in town. The domestication worked well for them both, and she liked cooking for him. Enjoyed taking care of him like that...for this brief affair, or whatever it was. "I hope you haven't eaten."

"You know I haven't." He stopped inside the kitchen. "Zara."

She gave an involuntary shiver from his low tone and drew the lasagna from the oven and bread from the warmer before turning around to see him lounging against the doorjamb. "Isn't this when you pour wine?" Her heart fluttered at seeing the contrast between her pretty butter yellow cabinets and the deadly rebel calmly watching her. "I have the beer you like."

"You always have the beer I like." He didn't move a muscle, and this time a warning threaded through his words in a tone like gravel crumbling in a crusher. "I asked you a question."

She forced a smile and carried the dishes to the breakfast nook, which she'd already set with her favorite Apple-patterned dinnerware and bright aqua linens. "And I asked you one." Trying to ignore the tension vibrating from him, she grasped a lighter for the candles.

A hand on her arm spun her around. She hadn't heard him move. How did he do that?

He leaned in. "Then I'll answer yours. I know what a woman looks like who's been hit. I know by the color and slant of that bruise how much force was used, how tall the guy was, and which hand he used. What I don't know...is the name of the fucker. Yet."

"How do you know all of that?" she whispered.

He lifted his head, withdrawing. "I just do."

There it was. He'd share his body and nothing else with her. She didn't even know where he lived when he wasn't on a case. From day one he'd been clear that this wasn't forever, that he wasn't interested in a future. Neither was she. He was her first purely physical affair, and that's why he could mind his own business. "Bully for you." She shoved past him for the wine waiting on the counter and twisted in the corkscrew with a little more force than was necessary. Why was he changing the game on her?

"Are you seeing somebody else?"

She stilled. Hurt, surprising in its sharpness, cut through her. "No." Yanking out the cork, she turned to face him. "We said we'd be exclusive for however long we, ah, saw each other."

He rubbed the scruff on his chin, studying her. "Part of exclusivity means nobody hurts what's mine."

She blinked twice at the possessive language. "I think we both know I'm not yours." What was going on with him? She studied him closer. Lines fanned out from his eyes, and a tenseness lived in his broad shoulders. "Are you okay?"

Without moving, he seemed to withdraw. "Yes. Been on a case."

"Is it finished?"

"No." A vein stood out along his tough-guy neck.

Ah. Ryker was a private detective who specialized in finding the hard to find. "Want to talk about it?"

"No."

Yeah, she'd figured. "Then let's relax." She poured two glasses of Cabernet and took a seat, carefully unfolding her napkin. Her toes ached in the sexy shoes, and for the first time, she wondered if all the effort was worth it. "We can have a nice dinner."

Slowly, he shrugged out of his jacket and draped it on his chair, drawing the chair out to sit, his movements controlled and with a hint of something...violent.

Her breath caught, and she filled their plates.

"I like your hair down," he rumbled, reaching for his napkin.

"Yet I kept it up," she said primly. They were on even footing. This was casual, and apparently they both needed a quick reminder. Sitting back, she took a deep drink of the potent brew, almost humming when it warmed her stomach.

He lifted his chin, amusement partially banishing the irritation in his eyes. "Have I done something to piss you off?"

Her gaze dropped to the food. "No." She wasn't being fair. Her law firm had hired him as a private investigator on a case, and one night after going through files together and drinking way too much beer, they'd ended up in bed for the most fantastic night of her life. He'd made it clear it was just temporary, *they* were just casual, and she'd agreed with her eyes wide open, meeting up whenever he was back in town. "You haven't done anything."

"Then why won't you tell me who hurt you?"

She sighed, her gaze meeting his. "Because that's not what we have."

"Oh?" One eyebrow drew up. "What do we have?"

She snorted and then caught herself, embarrassed. "We have this." She gestured toward the food. "And sex. That's all. Food and sex." He'd never proclaimed to be a knight in shining armor, especially hers, so why all the questions? "My everyday life doesn't include you.

You're a fantasy who shows up periodically for fun, and then you're gone. Stop acting like you're more."

If the words affected him in any way, he didn't show it. Instead, he reached for his wine, his gaze holding hers like a lion watching a doe, and drank down the entire glass. Setting it aside, he tossed his napkin on the table. "Are you hungry?"

"Not even a little bit." She was more out of sorts than she'd thought.

"Good." He pushed back from the table, stood, and moved toward her. "This is a conversation better had where I can touch you." Dipping his shoulder, he lifted her in corded arms.

She yelped and grabbed his chest for balance. "What are you doing?" she whispered. How was he so strong? Even for a healthy guy who worked out, his strength was somehow beyond the norm. Fluid and natural.

He turned, grabbed his jacket, and strode for the living room, dropping onto her couch and setting those thick boots on her glass coffee table. The jacket had landed next to him. One arm remained beneath her knees and the other around her shoulders, easily cradling her against his rock-hard chest. His lips snapped over her jugular with just enough force to make her jump.

Then, clearly indulging himself, he tugged the clip from her hair, which cascaded down. Burying his face in the mass of dark curls, he breathed in. "I love your hair."

She tried to perch primly on his lap and not snuggle right into him. His strength was as much of a draw as his passion. "What conversation did you want to have?"

He leaned back and waited until she'd turned her head to face him. "We agreed to keep this casual."

"I know." She played with a loose thread on his dark T-shirt.

"Then you started cooking me dinner."

She blinked. "I like to cook."

"Then you started keeping my beer on hand and lighting candles with every meal."

She shrugged. "Candles create nice light that helps with digestion." Could she sound like any more of a dork?

"Right." He played idly with her hair, heat from his body keeping her toasty warm.

Flutters awakened again throughout her body, and her nipples hardened. Good thing the bright red bra had plenty of padding. She tried to shift her weight, not surprised when he kept her easily in place. "I have not asked you for anything," she murmured, panic beginning to take hold.

"I like that about you." He punctuated the words with a tug on her hair. "In fact, I like you."

"I like you, too." The words went unsaid, but that's all they had, and that's all they were. It was an adventure, and she was truly enjoying the ride. She knew where they stood. "Stop playing with me."

"I'm not playing." His gaze dropped to her lips right before he leaned in to rest his mouth over hers.

Liquid fire shot from her chest to her sex.

He nibbled on her bottom lip, kissed the corners of her mouth, lightly whispering against her. "This is playing." The hand in her hair twisted, drawing back her head and elongating her neck. "This is not." He swooped in, angled his mouth over hers, and took. Deep and hard, he kissed her, his mouth alone having enough power to drive her head back against his palm.

Hunger slammed through her, and she moaned low in her throat. Pleasure swamped her, head to toe, vibrating in waves as she kissed him back. Her nails dug into his chest, and she tried to move closer into him. He controlled the kiss, taking her deeper, his erection easily discernible beneath her butt.

Finally, he lifted his head, his eyes the color of a rocky riverbed beneath a stormy sky. "Who hit you?"

The simple words struck like a splash of cold water in the face. Shock dropped her mouth open. Had he been trying to manipulate her by kissing her like that? Sure, he'd been passionate with her many times, but something felt different. A wildness she'd always sensed in him seemed to be breaking free. "Forget you." Slamming her hand against his chest, she shoved off his lap.

"Zara." One word, perfectly controlled. He held up a hand, showing a long scar across his love line. One that he'd never explained, even when she'd asked nicely.

Her knees shook, but she backed away until her shoulders hit the fireplace mantel. Anger and panic welled up in her, and she couldn't separate them and think, so she just spoke. "Unless we're eating or screwing, my life is none of your business." She was trying hard to keep her sanity and *so* did not need mixed signals from him. He didn't get to act like he really cared—not that way. "Got it?"

He stood, towering over her even from several feet away. "That may be true, but no way am I going to let anybody harm the woman I'm fuckin'."

Fuckin'. Yeah, that's exactly what they were doing. She was so out of her depth, she'd lost sight of the shore miles ago. "Stay in your own compartment, Ryker. My business is my own, and you're not to get involved."

For the first time, anger sizzled across his features. "Be careful what you say, little girl. I'll make you eat those words."

She blinked. Sure, he'd been commanding in bed...a lot. But outside the bedroom, she'd never seen this side of him. "Don't threaten me."

"Then don't be obtuse. If you think I'm going to allow a man who hit you to keep walking, you've lost your damn mind." He put both hands on his fit hips, looking like a pissed-off warrior about to bellow a battle cry. "We may be casual, but even I have limits. A woman who cries on my shoulder after watching a stupid movie with dogs is someone who should never be harmed."

She gasped. "It wasn't stupid." It was sad when Juniper had died, darn it.

"Yeah. It was one of the dumbest movies ever made, and you turned into my shoulder to cry it out." He took a step toward her. "You don't want to mess with me on this. Trust me. Just give me the name, and tell me what's going on." Another step.

She couldn't back up any more or she'd be in the fireplace. So she held out a hand. Panic cramped her stomach, and she sucked in air and tried for anger. There it was. "I created a situation, there was an issue, and I've taken care of it." The truth would change his opinion of her, and she kind of enjoyed the view from the pedestal he temporarily had her on.

"No way did you create any situation that resulted in violence." The tone was almost mocking.

"That's it. You don't know me." Her chin lifted.

Something too dark to be amusement lifted his lips. "Oh, don't I?"

"No, you don't." Steam should be coming out of her ears. She reached down and plucked a high heel off. It was time to stop pretending to be somebody she just was *not*. "I don't like these, and I sure as shit don't walk around at work in them." Her tone was two octaves higher than normal, and she couldn't help it. Angling back, she threw the shoe at his head.

With lightning-quick reflexes, he grabbed the strap before the shoe took out his eye. "Zara." The tone was low and controlled...like always.

"You wouldn't like the real me." She kicked off the other shoe, her mind buzzing and her temper flying free. Reaching under her skirt, she yanked off the G-string underwear that had been shoved up her butt, her legs wobbling when she pulled them down and over her feet. "*Nobody* likes these." She flung it at his head. "I only wear them for you."

He snatched the flimsy material with one finger, his cheek creasing.

She fought the urge to stomp her foot and look like an idiot. He wasn't getting it. "I don't even know where you live," she yelled.

His phone buzzed, and he held up a hand. "Put the tantrum on hold, just for a second." Drawing the phone out, he read the screen. Both his eyebrows drew down, and he lifted the phone to his ear. "We've had movement?" Then he held still. His jaw hardened even more. "Damn it. Okay, I'm going." He paused, and his eyes darkened. "Because you just got shot. It's my turn to go, and I'll be right there." He shoved his phone back into his pocket.

Her breath heated. "Who got shot?"

"My brother."

Ryker had a brother?

He took several steps forward to grasp her neck.

She stilled. He'd never grabbed her neck before. Sure, his hold was gentle, but his hand was *wrapped around her neck*. "What are you doing?" she squeaked.

He leaned in, pressing just enough to show his strength. "I know you don't wear shoes like that at work, and I know the underwear set is just for me. I like that." He pressed a hard kiss to her mouth before drawing away. "I have to go, or I'd stay until we reached an agreement tonight. That bruise on your face offends me, and I'm done coddling you about it. You've got until tomorrow morning to give me the name of the guy who hit you, so I can have a conversation with him."

Ryker released her to grab his jacket and stride for the front door.

"Or what?" she asked, her voice trembling.

He opened the door and paused, looking back at her. "Or I'll find him myself and take him out for good." He yanked on his jacket, looking exactly like the badass rambling man he was. "And Zara? About where I live?"

"Yeah?"

"I moved permanently to Cisco a week ago."

CHAPTER 2

Life didn't make any damn sense. Ryker leaned back against a tree and ignored the pounding rain. Blue and red lights swirled through the darkness as FBI techs hustled around the secured vacant land north of Salt Lake City, looking for evidence that wouldn't be there. This killer was too good to leave evidence.

Being this close to any law personnel gave Ryker a gut ache, but he didn't have a choice. At least his disguise wouldn't reveal his true identity, although to the best of his knowledge, the FBI wasn't after him. Yet.

Two guys wearing jackets emblazoned with yellow FBI letters finished setting up a tent to protect the body from the elements.

Ryker had caught a glimpse of the girl's matted red hair but hadn't gotten close enough to see her face yet. But he knew. Yeah. The body was Maisey Misopy, and he was too late again. The idea of some psycho hurting the innocent plunged him right back into his childhood, and he had to fight to keep in control of himself when all he wanted to do was punch the nearest tree.

Why did people with loved ones get killed while a guy like him, who for so long hadn't had anybody, still walked the earth?

"How the hell did you get the news?" asked an irritated female voice from his left.

He turned to see Special Agent Loretta Jackson stepping gingerly over broken bottles and what appeared to be a dead possum. "Connections," he said easily, raising his voice a few octaves to mask his normal tone.

She came to a halt, her battered brown boots sinking into newly forming mud. In her midthirties, she had deep brown eyes, very curly brown hair, and full lips that belonged on a supermodel, not a cop. "The family hired you."

"No." He smoothed down his nondescript paisley tie, which coordinated perfectly with his boring brown suit. Padding gave him a beer belly, and high-end costumery gave him a beard and mustache. Add brown contacts and a blond wig, and even the sharp-eyed agent wouldn't be able to draw a true picture of him. "My agency is going to keep working this until the guy is caught, whether we're paid or not."

The family of the fourth victim had hired them two months ago, and they'd failed to bring her back home alive. Yet another person Ryker had let down.

Jackson looked around him, spotting his rented Taurus on the deserted county road. "You're solo this time?"

"Yes." Usually Heath handled the crime scenes, but he'd been getting too emotionally close to the case, so Ryker had stepped up. "Can I see the body?"

She zipped up her dark jacket. "Sure. Tell me how you knew about the body, and I'll let you see it."

"We have an alert out for any suspicious deaths of young females in the western states," he said, giving her the truth and biting back his frustration. "When the hikers discovered this body and the local sheriff called you in, we were notified, and here I am."

"There's something not quite right about you guys, and I'll figure it out after I catch this maniac." She pushed wet hair away from her face. "If I insist on seeing your license for the state of Utah, you'll say you don't have it with you, right?"

"Yes." He smiled beneath the fake beard. "Then we'll send you copies of the license after I get back to the office." They'd have no trouble once again faking credentials by copying authentic ones and backdating them in computer systems. Thank God Denver was so good with computers. "I'll have my office send you our Utah credentials."

"I'd appreciate that." She looked toward the white tent, her shoulders slumping. "All right, one peek."

He kept the surprise off his face as he followed her across the uneven ground toward the tent. Mountains rose in the distance, silent observers of man's worst, and he fought a shiver.

As they reached the tent, he tugged up the flap and let her enter first.

The eighteen-year-old girl lay on her side, blood matting her hair to the right side of her face. In death, her pretty blue eyes were closed, but bruises marched down her face. Somebody had placed a sheet over her, and part of the potato sack she'd been dressed in peeked out the side.

The smell of death hadn't permeated the tent yet, but it would. His stomach clenched, and he dropped to his haunches next to the body. His chest ached. "God, she was young."

Jackson nodded and reached a gloved hand to tug the sheet down. "Just turned eighteen. Dressed in burlap, like the others, and..." Pulling farther, she revealed the knife marks in the upper chest that said MINE.

Ryker sucked in air. The gouges were deep and bloody, showing the bastard had cut her while she was alive. "Sexual assault?"

"Looks like it. We'll know more after we get her to the coroner's." Jackson settled the sheet back in place, her voice sober, her hands shaking.

Ryker wondered why she'd taken such a heartbreaking job.

Instinct whispered the agent had some serious shit in her background.

He wanted to smooth the bloody hair back from the dead girl, to get it off her face, but he knew better than to touch something in a crime scene. "She loved playing the piano," he murmured, forgetting to alter his voice. He'd even watched a couple of recitals from her grade school years, where she'd worn pigtails and a pretty white dress. The pain of her loved ones at losing her like this must be indescribable. "She was adorable."

"I know," Jackson said softly. "Did you know she volunteered at the local animal pound twice a week?"

Ryker nodded, his chest compressing. Emotion swirled through him, and he couldn't quite grasp the anger past the grief.

"Seemed like a nice girl." Jackson swayed and then quickly recovered.

Ryker stood in case he needed to catch her, noting her too-pale face and darkening brown eyes. "Why are you working with me?"

She threw up her hands. "This is the seventh case in six months, all family members or close friends of law enforcement personnel, and I'm at the end of my rope." She sighed and looked years older than her probable thirty-five. "You guys have been involved since the first case, your records hold up, and I want you to share any information you get."

He nodded, making a mental note to have Denver shore up their identities and histories a little better, because this woman wouldn't give up until she'd figured them all out. "No problem." The small body on the ground would haunt him forever. "Has her father been notified?"

"Yes."

He couldn't even imagine that type of pain. The girl's father was a bounty hunter who'd raised her by himself. Maisey had been kidnapped from a college in Spokane, held for a week, and then dumped in Utah. The killer tortured the kidnapped victims, which in turn tortured anybody who loved them. It was beyond cruel. He needed to be taken down and brutally. "So far the guy has taken women from Washington, Oregon, North Dakota, Idaho, and Utah."

Jackson nodded. "Yes. If you find any sort of lead, I expect you to give me a call. I have your numbers to find you."

He tugged out a new business card. "We've relocated to Wyoming."

She took the card, her eyebrows rising. "Because of this case?"

"No. It's a nice place, and we need a home base," he lied, wishing he could offer some sort of comfort to the agent. But there was no comfort while the killer still walked. "Keep in touch." Turning on his heel, he left the tent and headed for his car through the rain, which was rapidly turning into freezing snow.

"Ryker?" she called, peering out of the tent. "I don't mind you doing research, but stay out of the line of fire."

He turned back. "We're not looking for the line of fire."

"We both know your choosing Wyoming as a new office base isn't a coincidence." The wind blew rain to cover her pretty face, and she shoved hair out of her eyes. "I want to know what your plan is now."

To get the hell away from the FBI. "I'm heading to the airport and back to work...after drinking a bottle or two of Jack Daniels." Without waiting for an answer, he left the dead girl and his latest failure behind him.

CHAPTER
3

Night, Grams." Zara hung up the phone after a nice call from her grandmother, who was on a seniors trip to various casinos in the Pacific Northwest. So far Grams had won nearly twenty dollars.

The woman was a wild one. Zara grinned. Her grandmother had raised her from the age of ten, and they still talked every day. When Grams was at home in town, they got together for coffee or dinner several times a week. When Zara had told her about buying the uncomfortable G-string to wear for Ryker, she'd laughed her head off.

Zara hummed softly to herself as she finished her once a week routine and slipped into bed. She'd painted her fingernails a pretty pink, her toenails a darker pink, and her face green with an avocado mask. After an early childhood of moving constantly with her flighty mother before Grams had taken her in, she needed a home base, and she'd created a lovely one where she could ground herself in rituals. She loved her beauty regimen almost as much as she needed a good routine.

Did Ryker have any routines?

She stopped humming. No more thinking about Ryker, darn it. The badass kept popping into her head even after nearly a week of no contact. He hadn't shown up, hadn't called, and obviously hadn't thought about her.

Her phone rang, and her breath caught. She fumbled for the light and grabbed her phone, reading the caller ID to see it was her friend Julie, not Ryker. Her shoulders slumped, and she shook her head at her silliness. It wasn't her place to worry about him or whatever case he had left so quickly to work on. Zara kept the disappointment out of her voice as she answered. "Hi, Jules. Everything okay?"

"Everything is fine." Julie sighed. "I was just lonely and thought I'd give you a call."

Zara sat up. "Are you sure you're all right?" They'd been friends for nearly eight years, although they'd lost touch for a while. She didn't have many friends, and Julie was somebody she actually trusted. "You can stay here, you know?" She didn't like the dive motel Julie was shacked up in.

"Jay will look there, and you know it."

"I know. Well, maybe." Zara pushed hair away from her avocado mask. Julie was hiding out in a motel until her divorce from her dickhead of a husband became final. Zara tried to keep her voice gentle without the anger. Julie had faced enough anger from her ex and needed support. "I get paid next week and can help you out some more."

"I hate that. You shouldn't have to loan your money to me." Julie's voice wavered. "I will pay you back."

Zara batted away tears for her hurting friend. "I know. As soon as you get your settlement, you'll be rolling in it." She forced humor into her voice. "Well, if you pass your competency hearing next week."

"Can you believe that? Talk about dirty pool," Julie growled, finally sounding angry and not defeated.

"I know. Your husband is an ass." That he'd convinced a judge that Julie needed a competency evaluation before the divorce could go through was unthinkable. Of course, it was Zara's law firm that was coaching Jay, which made the entire situation even worse. "It'll be okay."

"How's your face?" Julie whispered, her voice cracking.

"I'm fine. Next time teach me not to get in between you and Jay the asshole when you're fighting." Zara almost touched the bruise across her cheekbone but remembered about the avocado. "The bruise is almost gone."

"I'm so sorry," Julie said, choking up. "I don't think he meant to hit you."

Zara shrugged. "I'm not sure, to be honest." Jay had found Julie at another dive motel when Zara had been visiting, and he'd rushed her. Zara had moved between them and taken the hit. "Either way, I wish I could turn him in." But if she did that, she'd get fired for helping the opposition, and she needed her job.

"Once the divorce is final, we'll egg his house."

Zara laughed, her spirits rebounding. "That would be fun. It's a date."

"All right. Enough about me. How's it going with Hottie McHottiness?"

Zara lost the smile, and her shoulders slumped. "I think we're almost over."

Silence ticked for a few seconds. "I'm so sorry to hear that. You've been happier since you've been dating him."

Zara shook her head. "We're not dating. It's casual, which is what we both wanted, but I think it's getting a little odd, you know? We have to either go forward or stop, and neither one of us is willing to go forward."

"Are you sure? He sounds like the total deal."

Zara snorted. "Because he delivers multiple orgasms?"

"Hell yeah."

She laughed again. "I don't know a thing about him. He was here the other night, and he mentioned he had a brother. I didn't even know that." She plucked at a loose thread on the bedspread. If Ryker wanted something serious with her, he would've at least mentioned family.

"Oh. Maybe if you made the effort, he would, too? It's time you stopped holding yourself back. Not all guys will leave like your dad did or die like your mom did." Julie cleared her throat.

Zara breathed out, her mind spinning. "Maybe not, but Ryker's a leaver." No way would the tough private eye be a soccer dad or attend ballet recitals. Zara wanted kids and a stable home someday, and Ryker just didn't fit in that picture. She couldn't think about it any longer. "Anyway, let's concentrate on you."

"For now." Rustling sounded. "All right, get some sleep. And Zara?"

"Yes?" Zara settled down into the pillows.

"I, ah, I could use that loan for a couple of bills when you get paid. I promise I'll pay you back."

Zara reached up and switched off the light, hurting for her proud friend. "Of course. Night."

"Night."

Zara turned over and set the phone on the nightstand. Poor Julie. Her husband had turned into a total prick who liked to hit. Why were so many men assholes? Her own father had disappeared when she was three, and she'd learned at eighteen that he'd died a few years after that in a tractor accident. Who the heck died in a tractor accident?

Her eyelids fluttered closed, and she dreamed about chocolate and rivers before the phone jerked her out of the nice sleep. "Julie?" she mumbled as she answered.

"Um, no," a raspy male voice said. "This is Sal from Sal's? On Sixth?"

She blinked and sat up. The dive bar on the other side of town? "Huh?"

"Sal's Bar. Ryker lost this phone in the fight—"

"Fight?" She flipped on the light, her heart roaring to life. "Is he okay?"

Sal cleared his throat. "Define 'okay.'"

Zara swung her feet to the floor.

"Listen, lady. I found this phone, and your number is the only one on it. Either come down and get him, or I have to call the cops. Enough is enough," Sal muttered.

"I'll be right there. Don't call the cops," she breathed. "Just give me a few minutes."

"You've got ten." The line went dead.

Ryker had been fighting in some bar and she was the only contact on his phone? That seemed like a bad thing. Was he hiding her from somebody? No way was he married. Now she had to pick him up at a bar? Well, didn't that bring back memories of several of her mom's boyfriends? Zara hurriedly dressed in yoga gear and washed the face mask off before pulling her hair into a ponytail. How could her number be the only one on his phone?

A quick glance outside showed a dry but probably cold night. She yanked on tennis shoes and a jacket before heading into the garage. Was this a mistake?

Probably.

The drive through town took fifteen minutes, and she breathed out as she pulled to the curb in front of the dingy bar. A battered Ford was in front of her and a few Harleys behind her. The street was fairly deserted with no police cars. Good.

Jumping out, she hustled through the dark door. Smoke and the smell of tequila hit her a second before she winced at the loud rock coming from a jukebox in the back. Round and scarred tables littered the peanut-shell-covered floor, and at this hour, only a few diehard drunks slouched in chairs. Two broken chairs had been tossed in a corner. A long bar ran the length of the north wall, and a bald man sporting an outrageous mustache wiped down glasses. She moved toward him.

His sober brown eyes raked her. "I'm thinkin' you're Z."

"Z?"

The bartender shrugged. "There's just a Z in the phone contacts."

She tried to make sense of that. "All right. I'm Z."

He handed over a nondescript black phone. "Your man is toward the back. Get him out of here."

Her man? Yeah, right. She swallowed and turned toward a series of booths. They were empty save the last one. Ryker leaned against the wall, his head back, blood on his chin. His eyes were shut and his legs extended beneath the table, showing his motorcycle boots. She hesitated and then approached him slowly, her heart thundering. "Ryker?"

His eyelids flashed open. "Zara?"

She nodded and kept her focus squarely on him. "The bartender called me."

Ryker wiped off his chin, his gaze not quite focusing. "What the fuck?"

"Ah." She faltered. Man, he was big…and drunk. She didn't know him like this, and yet a glimmer of vulnerability showed in the man she would've bet had none. That drew her to him as much as the desire to help him.

His leather jacket was unzipped and showed a large rip in his T-shirt. Blood dotted his jeans from what looked like a violent altercation. What the holy hell was she doing in the bad part of town at midnight? She knew better than to be in such a place, and she didn't know Ryker like this. "The bartender said he was going to call the cops if I didn't come get you."

Ryker shot from the booth, grabbing a worn duffel bag. "No cops." He slung an arm around her shoulder and herded her toward the bar where he slapped down five hundred-dollar bills. "This should cover tonight."

Sal took the money. "Last time, Ryker. Next fight you start, I'm callin' the cops."

Did he fight a lot? That didn't sound like Ryker.

"Whatever." Ryker turned Zara toward the door, leaning heavily on her. He turned back. "There's a fight in the back alley—two guys arguing over a woman named Bernadette. They're too drunk to fight, and somebody's gonna get hurt." He turned back to the door.

"How did you know that?" Zara whispered.

"I can hear them," Ryker mumbled.

Zara turned her head but couldn't hear anything. It wasn't the first time Ryker had heard or seen something that seemed impossible. How were his abilities so fine-tuned?

More important, how drunk was he? She let him stumble them both outside, where a fresh wind pierced her with cold. She shook off the bar's smoke. Taking him home was a bad idea. Not once had she seen him drunk or out of control, and he appeared to be both at the moment. The guy was solid muscle and could easily harm her, although she couldn't imagine Ryker hurting a woman. Even when he'd grasped her neck the other night, it hadn't hurt.

She opened the passenger-side door of her old compact and shoved him in. "I'll take you to wherever you're staying." Without waiting for an answer, she crossed to the driver's side and started the engine. Soft snoring came from the man at her side.

She looked at him. Long, dark lashes lay against his rugged face, and in sleep, he looked no less dangerous than while awake. Tension all but rolled off him, along with a hint of something else. Something…sad. She sighed and brushed his too-long hair away from his cheek. "What am I going to do with you?" she asked softly.

What was it about a wounded man that all but called for her to fix him? To heal him? Wounded tough guys were like catnip to a good girl like her. When he looked at her, when he touched her, she felt special. Ryker didn't look at many people, and he more than likely didn't let anybody see him like this. His draw was dangerous to her heart, and she knew it. "I'm smarter than this," she muttered, swinging the car into the road.

They were halfway home when his voice made her jump.

"She was dead," Ryker murmured, his head back and his eyes closed.

Zara shivered. "Who was dead?"

"The girl. Another one. He got another one, and I can't find him. He enjoys causing them pain, and he has to be stopped. Yet another bully—this one psychotic." Ryker scrubbed both hands down his face. "What day is it?"

"Um, Thursday." She turned down a different road. "Is this a case you're working on?"

"Yeah. For months we've been working on it." His words slurred a little, but she could make them out.

"You and your brother?" she asked softly, feeling like she was walking on cracking ice.

"Brothers," he mumbled. "I have two."

She turned into her driveway and pressed the button to open the garage. Her chest gave a little hitch. "It seems like I should know that about you already." While they hadn't been building a relationship, he could've shared a little about himself. Of course, neither had she. "I have a grandmother."

"I know," he said. "Her name is Patricia Remington, and she lives over on Orchid Street. Is on an old people's trip right now."

She jerked. "How do you know that?"

"I checked you out after the first night." His eyelids opened, and those odd greenish blue eyes homed in on her. "I know who I'm bangin', darlin'."

Words escaped her. Not once had she ever considered herself the type of woman who'd be *banged*. "You're the one who keeps coming back for more," she muttered.

He snorted.

Turning away, she drove into her garage, scrambling for something to say. "Why are you getting into fights in dive bars?"

"The nicer bars are too expensive to fix." He shoved out of the car and strode toward the kitchen door, his usually graceful gait now lurching. Without waiting for her, he moved into the house and dropped his duffel bag on the kitchen table.

She stumbled as she followed him, her mind spinning.

They reached the bedroom, and he started shedding his clothes onto the floor.

Whoa. "What are you doing?" She couldn't help but appreciate his hard chest and cut abs.

"Bed." Remaining in black boxer briefs, he slipped beneath the covers. "Come, Zara."

She blinked. "Wait a minute."

"Tomorrow. Fight tomorrow." He tossed back the covers on the other side of the bed. "In."

She hesitated for a moment. Her rescuing him from the bar seemed to be a line she'd crossed. She'd just helped him, and he had offered to help her with the guy who'd bruised her. They were edging toward taking responsibility for each other. Was she ready for that? With him? How could she decide that when she didn't really know him? Plus, he hadn't called her for help—the bartender had. If she was smart, she'd end this right now.

"Bed, Zara," he mumbled.

She was tired. Maybe a good night's sleep would help—one more night of sleeping next to him. Then she had to do the smart thing. "Fine. But we are *so* talking tomorrow." She turned off the light and quickly slid into bed.

He pulled her against him, her back to his front, and wrapped around her. "You smell good."

She took a deep breath, snuggling into him naturally. She'd miss this. "Go to sleep."

"I like you," he mumbled against her hair. "You're nice and sexy and sweet. You cook."

Her traitorous heart warmed and thumped. "I can see we're at the 'I love you, man' part of the drunken evening." It was good to know he wasn't a mean drunk.

He chuckled and stirred her hair. "And funny. You're funny and sweet."

"You already said 'sweet,'" she murmured, really not wanting to be touched by the kind words, and yet...

"Because you are. I've never met anybody as sweet as you. No woman is as sweet as you." He pulled her closer into his heat, enfolding her in dubious safety. "You should be protected at all costs. They're gonna find me at some point. *He's* going to find me. You can't be there."

"Who?" she asked, her lungs seizing.

His breathing deepened against her, and his body relaxed. "When I was at the end, drinking that last drink, you're the one I wanted to call. Only you." He slipped into sleep.

Her eyes opened in the darkness. What exactly did that mean? He hadn't called her, after all. The bartender had found the phone...the odd one.

For thirty minutes, she tried to sleep. Ryker dropped into a deep booze-induced slumber all around her. Finally, she carefully dislodged his arm and maneuvered from the bed, turning to make sure he didn't awaken.

He slept peacefully, his hair ruffled, his jaw relaxed. One muscled arm was out of the covers, and even in sleep, a sense of power surrounded him.

She had to know more about him and that damn phone, but if he caught her snooping through his belongings, he'd be seriously pissed. The truth seemed important to Ryker, even if he didn't share much of it. While the smart move would be to end things with him, it hurt to think they'd end with anger.

Yet she had to know. The mystery was eating at her.

She tiptoed across the room, closing the door as she passed into the living room. This was so wrong.

Padding on her toes, she made it to the kitchen.

His duffel lay on the table next to the phone the bartender had given her. She reached for it and located the contacts. There was one. Z. Not even her full name. Just a Z. Was this a burner phone? Why would Ryker have a burner phone just for her? The only thing she knew about burner phones was from watching detective shows on television.

She looked at the innocuous bag. Oh, she shouldn't. Yet she reached out and released the zipper.

Clothes. A pair of jeans, a couple of shirts, and some underwear. She rummaged beneath the jeans and found two guns, a knife, and three more phones.

Three phones?

A look at the contacts revealed one in each phone. One for a *D*, one for an *H*, and one that said FBI. Why would he have a burner phone for the FBI? More important, who were D and H? Women in other cities?

Man, she was tempted to dial H and D to see who they were. Instead, she quickly replaced all the contents in the duffel.

She glanced toward the quiet bedroom. Just who the hell was Ryker Jones?

CHAPTER
4

Ryker finished in the shower and drew on his clothing, then walked into Zara's kitchen and stopped short.

She sat at the table with his duffel bag in front of her. "Who are H and D?" Her eyes were guarded and her voice low.

Shit. He shoved wet hair away from his face.

"I went through your stuff. I wasn't going to tell you, but I did, and we're over, so you don't have to tell me, but I still want to know." Her words had run together so quickly it took him a second to make them out.

"We're not over." The statement burst from him before he could think, and heat climbed up his throat. Was that panic? Think. He needed to think. "D and H are Denver and Heath, my brothers. We have burner phones because we're on a case where we don't want to be connected to each other." He couldn't tell her the full truth, and damn if that didn't piss him off.

"Fine. Let's go." She moved toward the garage, and he followed.

The trip back to the bar was made in silence. He wanted to talk to her, but his head felt like a mini war was going on inside of it, and he needed to puke. The hangover had him and bad.

At some point, he needed to really get through to her—when he could concentrate again. Somebody had hit Zara a week ago, and she didn't trust him enough to take care of it.

Not that he could blame her. It wasn't like he'd offered her any sort of relationship. Now she'd said they were done, and a shocking panic had taken hold of him. The idea of not having Zara around, her warmth and kindness, sent him back into that cold he'd been trying to escape since childhood.

Yet what could he offer her? Really? A life on the run, looking over her shoulder? Burner phones? Sick cases with psychopaths winning?

She pulled up next to his motorcycle. "Bye, Ryker."

He grasped her arm, keeping his hold gentle. "It's not good-bye."

She sighed. "I don't understand your life, and after snooping in your bag, I'm uneasy. Worse yet, I'm angry I had to snoop. We made a deal to just have some fun with no hard feelings when it ended. Let's stick to the deal."

The deal was to keep things casual, and yet he felt even that slipping away. "I don't want to stop seeing you. Let's just forget that last week happened and go back to being casual."

She looked at him, temptation in her gaze. Oh, he could read people, and she didn't want to end it, either. "I'm not sure." She flattened her hands on her skirt, her lip twisting. "I've had fun, and I like you, but the burner phones are a huge red flag. Are you wanted by the authorities?"

"I have a phone for the FBI. We're working with them." Truth, but not all of it. He released her. "You have to know, even if we split, I'm going after whoever hit you. It's who I am, and I won't rest until I make sure you're safe." He wanted to be honest with her, but her eyes fired up again, so he slid from the car before his head exploded. "I'll see you later today, and we can discuss us. We're not over." He shut the door, and she sped away from the curb.

He swung his leg over his bike and stroked the engine to life, quickly taking off. Soon he angled toward the edge of town, enjoying the feeling of the Harley Fat Boy beneath him.

Cold air whipped against him, belying the odd fact that no snow dusted the ground in November. It was a record dry season, but snow-fall was coming…He could smell it. Soon he'd have to put the bike away until spring.

Mountains, already clipped with white, rose up all around him like watching sentinels. Snow had fallen to coat the highest peaks finally. He reached the end of a deserted street and parked behind a black 1970 Plymouth Hemi 'Cuda, his mind still on Zara. Heath must already be inside. Ryker swung off the bike and read the newly painted front window: LOST BASTARDS INVESTIGATIVE SERVICES: WE FIND THE LOST. He shook his head.

Heath opened the front door of the weathered brick building that had an underground garage, first floor offices, and second floor apartments. He leaned out, his brown hair scruffier than normal and in contrast with his white dress shirt and blue tie. Tension rolled off him, and lines near his eyes showed he still wasn't sleeping. "Denver did it."

Of course, Denver had done it. "We're probably going to get in trouble with the town." They couldn't have the word *bastard* on the window, could they? "Plus, while I understand the need to be present, there's such a thing as too attention grabbing, and we can't afford that." Their business had been doing just fine the past five years without a permanent location, a website, or advertising.

"Agreed." Heath held the door open for Ryker. "But Denver is nesting like a pregnant chick."

"I heard that," Denver bellowed from his office in the back. Those three words from Denver said a lot more…He wanted the sign to stay.

Heath shook his head.

"Scratch it off when he's not around," Ryker muttered. "We don't want business off the street." Which is why they'd chosen Cisco, Wyoming, for this case. He'd spent enough time in the town to enjoy the mountains and wild weather...and there were several ways out of town if they ever had to run. "Why are you wearing a tie?"

Heath tugged on the garment, loosening the knot. "Got sworn in to practice law in Wyoming today. Just in case and also so we look legit here. Temporarily."

Ah hell. "I missed the ceremony." Ryker leaned against a battered reception counter. "I'm sorry, man."

"I hate ceremonies, so don't worry about it." Shrewd greenish brown eyes took his measure. "You've been in a bottle for days. You out now?"

It had been a lot more than one bottle of Jack. "Yeah. I'm sorry."

Heath clapped him on the back. "We've all been there. This case is killing all of us. It's a tough one."

Tough? Yeah. Finding the vic dead and buried had been more than tough. Sometimes *the lost* were dead. They had to find the fucker killing young women. "I should've been at your deal today."

"Why?" Heath frowned.

Ryker lifted a shoulder. "I don't know. It's what you do, right?" They were family, and he'd die for his brothers. The least he could do was attend a ceremony and be supportive. He wouldn't have had a chance in life without Heath.

"Hell if I know." Heath turned on his motorcycle boots to maneuver by several abandoned chairs. Beyond the reception area, there was a wide, open room with two long tables. To the right lay three offices and a small kitchen. "Let's see what Denver found."

Ryker followed, his temples starting to ache. "Did you wear those boots today at the courthouse?"

"Yeah." Heath stomped into Denver's office. "Why?"

"They don't go with a suit," Ryker said slowly.

Heath moved past a well-polished cherrywood desk to sit in a winged leather chair of dark green. "I wore these pants with a tie. Didn't need a full suit, which is good, because I don't have one."

Shouldn't a lawyer have a suit? "You don't have to act like a lawyer if you don't want to," Ryker said. Heath was always trying to save everyone, and he'd definitely do a job he hated if it helped the agency. Ryker needed to do a better job of making sure Heath didn't lose himself in his drive to fix things. "We don't need a lawyer."

"I'm fine, Ryker. It's only for emergencies, and I am a lawyer, so why not use it?" Heath rolled his eyes. "I'd rather be in the action, but my brain is better than yours."

"Huh." Ryker grinned. "If that helps you sleep at night." He took the adjacent chair, noting the matching bookshelves and file cabinets. "Jesus, Denver. Where did you get the furniture?"

"Internet," Denver grunted. He glanced up from pounding on his keyboard, his hair ruffled and his blue eyes slowly focusing. A bandage peeked from his open collar, covering a minor bullet wound. He'd been shot the week before while chasing down a guy who owed child support. "Got some furniture for you, too."

Ryker cut Heath a glance. "Is he pregnant?"

"Shut up." Denver threw a brass paperweight at him, and he caught it.

"He has a *paperweight*," Ryker whispered to Heath.

Heath chuckled. "I told you. Nesting."

"Receptionist?" Denver asked.

"No," Ryker and Heath said in unison.

Ryker tossed the paperweight onto the desk, where it clattered. "We're not exactly working within the law here, guys. A receptionist would just complicate things."

Denver leaned back to rub his scruffy jaw. A wide oil painting of the Rocky Mountains spread across the entire wall behind him, its vibrant hues of pink and green adding even more warmth to the area. "The phone?"

"We can take turns. Hopefully it won't ring much. Keep in mind we're setting down temporary roots just to catch this nutjob killing redheads," Ryker said. "We need a virtual redhead to be dating one of us. Somebody just on paper, not real, that will draw the killer in. Then we get him as he tries to find her."

Heath nodded. "We do have to look like we're relocating here for good. It has to look natural, or the asshole killer won't go for it." His fingers drummed impatiently on his jeans. "We're fighting a ticking clock. The bastard already knows his next victim, I'm sure."

True. Frustration for the innocent victims made Ryker's hands clench, and he purposefully relaxed them. He glanced at all the wood. "Please tell me my furniture doesn't look like a ninety-year-old lawyer uses it."

"I like cherrywood, and, no, your office fits your personality," Denver muttered, tapping the long scar along his jaw, which he'd gotten in a knife fight years ago. It was a habit he resorted to when he became irritated.

"What's going on, Den?" Ryker asked.

"We got hacked." Denver glanced over at the computer. "Our files, our backgrounds, and the encrypted stuff. Even the stuff on the dark web that allows people who need a job done quietly to find us."

Ryker frowned, and his shoulders shot back. That was two entire sentences from Denver at once. The guy was pissed off. "Even the encrypted stuff?"

"Yeah." Denver rolled his neck. "I'm good, but this guy hacked through my levels of protection like a buzz saw through butter. Kicked the door wide open and left a calling card." He flipped the screen around to show a picture of a hand giving the bird.

Ryker coughed out a laugh. "What a dick."

"Yeah." Denver sighed.

"Did he spend extra time in any of the files?" Heath asked.

Denver nodded. "Yes. The files of our last three cases. He read through them and downloaded copies of everything."

"Do you think it's the serial killer?" Ryker asked, his fingers tapping restlessly on his thighs.

Denver shook his head. "No."

Heath nodded. "That doesn't feel right. Mainly the picture flipping us off—it's too immature. The killer is methodical, psycho, and determined. I think this hacker is somebody else entirely. Maybe it's somebody looking to hire us. Folks usually find us on the dark web."

"That's not all," Denver said.

The hair on the back of Ryker's neck rose. "What?"

"He left this, too." Denver pointed to a URL.

"Where does the link go?" Ryker asked, his instincts kicking in hard.

Denver clicked his mouse, and a newspaper article came up: LOST SPRINGS HOME FOR BOYS BURNS DOWN: TWO DIE.

Ryker read the headline twice before the words made sense and he could concentrate. His chest compressed. "Well, fuck. Looks like somebody knows who we are."

"How?" Heath asked, tension cutting lines on either side of his mouth. "How in the hell?"

"Dunno," Denver said, shoving the sleeves of his long T-shirt up his muscled arms.

Ryker fleetingly wished for another bottle of booze. "Can he trace us here?"

"No. I used false identifications to create a series of corporations that own the building as well as the business. If the three of us walk away, *again*, nobody can trace us," Denver said.

"We didn't have to leave Alaska," Heath muttered. "It was your choice to leave Noni there."

Ryker blew out air. "Sheriff Cobb was closing in again, and there's no statute of limitation on murder, boys. Leaving her might've been the best thing for her." Someday they were going to get caught. Could he leave Zara? He might have to flee if this hacker discovered their location.

Denver tapped his scar. "Leaving Noni was my decision, and I've asked you not to say her fucking name. So stop saying her fucking name."

Ryker studied the newspaper picture on the screen of a younger Sheriff Cobb, strong and tall, standing in front of a smoldering pile of rubble, his hand on his nightstick. Ryker had felt the pain of that damn thing more times than he could count, and looking at it now made his gut ache. "He'll never stop coming for us."

"We could put him down," Denver said darkly.

"We'll probably have to at some point," Heath said.

Ryker extended his legs. "Haven't we killed enough?" Hell, they'd started killing as teenagers, although they hadn't had a choice. Not really. "I say we keep dodging the asshole. We can't be the only ones who want him dead." How many kids had he beaten through the years? "For now, we need to clear out the garage space in this building, because I smell snow coming."

Heath cleared his throat. "We cleaned it out yesterday. You can park the bike inside now."

Guilt blasted through Ryker. "Ah shit. I'm sorry I didn't help."

"It's tough to concentrate when you're knee-deep in booze," Heath said. "The case was a tough one, and you took point, so you got to know the kid before you found her. A week in a bottle is healthy, if you ask me."

Ryker had used every odd sense he had to find that girl, and in the end, he'd been too late. He'd still failed. Sometimes he could read a situation, or even a person, with nearly supernatural abilities. All three of them had special gifts, ones they'd never been able to explain, and if they were going to be freaks, then why the hell shouldn't they save people? Why did bad guys win and good people die? Ryker cleared his throat. "Are we making a mistake? Having a building and an office?"

"Probably," Denver said.

Heath kicked dirt off one boot. "But we need the setup to find this bastard, and if we do it right, we'll be gone before Sheriff Cobb finds us again."

"When have we ever done anything just right?" Ryker muttered, rubbing his left eye.

Denver snorted. "I like it here."

Heath, as usual, interpreted Denver's sentence. "I agree that I'm tired of living out of motels and eating fast food. Even if we stay here just long enough to draw the killer in, it'd be nice to cook a meal once in a while. Even relax a bit after we catch the guy?"

"We relax, we get caught," Ryker countered. The only reason he'd agreed to a permanent building was because they'd had no luck finding the killer so far.

"Maybe we should've kept the identities we used that time in Florida," Heath said.

Denver shook his head. "No."

Ryker nodded. "Yeah, you're right. It was good we faked those deaths. Nobody will ever come looking for them." He glanced at the computer screen. "Lost Bastards Investigative Services doesn't have our names attached to it."

Denver pulled the screen back around.

"Do we have any new cases?" Ryker asked quietly.

"No," Denver said. "Nothin' new on ours, either."

Ryker nodded. He'd been abandoned as a baby at a church in New Orleans and then spent time in several orphanages, ending up in Lost Springs, North Carolina. He knew he had family out there, and someday he'd find them. Maybe. "No luck on finding the lawyer who did my adoption?"

"No." Denver started typing again. "No news on your lawyer, Heath's mom, or my so-called uncle who just wanted the money from the state for taking me in. We're all still fucking lost, men."

"Sometimes we depress the shit out of me," Heath said. "So let me get this straight. Sheriff Cobb is still after our asses, we're setting ourselves up to be attacked by a serial killer who is killing family members of law-enforcement-type people, and now we have a mystery hacker who knows who we are."

"Yep," Denver said.

"We're fucked." Heath shoved to his feet, his concerned gaze on Ryker. "At least we have each other, right? I mean, you're back amongst us and plan to stick around and be sober for a bit?" No judgment, only acceptance, was in his tone.

"I'm fine now," Ryker said. "Drank the demons away this time."

Denver grimaced and kept typing. "Your lady?"

Ryker rubbed the center of his chest. He wanted her to remain his lady. If being casual was what it would take, he could do that…except for whoever had hit her. A threat to her couldn't exist or he couldn't concentrate. "Didn't go great. Do you have time to do some digging? Check into her financials, her schedule at work, anything you can find."

Denver's dark eyebrows rose. He cut a look at Heath and then back. "Full background?"

Ryker swallowed but kept his face stoic. "Yeah, everything. Especially anything that sets up red flags about her safety."

Heath paused by the doorway. "You're investigating the woman you're dating. While I appreciate the new approach for you, this can't be a good idea."

"New approach?" Ryker snapped.

Denver snorted.

Heath paused. "Yeah. You meet somebody, have short-term sex, and move on. You avoid letting anybody but us in…because if not, you'd have a whole houseful of people you'd be protecting all the time. You can't do halfway with people. I get it. I really do. But right now we have no time for any distractions, and investigating a casual, ah, friend can't be a good idea."

Was Heath a shrink all of a sudden? "It isn't a good idea," Ryker returned, knowing his brother was right. "But I can't sleep until I make sure she's safe. Then I'll go back to distant and cold."

"Right." Heath eyed him as if studying a specimen on a slide. "It's okay if you want more with her, you know," he said quietly.

Ryker scoffed. "I don't bring home broken-winged creatures, Heath. You do." Which was one of the things he'd always admired in his brother. "Besides, Zara isn't broken. She just might be in danger. I have to know."

"All right," Heath said, dropping it.

"Thanks," Ryker said, knowing Heath had let up because Ryker needed him to. "Denver?"

Denver drew out a legal pad and started to jot down notes. "Another lover?"

"No. I asked her, and she said she wasn't seeing anybody else." Ryker stood.

Heath winced. "Women lie, brother. If your instincts are telling you something is up, then you're probably right."

Zara wasn't a woman who lied, but if anybody could lie to him, it might be her. While he could usually tell if somebody was lying, when his feelings were involved, he lost the edge. "I'm sure she's not seeing anyone, but if you find anything in her financials, let me know."

"You asked for it," Denver said, his gaze concerned.

"Fine. I'll go contact the FBI and see if the luscious Special Agent

Jackson is desperate enough to work with us yet." Heath shook his head and then left the room, muttering about stubborn bastards all the way through the building.

Ryker headed for the doorway and then stopped. "Check Zara's medical records, too. Anything out of the ordinary…any injuries that seem suspicious." Had he missed something in the times they'd been together?

"Injuries?"

"Yeah. She had a bruise on her face and wouldn't tell me where she got it."

Denver shook his head. "Not good, brother."

"Why not?" Ryker already knew why not, but if Denver wanted to weigh in, he needed to keep using complete sentences.

Denver rolled his eyes. "If she's protecting some douche bag who hit her, then she's seeing somebody else. Prepare yourself, because I can't dig you out of the booze train again so soon."

"She's not." Ryker slapped a hand against the sturdy doorjamb. Zara wasn't a woman who lied or cheated. Yeah, he might have her on a pedestal, but if anybody belonged there, it was her. "Did you happen to order furniture for the apartments upstairs?"

"No. Order your own. I did the offices." Denver turned back toward the computer screen, the words seeming to come easier with practice. "I'll start investigating your woman after shoring up our defenses against our mystery hacker. He's not getting back into our files."

"Great. Thanks."

"Ryker?" Denver asked.

Ryker lifted an eyebrow.

"I know you. While I'm digging up dirt behind her back, what's your plan?"

Ryker headed out of the office. "I'll be in her face."

CHAPTER
5

Zara clipped in sexy black heels through the law firm hallways in the midafternoon, trying to move her hips to get the black G-string out of her butt. What had she been thinking, wearing it? Yeah, she'd wanted to prove that the underwear was for her and not just some pathetic attempt to be a femme fatale with Ryker.

Now she had floss up her ass, damn it.

A low whistle stopped her, and she turned around to see Brock Hurst, one of the junior attorneys, digging through a file cabinet. "Don't sue me for harassment, but you look good." He smiled, perfect teeth in a charming face.

Okay. So she might've worn a pin-striped pencil skirt with a shimmering red top in an effort to make herself feel better about the odd night with Ryker and the thoughts of whether or not they should break up. Feeling sexy should help. "Thanks." She kept moving down the hall to her small office next to the two attorneys she assisted. Although, did casual affairs just break up? Probably not. They probably just ended.

She'd just settled into her chair and booted up her computer when a shadow crossed her doorway. She glanced up and her breathing hitched. "Ryker."

He strode into the room and slid a fragrant pumpkin-spice latte across the desk, planting it right next to a picture of Grams

Rollerblading the previous spring. "You missed breakfast and lunch, I believe."

Her mouth watered, and not just from the coffee. Today he wore a deep green T-shirt that only enhanced his wild eyes, faded jeans, and those tough boots. "What are you doing here?" she asked, even though he had said he'd see her later. She'd thought it was just an expression.

He dropped into one of her two pin-striped guest chairs, overwhelming the room with the sense of male. "I figured we should talk."

"I'm not ready to talk." Her fingers itched to grab that coffee.

"That's unfortunate." He leaned back, his gaze roaming the red shirt. "I'd love to see the everyday bra and panty set." He grinned. "You know, to compare with my sets."

She'd forgotten about throwing the sexy underwear at his head last week. The other sets weren't *his*. They were hers, darn it. She gave in and reached for the coffee. "You've already seen this set."

His eyes flared. "Oh?"

"Yeah." She took a deep drink and hummed as the spice exploded across her tongue. "Black satin, red bows, another stupid G-string."

"That's one of my favorites." His voice rumbled dark and low.

That tone. That damn tone had the ability to tighten her entire body with need. Her attempt to mess with his head was definitely backfiring. She tried to focus. "I'll launder it and send it to you."

"I'd rather take it off you with my teeth." His eyes smoldered.

God. How did he do that? Butterflies winged through her abdomen, and her breath quickened. She forced herself to look bored. "I have work to do, so thanks for the coffee, but you need to go."

"No." He cocked his head to the side, pinning her in place.

She frowned. "Yes."

"That's not how we're doing this, baby."

Baby. He called her baby in bed…usually when he was telling her what to do in that dark commanding voice. She shivered and discreetly crossed her legs. "I'm pretty sure we're deciding to take a step back or end things, so there is no 'this.'"

"Who hit you, Zara?"

"Keep your voice down," she hissed, panic rippling through her desire. Man, she thought he'd let that whole situation go.

He lifted an eyebrow and casually reached over his shoulder to push the door closed. "Who are you protecting?"

"Myself." She played with the coffee cup. "I was somewhere I shouldn't have been, I did something I could get in trouble for, and you need to drop it right now."

"Trouble?" He leaned forward, his elbows on his worn jeans. "What kind of trouble?"

"The kind that gets me fired." She sighed. "Trust me that I handled the situation, and please drop it."

"No." His voice remained matter-of-fact.

Her mouth dropped open. "Listen, Ryker. I'm giving you an easy out here. Take it," she snapped.

"I don't want out."

Her head jerked. "Casual sex doesn't work for me any longer."

"There ain't nothin' casual about our sex, and you know it."

A quick knock sounded on the door. The door opened, and Brock poked his head in. "You busy?"

"Yes," Ryker answered for her.

She turned to Brock. "What's up?"

Brock glanced from Ryker back to her, red tingeing his cheeks. "We received discovery on the Pentley case. Want to discuss it over dinner?" Curiosity glimmered in his gaze.

"We just made dinner plans," Ryker said quietly, his focus remaining on her.

Her temper simmered hotter, but she didn't want a scene in front of her boss's son. "Brock, I do have dinner plans, but I'm free this afternoon to go over the documents."

Brock nodded, studying her. "All right. I have a meeting at two but should be finished within the hour. We'll meet in the conference room. It's nice to see you, Ryker." He shut the door behind himself.

"Knock it off," she said, crossing her arms, her jaw aching from clenching it so tight.

"He's interested in you," Ryker said evenly, his chin lowering.

She rolled her eyes. "If he is, it's none of your business."

"Boy, do you have that wrong." Ryker shook his head. "I can feel that you're scared, and I can tell that your stress level is at an all-time high. Are you frightened of me?" He rubbed a hand across his sharp jaw. "I mean, after last night? I don't usually drink like that." Vulnerability flashed through his eyes to be banished by the steady strength.

She sat back, wanting nothing more than to delve into the vulnerability and then burrow into his strength again. "I'm not afraid of you."

"Good. Are you scared of whoever put that bruise on your pretty face?"

She blinked and tried to give him the truth without revealing the entire situation. "I'm, ah, concerned about the situation, not the idiot who hit me."

"I can protect you." The words were determined and the tone absolute.

"If I needed protection, I'd call you." She wasn't stupid, for pete's sake. "I got into the middle of a domestic situation, and my face was in the wrong place at the wrong time." It was the truth. Speaking of which, she glanced at the time on her computer. Julie should be calling soon, so she needed to get Ryker out of her office. "I have to work."

His gaze narrowed until she wanted to squirm. "Was the domestic situation part of a case you're working on?"

"Yes."

"Divorce?"

"Yes." She unfolded her arms and reached for her warm coffee cup. "I can't discuss a case with you, and you know it. Privilege applies."

"Hire me as a consultant again. Then privilege extends to me." He glanced at the stack of files on her desk.

She fought the urge to put her hand over the files. "I don't need a private investigator on the case, but thank you." What she needed was for him to get out of her office so she could breathe again. He was throwing her off balance, and she had to be quick on her feet today. "I believe you have your own cases to worry about. We're finished now."

"No. We are nowhere near finished." He stood. "I'm glad you're not in danger, and that definitely eases my mind. However, I still want the name of the guy who hit you."

"Why?" she snapped.

Ryker's eyebrows drew down. "So I can beat the ever livin' shit out of him, darlin', and make sure it never happens again. Anybody who'd hit you is a bully, and a bully needs to be knocked down completely so he doesn't do it again. That's what happens now."

His tone spoke of knowledge and old hurts. How could he be so calm talking about hitting people? "That's illegal, Ryker. I'm not in danger and don't need defending, so if you go batter some moron, you'll end up in jail."

"I don't think he'll press charges," Ryker drawled.

Yeah, Mayor Jay Pentley was exactly the type of guy who'd press charges. "You going after this guy would get me into trouble, so it can't happen." Although somebody should beat the heck out of Jay, considering he'd been smacking his wife around for years.

"How?"

"Can't tell you."

"*Won't* tell me." Ryker stood by the door. "You're forgetting what I do for a living."

She wiped a hand across her eyes. "Ryker, I'm asking you to leave this alone." He was the best at what he did, and he'd discover every little secret she had if he set his mind to it. Why was he acting like they were more than they were? Was it just ego? "Please. I took care of the situation."

"How?"

She huffed and tried to keep from yelling at him. "I kicked the bastard in the balls and ran." After getting Julie Pentley into the car and to safety.

Ryker's lips twitched. "Actually not the most effective move, and we'll work on that later. What I don't understand is that if this guy hit you, and he's on the other side of a domestic case, why not use that information in the divorce? Why not get his ass arrested and help your client in the process?"

"You're right. You don't understand. So let it go." Ryker would have it figured out by dinnertime if she didn't get him to back off. She stood and moved around the desk toward the door. "It has been good to see you, but after last night, I think we should cool things a little." She reached for the doorknob.

His hand enfolded hers. "You don't like our relationship being taken out of the little box where you put it, now, do you?"

Heat from his body washed over her, but she lifted her head to meet his gaze. "We don't have a relationship."

He smiled then, and the curve of his lips held more determination than amusement. "I'm not letting you run, and I'm certainly not letting you hide, baby. Although neither of us has been in this for the long haul, I'm staying in Wyoming for the moment. The first thing that's going to happen is I'm going to figure out who dared put a hand on you and make sure it doesn't happen again."

For the first time, she saw a side of him that gave her true pause. In the long haul, he'd be unbearably possessive. Why did that give her an intriguing sense of safety? "Knock it off," she snapped in his face. "Get out of my business."

That quickly, she found her back against the door and her front pinned by hard male. His hands planted on either side of her neck, his thumbs at her jaw, forcing her to look at him. "Something you need to understand and pretty damn quick is that your business is my business right now." His thumb swept up and over the offensive bruise on her face.

"Step back." Her voice trembled.

He ignored the very calm order. "No. You don't want to tell me who did this? Fine. I'll find out on my own, and I'll have the name by the time I pick you up for supper. What you don't want to do is deal with him or his case until I have that name. Kicking him in the balls might've just pissed him off more, and now you've let a bully stew on it for a while, which might be dangerous for you. Got it?"

"You have no right to interfere," she whispered.

"Baby, I've been fuckin' you for months. That gives me every right." Anger glowed dark in his eyes.

"We're done. Get out."

His eyes softened. "You shouldn't make statements you can't back up."

She shoved against his ripped abs.

He didn't move a millimeter.

And then he did.

His head dipped, and his mouth found her neck and wandered up to her ear. His teeth scraped, and then his tongue licked the slight wound.

Of its own volition, her body did a full tremble.

He leaned back. "That."

Her mind fuzzed.

His mouth slammed down on hers. She knew his kiss—often dreamed about it. Not soft and sweet...not even lustful. It was dangerous. From day one, she'd tasted danger on his tongue, and it burned her hotter than she'd ever been.

Never had she dated a bad boy, but after living her desired routine-driven life for years, she'd craved adventure, and he filled that need. He drew out a wildness she hadn't realized she possessed.

He held her flush against the door, kissing her hard, sending a craving along her nerves that almost hurt. His tongue went to work, his left hand keeping her jaw open for him. His right hand found her hip and dragged her against the obvious bulge in his jeans. By the time he released her, she'd stopped thinking completely.

"What time are you finished today?" he asked, his breath heating her face.

"Fi-five," she stuttered.

He leaned back and gently put her to the side. "Stay in the office until I come for you at five, Zara." He ran his thumb across her bottom lip. "Cross me on this, baby, and I ain't gonna be gentle." He had already shut the door behind himself before she could take a whole breath.

She blinked several times, her fingers going to her still-tingling mouth. What had just happened?

CHAPTER
6

Ryker pulled up to the business just as Heath finished scraping off the last of the logo on the front window. "Thanks for letting me borrow the Hemi," Ryker said, tossing the keys to his brother. Life, not genetics, had made them family, and he'd die for either Heath or Denver.

"No problem." Heath wiped the window with a clean cloth, his jeans nearly threadbare beneath a tattered Grateful Dead T-shirt. His movements barely contained his fury as he waited for something to break in the serial killer case.

"You do not look like a lawyer."

Heath turned, his eyes sober. "I'm not a lawyer. Well, I am, but I don't want to practice law. I just have the degree to get us out of trouble when it comes knocking."

Sometimes Ryker saw in Heath the angry and scared-shitless kid he'd met at Lost Springs so many years ago, determined to fight any bully who threatened him, no matter how big the bully. "Even so, now that we have this place, you should probably get some clothes."

Heath glanced down at his torn jeans. "Why?"

Ryker opened his mouth and shut it again. "I don't know. I mean, don't people who have dressers buy shit to put in them?"

Heath's eyebrows rose. "We don't have dressers."

Oh yeah. "I guess we should get some?"

Heath leaned in. "I don't know why. We'll be out of here as soon as we find the fucker killing redheads. I mean, if Denver gets the bug for nesting out of his ass."

"That ain't it with Den."

"Then what is it?"

Ryker rubbed the scruff on his jaw. He should probably shave at some point. "He's running from Alaska, and he's trying to convince himself that he needs to stay here." Probably to keep himself from hurrying back to Noni.

"Do you think he's really done with her?"

"No." Crisp and cutting, the wind scattered dead leaves across his boots. "But he has to make that decision himself."

Heath nodded. "He had a splash of coffee with his booze today, by the way."

Ryker scrubbed both hands down his face, jostling his aviator sunglasses. "I can't really criticize him there. Pot and kettle, you know."

"Yep. Just something to watch." Heath moved off the step and headed for his car. "He has info for you on your girl, and I'm chasing down a lead on the Copper Killer case. I need to do something, anything, so I'm going to talk to some folks from the first victim's circle."

Ryker wanted to go with him, but he needed to figure out Zara's problems first. "Is your head on straight?"

Heath paused. "I think so."

Ryker studied him. Heath lost himself in cases, especially in the impossible ones. Always trying to fix broken wings. "Stay in contact and stay safe. What about Zara?"

Heath's jaw hardened. "She paid for three nights at the Lonely Trail Motel outside of town last week."

"Motel?" Ryker asked, his gut clenching.

"Yep. Told you this wasn't going to end well." Heath opened the car door and slipped inside, his flippant words contrasting with the very real concern in his eyes. "I can handle only one of you falling apart at a time, and your turn is over."

Ryker nodded, his chest filling. "Understood."

Heath started the engine and sped down the quiet road, the Hemi making a badass statement even in quiet mode.

"When is it your turn, Heath?" Ryker murmured. At some point, Heath was going to try to save somebody he couldn't, and it was going to be ugly. Ryker drew in air before heading through the building to Denver's office. "Heath told me you found something."

Denver looked up from his computer, his eyes only a little cloudy. "He told you about the motel."

"Yeah."

"Okay." Denver tapped a few more times on his keyboard. "Zara has withdrawn nine thousand dollars from her savings account in three-thousand-dollar increments in the last three months."

Ryker dropped into a leather chair and shoved his sunglasses up on his head. "Cash?"

"Yep."

Blackmail? "To spend where?"

"Dunno yet." Denver stretched his neck. "Don't see blackmail here. Investing?"

"With cash?" Ryker drew air in through his nose, trying to rein in his temper. "Bullshit." What the hell was Zara involved in? She'd damn well give him the truth, because he was done being patient. "What else?"

"That's all I have so far. The cash doesn't look good, though."

"Thanks." The anger turned into something deeper…something that hurt. Ryker moved out of the office, waiting until Denver had joined him. "You can take one of the bikes."

"No, thanks. I'll stick to my truck." Denver yanked on a worn leather jacket and headed for the basement garage. "Your office furniture arrived."

Ryker hesitated and then called out. "Denver?"

"Don't want to talk about it, brother." Denver disappeared out the door.

The guy never wanted to talk, so that wasn't exactly a newsflash. Yet at some point Ryker would have to drag words out of him. Or at least some of the hurt. But apparently not today.

Ryker turned toward the middle office and stepped inside, stopping short. Glass and chrome. The entire office was glass and chrome with black leather accents. Whoa. A glass-topped desk, black leather chairs, and chrome file cabinets. A large black-and-white picture of Ryker's Harley Davidson Fat Boy was framed on the wall behind the desk, and a wide window to the side looked out at the mountains. "Shit, Denver," Ryker murmured as he walked around the desk to see the computer already set up. He sat. The office felt like home.

He'd never had a home. His sunglasses fell down onto his nose, and he tugged them off and tossed them onto the desk. The light from the window was comforting, even with the chill in the air.

A wisp of sound came from the other room, and he stilled, his senses going on alert. "Denver?"

"No." A kid walked into the office, his stride long and his expression hard. He shut the door. "You're Ryker."

Ryker sat back, tension swamping him. The kid was about twelve and large for his age, and he moved like he could handle himself. His brown hair reached his shoulders, and his eyes, a lighter shade of brown, held secrets and sadness. "Who are you?"

"Name is Greg." The kid sat, meeting his gaze evenly. "I want to hire you for a job."

"We're an eighteen-and-older type of service," Ryker drawled, his body remaining on alert.

The kid flashed a grin. "You help find the lost, and boy have I lost somebody."

Even with the smile, the kid oozed danger. What the fuck? "Sorry. We don't work for kids," Ryker said.

"Change your mind." Reaching into his back pocket, Greg yanked out a wad of hundreds bound with a rubber band. "As a new business, you probably require capital." He tossed the wad toward Ryker.

Ryker lifted one eyebrow. "Where did you get the cash?"

"Doesn't matter, and there's more if you do the job right." Greg didn't blink. "What do you say?"

More than a little curious, Ryker still shook his head. "Where are your parents?"

"Where are yours?"

Quick. The kid was very quick. "You're a minor."

"A minor with tons of cash and no parents." No emotion showed on his young face. "Nobody is looking for me, so there's no interference."

Lie. The kid had just lied. Ryker tilted his head to the side. "Not interested."

A slight tightening of the skin around kid's eyes was his only reaction. "All right. Let's move on to blackmail."

Ryker clasped his hands together on the glass desktop. "Am I blackmailing you?"

"No." Greg smiled again, showing a dimple in his right cheek. "How about you just find one person for me, and I don't call Sheriff Cobb and tell him the three boy fugitives he's been searching for his entire fucking life happen to be right here in Cisco."

Well, shit. "You hacked our files." Ryker frowned but kept his voice level, as if they got hacked every day. Giving the kid the upper hand would be a mistake. Who the holy fuck was this kid?

"Yep. The encryptions were good but…" He shrugged.

"If you're that good, why can't you find your own missing person?" Ryker asked, looking for the setup.

"I've tried. Believe me, I've tried." Greg rested his hands on his knees. "But your track record shows you're the best, almost to the point of being supernatural about it, and I need the best. So far I've been unsuccessful."

"You believe in the supernatural?"

"No." Greg shook his head. "But I think certain people have special gifts, and from your record, you're one of those people."

Everything in Ryker stilled. "I don't have any special gifts."

"Whatever helps you sleep at night, pal."

Ryker dropped his gaze to the wide hands. "You have a gun in your boot, kid?"

Greg's eyes hardened. "Gun in right, knife in left. If I wanted you dead, buddy, you'd already be dead."

A chill spread down Ryker's back. "How old are you?"

At the question, a desolateness filtered across Greg's sharp face. "Too old, man. Way too fucking old."

Ryker leaned back, more than prepared to go for the gun in his boot. Greg shook his head. "I'm faster than you."

"I doubt that," Ryker said softly. His gift in reading people didn't come close to the speed of his reflexes.

Greg's gaze sharpened, and he studied Ryker closely. "You gonna help me or not?"

"Our files don't indicate anything about Lost Springs," Ryker said. "The connections out there have been severed."

"Obviously not." Arrogance, probably well earned, echoed in Greg's tone. "There's always a string to pull, and I found yours. If you help me with my one little case, I'll show you how I found you and how to cut that string to the past for good."

Now, that was an intriguing offer, and there was something about

Greg that drew Ryker. Heath would take the kid in and buy him a milkshake. "Who do you want me to find?"

Greg reached into his front pocket and brought out a piece of paper, which he quickly unfolded. He took a long look at it and then slid it across the desk.

Ryker lifted the sketch of a middle-aged woman with blue eyes and jet black hair. His entire chest heated and then chilled with the force of a glacier. It was Sylvia Daniels…but older than he remembered. In the picture, she had a few wrinkles but still had the cold, intelligent gaze that had given him the willies as a child. For two seconds, he was a lost kid again, scared and alone. Then he regained control. "Who is this woman?" His voice remained steady, which shocked the hell out of him.

"Just a woman I need to find."

Ryker's head spun. "Your mother?"

"Hell no." Anger sizzled from the kid.

Ryker set down the paper. What was going on? "I'm not finding somebody for you to hurt." Although now he was going to find the woman no matter what.

"Don't want to hurt her. Just need to find her." The kid crossed his arms. "You gonna help or go to jail?"

Ryker flattened a hand over the carefully drawn sketch. He'd been running for a long time, and some kid wasn't going to turn him in. But he'd have to leave Cisco, and he didn't want to leave Zara until he figured out what was going on between them. The fact that this kid wanted to find Daniels…Shit. Something was going on, and it was way out of his wheelhouse. "I'll help."

Greg sat back. "Wise choice."

"Who is she?" Ryker studied the fine lines of her face. If he found her, he'd be digging up a past he'd spent ten years burying. Hell. Fifteen years.

"Her name is Dr. Isobel Madison, and she disappeared from a covert military facility in Utah last year," Greg said.

A covert military facility? Ryker eyed the kid. Why did the woman have two names? "If she isn't your mother and you don't want to hurt her, why do you want to find her?"

Greg ran his hands down his legs, his jaw trembling until he visibly controlled himself. "She's my last hope, man."

* * *

Several hours after Greg had disappeared from the office, Ryker leaned back in his chair, his emotions rioting. Every once in a while he could feel control slipping away, and he grabbed it back with ruthless hands. He'd been on the computer, doing searches, and nothing had popped, which didn't surprise him. Heath and Denver were still away from the office, and he hadn't discovered Zara's secrets.

At the moment, he wasn't doing anything right.

Taking a deep breath, he kicked his feet up onto his desk and closed his eyes.

Memories battered him, and he let them come, trying to find a pattern in the past. Just who was Isobel Madison?

He was twelve years old, had just taken Denver under his wing, and was worried Heath would try to recruit more members into their sad little team. He could cover only so many people, and two was his limit.

Even though it was Sunday, he'd been told to report to one of the two classrooms and continue working with Sylvia Daniels.

A thought played through his mind that he could just up and leave and nobody would find him, but he couldn't leave Heath and Denver. How could he take care of them if they all ran now?

Time. He was smart, and he'd bide his time.

The classrooms were on the second floor of the main building, and on Sunday, the entire floor was empty. He plodded down the empty hallway, his footsteps silent.

A woman's cry stopped him short. Chills darted down his back. He inched down the dingy walls and stopped, peeking into the classroom. Daniels was on her back on a table, her legs up over Sheriff Cobb's shoulders as he stood beside the table, and his pants were down around his ankles. He was holding her hips and thrusting hard, grunting each time, his butt in full view. His body shuddered, and he groaned.

Ryker jerked around, put his back to the wall, and kept out of sight. His stomach heaved. Old people having sex were grosser than he would've thought. Cobb had to be almost thirty, for pete's sake.

"That was lovely," Daniels said, her voice drowsy.

The sound of rustling clothing echoed. "When are you going to move here for good?" the sheriff asked, his voice growly.

Daniels sighed. "I have work elsewhere, and you know it. We have what we have, Elton."

A belt buckled. "What is it with these kids?" the sheriff asked. "Why these three, and why do you keep studying them?"

Ryker leaned closer to the door, his heart rate picking up.

Daniels laughed. "They're mine...just mine. I'm doing a study on kids in homes, and these three boys are exemplary. It's my private little study, which I don't share with anybody."

They were part of a study? She'd always said that, but instinct whispered to Ryker that it was something more. He leaned farther so he could see.

The sheriff helped Daniels set her clothes to right and kissed her—gently, really—on the forehead. "Whatever your reasons for being here, I'm glad my brother introduced us when you approached him about your little study."

"Me too." Daniels slid her hands over the sheriff's chest. "I really do like you, Elton. You're just for me, too. One more thing that's all mine."

Ryker shivered in the hallway. Her voice was so possessive. Who claimed other people like she did? Something was seriously wrong with this woman. Even though the Cobb brothers liked to beat kids, instinct told him she was the biggest threat in his life.

As if to confirm that fact, she glanced around Sheriff Cobb's shoulder and winked at him. Oh God. She knew he'd been watching.

Ryker sat up in his chair, shaking. He'd always known he'd have to confront the past, but he'd hoped to be able to run a while longer.

His time was up.

CHAPTER
7

Zara pulled her compact into a parking spot behind the Lazy Horse Motel, her stomach cramping. She'd told her receptionist that she had to run out for a few minutes, and now she had only an hour to get back to the office building before Ryker showed up for dinner. She really didn't want another confrontation with him. He was acting like a boyfriend, not a casual lover, and she wasn't sure what to do with that.

Did she want a real shot with him? An affair with a sexier-than-hell rebel was one thing, while a real relationship with a guy like him held certain danger. He was a rambling man, and the idea of him settling down didn't seem possible. For years she'd watched her mother fall for the wrong guy and then get her heart shattered when he left. In fact, her relationship with the wrong man had led to her death.

Rebels left.

They were hell on wheels for a short time, but they eventually rambled on.

She never felt more alive than when he was in town, and she never felt safer than when he was in her bed. That was the danger of a guy like him.

Drawing her coat around her shoulders, she stepped from the car. The wind kicked up, biting into her skin with cold. Winter was coming to Cisco. She shivered. The torn asphalt tried to grab her heels as she made her way to the back entrance of the decrepit motel. She already knew the lock didn't work on the faded door. Sucking in air, she nudged the door open. The breeze threw pine needles and leaves against her back, and she hurried inside the narrow hallway. Hunching her shoulders, she strode down the ugly orange carpet, ignoring the wall canisters selling everything from flavored condoms to tampons. The only open door in the hallway was near the front entrance, and one look inside the office showed the young clerk dead asleep in his chair.

Perfect.

She pushed open the dirty glass front entrance door to step out onto the main breezeway, then quickly made her way to room 4. She knocked. "Julie?" The door opened, and she slid inside to hug the small woman waiting for her.

"Were you followed?" Julie asked, stepping away.

Zara shook her head and leaned back against the door. The smell of rust and mold commingled around her, and she fought a sneeze. "No. I made sure." She studied her friend. Julie was short and curvy, even though she'd lost so much weight lately. Her green eyes were subdued, and dark circles lined them. "You look terrible."

Julie tossed back dark curls and laughed, the sound a little hollow. "I feel like shit. This isn't fair to you, and we have to stop it before you lose your job or worse."

"No. It's fine." Zara reached into her pocket. She'd been so sad when she and Julie had lost touch, ostensibly because of Jay, and now it was like they'd never been apart. "I have only two thousand left, but that should last you until the trial since you paid another retainer to your lawyer."

Julie eyed the cash. "I can't take all of your savings."

Zara pressed the money into her friend's hand. She'd been so focused on getting her degree and then building a stable life that she hadn't had much time to make friends. Julie meant a lot to her, and they'd stay in touch for sure this time. "You can pay me back with your divorce settlement. No matter what, you'll get something from Jay in the divorce." She leaned in to study the fading bruise across Julie's temple. "How's the head?"

"Better."

Zara rubbed her eye. Why did life end up so unfair for good people? "I still think you should go to the police and press charges."

Julie stepped back to sit on a dirty floral bedspread. "Why? It's his word against mine. I have no medical reports, and I have no proof. You can't even testify that you've seen him hit me or you'll lose your job." Julie remained matter-of-fact. "He's smart, Zara. You know that. And he has the best lawyers in the West on retainer."

Zara winced and took in some cigarette burns along the top of the television. "I know. I work there." It wasn't her fault her firm represented Jay and his business assets. Her temples began to pound, but she held firm. Right was right, and she was helping her friend, no matter the cost. Julie had called her a month ago, nearly desperate since she'd escaped Jay, and Zara had instantly felt guilty for letting their friendship lapse because she'd been working so hard to establish herself at the firm. "I'm sorry I didn't know how bad it had gotten." It was almost textbook how Jay had isolated Julie from everyone.

"I should've called you earlier," Julie said, her small hands fluttering. "It's my fault."

"No, it's mine." Especially since she'd introduced poor Julie to Jay years ago. What a mistake that day had turned out to be. "Things will get better as soon as the divorce goes through. Both sides have finished answering discovery. Your lawyer should amend to add an allegation of domestic violence."

"Why?" Julie frowned at the filthy-looking bedspread. "There's no proof, and you know his family knows all the judges. I just want out, Zara. I just want the divorce to go through so I can go on my way."

Zara sighed, her heart aching for her once upbeat friend. "You could leave town."

"I will as soon as I finish the medical examinations to prove I'm competent." She shook her head. "I can't believe he's alleging I'm mentally incompetent and I need a guardian."

Yeah, it was unfair, without doubt. Zara's heart ached for her friend. "He's convinced the lawyers at my firm that you have serious problems, and if I speak up, I won't be able to help you." She chewed on her lip. "I don't know much about your lawyer, but I'm not sure he's the best."

"I know, but he's what I can afford. It'll be okay. And he says I can leave town as soon as I prove I'm not nuts." Julie smiled, but her lips trembled. "I owe you so much."

"We're friends." That summed it up. Julie was one of her few friends, and she should've done a better job. It hurt to see the bright, spunky woman so defeated, and Zara wanted nothing more than to protect her.

When Zara had moved to Cisco after getting her degree eight years ago, Julie had instantly taken her under her wing and shown her around, drawing her into a singles Bunco group as well as the local Business Coalition for Women.

How odd to have their positions reversed so completely.

Julie looked at the bruise on Zara's face. "I can't believe he dared to hit you."

"He had nothing to lose." Zara shrugged. "If I report him, I'll have to admit that I'm assisting the opposition on a case taken by my firm. I'll lose my entire career and never get to be a paralegal again. He knows that, which is why he hasn't said anything, either." The jerk thought he'd win, without doubt. She steeled her shoulders and glanced at her watch. "When is your examination with the shrink?"

"Tomorrow afternoon. All I want is half the community property

and the jewelry my grandmother left me, which he won't turn over."
Julie looked down at her shaking hands. "And to start over. Just to
start over. Maybe with real love this time."

"I agree. You have plenty of time," Zara said.

A small smile brightened Julie's face. "Sometimes the right guy is
just around the corner in an unexpected place, right?"

Whoa. Zara shook her head. "You're not actually interested in anybody, are you?" A rebound would be a huge mistake. She'd seen it
happen with other clients, and Julie was so vulnerable right now. The
woman needed to regain some strength and stand on her own for a
while. Zara didn't think Julie could take another painful experience.

Julie paused, and her smile slid away. "No, but there are good men
out in the world, right?"

"Yes."

"Well, maybe I'll find one." Julie didn't quite meet her eyes.

Zara's instincts were piqued. "You haven't found one already, have
you?"

"No. But I would love to find a good guy. Jay and I made so many
mistakes. Some of the things we did—"

Zara frowned. "Did? What do you mean?"

Julie looked up and tried to smile, but her lips seemed to tremble.
"Nothing. We just tried some crazy things to keep our marriage
fresh, and they were mistakes. Nothing you need to know about.
Trust me."

Eesh. It sounded sexual, and she so did not want to go there. Her
poor friend, having to feel ashamed of her own marriage. There
should be freedom and trust no matter what in a marriage. "I do trust
you. Just think twice before starting to date so soon. Okay?"

"Okay." Julie sighed. "I just want to be with somebody strong and
good, you know? Someday."

Zara leaned down and hugged her friend. "You will, I promise.

Right now I have to get back to work. I'll let you know what his discovery answers are."

"Thank you." Julie stood and returned the hug. "Be careful. You don't know what he's capable of."

Zara swallowed and nodded, slipping back outside. She had an idea of what Jay could do fading from her cheek right now. What a complete dick. She should let Ryker have a go at him, but that would screw up the case, and she couldn't do that to Julie. Not right now, anyway. Plus, it was professionally unethical for Zara to even talk to Julie.

She kept her head down and made it back to her car, then quickly drove out of the dismal lot. The motel was located outside of town in the middle of a mountain pass, perfect for lost and exhausted drivers, and during the day, it was deserted. Good thing. She carefully pulled onto the main road, and her shoulders began to relax.

A country song crooned through the radio, and she began to sing along. The grade steepened, and she pressed on the brakes.

Nothing happened.

She frowned and pressed harder, the pedal finally reaching the floor.

The car sped up, careening down the hillside on its own. Her eyes widened, and her heart beat faster. Her breath panted out. She pressed on the brakes.

Nothing.

She tried to focus and not give in to the fear. The brake pedal was useless. Gingerly, she twisted the key in the ignition, and it wouldn't release.

Her phone buzzed on the seat, and Ryker's number came up. Ryker! Relief and hope hit her at once. Her knuckles turned white on the wheel, and she tried to hug the hillside. No cars were in front of her, but at some point, she'd be in trouble.

The car continued to accelerate. Panicking, she pumped the brakes several times, trying to get them to engage.

The phone buzzed again. She reached over and fumbled for the speaker. "Ryker? I'm in trouble."

"What kind of trouble?" he asked, his voice steady.

"I'm coming down Thompson's Hill, and my brakes aren't working. I've pumped them several times and nothing." Her voice rose on the last words as she instinctively waited for him to help her.

Quiet ticked by. "Is anybody in front of you?"

"Not yet." God, what should she do?

"How's the drop-off to your left?" His tone remained calm and focused.

She glanced to the side and tried to follow his lead. "Steep and full of trees."

"Have you tried to free the key?"

"Yes."

"Shove the car into park and then neutral really fast. Wait. Is your seat belt on?"

She nodded and then remembered he couldn't see her. "Yes," she said.

"Okay. Do it and prepare for a jolt."

She sucked in air, grabbed the shifter, and shoved the car into park and then neutral. Something clanked, the engine trilled, and then the car went dead. She angled the steering wheel into the hill, and it rolled forward, hitting a large pile of rocks along the shoulder, stopping with a crash. "Oh God." Her heartbeat echoed loudly in her ears.

"Zara?"

She gulped. "I'm okay. The car stopped." Silence descended on her, ominous and pounding. He'd been right. She'd turned to Ryker, and he'd known what to do. "Thank you."

"Stay in the car. I'm on my way."

* * *

The wind blew through the open truck window. Ryker had moved quickly to take his Hummer, more than a little thankful his brothers had dragged it out of storage for him. Winter had arrived.

Her brakes had stopped working?

He'd told Zara nearly a month ago that she needed a new car. He'd offered to help pay if she didn't have the funds for one...and of course, she'd rejected the offer immediately. But a newer car wouldn't have shut off by pulling the key out, so maybe it was actually a blessing.

If this wasn't an accident...

It had to be an accident. He planted his foot on the accelerator. The idea that she'd been in danger unfolded something inside him...something dark. He struggled to remain as calm as he'd tried to sound for her, but emotions, dark and angry, rose up in him. She could've been hurt, damn it.

He was a master at compartmentalizing his life. Family—Denver and Heath—in box one. Jobs and clients in box two. The past in box three. Women in another box.

But Zara. Something about her was different. A whisper inside his head, coming from deep down, hinted that she'd escaped her box. He'd loved two people in his life, Heath and Denver, and now Zara was right in his chest, mingled up with the emotions he'd never been able to sort out.

The thought that anybody would try to harm her clenched his teeth and forced an energy to the surface he'd worked hard to banish. His chest burned, and the world widened until he couldn't focus. He pounded his fist on the steering wheel.

His hands shook, and he wanted to yell. Anger had ruled his life for too long, and he'd finally learned to control the rage when they'd escaped the boys home. He hadn't had to fight his baser nature in years, but now, with the mere thought that Zara had been in danger, it rose closer to the surface.

It almost erupted the second he rounded the next corner and saw her, pale and trembling, leaning against the hood of her shitty car. Mud coated her entire right side.

He was out of the truck and barreling into her before he could take a breath.

She lifted both hands to press against his chest. "Ryker?"

"Why the hell are you out of the car?" he snapped, drawing her around the vehicle to put the rocky hillside at her back, holding her too roughly but unable to stop himself.

She blinked. "What?"

Jesus. She was just standing there, totally exposed.

He sucked in air to yell and stopped himself just in time. Control. He needed control. So he blew out a breath, keeping a firm hold on her arm. Smells hit him first: Scrub grass, cattle in the distance, her perfume. The scent, too sweet, of fear. Sounds next: Her ragged breathing, her heartbeat, birds, wind, life. Nothing near. No presence.

Even so, he took a moment to survey the area, not finding anything out of place. Then he eyed her, head to toe, his breathing leveling out. He forced himself to take several more calming breaths before he could speak evenly. "Are you hurt?"

"No." She pushed hair off her face, and her hands shook. "Nothing hurts. I looked around the car and fell in the stupid mud. I'm just in shock, I think."

He nodded. If she didn't require medical attention, he needed to get her to safety in case this had been deliberate. "Okay, honey, get in the truck."

When she didn't immediately move, he did, all but dragging her toward the H3 Alpha and lifting her into the driver's side. "Scoot over, sweetheart." He kept using endearments to calm her and to keep himself from freaking the hell out. His hands had started shaking again. Man, he needed to get himself under control. This wouldn't do at all.

She pushed across the seat, her eyes wide.

He returned to her car, crouching down for a better view. Wet brush at the side of the road dampened the bottoms of his jeans. Scratches marred the right side and front bumper of the car from hitting the rocks. He punched the ground, hard, and pain lanced across his knuckles.

Okay. One punch. That's all he got.

Brush blocked his view of the underside of the car, so he stood and grabbed her purse before striding back to the Hummer and jumping in.

She leaned forward to look past him at her silent car. "I can't leave my car here."

"I'll have somebody come get it." He'd call Denver on the way out. "I'll take care of it." Heat built up inside him, shoving against his sternum, making his arms tense with the need to hit something again and hard. Nope. One was all he got. Slowly, deliberately, he shifted the vehicle into drive, keeping a handle on himself with sheer will.

Allowing Zara to see the real him, the asshole at his core, was not an option. Hell. She'd seen the asshole, but she hadn't seen the monster—the one ruled by emotion and unable to think clearly to protect everyone.

Anger ruled the monster, and Ryker ruled the anger, so he won. Every time he controlled his temper, he beat every bully who had ever tried to make him something else. Somebody else.

He kept his grip light on the steering wheel, once again fully in control.

This time.

CHAPTER
8

Zara's hands were still trembling as she followed Ryker up the stairs from an underground garage. She'd recognized his motorcycles but hadn't before seen the black muscle car with shiny rims. They bypassed the first floor.

"Our offices are here, and I'll show them to you later," Ryker said, his hand firm and warm around hers as he turned to take another set of stairs. The sense of protection and safety he provided tried to burrow into her heart and stay. He reached a landing and put his shoulder to a scratched metal door. The thing opened with a groan, looking beyond heavy.

Her mind cleared as she looked around a spacious foyer, empty of furniture. Blue metal doors were set into each of its walls.

"We replaced the doors with something sturdier." He strode across the black-tinted concrete floor to the door at the far right and opened it. "Though I should probably start locking this." His hold on her gentled, and he drew her inside an apartment with a sprawling open floor plan. Floor-to-ceiling windows showed the mountains in the distance while heavy metal beams were stationed throughout, no doubt as support. The kitchen was a cross between ultra-modern and stark, with stainless steel appliances, concrete counters, and empty white cupboards.

She blinked at the bare living room. Sure, she'd spent a little bit of time wondering where he lived when he wasn't in town. The room already smelled like him—male and strong. "I figured the bat cave would have more gadgets. Or at least a sofa."

He chuckled. "I guess we should start shopping."

We? She tugged her hand free. "Um, why do you suddenly have an apartment and offices?"

"We need them for now." He shut the door.

Strung-out butterflies flapped their way through her abdomen. She scratched her arm. The mud had dried, and her entire right side felt sticky. "I don't understand. What do you mean by 'for now'?"

For an answer, he dug her cell phone from her purse and handed it to her. "Call in sick for tomorrow."

She shook her head. He was taking over, and a part of her—one she didn't much like—was tempted to let him. But how many times had she seen her mother give up control to a man, seeking some sort of security, only to lose everything? Was the need to rely on a strong man a weakness for all women or just the women in her family? She could handle her own life and ignore those unreliable needs. "I can't call in sick. Too much work."

He studied her with no expression on his rugged face. "You need cover until we double-check your car and see why the brakes stopped working. Either you stay here or I spend tomorrow at your office. Your choice."

That didn't sound like much of a choice, now, did it? Yet curiosity, the burning kind, had her looking around the apartment again. He intrigued her in a way she couldn't understand. "Who lives behind the other blue doors?"

"Stay here, and you'll meet my brothers." His cajoling tone nearly made her smile.

As a carrot, it was dangled perfectly. The D and H...Denver and Heath. She hated—*oh, she hated*—the fact that she wanted to know more about him. What kind of men were his brothers? Were they like him, full of secrets and sexiness? She frowned. "You always seemed like such a lone wolf." Sure, she'd figured he had other people on the payroll or people he contracted with for help but not family. "You trust them?"

"Yes. They're my brothers." His eyes darkened. "I trust Denver, Heath, and now...you."

He'd just included her in his family. She took a step back as hope dared to flare in her. "This is happening too fast."

"We've been dating for months."

Her eyes rolled of their own accord. "You can't call what we've been doing dating. We've never been out together. Not really."

"You want to go out to dinner?" One of his dark eyebrows rose.

"No," she breathed, her legs twitching with the urge to run. She had to get away from him and think. Definitely think. Sure, she'd had fantasies about him staying, but the reality was freaking her out. He kept too many secrets. The darkness in his eyes that he thought she couldn't see...Oh, she did more than see it. Sometimes she could *feel* it.

She'd been on the run before, when her mother had dated a convict, and she knew—she just fucking knew—he was running from something or someone. This apartment, this building, was just a temporary stop. Part of her believed he was different from the jerks her mother had dated, but what if her instincts were just as bad as her mother's had been? What if she allowed herself to get all caught up in one man? That led to disaster. "Ryker, we need to take a step back." Why was it so hard to breathe all of a sudden?

His head lifted while his eyelids half lowered.

She shivered.

"I know the right thing to say, and I know the right thing to do," he said slowly, his voice gritty.

"Which is?" she breathed out.

"To nod and take you home, telling you to let me know if you want my help." His head cocked, just a millimeter, to the side. Tension rolled from him, taking over the atmosphere with the sense of maleness.

She swallowed, and a heated tornado of air, one borne of instinct, whirled through her chest. "Exactly."

"But I'm not going to do that." Determination hardened his already implacable face.

She reared back. "You're not."

"No." One of his muscled shoulders lifted. His angled jaw tightened. "The right thing be damned."

She started to shake her head and stopped when he took a step toward her. The breath whooshed out of her lungs.

"You showed me you, Zara. Whether you meant to or not." Another step, and the heat from his body washed over her. "When you cooked me meals and cried on my shoulder. You're sweet and you're kind...and I'm neither of those things. I'll protect you now whether you like it or not."

The anxiety slid right into temper. "The hell you will."

"Think you can stop me?" he asked softly.

Her head jerked. His behavior was unacceptable and totally not the norm for a modern man...and U.S. law. The more emotional she became, the calmer he became, which provided a warning...one she couldn't quite decipher but instinctively knew to heed. Yet damn if it didn't intrigue her as well. "You can't just do whatever you want."

"I gave up on doing the right thing years ago, baby. It's too late, and even if it weren't, I don't give a shit."

There was the part of Ryker she'd always sensed beneath the surface: an immovable rock of sheer stubbornness, of something not quite tame. And his earlier question had been a good one. Could she stop him? "You're forgetting a couple of things here." To her shock, her voice remained steady.

"Which are?" The street showed in his eyes, was stamped hard on his face.

"One, I'm not in any danger. The car was old. Two, I could stop you." Her voice rose, and she tried to tamp it down, to meet him on even terms. But she knew he had an edge she'd never seen and didn't have.

He smiled then. "We'll see about the brakes, but that bruise on your face? Yeah, that's danger. Two, how are you going to stop me?"

How indeed? Her mind spun for answers. "This is kidnapping. If you follow me, that's stalking and harassment. Don't think for a second I won't turn your ass in." Yeah. She'd use the law.

"You even think of turning my ass in and I'll turn yours a bright red."

She gasped. Oh, she'd been bluffing, but something told her he wasn't. Heat flared through her chest. "I'm not liking you very much right now," she hissed, feeling both trapped and traitorously interested in this new side of him.

"I can live with that," he said evenly.

She opened her mouth to let him have it when a hard knock sounded on the door.

Ryker strode past her, brushing her with heat. "What?"

"Have the car up on the lift," said a deep, very deep, voice.

Ryker opened the door and moved aside. "Zara, this is Denver."

Zara walked toward a man every bit as big as Ryker. This one had black hair and deep blue eyes, flecked with gold, that revealed absolutely nothing. A scar along his jaw gave him the look of a battle-worn soldier. He wore a ripped T-shirt and frayed jeans. Man, she wished she wasn't half covered in mud at the moment. She held out her hand. "Hello."

He finished wiping his hands on an oil-covered rag and then gently took hers. "Hi."

She nodded, noting a scar across his palm. One just like Ryker's.

Denver released her and shoved the rag into his back pocket. "Bad brake lines."

"How bad?" Ryker prodded.

"Worn and leaking." Denver glanced at her. "Really worn."

Well, geez. It wasn't like she'd had time or money to hit a mechanic's. "I'd noticed the brakes were getting tougher to use, and I thought to get the car into the shop next week." Relief, the full and blooming kind, whipped through her. She'd almost subscribed to Ryker's goofy notion that somebody had tried to harm her.

Ryker's expression didn't change. "Any chance somebody did it deliberately?"

Denver shrugged.

Ryker kept still. "If I wanted to sabotage somebody, and their brake lines were that bad, then it'd be easy to use a wire sponge and finish the job. Hell, even sandpaper might've worked with worn brakes."

She shook her head. "Nobody wants me dead."

Ryker ran a knuckle across the barely there bruise on her face. "Uh-huh."

Her knees wobbled. One little touch, and he sent her body into overdrive. She should panic, but instead, she wanted to crawl up onto him and plaster herself to his hard body. Man, she needed a vacation.

Denver cleared his throat. "I doubt it."

Ryker's lips pressed together, his patience obviously dwindling. "I need more, Den. I'm having trouble interpreting your meaning right now with the monosyllables."

Denver glanced down at the floor and steeled his shoulders. "As a means of harming somebody, especially on such a small hill, it sucks.

My guess is that the brakes were just worn down." He looked at Zara, his words rushed. "It'd be easier to just shoot the car from the hill-side." He sucked in air as he finished speaking.

"Yet we're not sure if anybody did anything," Ryker rumbled, clapping his brother on the back as if in support. "So if they wanted to stay under the radar, they have."

What were these odd undercurrents? Zara shook her head. "My engine went out six months ago, and the transmission was next. The mechanic told me the brakes were bad, but—"

"But what?" Ryker asked, way too softly.

Denver looked from Ryker to Zara and back, his gaze contemplative.

A ruckus came from outside the door. "Hey. Why is there a piece-of-shit car up on the lift?" A guy wearing a black coat loped into the hallway, his greenish brown eyes sizzling and his brown hair shaggy across his collar. "Oh. Hi."

Denver jerked his head toward Zara and lifted his eyebrows.

Ryker nudged Denver in the ribs with an elbow and then stepped aside. "Zara, this is Heath."

They shook hands. Another scar. Zara ran her finger along it as he drew away. Interesting.

"The car is Zara's," Denver explained, his gaze not leaving hers, a smile tickling his lips.

"Oh. Sorry about the 'piece-of-shit' description," Heath said, also not looking away.

She nodded, trying very hard not to feel like a bug under a micro-scope. The men watched her, studying her, their gazes more than a little curious.

"Stop looking at her like that," Ryker snapped.

Denver looked at Heath and shrugged.

Heath smiled. "Like what, brother?" he drawled.

Ryker coughed. "Like we're back in high school and a pretty girl has dropped by."

He'd just called her *pretty* in front of his brothers. Zara fought the insane urge to preen like a teenager.

Denver snorted.

Heath nodded. "Like we ever went to high school." He traded smiles with Denver.

Ryker's sigh was full of suffering. "Heath, why are you dressed up?" He looked down at Heath's boots. "With boots again? I told you to get shoes."

Heath shrugged. "I had to do a local sign-in with three other new attorneys and meet the judges, which was a pain in the ass. I haven't had time to get shoes."

"You're an attorney?" Zara asked.

"Just got sworn in yesterday," Heath said, his tone bland.

Zara kept still, her mind spinning. "And the three of you own a business?"

The other two men finally stopped looking at her and turned their attention toward Ryker, obviously giving him the chance to reply.

He nodded. "Yes. I'll tell you about it later."

More secrets. Zara frowned. "Why did you guys move into town?" So much wasn't adding up, and maybe the two men now shuffling their feet would tell her more than Ryker ever had. Although, that was all sorts of screwed up. Now she felt like she was back in high school, playing it coy. That wouldn't do at all.

"We won't be here long," Heath muttered, his upper lip twisted. "Sorry."

She shoved a piece of hair out of her face, a little intrigued by this more-than-honest brother. "I figured."

Ryker cut her a look then, and it sure as hell wasn't full of patience. "I need a moment with Zara."

Her chest grew heavy.

Heath made a quick exit, and Denver followed, pausing at the door. "The car?"

The guy really didn't use many words. Zara opened her mouth to answer, but Ryker beat her to it.

"Scrap it," Ryker said.

"No." Zara moved toward Denver, only to have Ryker block her path. "That's my car. Do not scrap it."

Ryker's nostrils flared, and he kept his gaze on her. "Take the car off the blocks, and I'll let you know our plan tomorrow morning."

Denver shut the door quietly behind him.

She looked at the closed door. "What's up with him and monosyllables?"

"He doesn't talk much," Ryker said, "doesn't like to talk, but he makes an effort for us."

There was a well full of information being left out, but Denver wasn't really her business. "All right." She turned back toward Ryker.

"What's it to be? Are we staying at your place or mine tonight?" Ryker asked.

She worried her bottom lip, her mind turning events over. Never, not once, had she been a coward, and she wasn't going to start now. "I haven't decided. Now you start explaining who you guys are and why you're suddenly renting offices in Cisco."

He leaned back against the door. "Oh, you're going to explain where you were today first, after you have a shower and get rid of the mud. Do you need help getting into the shower, or would you like to handle that yourself?"

CHAPTER
9

Ryker waited until Zara had fled into the master bathroom, insanely grateful he'd purchased bath towels the previous week, and then he went out into the hallway.

Heath leaned against the door to his own apartment, ankles crossed. Exhaustion had turned his eyes bloodshot. After Zara's accident, he'd stayed in town and been on the phone or computer, still obsessed with the serial killer case. "She's pretty."

"Yeah, she is," Ryker said.

"You can't be seen publicly with her, Ryker. I know she's not a redhead, but she could still be in danger by being close to us."

Ryker breathed out heavily. "She might be in her own set of danger, so I can't leave her alone. I'll stay under the radar with her, so when our good old serial killer comes knocking, he won't know anything about her. Any luck with her medical or financial records?" Ryker kept his voice low in case she finished showering.

"Not yet, but Denver is working on it." Heath drew in air. "Why don't you just ask her?"

Ryker nodded. "I'm planning on it, but considering she's been keeping secrets, I'd rather know the truth before asking."

Heath snorted. "That is not how trust works, brother."

Yeah. Good point. Ryker reached into his back pocket. "The guy who hacked our system came into the office earlier and wants to hire us for a job."

Heath shoved off the wall. "Really?"

Denver pushed open the door to the stairwell and stepped inside, his gaze going from one to the other. "We're meeting here?"

"Yeah. I was just telling Heath that I met the person who hacked into our system. We need to scout the security cameras and see where he went next." Ryker slowly unfolded the paper Greg had given him.

Denver sighed. "An external source wiped the security cameras. The hacker is good."

That fuckin' kid seriously knew his electronics. "The hacker is about twelve years old, named Greg."

Denver's eyebrows drew down. "Twelve?"

"You could've done it as a teenager," Heath said slowly.

Denver nodded. "Yeah, but we're not normal."

"Amen to that," Ryker said. "I'm thinkin' maybe this kid isn't normal, either." He handed over the picture of Sylvia Daniels.

Denver took it silently and handed it to Heath.

"Greg wants to hire us to find her. Says her name is Dr. Isobel Madison and that she's part of some covert governmental agency," Ryker said.

Heath shook his head, his eyes firing. "No way."

Ryker kept a wince off his face. The woman had shown up at the boys home periodically through the years to test their scholastic and physical abilities. For a while, she'd claimed she was leading a governmental study about kids raised as orphans, but once Ryker had learned to discern a lie, he knew that was untrue. Why she'd studied them, he still didn't know. "It's not a coincidence this kid wants to find her."

Heath's chest lifted with a huge breath, and he blew it out through his nose. "I thought we were done with that witch."

"Me too," Denver said, staring down at the picture.

Heath growled. "Is the kid messing with us? I mean, he did hack our files. Maybe this is just another 'Fuck you.'"

Ryker replayed the entire meeting in his head, his heart hurting for Greg. "I don't think so. He's almost desperate to find her, to the point where I could smell it on him."

"Wait a minute. If he's good enough to hack us, then why doesn't he just find her himself?" Heath asked slowly, his hand shaking a little.

"Says he can't." Ryker rubbed his chin. "Says he read our files and saw how we find people nobody else can." With skills they shouldn't have, really. "Greg said he couldn't find her but thinks that we can."

"He knows about us?" Denver asked, his head going back.

That was good. That Denver was still speaking in complete sentences when talking about the past was a good sign.

Ryker shook his head. "There's no way for Greg to know much about us, but he suspects we're able to do something most folks can't. He can't understand the rest of it." Unless the kid had his own special gifts. "It's not a coincidence that Sylvia—or rather, Isobel Madison—studied and taught us...and this special kid, the best hacker we've ever found, is looking for her."

"We cannot open that fucking can of worms," Heath snapped, his eyes wild. "Everything will unravel, and we just got to safety. Of a sorts."

"I know," Ryker said. "But what choice do we have? If we don't help the kid, he's going to turn us in to Sheriff Cobb."

Heath scrubbed both hands down his face. "Damn it, I know. Even if the little shit wasn't blackmailing us, we have to figure out what's going on. I've always wondered about Sylvia, and it appears there's more to her than we thought. Maybe—"

"Don't say it," Denver grumbled.

Heath cut him a hard look. "Maybe she has the answers about us. I mean, why we're different. Why we have high IQs and super hearing. Why we can read a lie on most people. The weird stuff."

"Maybe she knows about our families, the people we've been searching for," Ryker added. It wasn't a coincidence they'd created a detective agency to find the lost. "This kid may lead us to the answers we've been hunting for since escaping the home."

Denver slowly shook his head, his eyes stark. "We have lives, and things are good. Digging up the past will lead to pain and death. You *know* that." His voice broke, and heat swelled from him.

"What I know is that the past has *always* been coming for us. Now maybe we have a chance to get there first," Ryker said quietly. He pulled out another drawing to hand over. "After Greg left, I quickly sketched his face." The kid wasn't the only one who could draw.

Heath studied the picture, his shoulders straightening. "Strong bones, sad eyes."

"Yeah, and no doubt dangerous. Definitely dangerous," Ryker added. He couldn't let Heath try to save another kid in case everything went south.

Heath lifted an eyebrow. "Wait a minute. All hell is breaking loose, and you have a woman in your shower right now. You really think it's time to bring Zara into your life?"

Ryker stilled. Heath was right. "No. Now is a shitty time, but Zara is in danger, and I've promised to protect her. Or at least to find out if she's in danger. Somebody punched her, and I want to know who it is. Zara is in now, and I'll keep her safe."

"She's not in," Heath countered. "We could leave here like we did Alaska and start over in a different town to hunt the killer. Leave Zara safe and free."

"The woman had a bruise the size of a tangerine on her face," Ryker growled. "She ain't safe." That was why he was staying, damn it.

Heath threw up his hands. "Maybe not, but she sure as shit isn't asking for your help or telling you the truth. She's bruised, she's been paying for motels, and she's been giving somebody cash, brother. That woman is a fuckload of trouble, and she's not leveling with you about it."

Ryker ground his teeth together even as his hands fisted. Everything Heath was saying was true, and that just pissed him off. "I can handle Zara."

"Right," Heath mocked.

Fire flushed so hard through him it burned. Ryker moved then, and Denver planted himself firmly between the two men, his hand flat against Ryker's vibrating chest. "Whoa now. We're brothers."

"Doesn't mean we can't beat the hell out of each other," Ryker said evenly, his gaze on Heath over Denver's shoulder. While he couldn't stop the voices inside his head, mocking his reasons for staying, he could sure as shit hit Heath a few times.

"Any time and any place," Heath returned, fury flashing in his eyes.

Denver shoved Ryker back. "Jesus, you fuckwads. Knock it off. We have enough problems."

Heath blinked and then leaned back against his door. He took several deep breaths. "You're right. I'm sorry."

Regret slammed into Ryker. "No, I'm sorry. Really." God, he needed his brothers. Without them, he wouldn't have made it to adulthood. "I'm an ass."

"We both are. I'm off—had a rough day at court," Heath muttered.

Denver frowned and partially turned. "Huh?"

Heath shook his head. "Nothin'. Just a rough day." He turned and shoved open the door to his apartment, and his shoulders slumped. "Ryker, I'm sorry about what I said. If you want to keep her, I'm here for you. But that don't mean it'll end well. It never does." He moved inside and shut the door behind himself.

"Well." Denver looked at the closed door. "He's a fucking ray of sunshine."

"Something's up," Ryker said, his chest growing heavy. He'd been so focused on Zara and the visit from Greg that he was missing signals. "What happened today at court?"

Denver turned toward Heath's door. "You go figure out what's up with your lady, and I'll dig into Heath's psyche."

Ryker nodded. "We can meet in the morning and determine our next plan." He paused. "If we have to talk about that woman again, let's use Isobel Madison as her name, okay? That way we don't ever have to say 'Sylvia Daniels' again."

Denver blinked. "Yeah."

"Good. Also, I think Heath should talk to the FBI about the Copper Killer case. He's pacing the office like a caged tiger, and he needs to have a meeting with them just to do something. Okay?"

Denver nodded.

Ryker sighed. "Denver?"

"Yeah, I know. You're welcome." Denver opened Heath's door and then disappeared.

Ryker breathed deep and headed back into his place to talk to Zara. It was time she leveled with him, whether she liked it or not.

* * *

Zara stepped out of the bathroom, tucking the towel securely at her breasts. She stopped short at seeing Ryker on the bed, which was the only piece of furniture in the room. "I don't have spare clothes."

"You're not gonna need them." His eyes darkened as his gaze ran over her freshly scrubbed skin. He still wore the faded jeans and T-shirt, but he'd ditched his boots and leather jacket. Sitting on the end of the bed, his elbows on his thighs, he was the perfect picture of masculine intent. A tension, one she didn't recognize, swelled through the room.

She swallowed and pushed her hair off her shoulders. Her body started to thrum in a way unique to being with Ryker. He brought out something in her she didn't quite understand. Even if her mind and heart had doubts, her body was all in. "Listen. I'm not going to lie."

"That'd be a nice change."

Her chin went down. "Hey—I've never lied to you."

"You haven't told me shit." Even the clipped words held a sense of…dominance—a state at home in him, on him, around him. Why she responded to that with wild tingles, she'd never understand. But she had to shake her head to focus.

"You don't get to know about my life, Ryker. We've gone over this." Heat rose from her chest to her face. "You set the parameters from the beginning." The concrete floor chilled her bare feet. Wearing nothing but the towel, she shivered with an unwelcome vulnerability, even through the ever-present desire. "You can't change them now."

"They're already changed." He clasped his hands loosely between his knees. "Come here, Zara."

That voice. Deep and dark, with a commanding, sexual edge. Her body reacted instantly, her nipples hardening as she became wet. "Don't tell me what to do," she whispered, fighting need along with her temper.

"You like me telling you what to do."

"Only in bed," she burst out.

He smiled, the expression gentle and dangerous all at once. "Then get in bed."

She shook her head just a little. If she got in that bed, she'd forget all about her anger, her independence, her safety. Oh, he'd keep her physically safe, but she'd known from the first kiss that he'd shatter her heart if she let him. "Not until we reach an agreement." She clutched the towel like it was a lifeline.

"If you make me come and get you, I'll make you beg tonight."

A full-body shiver took her, and it had nothing to do with fear. Oh, she'd begged him before, and the result had been multiple orgasms that still filled her dreams. Her breath quickened. A flush worked under her skin, sensitizing her breasts. "You have to listen to me."

"I plan to listen to a whole lot from you." He stood, so tall and broad he took her breath away. "After we take the edge off."

The sense that he'd stopped playing focused her attention solely on him. But it wasn't that simple, now, was it? His taking the edge off would make her mellow, even pliant. She'd start dreaming about forever, and she knew better. It was all right to have a weakness if one acknowledged and fought it. Falling for him could be her weakness. So she lifted her chin and met his gaze directly. "We're friends with benefits."

"Is that a fact?" He stepped closer, leaving only a couple of feet between them.

"Yes." Her voice stayed strong and sure, thank God. After dating for a month, they'd both had checkups, and she'd gone on the pill. For him. Okay, for her, too. "Accept the parameters, Ryker. You have no choice."

He flashed his teeth. "So you just want to get fucked?"

The coarse language in that throaty tone nearly sent her over the edge. Her thighs trembled—with the need to run toward him or away, she wasn't quite sure. "That's what we have," she whispered.

He reached her then, tucking one finger in the towel. His head lowered, his mouth next to her ear, brushing heat against her skin. "Tell me, then."

Her mouth went dry, and her abdomen rippled. "Wh-what?"

He tilted his head until his gaze could capture hers. "Tell me again. What we are. What you want."

"You know," she whispered back, her gaze dropping to his full mouth. Oh, the pleasure he could bring with those lips.

"Just fucking." His fingers traced up her neck and around her nape, sensations tingling through her.

She tried to swallow. "Yes."

His fingers tangled in her wet hair. "Ask me, then."

"Wh-what?" she breathed.

He twisted his wrist, securing her and tugging her head back. The finger tucked in her towel tugged, and the material loosened. He leaned closer, his gaze on hers, his mouth right over her lips. "Ask me to fuck you."

The erotic pain cascaded along her scalp. Her mind fuzzed and shut down as hunger shot through her. Even so, caution whispered deep inside her. Something wild was being unleashed in Ryker... something she'd sensed but never seen. "Ryker—"

His hold tightened, stealing her breath. His eyes darkened. "Ask. Me."

Desire spiked to lust inside her, forcing her nerves to riot. God, she wanted him. But pride wouldn't let her just ask. Not yet, anyway. She reached out to cup the rock-hard erection beneath his jeans. "Maybe you should ask *me*," she murmured, using pressure and tapping her fingers along his length.

His nostrils flared.

Quicker than she would've thought possible, he grabbed her wrist and snagged the other one in a strong grip as the towel fluttered to the floor. With his hold on her hair and the other hand on her wrists, she couldn't move.

The reality of that flushed need through her so quickly her knees wobbled.

His hand secured hers against her abdomen. His thigh slipping between her thighs to press against her pulsing core. The hand fisted in her hair drew her back more, elongating her neck and putting her in an even more helpless position.

Delicious heat sparked through her. She bit her lip, but a moan still escaped.

His mouth still hovered above hers. "Ask me." Each word was punctuated with a flexing of his thigh muscle against her clit. Mini explosions rocked her lower body.

She panted and her eyelids closed.

A sharp nip to her lips had her gasping and opening her eyes. Ryker kept her gaze and soothed the small wound with his tongue. "Now, Zara," he growled.

Her lips smarted and yet needed more. He wanted the words? Fine. "Fuck me, Ryker." She lifted up onto her toes and took his mouth, pushing hard against him.

CHAPTER 10

When her lips touched his, the beast inside Ryker—the one he secretly believed made him different from normal people—roared to the surface. For his entire life, what he'd wanted had been held out of his view, out of his grip.

Including this woman.

Oh, she was flush against him, her mouth working his, the dampness from her skin edging through his T-shirt. Yet she held herself away, wanting to limit what they had. What they were.

Which should be exactly what he wanted. Instead, what he wanted was to blast right into her heart, where it was safe and warm and good. Where he could finally relax and be himself.

But she was refusing to take a chance and wouldn't tell him why. Unless...she sensed who he really was and knew better. Knew that he wasn't quite right.

Maybe Zara could be the one person, the one woman, who could accept all of him. The thought brought out a hope, a dangerous one. If he had her, really *had* her, he'd do anything to keep her. Maybe she was smart to keep her distance.

He took over the kiss, his fingers stretching to release her hair so he could cup her scalp. As his tongue met hers, she made a low sound deep in her throat. A sound of welcome.

Created just for him.

Such a small sound, and it skated right through his heart and straight down. His cock pounded to be inside her...now.

He snaked an arm around her bare waist, twisted, and pressed her down onto the bed. She tasted like mint and something sweet—all Zara. Stretching atop her, he balanced his weight on his elbows. When she opened her legs, allowing him to settle in, his heart skipped.

Then his cock hardened until his zipper caused pain.

Zara was something special, even among good people. She was smart and kind, and she made choices with her eyes open. He wanted to be one of her choices.

Her hands tunneled through his hair, her nails scraping. She reached down and tugged his shirt up. He had to release her mouth as the material was yanked over his head, but the second it was free, he found her again. Soft and succulent, her lips met his.

He wanted to go slow and show her tenderness.

Then she wrenched her mouth away with a small chuckle. A challenging one.

Right or wrong, such defiance burned electricity right through him. It crackled in the air around them. Fine. She wanted to play? Next time he'd go slow. A rumble came from his chest and sounded suspiciously like a growl.

Those stunning eyes widened. Her pink lips gaped in an O, and desire glimmered in her sky blue eyes. A flush covered her high cheekbones, and the smoothest skin imaginable stretched tight across very fragile bones.

"God, you're beautiful," he breathed, angling to the side and releasing his jeans. A couple of shimmies and quick kicks, and they dropped over the side of the bed.

She sucked in air. "You are too, and you know it." The slow caress down his back served to calm him a little.

He nipped under her jaw and kissed her full breasts. It had taken a couple of months to get her comfortable with being nude with him, and he'd fully meant it when he'd assured her he liked curves. Lots of them. "Stunning, Zara." He took a nipple into his mouth, trying to be gentle when all he wanted to do was bend her over and make her scream.

She arched against him, all woman.

He flicked her nipple, knowing she liked a small bite of pain. She gasped, and he fought a grin. Not once in his life had he experienced this type of need. Only with Zara.

"Ryker," she breathed, her nails scraping across his ass.

His dick jumped against her, and she purred. The woman fucking *purred*.

She dug in her nails. "You said you'd take the edge off. Do it. Fast." Her legs widened, and her inner thighs gripped his hips.

Liquid heat coated his balls. Wet and ready. "Fuckin' amazing." He released her breast and kissed up her chest, angling his mouth over her fragile collarbone. Sometimes, the very smallness of her bones caught him off guard. His need to protect her came from instinct, not thought. He *felt* her inside his chest. Murmuring, he licked up her neck and enjoyed the full-body shiver that engulfed her.

The woman had a very sensitive neck. *His woman*. For the first time, he let the reality firmly take hold. He was done fighting it. Now all he had to do was convince her. Finally, he reached her mouth for a long kiss that sent his senses reeling. He leaned back and grabbed his dick to press into her. "After this, we're gonna talk," he whispered against her lips. When he could think of more than the wet heat waiting for him.

Her mouth curved under his. "Uh-huh."

Oh, she did like to mess with his head. He kept her gaze and worked his way inside her, stretching her and fighting the overwhelming urge to shove in. His arms shook with the effort, but he went slow, giving her time to accommodate to his size before he went farther.

Her thighs trembled against his legs.

She swallowed and breathed out. "Each time…"

Yeah. He rested his forehead on hers. Each time felt like something new. Finally, after a century or two, he rested, fully embedded in her. Heat surrounded and caressed his cock, and he had to inhale to keep himself in check. "You okay?"

Her smile nearly lit him on fire. "I'm better than okay." She punctuated the words with her nails on his ass. "I've missed you, Ryker."

Those words. She had no idea what those small words did inside him. Hell. He didn't understand it and had been running from it, rather unsuccessfully, from day one. The feeling should be soft and sweet, when actually it was raw and fierce. She created something in him that was almost primal. "Then it's about time you trusted me." The words came from deeper than his consciousness and were out of his mouth before he could think.

The sense of unexpected vulnerability, one he hadn't felt since he was a kid, loosened something dark inside him. He grasped her arm and tugged up, winding his fingers through hers and pressing her hand to the mattress. His other hand secured her hip, and he pulled out only to shove back in. Hard.

She arched her back, revealing the long line of her neck.

"This is what you wanted, right?" He pulled out and started pounding into her, knocking the headboard against the wall. By the time he was through with her, she was going to want so much more. She had to.

"Yes," she breathed, her thighs tightening against him. Her fingers wrapped around his, and her hold strengthened.

So he gave it to her, not holding back, hammering inside her until her sex began to quiver around him. Then he slowed down and stopped, balls deep, inside her.

Sweat dotted her forehead. She blinked at him, fine tremors going through her that he could actually feel. "Ryker?" The hoarse tenor of her voice almost made him come right then and there.

"I think we're more than this." Although *this* was pretty damn good.

Her head fell back onto the pillow, and her hips rolled against him. He flattened his hand across her ass, pulling her closer to him, somehow forcing himself even deeper inside her. Electricity shot through his balls. A groan rumbled up from his chest.

She tried to move again, and he prevented her. Her eyes darkened, and her womb convulsed around him. Someday he wanted to tie her up. Based on her reactions, she'd fucking love it. For now, holding her where he wanted her was enough to nearly send her over. So he held perfectly still and made sure she did the same.

He forgot about her one hand still on his butt.

The nails dug in while challenge—oh, that was definitely challenge—filled her stunning blue eyes. She did something with her internal muscles that gripped his cock stronger than any vise. Ecstasy blasted through him.

"Oh, you're gonna pay for that," he gritted out. "Later." It was way too late now.

Holding her tight, impressed as hell with the dangerous woman, he pulled out and shoved back in, setting up a hard rhythm that had her gasping. She went over first, waves crashing through her body to undulate around him. Sparks, flying fast, ripped down his spine to his testicles.

He dug his face into her neck, his entire body shuddering as he came.

Slowly, his heart rate calmed down. He chuckled against her damp neck as she relaxed beneath him. Now, that hadn't gone exactly according to plan.

Yep. Definitely a dangerous woman. He had to keep her—it was too late to turn back now. The sense of possession gripped him hard, compressing his lungs. Slowly, muscle by muscle, he released the tension. That was that, then.

* * *

Zara's body turned to mush, and her hand slid from Ryker's ass to the bed. Her other one was trapped beneath his, but right now she didn't really care. Her eyelids fluttered shut.

"Oh no." He pressed harder inside her, sending quakes throughout her abdomen.

She lifted one eyelid, beyond exhausted. "Tired."

"Talk."

"No." She wiggled a little beneath him. Her excitement had ebbed, but the guy was apparently still semi-hard inside her. "You're an impressive man, Ryker." She yawned.

"Jesus." He withdrew and shoved from the bed to pad toward the bathroom, masculine irritation deepening his tone.

God, she loved that tattoo. Fierce and strong, a wild bird decorated his right shoulder with its wings spread and rising out of fire. Two intricate *B*s combined in the center. She'd asked once what it meant, and he'd shrugged.

She smiled as she shimmied her butt up, grabbed the bedclothes, and slid beneath cool, clean sheets. A small groan of pure pleasure erupted from her, and she stretched before curling onto her side. A minute later, the bed shifted, and warmth enclosed her.

"What do the *B*s stand for?" she mumbled.

"Blood brothers," he said against her hair. "We thought we'd name the agency that, but we don't want it traced, so we went with Lost Bastards."

"Blood brothers?" she murmured, realization dawning. "The scars on your hands?"

"Yeah. We didn't have family, so the three of us created one with an old knife and blood."

"How old were you?" She blinked. They'd created their own brotherhood. There was so much more to know about him.

"Twelve. I'll tell you more tomorrow," he whispered, sounding drowsy.

How sad and sweet at the same time. "Tomorrow sounds good." She snuggled right into Ryker's hard warmth and fell into dreamland.

The dream caught her around the neck and threw her into the past.

She was ten years old, humming quietly in the backseat of her mother's clunky car on the way to yet another farmers' market, this one in northern Washington State. She liked the trees and wildlife in Washington, and hopefully her mother would stay with this boyfriend for a while before they moved on again.

Well, usually the boyfriend moved on. Sometimes with screams and shouts, and sometimes in the dark of night…while taking any money they'd found. But Chuck seemed like a nice guy, even though he had three cats, four dogs, and a llama. Who the heck had a llama?

Lightning flashed outside, and Zara frowned, peering out the wet window. "I forgot my umbrella," she muttered, patting her nice and dry jeans. She'd learned early to plan for herself.

Her mom turned around from the driver's seat with a wide smile, her hair in a wild mane and her face freshly scrubbed of makeup. Apparently Chuck liked the natural look. "It's fun to get wet."

Actually, it wasn't fun to get wet. Not really. "My hair gets all wild and curly, and then I sneeze." Zara shook her head and focused on Chuck in the passenger seat. "Did you remember the ledger?"

He turned, his green eyes dilated. "No, dude. Totally forgot."

Zara sighed and started organizing her hair into two neat braids the rain couldn't ruin. "We need the ledger to keep track of how many of the pottery pieces you sell, Mom."

Her mom laughed and concentrated on the road while shoving back curly black hair. "Why? I mean, if we have money, we sold some. If we don't, then it wasn't a good day."

Zara shook her head. The old jeans barely fit her, and she just didn't understand why her mom didn't care. Somebody had to be a grown-up and take care of things. The world was dark and scary. She shivered.

They'd never go global with the pottery pieces without organization. While she'd given up any idea of having a college fund, it'd be nice if she could start a savings account for her mom, for when she went to college. On loans, no doubt. College was her way out, and then, to get rid of the guilt of leaving, she'd send money to her mom.

If she made it into college. Fear clawed up her throat, and she swallowed it rapidly down. She eyed the marketing book she'd borrowed from the library. "Have you contacted that distributor in Seattle?" It had taken her three days to understand exactly what a distributor did, and she figured they needed one now.

"Um, no." Her mom leaned forward as thunder ripped across the sky. "I will later today. Promise."

"Right." Zara wrapped rubber bands around her braids and kicked out her feet. There were holes in the bottoms of her tennis shoes. If they made any money today, she'd have to grab some before Chuck got it all and bought more pot.

Chuck turned, his frizzy blond hair drifting around. "Whoops. Did you feed the dogs?"

"Yes. The dogs, cats, and llama." Zara sighed.

Chuck laughed. "Sounds like a nursery rhyme."

"Sounds like a moron," Zara muttered quietly to herself. But at least this one didn't hit, yell, or look at her funny. So she smiled at him. If they could just stay in one place for a little while, her mom could make a bunch

of the pretty pottery to sell, and then maybe they'd get to eat regularly. Her stomach growled as if on cue. "The animals are fine."

The rain pounded harder, and she wished for a warmer jacket. Or even for one of those rain slicker kinds that kept people dry. A girl in her class, Mandy Martini, had two of those jackets. One was purple and one was blue. The blue one was super pretty. Mandy's dad was a lawyer.

Lightning cracked again, and she shivered. Maybe she'd be a lawyer. Well, she didn't like to fight with people, so maybe she'd be a paralegal. That was stable, and the lawyers she'd seen on television wore cool clothes.

Something popped. Her mom shrieked and wrenched the steering wheel around. The car turned left and plunged down an embankment. Trees flew by.

Zara screamed. Terror ripped into her, and she flung her arms out.

Glass shot inside. The car hit a tree, and the sound of metal crunching destroyed the day. Zara blinked blood from her eyes. "Mom?" she yelled.

Zara bolted upright in bed, sucking in air. Sweat dripped down her back, and she couldn't breathe. She clutched her chest and shook.

"Whoa." Ryker snagged her around the waist and pulled her to him, settling her face against his neck. "What the hell, darlin'?"

Breath whooshed out of her lungs. She sucked in air. Breathe. She could breathe.

She blinked away tears and exhaled slowly. Okay. It was just panic. She wasn't having a heart attack. Thunder rolled outside, and sleet pinged against the windows. Fairly strong light filtered in. "Bad dream," she burst out.

"No shit." His voice was sleepy, but the hand caressing down her back was very comforting. "You've had it before. What happened?"

She stilled, although the comfort he offered settled something deep inside her. Something warm and safe. "I, ah, don't really talk about it."

"That sentence is easy to change." The sleep cleared from his voice, the tone commanding and oddly comforting.

Her feelings were, too. For once, she was tempted to share her story. So she told him about the wreck and her mother dying. "I was trapped in the car with them, both dead, for several hours." She shivered, remembering how terrified she'd been. How sad and alone.

Ryker's head had lifted, and his eyes burned. "Oh, baby. I'm so sorry. I wish I could fix that."

Tears pricked her eyes, and she battled them away. He'd fix everything for her if he could. A sweetness lived in Ryker that she doubted many people in his life had seen. "So I went to live with my Grams. That's all."

"Sounds like a lot." Ryker pressed a kiss to her head, his strong shoulders shielding her. "All I know about your grandmother is what I read in a file and that she moved here to Cisco when you did. You never talk about her."

"She's mine." Zara smiled.

Ryker was silent for a minute. "I get that. Denver and Heath are mine, and I hold that close." He rubbed a large hand down her back. "I guess I didn't realize other people felt that way, too."

She pressed her lips against his neck. The nightmare attacked her every once in a while, and she'd awaken to a cold and lonely bed. Having Ryker comfort her, having his sheer strength and warmth surrounding her, made the past not so frightening. "Grams is a combination of my flighty mother and my responsible self." She stiffened and then relaxed as she opened her heart and shared what was in there.

He kissed her head as if knowing the huge step she'd just taken. "How so?"

"Well, she took me in, gave me a nice home, and did all the things a mom should've. She was the grown-up, and I got to be the kid. Usually." She smiled.

"Usually?"

"Yeah," Zara said softly, warmth spreading through her at the memories. "Once in a while, she'd decide we needed girl time, so we'd drive to the Grand Canyon for a few days."

"Sounds like fun."

"It really was," she murmured. Something buzzed by her head. She frowned and glanced at the alarm clock. They'd slept in until almost noon. Wow. She never slept that long. "Crap. I have a meeting at work."

"It's Saturday," Ryker said, his voice a little too calm.

"Discovery and trials don't pause for weekends." She pushed from the bed and hesitated. "I need a ride to my place to change clothes. Any chance my car is working?"

"Not a chance." Ryker stretched from the bed, and in the strong light, he looked like a fucking ripped god. He stretched all of that smooth, honed muscle.

Butterflies heated in her abdomen.

Then he turned and pinned her with a dark look. "Who hit you?"

That quickly, she was just tired of keeping secrets. Maybe great sex had mellowed her, or perhaps it was time to let Ryker in. She'd told him of the worst day of her life, and he'd comforted her. It was time she stopped being so afraid and started to live. Sure, opening up to Ryker was a huge risk, but he was worth it. She felt it. So she swallowed several times and decided to trust completely, feeling every bit like she was jumping off a cliff. She was tired of being completely alone. "Jay Pentley hit me."

CHAPTER
11

Ryker rocked back, anger trying to claw through him. "Jay Pentley—the mayor and your client?"

It sounded even worse put that way. "Yeah. He's a wife beater, and I've been helping his wife out, so he felt free to challenge both of us." She shrugged. "I'm violating legal ethics by helping Julie, and if I get caught, I'll be fired and the firm will be sued for malpractice."

Ryker scratched his head, warning tickling at the base of his neck. "Are you giving her legal advice?"

"No." She shook her head. "Just a couple of loans." She looked down at the bed.

Oh man. The woman was a terrible liar. Just terrible. For some reason, amusement attacked him. Yet he tried to keep it out of his voice. "Zara. Are you telling Julie about your case?"

She winced. "Kind of. I mean, we're turning over all discovery requests, but I might have directed her to tell her attorney where to look for hidden assets."

Ryker huffed out a laugh as he tried to order facts in his mind. "That's totally malpractice."

"I know." Zara wiped her hands down her face. "But Jay is such an ass, and he has all the money, and Julie's attorney sucks. You know who Jay's family is."

"Yeah. Isn't he supposed to run for governor or something?" Well connected or not, the man was about to take a beating for touching Zara.

"The U.S. Senate," she mumbled. "He's announcing early next year, after the divorce is all complete. By then he'll probably be dating a perfect debutante, and their romance will be part of the campaign strategy."

Ryker shook his head, grateful she'd told him the truth about the bruise. Finally she was trusting him, and damn if that didn't feel good. He could do what he did best and shield her. He now understood where the threat was, which put him in control of the danger. His heart warmed that she'd let him in. "Why Julie?"

"Huh?" Zara focused her pretty blue eyes on him.

"You believe in the legal system, and you're a straight shooter normally. Why are you sticking your neck out and breaking rules for this woman?"

Zara stretched her neck. "She's my friend. I mean, we became really good friends when I came back from college, and Julie got me out into the world and out of books and work for a while." She cleared her throat. "We kind of lost touch when she married Jay five years ago, and I should've seen what was happening." Color tinged her cheeks.

"Wasn't your fault." Ryker shoved a hand through his thick hair. "Is Pentley dangerous to you?"

Her eyebrows drew down. "No. Julie was staying at a different motel, and he found her. I happened to be dropping off some essentials for her, and there was a fight. We got away."

So the bastard thought he could hit Zara since she couldn't tell anybody what she was up to. Ryker would have to discuss that with the mayor. "What about the three thousand dollars you've been withdrawing each month?"

She jerked back, and fire flashed in her eyes. "You've been *investigating* me?"

"Yes."

She really was pretty when furious. "How dare you."

"You should've leveled with me, baby," he drawled, fighting his own temper. "Money?"

"None of your business," she ground out, her teeth definitely clenched.

"That's where you're wrong." He was about done being reasonable.

Whatever she saw in his gaze had her blinking. He could actually see the very second she decided to work with him instead of against him.

She drew back and nodded. "I may need your help in getting Julie to safety after her competency hearing on Monday. Her stupid husband is challenging her sanity."

"If her lawyer sucks, I can ask Heath to represent her." Although what a clusterfuck that would be. Heath had a serious blind spot when it came to battered women, and he hated being in court. Plus, Jay Pentley was the mayor, and the news outlets might be covering the divorce. Not to mention they needed to keep a low profile. "How bad is her lawyer?"

"Terrible. New kid right out of school…and if you ask me, it's shocking he got *into* a law school. Guy's a moron." Zara's body visibly relaxed. "Julie has bills from before they were married—mainly school, credit cards, and her car—and so far, the court hasn't ordered Jay to pay them. I've been loaning her three thousand dollars a month just so she can keep her head above water."

Well, that explained the money and the motels.

"There's more." Her voice hitched.

Of course there was more. "Tell me."

She worried her bottom lip with her teeth. "I actually introduced

Julie and Jay. After I first came back with my paralegal degree, I interned at the mayor's office. Jay's dad was the mayor then, and Jay worked for his dad."

That wasn't all. "And?" Ryker asked, going on instinct, warning tickling the base of his skull.

She winced again. "I may have dated Jay a little bit. I mean, we went on a few dates, but it wasn't serious. Not at all."

"Wait a sec." Ryker ran through the new tidbit of information, an unwelcome jealousy ripping into his gut. "How did Julie end up with him?"

Zara shrugged. "I wasn't feeling it with him, so I called it quits. Julie showed up to meet me for lunch one day, and they hit it off. Turns out I was right about the guy."

"Did he hit you?"

"No. We just didn't…mesh." She sighed. "I'm so relieved it didn't work out between us, but I still feel a little guilty about encouraging Julie with him."

Ryker breathed out, irrationally glad she'd dumped Jay. "It's not your fault."

"I know, but still…"

Ryker watched her carefully. "Did you sleep with Jay?"

She tilted her head to the side. "Would it matter?"

"No, but I'd like to know." He had no right to ask the question, but it didn't stop him. Right and wrong rarely had.

"No." She faced him head-on, the truth glimmering in her eyes. "I broke it off before that point. Well, mainly because he was pushing that point, and I just didn't trust him."

Good instincts. Relief, wrong and inappropriate, still filled him. "Thanks for telling me the truth."

"Always. You and I are always honest with each other. We just don't share much, do we?"

"I'd like to change that." He blinked as the words flew out of his mouth.

"Would you? Really?" Her upper lip curled. "I think you'd like for me to tell you everything and for you to not have to say a word. I don't know a thing about your childhood except for the scars that you share with your blood brothers."

He could give her more than that. "We lived in a hellhole masquerading as a boys home. Those were pretty bad years, and I don't like to talk about them. Heath and Denver really don't like to talk about those days, so please don't ask them." All he needed was Zara poking into the past he was still shielding them all from.

"I won't," she said softly, her intense gaze proving she probably noticed much more than he wanted her to see. "I like, ah, knowing more about you. The real you." Vulnerability shone in her eyes.

His chest thrummed. "You can trust me, Zara." She didn't need to feel vulnerable with him. Ever. "I'll protect you."

"That's what you do, right?" she asked thoughtfully.

He opened his mouth and nothing came out. Then he cleared his throat and gave her the truth, because he'd said he would. "Yeah. That's what I do." It's who he was and who he needed to be. "I imagine it's not easy being on the other side of that."

She smiled. "We'll see, won't we? For now, I, ah, have to get to work. Jay Pentley is actually compiling documents for us today so we can answer discovery requests from Julie's attorney. Kind of answer, I guess."

Yeah. Enough sharing. That meant Pentley would be at City Hall, working on his discovery documents. Ryker nodded. "We'll swing by your place for fresh clothes, and then I'll drop you off at work." He held up a hand to stall her question as she started to ask it. "I don't know when your car will be ready, but I'll find out. Denver can fix anything." Although, the idea of having Zara dependent on him for transport, especially while Jay Pentley was still walking, held definite appeal.

By her quick snort, she somehow read his mind.

Good thing she couldn't read past that.

* * *

Zara tugged down her moss-colored sweater and walked into the conference room, where Brock had files and notebooks haphazardly spread out. She gasped. "What in the world have you done?"

The lawyer looked up. "I've been trying to put all the data into some sort of order."

She'd had it in order. "I see." Pulling back a chair, she dropped down and slid manila files into organized stacks. Why was it that the smarter the man, the more chaos he created? "How far have you gotten on the discovery requests?"

"I've gone through all the documents supplied by Jay, and I read over his answers to interrogatories. We need to tweak a couple." When he worked on weekends, Brock wore a dark blue golf shirt that emphasized his broad chest. "I also went through the affidavits you drafted for us. Good job on those."

"Thanks." She smiled. Brock was a stickler for procedure, and a compliment from him meant something.

He leaned forward, his gaze somber. "I know you and Julie Pentley were friends a while back, and I'm sorry you're on this side of the aisle."

She nodded. "I'm not sure Jay is such a great guy, you know?"

"He's a politician." Brock smiled. "Aren't they all slightly less than great?"

"Says the lawyer," she teased. An easy friendship with Brock was one of the best parts of her job.

Brock barked out a laugh. "Very good point." He shoved a manila file toward her. "Here are the financials."

She flipped the file folder open to read down a list. "Are we sure he gave us everything?" According to Julie, there was a lot more money than what was neatly laid out there.

"As far as I can tell. Why? Do you know something I don't?"

Definitely. "No, but it seems like a man like Jay Pentley, with his family and trust funds, would have more income than this." She pushed the file toward Brock. "I'd double-check with him. If Julie's attorney hires a private detective or a forensic accountant, then we don't want to be unprepared."

Brock spun the file around with one finger. "It sounds like you do know something."

"No." She worked for Brock, darn it. The man was a master in trial and certainly didn't need her help. "I just think Jay has more money than he's showing. When I worked for the mayor way back when, Jay was always throwing cash around."

"I'd forgotten you dated," Brock said slowly, his eyebrows rising. "Was it serious?"

"Not at all." She tried not to squirm.

Brock grinned. "Good."

Hmmm. She reached for a ledger showing a breakdown of marital versus separate property. Jay had left a few items off. But she couldn't tell Brock that. Not right now.

"So, ah, Zara. Are you still seeing Ryker? He seemed pretty intense in your office yesterday."

Her gaze shot to Brock, and her instincts kicked into gear. Oh, he couldn't want to ask her out again, could he? "Um, yeah." That was definitely the safest answer, even if she had no clue where she and Ryker really stood.

"I think you could do better," Brock murmured.

Zara couldn't help the small grin. "You're impossible."

"I know." He rolled his neck. "Even you have to admit that we make a perfect team in the office. Who knows how much fun we could have outside these walls."

Yeah, and if Ryker hadn't already thrown her world into a tailspin, she'd be lucky to date a guy like Brock. He was the total package, and he didn't seem to flaunt it. "I'm glad we work together, and I'm happy we're friends."

"I'm not giving up." He reached for a stack of ledgers, his tone cheerful.

"What ever happened to the doctor you were dating?" Zara pulled a legal pad closer to start making some notes about the interrogatories.

"She got too clingy." Brock tossed the ledgers toward Zara. "Would you sum up the assets for the trial binder? And, um, create a trial binder?"

She rolled her eyes. "Seriously, Brock. I already have one started. It's the big blue one over on that chair. You know. The ones that says TRIAL BINDER on it?"

"Oh, good." He reached for the binder and chuckled. "Everything should go a lot smoother after the competency hearing on Monday."

Zara's pen stopped mid-stroke. "I know Julie and she's competent."

Brock shook his head. "Her shrink, the one she's seen for three years, will testify otherwise. Julie is unstable, Zara, and she does drugs." His eyes softened. "I'm sorry."

"No, she doesn't," Zara burst out.

"Sure, she does. She's been borrowing money from several friends each month, pretending that she needs help with bills." Brock scratched his head and opened another file.

Zara's mouth dropped open only to snap shut. That couldn't be right. She knew Julie much better than Brock did. "Maybe Julie does need help with bills."

Brock leaned over and tapped his fingers on the ledger. "Jay has paid all her expenses since the separation. Car, student loans, credit cards." He pointed to a column. "In fact, Jay paid off all her debts. See?"

Zara looked down and read the neatly printed numbers. Her breath heated, and unease dropped like a rock into her stomach. "We have proof?"

"Sure. Receipts for everything."

Well, hell.

CHAPTER
12

After dropping Zara off at the law office, Ryker turned down a side street and headed across town. Snow began to fall quietly and softly.

On a Saturday, City Hall was vacant and closed, but he could see lights on in the mayor's office. Zara had said that Jay Pentley would be in his office, and apparently she was correct. Excellent. After parking in a side alley, he loped around the building to the rear exit, taking a quick look around. No one. A twist with the tools he'd brought, and one of the back doors opened.

He slipped inside and quietly shut the door. The silence of an empty government building on a weekend pounded around him. Keeping his senses on full alert, he crossed the polished wooden floor and ran up the wide stairway, careful not to touch the intricate banister.

The mayor's office was situated at the front of the building, so Ryker turned on the landing and passed several closed doors before reaching the one room with a light on.

He bypassed a vacant reception area, using a swinging half door to finally reach the entrance to the office overlooking the quiet street. Heavy breathing and a woman's soft cry had Ryker stopping short. He peered around the open doorway to see a blonde on Jay's lap, pounding hard, her back to the door. Jay's arms were around her waist, and he was helping her move faster.

Jesus.

The slapping sound of flesh on flesh filled the office. Jay groaned and shuddered, dropping his head to the blonde's neck. The blonde threw back her head and screamed, her body shaking.

Ryker rolled his eyes and moved away from the door to crouch beside the receptionist's desk.

"Oh God, Jay. That was so good," the woman breathed.

"Yeah." Something rustled. "I have to get back to work, sweetheart."

More rustles as the blonde probably put herself back together. "We're going to be together now that you're getting divorced, right?" A definite pout lived in the woman's words.

"Of course." A smacking kiss could be heard. "As soon as it's all official, you and I will go public. Slowly. It'll be a good romance to delight voters." A zipper. "Now be my good girl and let me get some work done, okay?"

"Okay." The woman came into sight, slipping on a pair of high heels. "I'll see you tomorrow."

"Bye," Jay said, his voice preoccupied.

Ryker waited until the blonde had clopped down the hallway before standing and slipping inside the office. "Jay Pentley." Ryker shut the door behind him and locked it.

Jay looked up from a stack of papers on his desk, his reading glasses askew, and the sleeves of his white dress shirt shoved up his arms. The guy was over six feet and muscled…probably from working out with a trainer. His hair was mussed, his shoulders relaxed, and his eyes lazy. The sex must've been good.

Ryker smiled and crossed the room to the corner of the desk.

"Who the hell are you?" Jay reached for a phone, his head jerking.

Ryker beat him to it and yanked the phone away. The entire thing clattered to the floor. He moved in, smooth and calm, and grabbed

Pentley by the neck. "All you need to know is that I'm here for pay-back for Zara Remington." Without missing a beat, he punched Jay in the gut. Hard.

Jay doubled over and then swung out, his fist barely grazing Ryker's chest. "I'll have you arrested." He gasped.

"Then I'll just kill you and bury your worthless ass where they'll never find you." Ryker punched him in the thigh and then the ribs. His muscles bunched with the need to cause real damage, to protect what he'd claimed as his own: Zara.

But that would cause more problems for them all, so he held himself back. He'd keep his monster caged.

This time.

* * *

His knuckles still smarting a bit from his meeting with the mayor, Ryker kicked back in Denver's guest chair, the sketch of Isobel Madison in his hands. "If we go looking for her, we might find more than we want," he murmured.

Denver nodded from across the cherrywood desk, his gaze remaining on his computer. "Yep."

Ryker grabbed a ball of rubber bands from a corner of the desk and tossed it up in the air. "Isobel Madison had a thing with Sheriff Cobb, and no doubt they've stayed in touch. If we try to find her, we might bring attention to ourselves, right when we really need to stay under the radar."

"Yep." Denver's fingers flew over the keyboard.

Ryker smoothed the paper out on his thigh. "We could tell the kid to stuff it, or we could somehow lock him down."

Denver looked up, his blue eyes narrowing. "Hmmm."

"You're right. I don't like either of those ideas." Ryker breathed out. "I want to know who this woman is and why she tested us through the years."

"Me too," Heath said, loping into the office and dropping into the other guest chair. "At the time, I figured she was just some sort of social worker, but now..."

Yeah. Now that Greg seemed so desperate to find her, Ryker's instincts were humming, too. "Let's find her."

Denver waited for Heath to nod and again began typing furiously.

Ryker turned to Heath. "What was up with you yesterday?"

Heath tugged down a ripped T-shirt marred with grease. "I had to go to the courthouse and a chick was there, getting a protection order against her husband. She was beat to hell and about eighteen years old. Name was Molly." His tone darkened and deepened, upping the tension in the room.

"Molly. Sweet name." Ryker treaded lightly. Heath's mother had been murdered by her boyfriend after systematic beatings, which had often included roughing up Heath. "So the PO is a good thing, right?"

"Yeah." Heath held out his hand and frowned at the grease marks. "I saw her outside the courthouse after the hearing, clearly talking to the asshole over by his car." Heath shook his head.

Serious land mine there. "I'm sorry." Ryker glanced at the grease. "Do you want to talk about it?"

"There's nothing more to say that you don't already know." Heath tipped his head to the side. "Although I'd really love to find the asshole who killed my mother."

"We will. I don't know when or how, but we will." Ryker glanced at the stormy weather outside. When that day happened, he'd cover his brother. "Any news or leads or anything on the Copper Killer case?"

"No. It's like we're just holding our breath for the next blow," Heath muttered.

Yeah. That summed it up. While Ryker couldn't do anything on that case right now, he could help Zara. "How's Zara's car?"

"It's fine. Well, for a piece of shit, it's fine," Denver said, not losing a second with his typing, even though his gaze had strayed to check on Heath a couple of times.

Heath nodded. "He looked it over this morning and then asked me to replace the brake lines. She needs a new transmission, too."

"She needs a new car," Denver retorted.

Ryker nodded. "Yeah, but she doesn't exactly want to accept a car from me." What was the big deal?

"Maybe she thinks you'll want kinky favors," Denver drawled.

Ryker rolled his eyes. "We both know you're the kink bastard in the family."

Heath snorted, visibly shaking himself out of his mood. "Remember that leather club he visited in Seattle?"

"I was on a case," Denver said, his tone even, his fingers flying. "Why do you jerks always forget that part of the story?"

"You were a *master* at the case." Ryker snorted, enjoying bugging Denver enough that he had to speak. The more he spoke, the more he continued speaking. Physics at its best.

Heath chuckled.

Yeah. He'd made Heath laugh a little. Good. "Do you still have the leather pants and bullwhip?" Ryker asked, widening his eyes. "Maybe we could use those in Wyoming if we get a case on a ranch."

Denver stopped typing. "It was a flogger, not a bullwhip, and if you don't stop messing with me about it, I'm going to shove it up your—"

Heath held up a hand. "God, please don't say it. The image. It's a mental picture that would never go away."

Ryker bit back a grin. "We could always use Heath's clown outfit from that case in Jersey. The master and the clown. Man, I think we might have an idea for a sitcom. Denver can spank 'em, and then Heath can make 'em laugh."

Both of his brothers looked at him like he'd lost his mind. He tried to bite back a chuckle. Then Denver started laughing, a full rolling sound he rarely made. Heath swung his head and then joined in, the tension visibly leaving his shoulders.

Ryker settled. "Any news on Zara's medical records?"

"You sure you want to know?" Heath asked, clearing his throat.

"Yeah." Well, probably. "I'd rather she told me, but she hasn't, and if I ask her directly, she'll know I investigated her." More than she already knew he had, that was.

"Haven't found anything," Denver said.

If Denver hadn't found records, there weren't records to find. Good. That was good. Ryker tugged on a loose thread near his knee and ripped open a hole in his faded jeans. "Shit."

Denver glanced over the desk. "That's the style."

"Like you'd know shit about style," Heath retorted.

Denver grinned and read his screen. "I'm going to need about an hour to create a program that'll spot and hopefully shut down any backtracking software Madison might use. We're still calling her Madison, right?"

"Yeah. That name rings more true than the one she used with us. I always felt she was lying," Heath murmured.

"I wish I had that ability," Denver said.

Heath shrugged. "You have plenty of other weird ones, including the freaky computer skills."

"Maybe that's why she was studying us," Ryker said, his mind flipping the puzzle around. The woman had given them written test after written test and then watched them, recorded them, working out and playing sports. They'd even attended a military training camp once with her as their guardian. He shivered at remembering the way she'd looked at him when he started to gain muscle...like she wanted to take a bite. "What if we showed weird promise in some initial tests, and that's why she arrived to test us more? What if she wasn't some governmental social worker keeping an eye on orphans?"

Denver stopped typing and looked up. "But that would mean—"

"Yeah. It would be way too coincidental that we were all at the boys home at the same time being tested by the same woman." Ryker shoved down unease until a ball formed in his gut. His skin prickled. "No way could she have engineered our lives that way."

Heath pushed back in his chair. "You're right, so stop thinking such a bizarre scenario. That Greg kid got to you, buddy. There's no big conspiracy that put us in that shithole, and that Madison woman was just studying us as part of a governmental study, like she said. How orphans learn or something like that."

It was totally farfetched to consider any other explanation. "Why give us a fake name, not her real one?" Ryker asked.

"Maybe the kid gave us a fake name and her name really was Sylvia, like she told us," Heath said.

That was the most likely scenario. "The kid is wicked smart to have hacked us so well, but genius and madness, you know?" Ryker murmured. He settled back and tried to figure out the problem.

Heath glanced at his watch. "Did you see Special Agent Jackson on the news yesterday? She's becoming the face of the Copper Killer investigation, and damn if her hair isn't starting to look red."

"So we stick close to her," Denver said. "Right?"

"Exactly," Heath said, satisfaction tilting his mouth.

"Great. Us tailing the FBI. What could go wrong?" Ryker sighed.

"I'm with you there. I've tracked down Jackson, and she's still in Utah. I'm catching a flight in an hour to, well, bug her," Heath said. "She has to know more than she's told us."

Denver nodded.

"Okay." Ryker nodded too. "Denver, you keep working on Greg and finding Isobel Madison, and for the moment, I want to treat Zara's issue like a case." He needed to banish emotion until he figured out what was going on. Something had been nagging at his subconscious, so he tuned in. A buzzing sound. Barely discernible...but with a definite pattern.

He motioned to Heath, who instantly stilled.

Denver paused in typing, and Ryker shook his head, pointing at the keyboard. Denver nodded and continued typing, his gaze now wandering the room.

"We need to get furniture for the apartments," Heath said, his head slowly turning as he scanned the room.

Ryker nodded and stood, trying to follow the buzz, anger swelling in him. "Why doesn't Denver just do it? He did an okay job with the offices."

Denver snorted, his voice calm but his eyes sizzling. "You two morons can choose your own furniture. I've done my charitable deed for the year."

Ryker frowned and moved silently to the bookshelf near the window. Leaning around a potted plant, he saw the bug. It was rough and cheap, but it'd get the job done. His pulse spiked, and he had to take several deep breaths to keep from losing his mind. Son of a fucking bitch. They'd been bugged.

Nobody bugged them. They had an edge because of their abilities, and if somebody else was smart and smooth enough to bug them, then they lost that damn edge. Oh, hell no.

He walked toward the office's entrance, his hands clenching. "I'm starving, but I don't feel like cooking." Even though his fridge was fully stocked.

"Me either," Denver said, pushing away from the computer, his eyes glinting with a harsh light even as his voice remained cheerful.

Heath cleared his throat. "There's a place just down the road. Kind of a hole-in-the-wall, but it looks like they serve breakfast. Let's get a late one, and then I can return to this Internet search." He jerked his head toward the other offices, his jaw clenching hard enough to look painful. "Sound good?"

"Yeah. I just need to grab something from my office," Ryker said, heading out and walking along the worn wooden floor. It had to be the kid, right? Damn, he was good. A quick search of Ryker's office found a similar bug, and as he exited, he caught Heath's nod upon leaving his own. Shit. Were the apartments bugged also?

There was only one way to find out.

CHAPTER
13

The SUV handled so much better than Zara's crappy car as the rain-and-snow mix slashed down from an angry sky. She reached over and flipped on the heated seats, which warmed instantly. Brock had loaned her the car to go and get lunch, but first, she had an old friend to confront. How could Julie lie to her in such a manner? Zara had triple-checked the receipts provided by Jay, and they looked authentic. If he'd paid off all of Julie's bills, then what was she using the three thousand dollars a month for? Could it really be for drugs?

Zara rubbed her chest, which suddenly felt hollow.

She drove by where her car had died the day before and then pressed her foot to the gas pedal. She'd told Brock that she needed to run a couple of errands, but even so, she had to hurry so she'd have time to get sandwiches.

She pulled into the back lot of the almost-deserted motel and noted Julie's car, partially hidden behind a huge Dumpster. Good. Her friend was there.

The wind smashed against Zara's jean-clad legs as she jumped from the luxury vehicle and hurried across muddy potholes to trace her steps from last time. The wind pummeled her hair, and she ducked her head to protect her face even as a tide of hot anger swelled in her. Had she been made a fool of? When she emerged at the front of the motel, she hustled toward Julie's room and knocked sharply on the door. Then she waited.

And waited.

She pounded harder, her knuckles protesting. "Julie? I saw your car."

Nothing.

She pressed her ear to the peeling paint on the door and couldn't hear a thing. Then she twisted the knob, and the door slid open.

Glancing quickly around, she couldn't see anything or anybody. Only the trees moved, whistling a lonely tune in the wind. Gathering her breath, she shoved inside. The smell of mold instantly assailed her. "Julie?"

The bed was unmade, and Julie's suitcase was open on the table with all the contents neatly organized. Zara strode over grungy orange shag carpet to glance inside the dimly lit bathroom. Toiletries were lined up on the counter—all high-end and from Julie's time as the mayor's wife. They looked incredibly out of place against the avocado-colored counter and rust-stained sink.

Julie was nowhere to be found.

Zara's neck ached. Should she? Oh, she really shouldn't. While her angel fought with her devil, she moved toward the suitcase and lifted a white cashmere sweater out of the way. Underwear and a bra were beneath it. She breathed out. Well, she was already committed. She lifted the silk panties and quickly went through every compartment of the suitcase, finding nothing but clothing and some costume jewelry that was pretty but not worth any money.

God. No drugs. She knew it. Guilt tried to slither through her.

Then she glanced at the rickety, scarred furniture. Would a druggie hide the evidence in their own suitcase? Probably not. Wincing at the dirty surfaces, she rapidly looked through the battered dresser and bed table before glancing beneath the mattress. No drugs.

Her shoulders relaxed. Thank God. Then heat climbed into her face. She'd known Julie for years, and she should've trusted her. But where was the three grand a month going? Or had Jay somehow created false receipts, which didn't seem likely since it'd be so easy to prove.

As she straightened and headed for the doorway, she glanced around one more time. Reaching the torn curtains, she moved them aside to look into the empty parking area.

Where in the world was Julie?

* * *

In the late afternoon, Ryker parked the truck outside Zara's office building on a semi-quiet street. Three stories high and made of red brick, the place appeared imposing. The law firm was on the top floor. When he dropped her off that morning, he'd made sure she promised to stay inside until he picked her up. The firm had excellent security, and he should know, considering he'd installed it.

Rain splattered down, and he twisted on the windshield wipers.

He'd been working since lunchtime, trying to track Greg down after searching their building. They'd found seven bugs placed throughout the offices and none in the apartments.

It had to be the kid. Nobody else knew they were in town. At least nobody who'd want to listen in on their conversations. Part of him wanted to shake the kid until his teeth fell out. The other part...Well, that one was somewhat impressed with the little shit.

Denver had suggested leaving the bugs in place to lure Greg back in. For now, Ryker needed to pick up Zara while Denver figured out how the kid had hacked into their security systems without leaving a trace.

Just who the hell was this kid?

Not only was Ryker on the hunt for Isobel Madison, but he also had Denver set search parameters in place for Greg, the mysterious genius boy.

Ryker's attention shifted as Zara pushed out of the building, laughing at something Brock Hurst had said. The lawyer was on her heels, his briefcase bulging at his side.

Zara scanned the sidewalk and saw the truck. Her smile widened. Damn if that didn't feel good.

Ryker jumped from the truck and came around to open her door.

"Ryker," Brock said, hunching his shoulders against the rain.

"Brock." Ryker hooked Zara around the waist and lifted her into the truck, not missing the other man's close scrutiny of the act. Were they about to have a problem?

Brock paused and switched hands with the overloaded briefcase. Rain matted his brown hair to his face, but he straightened to his full height. "It's good to see you. How long are you in town this time?"

Ryker half turned from Zara to stand eye to eye with the lawyer. "Why?"

Brock blinked intelligent eyes. "We might have a job for you. It's a nasty divorce case, and there may be drugs involved. We'd need the investigation to be very low-key."

Sounded like the Pentley case. "We're concentrating on missing persons cases right now and don't do divorces, as you know." Three other times he'd turned down jobs from the firm regarding divorces.

"I've always wondered about your business. Employees, partners, other clients," Brock said, his focus narrowing. "You're such an enigma." While he spoke to Ryker, the words were obviously meant for Zara.

"We like to stay under the radar," Ryker said smoothly, planting his hand on Zara's thigh, heat flowing through him in a primitive warning.

Brock's eyebrow lifted. "It's probably better that way, considering you don't stay in town long," he drawled, all charm.

Ryker leaned toward the lawyer and released Zara, keeping her partially behind him. "You know, Brock, I like you and always have. You work hard, you play hard, and you don't pull any punches."

Brock widened his stance, his lips twisting in almost a mocking smile. "So?"

"I'd hate for us to have a problem, you know?" Ryker made his intention clear in his gaze.

Brock full-on grinned, his good nature and a new determination shining through. "So would I, buddy. But fate is fate, you know?"

"Fair enough." Ryker turned back to Zara, who was watching the interchange with curious eyes. "Bye, Brock."

"I'll see you on Monday, Zara," Brock said, turning to hustle through the rain and down the street.

Zara eyed him. "That was interesting."

Not really, but Ryker couldn't blame the guy. Zara was the entire package, and Brock was smart enough to see it. Too bad Ryker had made a move first. He leaned in and indulged himself with a kiss, drawing her sweet lips against his. "I don't share, baby."

She rolled her eyes. "For goodness' sake. I guess I'm lucky you didn't both try to pee on my leg."

Humor bubbled through him. The woman had a point. "How was work?"

"Okay," she murmured.

That wouldn't do. He tugged her sideways and pulled her core against his, the tension from his face-off with Brock making him rougher than he liked. The rain dropping on his head wasn't doing a thing to calm him, either. Her legs spread on either side of his hips. "What's going on, Zara?"

"Nothing. Just lots of work to do for the trial." Her fingers fluttered over his jacket, and her gaze dropped to track the progress. "We should probably get going."

What was she hiding? "Is there something going on I need to know about?"

Her gaze lifted to his. "No. Not at all."

Hmmm. The woman didn't get him at all. No more secrets. He leaned over her, enjoying her quick intake of breath. "Let me re-phrase that. Is there something going on that you don't want me to know about?"

A faint pink tinged her cheeks.

That's what he'd thought. "Did something happen with Brock?" The guy hadn't exactly hidden his interest in her.

Her eyes widened. "Of course not."

"Did he figure out you've been helping the other side in the di-vorce?" Ryker slipped his hands into her back jeans pockets and clenched. Her full curves filled his palms, and his groin awakened.

She blinked, and her eyes darkened. Her heated core warmed his dick through his jeans. "No. Besides, I haven't really helped Julie. Everything I've told her should've been in all the discovery responses, anyway. And lending her money? That isn't an ethical breach, I don't think."

The sweet paralegal was keeping secrets from him. He wanted to coax her into a more stable relationship, finally willing to give it a try, but every instinct he owned bellowed that she was courting danger. Even if the problems with her car were just from age, the way she was breaking legal rules for her friend promised a bucket of hurt if she got caught. "Why do I get the feelin' you're not leveling with me, baby?" he rumbled.

A slight tremor shook her torso. Oh, she might like her independence, but the woman liked it even more when he called her *baby*. She glanced toward the rain-covered windshield. The splatters were turning to a light snow. "I don't have a clue about your feelings, but you really should get out of the rain."

He hated secrets. Yeah, he recognized the irony there, considering he was one long line of secrets, but even so. The woman should trust him, and perhaps it was time he set some boundaries with her. "I'm gonna give you three seconds to tell me what's on your mind."

She stilled and then focused. Her breath came in a couple of cute pants. "What happens after three seconds?"

Ah, there she was. The curious smart-ass who loved to challenge him in bed until he pushed her right into orgasmic submission. Taking their relationship into the light of day would spur her curiosity, now, wouldn't it? He smiled slowly and pressed hard against the apex of her legs, holding her right where he wanted her. A woman like Zara only submitted with true trust, and suddenly, he wanted that trust more than his next breath. "Stop pushing me, Zara. Right now you have three seconds."

Her mouth opened and then closed. Her head tilted just enough to show intrigue.

"One."

She licked her lips.

"Two."

She lifted an eyebrow, and her gaze clearly challenged him.

"Three," he whispered.

She waited a beat.

He pulled her even closer to him, capturing her lips.

CHAPTER
14

Zara exhaled into his mouth. With his hands on her ass and his big body pressing her back into the seat, she couldn't move.

He kissed her hard, his tongue taking control, his lips firm. One of his hands tangled in her hair, tilting her head and forcing her core harder against his.

Hunger careened through her with the warm, wet, strong lash of his tongue. He plunged in, Ryker in full dominant bedroom mode, taking possession of her from head to toe and everywhere in between. A tide of white-hot desire flowed through her as his scent and heat consumed her.

His hold tightened, and he slid his hand beneath the back of her shirt to sear her waist. He stepped even closer, forcing her thighs farther apart and rubbing her center to the hard line of the erection trying to punch through his jeans.

Desire blasted through her, ringing through her ears. Her breasts grew heavy, and a pulsing echoed between her legs. He rubbed her against him, and shards of electricity rippled up her abdomen.

A horn honked.

She wrenched her face free, looking at the dash, her breath panting out. "Ryker. For God's sake. We're on the street." She could barely get out the words, she was breathing so hard.

His hold tightened, and he pressed his cock unerringly against her clit. Pleasure vibrated out to the point of needy pain.

She arched and moaned, her mind spinning. "What in the hell?" she gritted out, turning to stare up at his face. Her breath completely deserted her this time. Forget panting. His rugged face was set in hard lines of uncompromising determination and desire. His eyes, those clear eyes, glittering and molten. So much masculine strength, and all of it was focused on her. "Ryker?"

"Spill it, Zara, or I swear to God, I'm making you come right here on the street." Tightly leashed violence rode his voice, and instead of frightening her, it ratcheted up the sexual tension in her body.

This was new. Or rather, this side of Ryker, outside the bedroom, was new. Oh, she'd suspected something not quite tame lived in him, and she'd caught glimpses of it before. But here, on a public street, in plain view of everybody? The man truly did make his own rules. "Let me go," she whispered, more than a little wary and way too turned on to think straight.

"My way, baby. Right here and right now? My way only. Talk." His fingers curled into her buttocks.

Her temper stirred to compete with the lust. "We are about to have a huge-assed fight."

"Maybe, but you're gonna come first." His smile held more intent than humor as he freed one of his hands to flatten on her belly. "You sure you want to push?"

Oh, hell yeah. Not only did her pride demand it; so did her thirst for intrigue. Just how far would he go? Not that far, she'd bet. Yet something in her, deep down, wanted him to stay true to his word. To back it up like the badass he seemed to be. Yeah, she was crazy. "Let me up, or you're going to get kicked and hard."

He slid his hand down beneath her waistband and panties.

Heat spiraled up her torso, and she struggled to get up. "Wait—"

"No." A quick twist of his wrist and his thumb grazed her clit.

Her thighs trembled. Her body opened. "Wait a minute. I—"

He did it again and slipped one finger inside her.

Warmth roared through her ears. A car drove by, splashing water. It felt too damn good. "Ryker."

"The street is nearly deserted on a Saturday," he murmured.

A group of people laughed farther down the sidewalk. "Not enough," she hissed, fighting her body as much as him. "Let me up."

He slowly rotated his hand, and she saw stars. "Submit, Zara."

Oh, she fucking hated that word. But as the group of people came closer, panic won. "Fine. Let me up."

"No."

"I went to see Julie. Borrowed Brock's car, but she wasn't there. He says she's on drugs." The words rushed out of her so quickly she started to cough.

Ryker stiffened, and his gaze darkened. He slowly removed his hand and helped her to sit up.

Quivers consumed her abdomen. She pressed her thighs together to try to dispel the ache. Man, she needed an orgasm.

Without another word, Ryker shut her door and moved around the front of the truck to slide into the driver's seat. Rain had soaked his T-shirt and black hair. He started the engine and pulled out into the street.

Zara swallowed. Her body rioted, brought to the brink and not fulfilled. She dared a look at Ryker.

A muscle clenched in his jaw, his face impenetrable.

He had no right. "What the hell, Ryker? I mean, my car wasn't messed with, as you know. What's your problem?" she asked.

He paused at a streetlight and turned to look at her, his gaze thoughtful. "Not sure. A gut feeling that something is up, and it may have nothing to do with you. But you've been hit in the face, and then your car had problems."

"Jay hit me when he was trying to hit his wife, and he has no clue where she's staying, so he couldn't have messed with my car. Nobody had any reason to mess with my car, and your friends said it was probably just wear and tear." She tried to rub her hands down her jeans, but her entire body felt oversensitized. "I don't like your caveman act." Well, her body did, but she wasn't admitting that. Ever.

The light changed to green, and he pressed on the accelerator. "Don't you?"

"No." Forget the fact that her body was on fire.

"Hmmm."

If he pulled the truck over and told her to get naked, she was very much afraid she'd do just that. It should frighten her how well he played her body, but there was something intriguing about it, although she did feel vulnerable. A woman would have to be able to trust completely to be with Ryker Jones forever. They drove the rest of the way to his place in silence. "I should go home," she said.

"I need to check in with Denver, and then I'll take you home."

Good. She could take a cold shower, make out with the shower nozzle, and get some good sleep. "Fine."

His chuckle slid right under her skin in a lazy caress.

They drove into the underground parking, and he parked the truck before dragging her across the seat. Her butt hit his hard thighs, and she nearly groaned out loud. "Want me to finish what we started?" he asked, his voice beyond rough.

"What did we start?" she whispered, her body already swaying toward him. She grinned.

He put his face an inch from hers. Raw sexuality and masculine power glowed in his odd-colored eyes. "You know what."

"I guess." Her mind wanted to be mad and her heart wanted to be protected, but her body wanted relief. So her tone was teasing.

"Good." He stepped out of the vehicle, tugging her with him, and tossed her over his shoulder.

Vulnerability attacked her along with humor. She hung over his shoulder, easily controlled by a strength so much more primitive than her own. Yet something about him—a sense that he was searching so hard for something, for a connection—called to her. She slid both hands down his back to grab his very fine ass. If she could trust him even when he was being over the top, what would he give back? Her gut told her he'd give everything and then some. "I'm still mad at you."

He all but jogged up the stairs, and before she knew it, they were back in his apartment. The world tilted, and she ended up on her feet for the briefest of seconds before he spun her around to face the wall. "Hey—"

Firm hands molded to her breasts, and he pressed his erection against her butt. "Take off your pants," he rasped in her ear.

She shivered. "Are you playing?" Her voice trembled.

He paused. "I'd never hurt you."

She knew that, but still, the words mattered. Her heart thumped hard, and feminine power flushed through her. "All right, badass. Let's see what you've got."

He chuckled against her ear and plucked her nipples. Erotic pain shot through her, and her knees weakened. "Pants. Off. Now."

She unzipped her jeans just as he tugged her shirt over her head, his hands rough.

"Nice." He caressed from her breasts down to her thighs and back, missing the important parts.

She pushed back against his fully clothed body.

He chuckled and tapped down to her core, easily parting her with his fingers.

Her knees almost buckled from the excruciating pleasure. Her eyes closed, and she pushed against him. More. She needed so much more. "Ryker."

As she breathed his name, he took her down, flipping her onto her back. His hand cradled her head until she rested on the floor. The cool concrete chilled her back, and with her fully nude and him still dressed, vulnerability swelled inside her.

He kissed her hard on the lips and then moved down, his mouth finding her core. For a few seconds, the entire world disappeared. Her pulse slowed as he held her open and exposed. To him. Red wound beneath his bronze skin when he spread her with his thumbs. "You're mine, Zara." Hunger glittered in his eyes.

She couldn't speak, but in that second, she wanted to be his. Completely.

With a low hum, he leaned down and licked her, sending sensual flames ripping through her abdomen. She clamped a hand on the back of his neck. "Ryker, stop playing," she moaned.

He chuckled, and the vibrations nearly sent her over. "Man, you're bossy."

"Look who's talking."

"Fair enough." Then he went at her. Tongue, fingers, even teeth— he worked her until she was a mumbling mass of needy nerves.

Sweat dotted her body. Her thighs trembled. She was ready to beg.

Then he twisted his fingers inside her and sucked her clit into his mouth.

She detonated with a sharp cry. The orgasm cut through her like a blade and was followed by a series of deep waves. Finally, she came down with a small whimper. He was amazing and so dangerous. If she didn't check herself, she'd be climbing right into his world, where he called all the shots.

Maybe the mind-blowing orgasms would be worth it. Ryker had his own life, and it contained a bunch of secrets from what had to be a shady past. If he couldn't trust her with his life, how the hell could she trust him? Of course, maybe they were both just starting to trust each other. If she showed him trust, which she had, maybe he'd do the same. "Why won't you tell me about your past?" It was a question she'd never asked. Sure, she'd asked what his life had been like before they'd met, and he'd stonewalled her. At the time, she'd thought he just didn't want to be close.

Maybe it was something else.

He pushed himself up, the lazy slumber in his eyes sharpening to an intense determination. "Why?"

"I want to know you," she whispered, trying to sit up.

He planted a hand on her abdomen, effectively keeping her in place. Yet a warmth entered his eyes, and his cheek creased with what had to be pleasure. "My childhood sucked until I met Denver and Heath, and frankly, it sucked afterward as well. But then we were together, so it wasn't so bad."

She'd figured. "And?"

"The rest of it I need to clear with my brothers. I trust you, Zara, but it's not only my story to tell."

"All right." Maybe they could have a shot together. Her body relaxed into him.

He stood, lifting her easily and making her feel beyond feminine. Even cherished. "Round two is in the bed."

CHAPTER
15

Ryker yanked on worn jeans and a T-shirt, then padded quietly across the bedroom to yank on his boots. The rainy snow had ebbed, and moonlight filtered through the blinds to caress the woman in his bed. In sleep, she was soft. Delicately soft and so feminine he wanted to put her somewhere safe forever.

His chest ached, and he allowed determination to push his shoulders broader. While he couldn't hide her away, he could stand between her and any threat. To do that, he needed her trust, and for once, he actually felt like he was getting it.

For now, he had a job to do. He locked the bedroom and then the outer door to the apartment. He wasn't worried that anybody could get by both him and his brothers to get to her, but the locks added assurances.

He jogged down the flight of stairs to the offices. Long strides took him to Denver's office, where Denver and Heath already waited. "Quick trip, huh? How was Utah earlier today?" he asked Heath, wanting to know before they started.

"Got some info but nothing concrete," Heath said, making a get-to-it motion with his hand.

Ryker nodded. "Oh. Then what the hell are we doing here right now? Why the late-night text?" he asked, following the script they'd come up with earlier.

"I found Isobel Madison," Denver said. "You're not gonna believe where she is."

"Where?" Heath asked, rolling his neck, his body one tense line as he played his part.

"Read this," Denver said, making a production of shoving a stack of papers across the desk.

Ryker crumpled a paper and kept silent for several beats, his gaze on Denver as he pretended to read. "Shit."

Heath joined in. "Yep. So what now?"

"Tomorrow we go and talk to her," Ryker said, nosily pushing papers back toward Denver. "It's quite the coincidence that she's so close."

Heath grunted. "I don't believe in coincidences."

"What about the kid?" Denver asked.

Ryker waited and then sighed. "Let's find the woman and figure out who she is. Then I'll know better how to deal with Greg. The kid is lost, and I'd like to help him if possible."

Heath lifted an eyebrow.

Ryker shrugged. He would like to help Greg, so why not say so as the kid listened in? The lost look in the kid's dangerous and way-too-old eyes had haunted him since their only meeting. "For now, I have to get some shut-eye. How about we meet at eight in the morning and head out?"

"Copy that." Heath groaned as he shoved from the chair. "Has anybody ordered furniture for the apartments upstairs?"

"No," Denver said shortly, tapping keys. "Security measures are in place here. We're well protected."

Like hell they were. Greg had already gotten in once to plant all the bugs. "That's good to know," Ryker said.

Denver stood and quietly opened his bottom desk drawer. He reached in and tossed Glocks to both men. Ryker shoved his gun against the back of his waist, much preferring the knife already in his boot. "Night, guys." He loped through the offices and up the stairs to his apartment, where he opened and shut the door without going inside.

Then he turned and made his way back down to the offices without making a sound this time.

He gave a head jerk to Denver, who had already stationed himself near the reception area. Heath covered the back, and Ryker set up dead center and out of sight.

Then they waited.

The night ticked on, and the skies outside decided to open up again. Rain slashed down, but if the weather turned as it was predicted to, they might have more snow by morning.

Ryker remained in a crouch against the long row of file cabinets in the center of the office.

The air shifted. Not enough for most people to notice, but something—or rather someone—hovered near. He gave a hand signal to Denver, who nodded. Heath was already on alert.

Denver held up a small box that had gone dark.

The damn kid had managed to turn off the security system without giving an indication. He had to be close.

No sound. As hard as Ryker tried, he couldn't make out a sound that shouldn't be there. So he closed his eyes and concentrated. Denver's heartbeat...then Heath's echoed through his mind.

Should he be able to hear them? Shit no. But he could. He'd accepted the oddity years ago, and once he had, he'd gotten accustomed to using it.

Another heartbeat. Strong and sure and damn steady.

He gestured to his brothers again, waiting for their nods. They both had odd talents, including the bizarre hearing abilities.

The back door slowly slid open.

The kid was good. He didn't make a tick of sound. He whipped inside and waited.

Ryker forced himself to breathe evenly and not hold his breath.

The kid moved as silent as death across the room and past a waiting Heath, heading straight for Denver's office. Heath waited until the kid was between the office and Ryker before flipping on the lights. Greg whirled around, his knife already out.

Ryker stood, his hands held out. "No need for weapons."

The kid eyed him, his body relaxed and yet in a fighting stance. No fear showed on his tough face while his gaze seemed to track all three of them. "You found the bug."

"Bugs," Denver corrected, pushing away from the reception area.

Ryker kept a line on the knife Greg hadn't put down. "This is Denver, and that's Heath. They're my brothers."

At the word, the kid visibly blanched before going stone-cold again.

Brothers.

Ryker's heart thumped for the lost kid. His pain was palpable in the wide room, yet he stood so bravely and faced the three of them.

Able to read minds, Heath caught the look. "You have family, kid?"

"No," Greg said, his free hand folding into a fist. He reminded Ryker of Heath as a child...so scared and angry and willing to fight.

Heath grimaced. "I have a rare talent of knowing when somebody is lying their ass off to me. Just so you know."

Greg backed away, knife out, keeping all three of them in his sights. He sidled to the left—toward the stairs, which led up to the apartments and down to the parking garage.

"Stop moving. I don't want to take you down, but if you go for the stairs, I will," Ryker said calmly, planning how to do it without bruising Greg. No way was he going to harm Greg.

Greg eyed him and then stopped moving. "Where's Isobel Madison?" His voice shook. "I have to find her."

"Tit for tat," Denver said, taking a couple of steps toward Greg, awareness in his gaze. "*Who* is Isobel Madison?"

"Doesn't matter." Greg lowered the knife but kept a firm hold on the handle.

"Smart move," Heath said, his body still on alert. "Now we can talk. Who is she?"

Greg shook his head. "I just want her location, and I'll go. She's none of your business." A thread of vulnerability wound through his tone.

"Now, that's where you're wrong," Ryker said. There had to be a way to get through to this desperate child. "You're not going anywhere, so you might as well work with us."

The kid's shoulders rolled, and he drew out a small box from his right pocket. "I brought insurance."

Ah hell. Ryker squinted, horror spiking through him. "What the fuck?"

The kid turned the box around, and a green light flickered. "Place is wired."

Heath coughed, fury darkening his face. "You're shitting me."

"Nope. Give me the intel on Madison, and I'll leave this nice little box on the front curb. It'll only take ten minutes to defuse the bomb. I promise." Greg retreated until his back was against the wall.

The kid had planted a bomb. Anger swept through Ryker on the heels of panic. His lungs seized. He'd brought Zara right into danger. Locks on the doors wouldn't save her from an explosion. His hands started to shake, and temper roared in to coat his vision.

Greg turned and eyed him. "I doubt you want the pretty lady sleeping upstairs to end up in pieces. She will if you don't do what I say."

Ryker snarled and took a step toward Greg, his back going rigid.

"You can threaten me all you want, but you mess with my woman, and I'll rip your head off."

Greg blinked. "I really don't want to hurt her."

Truth. Definitely the truth. Ryker forced himself into a calm state before he drove the kid to push the button. "Then you probably shouldn't have planted a bomb that'll take down where she's sleeping. Let's defuse it and now."

"That's up to you." Greg's jaw visibly hardened, his emotions all over the board and difficult to read. "You're in perfect control, and it's up to you if she lives or dies."

Something wasn't quite right in the statement, but Ryker couldn't get a bead on Greg. Was he lying? If so, he was trained to do so.

Heath moved to make sure they all but surrounded the threat. "I did not see this coming." He sounded more bemused than angry, as if surprised that anybody could surprise him, but it was an act. Ryker knew his brother, and he was livid. "You're impressive, kid."

"Thanks. Do you want to die?" Greg asked, his voice calm, but raw desperation swirled in his eyes. He had a good hold on the box.

"How about we all live." Ryker ran through possible scenarios in his head, the need to go cover Zara nearly overwhelming him. Heat coated his throat and made it hard to breathe.

Greg shook his head wildly. "You can't get to me before I push the button."

Ryker kept his hands at his sides. "Do you want to die?"

"I don't know." Greg looked down at the trigger. "I mean, I was supposed to die, you know? But I didn't, and now I'm here, and I just want to go back home. But there is no home, so maybe dying is the option."

Well, fuck. Definitely not what Ryker wanted to hear. "I can get you home."

"No." So much pain sizzled in Greg's brown eyes that Ryker's chest hurt. "My home no longer exists."

"Then why Isobel?" Ryker asked, trying to slide forward to get that box. "Did she study you?"

Greg's head reared back. "Why do you ask that?"

Holy land mine. "She's a doctor, right?" Ryker murmured, angling a little bit more. If he could just reach the boy before he pushed the button, he could end the threat to Zara.

Greg nodded. "Madison is a doctor."

Denver cleared his throat. "Is she your mom or something?"

"No." Greg's hand visibly tightened on the box until his knuckles turned white. "There's no way, is there? You didn't find her. This was just a trap."

"Wait." Ryker stiffened, one hand held out. "Just wait. Okay. Trust goes both ways, right? Here it is, kid."

Greg focused solely on him.

Good. That was good. "We've seen the woman before. All three of us. She'd show up at the boys home, the one you know about, and test us for shit. But she went by a different name."

The color drained from Greg's face. "Bullshit, man," he whispered, his voice going hoarse.

Denver moved closer to him. "You're killin' me. I can almost taste your pain. Jesus. Let it out."

Greg blinked. "Wait a minute. Just wait a fucking minute."

Ryker had seen a wounded bear cub in the woods years ago. The little furball had been scared shitless and horribly furious, and it had kept striking out and retreating over and over. This kid was worse. Wild desperation glittered in his eyes, and resignation slumped his shoulders. "Wait, Greg."

"Why?" the kid sputtered.

"Because I'll help you find her. I swear to God, if you tell me the truth, I'll help you find who you're really looking for." Ryker took a step toward him.

Tears filled Greg's eyes. "If she tested you, she's everywhere. Don't you see? We can't win. I'm supposed to be dead, so I will be. That's how it is." He looked frantically around. "If she tested you, she's watching you now. Don't you see?"

"No." Ryker took point since the kid was focused on him. Though Dr. Madison had studied him through the years, she'd obviously had a greater presence in Greg's life for him to be so frightened. "Did she raise you?"

"Yes, and she can find us all," Greg hissed.

Ryker shook his head. "We've changed names several times, and we've been on the run. She can't watch us anymore." Who the fuck was the woman?

"I found you." No triumph and only sad fact lowered the kid's tone.

"You found us because of what we do now: We find the lost. We're fucking great at it, and you know it. She doesn't know that about us, about me. She never really figured out what made me different, although she tried." Ryker went on instinct and kept talking. "Did she find out what made you different?"

"No." Greg paused. "She never did."

Okay, don't push. He was getting through to the kid. "She would show up out of the blue and have us take a bunch of written as well as physical tests."

Greg glanced at Heath and Denver. "Them too?"

"Yeah. Then she'd run us through different obstacle courses and do a series of medical tests," Ryker added.

Greg turned then, his focus slamming into Ryker. "Did she teach you to kill?"

Ryker's chest compressed. "No. Somebody else taught me that."

"The commander?" Greg whispered.

Ryker studied him and, once again, went with the truth. "No. Who's that?"

Greg licked his lips. "If you don't know, then you don't need to know."

"Okay. At some point, if you really want to find Isobel Madison, you're gonna have to trust us with the entire truth. You know we can find her. But I have to know all of it." Ryker took another step toward the kid.

The door to the stairwell opened. "Ryker? Your phone—" Zara gave a startled "Eep" as Greg grabbed her around the neck, his arm banding around her larynx, the knife close to her jugular. He was at least three inches taller than a barefoot Zara, even at his young age.

"No," Ryker yelled, stiffening. Pure panic exploded in his chest, but he sucked in air and went cold. He needed to think without emotion.

If the kid knew what he was doing—and the kid really did look like he knew what he was doing—he could crush her windpipe before Ryker could get to her. "Let her go," Ryker said calmly.

Greg's eyes grew wild again.

The detonator was in his other hand, which was down by Zara's thigh.

"Listen, Greg. That's Zara, and she's a really nice paralegal who likes to cook lasagna and wear funky shoes." Ryker immediately set out to make her human to the kid, even as his ears started to ring. "I have a feeling you haven't known many nice ladies in your life, and you need to understand that the one you're scaring so badly is as nice as they come. Nice, soft, and unable to protect herself from you."

Greg blinked, and his hold appeared to loosen a fraction. "I don't want to hurt her." His voice rose with a painful desperation.

Zara held perfectly still, Ryker's phone still in her hand. "What's going on?" she whispered, her face draining of color.

"Get the info on Madison, and do it now," Greg said levelly. "I said I didn't want to hurt your lady, and I don't, but I'll do what I have to do. I *have* to find Madison." The stark emotion in his eyes matched his raw tone.

The knife at Zara's throat glinted in the soft light. So close to her jugular. Ryker failed to banish emotion. "You hurt her, and I'll rip you apart."

Greg nodded, his eyes desolate. "Okay. Get the info for me."

The boy was ready to die, damn it. Ryker fought the urge to start swinging. "Fine. I'll get the info." He moved toward the door to the stairwell and came abreast of the two. "Now, Zara," he whispered.

She jammed an elbow into Greg's gut, and the boy breathed out but didn't release her. Ryker grabbed both his wrists, using size and strength to yank Greg's arm off Zara's neck. She ducked beneath his shoulder and spun around behind him.

Ryker shoved both of Greg's wrists against the wall, trying to keep from hurting the kid, even now.

Greg hissed and released the box. Denver yelled and dove forward, catching the thing right before it hit the ground.

Ryker leaned into Greg, allowing his fury to show. "That was my woman you just threatened to kill."

Zara cleared her throat and slid a palm along his arm. "He's just a boy, Ryker. Let's talk about this." Her voice was wheezy from nearly being choked.

Greg met his gaze evenly, no fear showing. "You wanna go?"

Fuck no, he didn't *wanna go*. "Denver? Got the trigger?"

Denver rolled to his feet and studied the box. With a low growl, he ripped off the back.

Greg smiled.

"Jesus. This is just a blinking box," Denver snapped.

"No bomb?" Ryker asked, his hold not relenting.

Greg sniffed. "I wouldn't hurt a nice lady like Zara Remington. Geez. The chick bakes cookies for the old folks home every Sunday."

Zara gasped from behind him. "How did you know that?"

Ryker frowned. He hadn't even known that fact. Was there a questionnaire to dating he hadn't discovered?

Greg leaned toward Ryker as much as the strong hold would allow. "Oh, there ain't much I don't know about Ryker and the people in his life."

Ryker reared back and then went stone-cold. Finally. "Enough."

Greg ignored him. "In fact, lady, I'm pretty sure I know a whole lot more about Ryker and these guys than you do."

Zara stepped up to Ryker's side. "Is that a fact?"

Greg's Adam's apple bobbled. "Yep. Would you like to know everything?"

CHAPTER
16

Zara ignored her freezing bare feet and wished she'd pulled on sweats along with Ryker's discarded T-shirt. At least the thing was enormous and hung to her bare, chilled knees.

What in the world was going on, and why had some kid just tried to choke her while holding a knife?

"Zara? Please go back upstairs." Ryker's entire back undulated with barely banked violence. Tension swelled in vibrating heat around them, but his hold seemed gentle, as if he didn't want to hurt Greg.

"No." She tapped his waist with his phone to calm him. "Your phone has been buzzing like crazy, which is why I brought it down to you. Let that boy go." She eyed the kid. Brown eyes, shaggy hair, lost expression. Oh, he'd felt a lot older when he'd been choking her, but even then, it had seemed he was trying to keep from hurting her. "Who are you?"

"I'm a client. Name is Greg," the kid said politely. "Sorry about the neck."

"I'm fine. Sorry I elbowed you in the stomach." She glanced down at the kid's narrow frame. "Are you hungry?" Perhaps if she got food into everybody, they'd all calm down and explain what was going on.

"Always." He shrugged and didn't seem to notice that Ryker still had him pinned to the wall.

"All right." Zara smacked Ryker harder. "How about we all go up to Ryker's apartment, and I make us a nice breakfast. Then we can figure out what's going on and what we should do next. I'm happy to help one of Ryker's clients." The kid looked beyond lost, and he needed help.

So she'd help.

Everyone looked toward Ryker. "We are not going to have a nice breakfast, Zara," he ground out.

"I'd like a nice breakfast," Greg said, flashing her a smile.

Heath cleared his throat from just a couple of feet away, his gaze thoughtful on Greg. "I wouldn't mind eating something homemade."

"Me either," Denver chimed in, also watching Greg, his brow furrowed.

Greg turned his smile on Ryker. "It's time to let me go, man."

"Or?" Ryker asked.

Greg's lips firmed. "Or I knee you in the balls, take out your left knee, destroy your right ankle, break ribs eleven and twelve, and then knock you out with a punch to the temple. Then I'll go eat eggs with your lady."

Ryker shook his head. "Much as I'd like to show you why that wouldn't work, I'd have to hurt you, and I'd rather not do that. Yet." He pushed off from the kid and gently straightened Greg's shirt.

Greg blinked and then slowly lowered his arms, his gaze on Zara. "I totally think you could do better than him."

Warmth bloomed through Zara, and she grinned. The night had passed surreal and careened right into bizarre. "That's awfully kind of you to say." She held out her arm, and the kid hesitated before sliding his through hers, leaving Ryker behind them. "I don't suppose you have anybody in mind?"

"Well, that attorney you work with is a nice guy, and he volunteers as a coach with a Little League softball team every spring. His sister has a kid who plays." Greg switched arms with her so she had the railing on her other side, his hold hesitant and beyond gentle.

Surprise and unease invaded Zara's stomach. "You really have investigated me."

"Just a little. I had to know I could trust these guys before hiring them." Greg slowed his steps so she could keep up. "Don't worry. I didn't look into anything really personal."

Zara stumbled. "Um, thanks?"

"Sure thing." They reached Ryker's apartment, and Greg pushed open the door, walking inside first. He lifted his head and listened, doing a quick scan of the place. "Come on in."

Okay. That was odd, and she'd seen Ryker do the same thing several times with a little more finesse. "What were you looking for, sweetie?" she asked.

He shrugged. "Any threats. I figure when a pretty lady offers to cook a guy breakfast, he should make sure the area is safe, you know?"

What kind of upbringing did this kid have to be looking for threats before being able to relax enough to eat scrambled eggs?

She made her way through the empty room to the kitchen and opened the refrigerator, which was surprisingly stocked. "How about cheesy eggs, bacon, sausage, and some biscuits and gravy?" Turning around, she took in Greg's widened eyes.

He nodded and swallowed, looking like a hungry puppy.

Glancing past him, she bit back a grin at seeing Heath and Denver nodding as well, their expressions just as full of hope as Greg's.

Ryker, on the other hand, leaned against the wall, his arms already crossed and what could best be described as a scowl marring his rugged features.

"This might take me a little while." She jerked her head at Greg. "Find some bowls and pans, would you?" Maybe if she gave him a couple of tasks, he'd relax. She began drawing food from the fridge to place on the smooth granite countertop.

Greg launched into motion and tore open cupboards. "There's nothing here," he whispered, sounding nearly heartbroken.

"I have cooking stuff. Be right back." Denver turned on a heel and quickly disappeared out the door.

"Thank God," Greg muttered.

Heath chuckled. "I told you he was nesting."

Ryker cleared his throat. "Right now, Greg and Heath down to my office. We'll work until Zara calls us for breakfast. I've seen her cook—it ain't fast, but the end result is awesome."

"How about you guys work here? I'd love to know what's going on." If the kid was in legal trouble, she could even help. She gave Greg her most encouraging smile.

Greg smiled back, but his eyes darkened at the same time. "I think we should go to the office." He glanced longingly at the eggs. "We'll hurry if you will."

So the kid didn't want her to know his business? "I'm a paralegal, and I may be able to help you," she said softly.

He met her gaze then, his looking much older than it should. "Ryker's correct that you're a nice lady, and I appreciate your offering to help me, but there's nothing you can do. It's better if you don't know about me. Please don't mention me to anybody." He turned and headed for the door. "Let's get this over with."

Heath followed him into the hallway.

Ryker didn't move and caught her gaze. "The kid is right. I don't know his story yet, but I will, and something tells me it ain't going to be pretty."

She lifted her chin, her heart aching for all of them. "You said you wanted something real with me."

"I do."

"Then you can't leave me in the dark. Not like this." Everything in her wanted to soothe that desperate look in Greg's young eyes. She'd never been very maternal, but there was something about him she wanted to heal. "I might be able to help."

"You're a paralegal, and part of your job is keeping confidences. My job is the same way, and I can't talk about many of my cases." Ryker spoke evenly, his body relaxed, his tone as firm as steel. "Our work doesn't define our relationship, and you know it."

Yet something told her that he was leaving way too much out. She didn't even understand enough about his past to know what questions to ask him.

He shoved away from the wall. "Do you want help with making breakfast?"

She tried not to smile. Ryker was a disaster in the kitchen, and she knew that firsthand. "Thanks, but you go get the story from Greg." If the kid needed privacy to tell his story, she'd give it to them. For now.

He nodded, amusement tilting his lips. "Fair enough. Give a shout when breakfast is ready." Turning, he paused at the doorway and looked back, his eyes warming into a soft green, banishing the blue. "It's really nice of you to cook for everybody, and I hope you know how much I appreciate it."

Well now, if he was going to be all sweet with her, she'd have to struggle with remaining protective of her heart. Unless he'd finally let her in? "Secrets can't work between us, Ryker," she mused.

He paused. "If I have secrets, they need to stay buried for both of us. Trust me."

Denver showed up with two boxes in his hands. "I have pots and pans as well as some mixing bowls."

Ryker frowned and took the boxes. "Jesus. You are nesting."

Why did that sound like such a bad thing?

* * *

Ryker loped into his office, where both Heath and the kid had already dropped into guest chairs.

"I like your office," Greg said, his gaze on the picture of the Fat Boy.

"Thanks. You've seen it before when you bugged us." Ryker went around the desk. "Isobel Madison. Who is she?"

Greg sat back, a myriad of expressions crossing his face. "She's a super smart neurobiologist who studies kids with high IQs and special gifts. She studied me and my brothers in a kind of military school in Utah." He gave quick coordinates, and Ryker typed them in.

He read the screen, his instincts flaring hot and fast. "Those coordinates lead to a former military depot that was used for storing vehicles and weapons." He scrolled down. "There was an explosion last year, and the place burned down."

Greg swallowed. "It was also a training and research facility. I lived there with my brothers."

Ryker narrowed his gaze and studied the kid. "You and your brothers."

"Yeah," Greg said. Emotion, dark and deep, echoed in his low tone. He glanced toward the nearest exit, and his body stiffened.

Being truthful scared the shit out of him, now, didn't it? Ryker wanted to protect the boy, but first they needed answers. How could they get him to trust them?

"Where are your brothers now?" Heath asked.

"Dunno. You find Madison, and you'll find them," Greg said. Hope and despair crossed his face, and he visibly struggled to subdue all expression.

Ryker sat back as images of the exploding army depot filled his screen. Could be a cover-up. "Since you really want us to find your brothers, why not give me their names? I could search for them and skip the doctor." But he was sure as shit going to find that woman, and not just for Greg's sake.

Greg shook his head. "There's no record of me or my brothers. You've already tried to track me down, right?"

"Yeah," Ryker said. How could the kids not exist on paper?

"Find anything?"

"No."

"Exactly." Greg ran a hand through his shaggy hair. "Believe me, you won't find them either."

Denver entered the room and leaned against the door frame, his gaze thoughtful. "There have to be records from before you went to the depot."

"Nope. Not even birth certificates," Greg said.

Ryker frowned and tried to click facts into place. The kid seemed to be telling the truth but definitely not all of it. "Let me get this straight. You and your brothers were put into a training and research facility because you have high IQs, and this Isobel Madison studied you, and for some reason she had your histories wiped."

"Yes." Greg seemed to be barely breathing. It was costing the kid to be honest. What did he fear so badly? What he was saying was beyond belief.

"Did they hurt you?" Ryker asked, anger beginning to take hold for the lost boy.

"No." Greg didn't move. His eyes hardened.

Lie. That was definitely a lie. Ryker let it go, not wanting to flay the kid open any more than he already was. "Where are your parents?"

"Dead."

Ryker tried to concentrate on the kid's emotions, but they were so jumbled he couldn't get a grasp. "When did they die?"

"When I was too young to know the difference." Now the tone turned matter-of-fact.

Lie or truth, Ryker couldn't tell. "All right. So Madison somehow found you and your brothers and took you to some weird depot in Utah."

"Pretty much." Greg kept his gaze level.

Lie? Yeah. That was a lie. "I can't help you if you don't tell me everything." Ryker eyed the burning metal on his screen.

"Sure you can. I've told you plenty," Greg said, his voice low.

"Who's the commander?" Ryker had been holding that one close and he almost hated to spring it on Greg.

Greg swallowed and looked younger for just a moment. "He's the guy who ran the depot and dated Madison. Well, I don't know if they dated, but they were together, if you know what I mean."

Ryker nodded and bit back a wince. Hopefully Greg hadn't seen the same stuff Ryker had with Madison and Cobb. Seemed to be her MO, considering she'd screwed Sheriff Cobb. "What exactly did the commander train you to do?"

Greg's lids lowered. "Hand-to-hand, weaponry, hacking skills. You know, your basic military school shit."

Something told Ryker it was a hell of a lot more than that, and his chest ached for Greg. "If Madison tested Heath, Denver, and me...all at a boys home, that's weird, right?"

"Not really," Greg said. "I'd bet anything she had a hand in you guys all three ending up at the same boys home. No way is that some sort of weird coincidence, you know? She loved her experiments."

Nausea swirled in his gut. Were they all experiments? Ryker clenched his jaw and tried to find a controlled place inside him. Had Madison messed with his life like that? Had she maneuvered his entire existence into where it was right now? Bile rose in his throat, but he kept his face stoic and decided to underplay for the kid's sake. "This is getting beyond odd."

"Saying all this is true, how did you get free?" Heath asked.

"I didn't. I went on a mission, failed, and Madison left me on my own overseas. Said I could get back myself or just die." Greg hunched into himself. "I made it back, but the place was already destroyed. I have to find my brothers."

"How many brothers do you have?" Heath asked, kicking back in his chair when his vibe was anything but relaxed.

"Three." Greg's voice cracked.

Are your brothers also looking for you?" Ryker asked. If they'd set up searches on the Internet, he may be able to create a trap for them to find and then he could backtrack and locate them.

"No." Greg swallowed.

"Why not?" Heath asked softly.

The kid breathed out. "They think I'm dead."

CHAPTER 17

Dr. Isobel Madison leaned over the desk, her perfectly manicured nails clicking rhythmically across the keyboard. She had more traps set on the Internet than Lewis and Clark could've dreamed about, but her prey, unfortunately, was as brilliant as she'd made her traps. So far, she'd been unable to find the men she sought.

But they wouldn't be able to hide from her forever.

They were hers and hers only. Oh, she'd shared other creations with her one true love, the commander, and he'd trained them, but the Lost boys from the home were all hers. She missed them, truth be told.

The air-conditioning kicked on in her small office, and she stopped typing. "I thought you had that fixed," she said, turning away from the computer.

Todd Polk looked up from the stack of papers in his hands. At about fifty years old, the survivalist was getting a little soft around the middle and would soon outgrow his usefulness. Isobel had convinced him to shave his buzz cut a month previous, and now he looked more the part of a soldier, at least. His jaw was square, and his eyes were blue and rather blank. But he had a fighting force, and that she needed.

She smiled at the man who'd get her what she wanted, and then she'd throw him away. "It's November, darling. We live in Colorado, and it's snowing outside." For the love of all that was holy. "The A/C?"

He nodded, his gaze dropping to her chest. "I'll take care of it."

Good. "You do take such good care of me." She allowed her voice to lower to a purr even as her mind went elsewhere.

His eyes flared. "My soldiers are getting restless. We need to make a strike or conduct a mission soon."

A mission. How silly. The home-trained militia wouldn't know a true mission if it rode in on prized ponies and whinnied a bit while spitting caviar.

For the moment, she needed the survivalist, and it was almost too easy to manipulate him. "There's a lab in Denver conducting experiments dealing with stem cell research. If your men would like to blow up the facility, that would make a statement." Not that his cause interested her in the slightest.

Todd rubbed his smoothly shaven jaw. "How did you find that out?"

"I hacked their systems," she said smoothly. It had taken less than five minutes, actually. While Todd's pseudo-military group had a nice cache of weapons, they lacked computer resources. For now, she needed their might, not their brains. "Our Protect group must continue the mission and purify this land, right?"

"Of course." He studied her. As the leader of the Protect group, he felt it his duty to end all scientific genetic experimentation and purify the world, especially the men she'd created in test tubes to be...more. "Though that's not your only mission, is it?"

Sometimes he seemed smarter than he looked. "You know I want to find the anomalies I helped to create and set things right." Her life's work had been to create supersoldiers, super beings, in labs and see how they functioned in the world.

"By ending them?"

"Of course," she lied. Only a couple of the men she'd created in test tubes and helped train through the years needed to die. The rest could go back to working for her and being studied by her. It was time for the next generation to be born and trained. She might not be God, but she was damn close, and she needed their genetic material to keep her experiments going. "As soon as I find the men we made, you can take them all out." She wondered if she'd have to kill him. While she'd ordered deaths, she'd never actually killed anybody personally.

"What about the three boys you told me about? The murderers?" Todd asked.

She glanced back at her computer. "I've been trying to find them for years, as has the sheriff from that town. At some point they'll make a mistake."

"You'll let me kill them?"

She forced a smile. "Of course. I'm with you to atone for my mistakes, as you know. I believe in your mission, Todd." The second she no longer needed his forces, she'd forget he ever existed. After she found her boys and got back to work. The boys from the home had been created with different genetic material, mostly, than her other experiments. Maybe they could have children, and she needed their genetic material to find out.

It was time for the next generation to be tested. Someday she'd have the perfect soldier.

Todd stood and overwhelmed the small office in the mountain compound. "I'm glad we're on the same page."

"Of course." She leaned over so he could look down her shirt. "We will get rid of all genetic experimentation and test subjects. Life must be pure."

* * *

Zara eyed the men happily eating around the living room, all on the floor with their backs to walls, none of them talking. Way too busy chewing.

She'd found paper plates in one cupboard as well as some plastic forks. If Ryker was staying in town, he needed supplies and furniture. They were all well on their way through seconds, and if she didn't miss her guess, Greg was about to head to the counter for thirds.

"So, Greg. Where are you staying?" she asked, dishing more cheesy eggs onto his plate when he approached.

"Here and there." He nodded when she pointed to more bacon.

When was the last time the kid had eaten? She dropped a bagel onto his plate as well. "Will you be in town long?"

He shrugged, his gaze on the food. "It's starting to seem like it, but I'm hoping your man gets me my info soon."

"I have a spare room at my house," she murmured.

Ryker's head snapped up from across the room. "Not a good idea."

Greg turned to retake his place by the door. "Unfortunately, I agree. It's better if I stay away." He slid down, his gaze remaining happily on his eggs. "I'm fine where I am."

"No." Zara slipped the spatula back into the eggs. "If Ryker is helping you, then he will find your information, but you can't just wander around town underage. Where's your family?"

Greg paused with his plastic fork almost to his mouth. "No parents, and Ryker's supposed to be finding my brothers."

Eesh. Another orphan. She knew how he felt, and her heart turned over for him. But the good news was that the kid had family. Hopefully he had one brother over the age of eighteen who could be a guardian and protect him. "Then I insist you stay with me until your brothers are located." She waited a beat. "Meals come with the extra room."

Greg shoveled eggs into his mouth and chewed as if he hadn't eaten in days, temptation in his eyes. He glanced toward Ryker.

Ryker studied him and then gave a short nod. His gaze shifted into something warm. "It's a nice place to stay, and I'll be there, too."

Zara opened her mouth and then shut it.

"But if I discover you're in any danger, you're staying here, not at Zara's place," Ryker finished.

Greg wiped his hand down his jeans. "Nobody knows about me, so I'm not in danger as long as you don't screw up the search. If you get found out and they discover I'm, ah, around, then all bets are off. Danger doesn't come close to describing the situation."

"We won't screw up the search." Heath leaned forward and wiped his mouth on a paper napkin. "But you might need to be more forthcoming with information."

"You know all you need to know," Greg mumbled, reaching for his bacon.

What kind of danger stalked the poor kid? Oh, she'd get her answers once she had him safely at her house and eating regularly. There had to be something she could do with her legal background to help Greg. It sucked being without parents in the world.

The wind whistled loudly outside, and Zara gasped as white powder cascaded down outside the window. "It's snowing."

Dawn was barely breaking over the horizon, and ice speckled the window.

Greg set his plate down. "Before I decide, how did you get the bruise on your face?" His chest puffed out just enough to show aggression.

Geez. Feed the kid once, and he wanted to protect her. Her heart warmed. "Not from Ryker."

Greg eyed Ryker. "Didn't think so."

"Why not?" Ryker asked softly.

Greg lifted a shoulder. "If you hit her, you'd do a shitload more damage."

Ryker gave a short nod. "I don't hurt women."

"Good to know. Is the guy who hit her still standing?" Greg asked.

"Barely," Ryker said. "Well, maybe by now he's standing again." He shared a manly grin with Greg, who returned to his food.

Zara dropped her plate on the counter. Her arms went weak. "What did you do? Ryker? Seriously. What did you do?"

He glanced up from the lone piece of bacon still on his plate. "I told you I was gonna have a talk with the guy who hit you. We had a talk, and he'll never do it again. You're safe."

Zara shook her head. "He's a client of the firm," she hissed. "I can't have him coming after you."

"He won't." Ryker bit into the bacon with a hum of appreciation. "Trust me."

Heat prickled along the back of her neck, and she ground her teeth together. "I told you I had it handled." What if Jay let her firm know she was working with Julie? Or at least that she'd helped Julie? She'd be fired.

"Now it's really handled," Ryker said, his tone firm.

Denver and Heath watched the exchange with different degrees of amusement.

Zara breathed out, trying not to hurl the spatula at Ryker's stubborn head. "You threatened the mayor. Seriously. You threatened the mayor of the town." Her voice rose on the last.

Greg snorted. "The mayor? Nice."

Ryker nodded and shared another smile with the boy.

Zara shook her head. "That is so wrong. Did anybody see you?"

"Not really. I mean, I locked his door and everything, but if anybody sees him nude in the near future, they're gonna see bruises," Ryker drawled.

Denver chuckled. "The mayor's a dickhead. Wish I could've watched."

"Me too," Heath said, patting his belly. "The guy was at the court-house when I got sworn in. Definite asshole."

Zara bit her lip. The whole man-code thing was getting really old fast. She should've put a laxative in the eggs. She also didn't like them ganging up on her, damn it. "You're all crazy, you know that?"

Ryker cut her a look before focusing on Heath. "How's the Copper Killer situation?"

Heath stopped chewing. "The FBI decoy is in place, and they're hoping the guy makes a move on her. If he doesn't..."

"Then somebody else will be taken," Ryker said, shaking his head. "I hate waiting around like this."

"We have searches going on the computers for possible victims, but it's slow, and there are too many to narrow down," Heath said, frustration crossing his face.

Zara opened her mouth to ask about the case just as her phone buzzed from the counter. She frowned. It was barely dawn on a Sunday morning.

"Who's calling so early?" Ryker asked, pushing to his feet.

Zara read the screen. "It's Brock."

Tension swelled through the room, heated and wild, and definitely from Ryker.

Greg snorted. "I like Brock. A lawyer like him is a better choice for you." His lips tipped into a smile. Was he teasing Ryker? Maybe the kid was finally relaxing.

"Shut up," Ryker said without much heat.

Zara lifted the phone to her ear. "It's really early, Brock."

"We have a problem. How soon can you meet me at Jay Pentley's house?" Brock said, the sound of tires on asphalt echoing through the line.

Zara coughed. "Um, why?" Shit. Jay had turned Ryker in.

"I'm sorry to tell you this, honey, but Julie Pentley was found dead in a motel outside of town just before dinnertime yesterday." Brock swore. "Idiots don't know how to drive."

Zara gasped. Panic swelled through her. "Dead? How?" God. Not Julie.

"Multiple stab wounds. Somebody wanted her dead and bad."

CHAPTER
18

Red and blue lights swirled around from the police car in front of Jay Pentley's stately home. Well ensconced in a perfectly manicured subdivision behind secured gates, Pentley's brick house was surrounded by groomed bushes barely being dusted with snow. Streaks of light cut through the heavy clouds, showing the morning had finally arrived.

Ryker parked his truck against the high curb, leaving the cobblestone driveway clear.

Zara pushed her door open. "I'll have Brock bring me home."

"I don't think so." Ryker didn't like the itch between his shoulder blades one bit. He exited the truck and shut his door. "Your firm is about to hire me on this whether they like it or not." Even if Brock refused to hire Lost Bastards, Ryker was going to figure out what the hell was going on…especially since Zara was now in the thick of it.

He took her arm and led her up the driveway and to the front door. Protecting her was becoming a full-time job. If anything happened to her, he'd never forgive himself.

She stumbled, and he righted her. "You shouldn't be here, considering you hit Jay yesterday," she hissed under her breath.

It did complicate things. "If Jay wants to out me, then he will out you, and we'll go forward with wife-beating allegations." Pentley was the most likely suspect in his wife's murder anyway. Ryker rapped on the door.

Footsteps sounded, and Brock Hurst yanked the extra-tall wooden door open. He wore dark jeans, a polo shirt, and a dusting of whiskers along his chin. He paused. "Ryker."

Ryker nodded. "You need me on this case. I'm making an exception to our caseload to take it."

Brock frowned and scrubbed a hand through his already ruffled hair. "We'll ask the client, but I have to admit, I would like a private investigator on the inquiry. The police detective doesn't seem to like Jay much."

"That's because Jay's an asshole," Ryker said evenly. "But I'll find out the truth about what happened."

Brock seemed to consider the situation, his gaze sharp. "I'll need Jay's okay on it, but I really don't think he killed her. So we'll end up hiring you."

"Why don't you think he did it?" Ryker asked. Brock was a smart guy and wouldn't be easily fooled.

Brock looked over his shoulder. "Get Jay to hire you, and then we can talk without violating privilege."

Zara put a hand on Ryker's arm, her voice soft. "This is a bad idea."

Yeah, more than likely. Ryker planted his palm over hers and walked inside, pretty much forcing her into the opulent vestibule. She was nuts if she thought he'd let her work a murder case without him, especially since she had been in contact with the victim. A lot. Now he wondered again about Zara's malfunctioning brakes.

It was a nice place. A three-story chandelier cast light all around them while a living room with a stunning view of the faraway mountains awaited.

Pentley was seated on a couch, wearing slippers, thick gray sweats, and a matching T-shirt, his hair mussed and scruff covering his jaw. He looked up and focused bloodshot eyes. "What the hell?"

Brock hurried around a leather chair to sit next to Pentley. "This is Ryker, our investigator. He's the best, Jay. Finds leads where nobody else can, and he's able to keep quiet when necessary. We need him on this."

Ryker kept amusement off his face.

Jay absently rubbed the left side of his rib cage, which no doubt still smarted. "Not a chance."

A man, around forty or so, sat in an overflowing leather chair beside Pentley's, a blue ski jacket over his broad frame, a notebook in his hand. Shrewd brown eyes studied them all. He rubbed a hand through his thick brown hair. "Now that your lawyer, your paralegal, and your investigator are here, Mayor Pentley, you need to answer my questions."

Pentley glared at Zara and then Ryker before turning to Brock. "I said no."

Brock frowned. "Why not?"

Pentley opened his mouth and then shut it again, his gaze on the detective's tapping pen. "I didn't have anything to do with Julie's death, and I won't act like I did."

"Yet you won't talk to me without your attorney present," the detective said quietly.

Jay clasped his hands together in his lap. "Because I'm not stupid."

"That remains to be seen," the detective replied.

Ryker fought a grin. The cop really didn't like the mayor, now, did he? "In or out, Mayor? I will find out what happened to your wife." Yeah, it may have sounded like a threat, but if Jay caught the undercurrent not to mess with Zara, it was worth it. Either way, Ryker was investigating the issue.

Pentley cut him a harsh look, obviously ready to tell his attorney everything about their skirmish. But if he did, he'd have to go into what a wife-beating scum he was, and, boy, would that make him look guilty. Finally, he snarled. "Fine. I'll hire your little firm to investigate Julie's death, but I'm telling you, I have no clue who would've wanted her dead." He flashed his political smile. "Except for Zara here. I mean, Julie broke us up. Right, sweetheart?"

Irritation clawed through Ryker, and he lifted his chin.

The detective studied Zara. "Is that true?"

She rolled her eyes. "No. Jay and I briefly dated, and we broke up long before Julie ended up dating the egomaniac. Which, considering they're in the middle of a contentious divorce, didn't turn out very well."

"Contentious?" the detective asked.

Brock shot Zara a hard look. "Julie was mentally unstable and addicted to drugs, and Jay was trying to get her help. It's that simple."

"Nothing is ever that simple," the detective countered.

Brock turned his attention on the cop. "Detective Norton, I hope you keep your personal opinions to yourself and work this case with an open mind."

Detective Norton lifted an eyebrow. "My mind is wide open. Now, where were you yesterday afternoon between noon and three, Mayor?"

Zara stiffened next to Ryker. He kept his gaze on the cop, but his mind ran through the day before. Exactly when had Zara visited Julie at the motel? Had Zara just missed the murderer? Time slowed down, and his system went on full alert. God, what if she had been there? His muscles involuntarily bunched like an attack dog's. He forced himself not to look at her and to keep the concern off his face.

She dug a notepad out of her pocket and began taking notes, her hand visibly shaking, as she leaned against the wall. Her teeth bit into her lower lip.

As soon as he got her alone, he had to question her about her timeline. Had she left any evidence? Or had anybody seen her? The murder took on a personal hue. Panic coated his throat. For a second he felt powerless, and then his mind took over. In the worst-case scenario, he could get her out of town and to a safe place to live, but what about her grandmother, who was still on vacation?

Vans screeched to a stop outside.

Pentley craned his neck to look out the window next to the door. "The press is here."

Ryker took a step back and out of the line of sight from the door. The absolute last thing he needed was to be caught in a photo or on video.

The detective cleared his throat. "Mayor? My question?"

Pentley placed both manicured hands on his sweats. "Yesterday during that time I was working in my office." He jerked his head toward Brock. "In fact, I was on the phone with my attorney several times, because we were working on answering discovery requests for the divorce. I made several copies of insurance policies, land deeds, and vehicle titles to fax to Brock."

The detective looked from Pentley to Brock and back. "Can anybody besides your attorney corroborate your alibi?"

Jay glanced at Ryker. "Not right now, but I'm sure my new private investigator will be able to round somebody up. Right, buddy?"

The detective narrowed his gaze and looked from the mayor to Ryker. "Do you two know each other?"

"No," Ryker said easily, "but I'm about to know everything about the mayor."

Jay's lips tightened.

Ryker rolled his shoulders. What time had he smacked Jay around? Obviously Jay thought explaining the situation would end up working against him, for now. It had to have been around one in the afternoon. Jay could've still had time to drive to the motel and kill Julie before three in the afternoon, although he would've been sore from the fight. "How certain are you about time of death?" Ryker asked.

"Preliminary report sets TOD between noon and three, but after the autopsy, we'll have a better idea, hopefully." The detective scratched in his notepad. "So nobody was at City Hall with you, Mayor."

"I was the only person working in City Hall yesterday." Jay kept his voice level, but his eyes flashed. "Not many public employees work weekends, Detective. I will keep thinking about the day and if I saw anybody. Right now nothing is coming to mind, but I'm a little bit in shock. While Julie and I were having problems, I just can't believe she's dead."

Ryker studied the mayor. He wasn't mentioning the blonde, and that made sense, because cheating spouses always looked bad to the law and juries—especially during a divorce. Or was Pentley actually protecting the woman? It was doubtful, but Ryker needed to calm the hell down, look at all angles, and stop just reacting out of fear for Zara.

"I'm sorry for your loss," Detective Norton said. "Who filed for divorce?"

"She did," Jay said. "But I'm fairly certain she was seeing somebody else."

Look who was talking. Ryker made a mental note to find out who the blonde on Jay's lap had been.

"She was not cheating," Zara burst out, her face turning red.

Detective Norton's head snapped up. "Who was she seeing?"

"Dunno," Jay said, scraping both hands down his face. "It was just a feeling I got last time I talked to her. She said something about knowing what a real man was like."

"But no names or other clues?" the detective asked, his focus zeroing in.

"No," Jay said, his shoulders slumping.

"I'll need copies of all correspondence between you." The detective wrote something down.

Jay nodded wearily. "We'll get everything to you."

"When was the last time you saw your wife?" the detective asked, his voice a low rumble.

Jay's gaze strayed to Zara. "I saw her last week at a motel on the north side of town. She asked me to drop off some of her clothing, so I did."

Zara drew in air next to Ryker. Was that when Jay had hit Zara?

Ryker stood straighter in place, a ball of lead in his gut. The entire situation sucked, and his fingers curled into a fist as he felt the desire to punch Jay again. "Have you spoken with her since?"

"No. She was upset about the competency hearing, and she became abusive. Kicked me and hit me, so I had to leave." Jay shrugged his shoulders. "It wasn't her fault. She truly wasn't herself." He sighed heavily. "Is there any chance this was a drug deal gone bad? I mean, I know she was using again."

"Julie didn't do drugs," Zara blurted, her voice heated.

Triumph surged into Jay's eyes before it was quickly veiled. "You and Julie haven't been close for years, so you wouldn't really know. She did do drugs, and that was part of the competency issue. My wife was horribly clinically depressed, Detective."

Brock spread his hands sympathetically, his gaze on Zara. "We have evidence of self-destructive behavior that includes everything from suicide attempts to picking up strange men for the night. She needed help, and we were trying to get that for her through the competency hearing." He leaned forward and read several lines from a notepad. "The doctor would've diagnosed her with a drug problem, we're certain."

Zara vehemently shook her head, and Ryker gently slid an arm around her shoulders to play with her hair. She settled immediately. Yeah. He could do this. He could cover and protect her calmly and rationally without losing his temper or drawing attention to his brothers.

"We wanted to help Julie, not hurt her." The lawyer was smooth with just the right amount of concern and genuineness. No wonder he often won in court.

There was only one way to get to the truth of whether or not Julie was doing drugs. Ryker focused on the detective. "When will the autopsy be concluded?"

Norton glanced at his watch. "I've put a rush on it, but that could still mean the end of next week."

"I'll get it done sooner." Jay reached for his phone and texted something, his hand shaking. "My chief of staff will light a fire under the coroner. We have to find out what happened to Julie."

The doorbell rang.

"I'll take care of the press," the detective said, standing. "Do you want to make a statement or have the officers outside escort them out of the subdivision? They're technically trespassing."

Jay stood and smoothed back his hair. His handsome face fell into sad lines. "I should probably make a statement." Without looking at Ryker, he moved past them to the door.

Ryker rolled his eyes.

The detective nodded, his expression veiled. "I'll come with you." They left with Brock in their wake.

Zara moved toward the door. "Oh, I want to watch this," she whispered.

Ryker grasped her arm and held her back. "Stay out of the picture for now, darlin'. Considering you were probably the last person to see the victim alive."

Zara stumbled and paused. "Besides the killer, you mean."

That was exactly what he had meant. He had to shove down the thought that the killer could've gotten to her that day, too, or he'd lose his fuckin' mind. His entire body flushed with heat, and he took a moment to regain control. "I want to hear what else Jay says to the detective when he gets finished using this whole thing to his advantage with the press," Ryker said. "At that point, we have to sit down and figure out what kind of mess you're in. Did anybody see you yesterday?"

She paled. "I don't think so, but I can't be totally sure." She winced. "And I went through all of Julie's things."

"Why?" Ryker asked, the blood rushing through his head.

She looked down at her notepad. "Brock had made some allegations about drugs, so I looked around her stuff to see if I could find any. I didn't find one tiny bit of evidence that Julie was doing drugs. Not one."

Ryker grasped her chin and lifted her face to meet her eyes. Shit. This was getting worse and worse. "Did you touch anything?"

She blinked. "Yes. I searched the whole room."

Well, fuck. He automatically sought for an exit. This was bad. She was in trouble, and running might be the only option until Ryker found the real killer or proved that Jay did it. "They'll dust for prints, darlin'. You haven't been arrested before, have you?" he asked, trying to keep his voice calm for her.

"No." Her eyes widened, and the pulse fluttered in her neck.

"Are your prints on file to be a paralegal?" This was beyond bad. It put in danger not only Zara but also anybody around her, including his brothers.

She slowly shook her head. "No. Only people taking the bar exam get printed, and paralegals don't take the bar exam. Nobody has ever fingerprinted me."

"Okay. That's good." It was also probably only a temporary reprieve. If anybody tied Zara to Julie, the cops could probably get Zara's fingerprints, and that would put Zara at the scene of the crime.

"Am I in trouble?" she whispered, any remaining color draining from her face.

He slid an arm around her, offering her warmth and protection. "Yeah, baby. You're in deep shit." But he'd get her out of it if it was the last thing he did. For now, he had to protect his brothers and stay away from the cameras flashing outside.

Oh, moving to Cisco had been a fucking terrible idea.

As he tucked Zara close, something in him roared to life: the fighter he'd tried to quell for so long. He'd known someday the showdown would occur, and he'd figured at some point Sheriff Cobb would win.

Not now. Now Ryker had way too much to lose. "We'll figure this out, Zara. I promise." As the cameras flashed again outside the door, he wondered if they'd all have to run this time. Maybe getting lost was his only option once again.

CHAPTER
19

Zara couldn't believe it. Julie was dead. Really dead. The words kept going through her head all day, and she couldn't get them to stop. It was unbelievable and so unfair.

Her heart hurt, and her stomach ached. Her temples pounded until her eyes stung. Julie had been a good friend, and somebody had brutally stabbed her. How frightened the poor woman must've been before death.

Zara had hung around while the detective questioned Jay Pentley for a few hours, handled the press for another hour or so, and then finally sat down with a game plan for dealing with the publicity. Brock had steadfastly sat by his client's side, once in a while cautioning Jay not to answer, but for the most part letting the detective take the lead. Ryker and Zara had watched and listened before finally heading to Zara's home after darkness had fallen. They'd grabbed burgers and eaten on the way, taking several home to Greg, who'd been dropped off earlier by Denver.

Zara batted away tears as she changed clothes in her bedroom while Ryker got Greg settled into the spare room. During the horrible day, she'd forgotten all about poor Greg. He'd descended on the burgers like a normal teenager.

The door opened, and Ryker entered, shutting it behind himself. "That kid ate all the leftover burgers."

Zara finished tugging down her T-shirt and turned to sit on the bed, her entire body exhausted. "Growing boy and all that."

Ryker studied her for a moment and then crossed the room to crouch between her knees, his warm hands flexing on her thighs. His gaze was steady and concerned. "I'm sorry about your friend."

A tear escaped her furious blinking. "Who would kill her like that?"

His eyes darkened. "Best bet is the husband. He would've lost half of his assets in the divorce, and that guy's an egomaniac. Anybody else would've thrown you to the wolves and had me arrested for hitting him. He's too embarrassed by us both—it's all ego."

"Maybe, but I don't see him taking a chance like that. Although he did like to hit Julie. The idea that she was really leaving him would've pissed him off." Zara set her hands over Ryker's. "Thank you for being with me today during all of that. I felt better having you at my back."

He nodded, his gaze sober. "I'm planning to stay right here with you, baby."

She warmed and leaned toward him. "Thank you."

He rubbed reassuring circles on her legs. "We need to figure out who killed Julie before you become an official suspect. It's your best way to keep your job and freedom."

"Okay." It was almost surreal. She'd never kill anybody, and it was nice that Ryker hadn't even once considered that she had.

"Tomorrow we're going to run through everything you know about Julie and Jay." Ryker's hands tightened. "You don't talk to the police or Brock without me, okay? And you *never* talk to the media."

She nodded. "I understand. But you have to keep working on Greg's case, too." She frowned. "What exactly is his case, anyway? He mentioned losing his brothers and needing you to find them. What's that all about?"

Ryker shook his head. "Client confidentiality. If he wants to share his story with you, he will. Not that he's told me everything, either."

Zara frowned. "Do we have a duty to notify the authorities since he's a minor?"

"Probably, but as two adults who were subjected to the system as kids, do we want to do that to him? I'd rather help him a different way."

"I just wondered if we had a duty. No way would I give that kid up to the system." Her urge to protect Greg caught her off guard, although she'd been a lost kid once, too. Not everybody had a Grams waiting with open arms to make the world right again. Maybe Zara could make the world a good place for Greg, or at least help to do so.

"So Greg stays with us for now." Ryker rubbed his hands down her legs to caress along the arch of her foot.

Pure pleasure ran up her calf. "That feels good." Was Ryker trying to distract her? "Is Greg dangerous?"

"Undoubtedly." Ryker dug both thumbs into the arch. "But that kid would cut off his right arm before harming you. You're probably one of the few nice people he's ever met, and you're more than likely the only one to make him breakfast, if you ask me. He's safe for you."

Her heart broke even more for poor Greg. "You read people so well." She'd always wanted that talent but was often totally off the mark with others. "Must be nice."

"Sometimes it sucks, but it does help with the business." Ryker shrugged. "Besides, I see a little of myself in that kid. He's ready to strike out at a moment's notice, but you give him one ounce of kindness and he'll die for you."

She studied his eyes, more blue than green today, as he revealed more about himself. There wasn't a doubt in her mind that Ryker would jump in front of a train to save her. "Your childhood hurt."

"Yeah." He gave a lopsided smile.

Her heart warmed even while it ached for the angry kid he must've been. "I'm sorry." Could she help him heal? Show him that life could be better than good?

He shrugged. "Wasn't so bad when I met up with Heath and Denver. Then at least I had a family."

He was being so open she couldn't stop her thoughts from rolling out. "You scare me, Ryker."

He lifted an eyebrow and gentled his touch. His head jerked like he'd been punched. "I'd never hurt you."

"You'd never *mean* to hurt me," she murmured. "But you're all or nothing. Pure trust or none at all. Full dependence or none." The words rolled from her tongue. Did he understand that kind of pressure? What if she let him down? He'd been let down too much in life already, she suspected. What if she screwed up and he reacted by leaving? Her heart hurt just thinking about it.

He rubbed his chin and turned his full focus on her.

She swallowed.

"I don't see you being anything but independent, darlin'."

The drawl. Every once in a while, he drawled a sentence in a deeper tone that shot right through her like fine whiskey. "You want everything," she countered, trying to make sense of the rioting feelings inside her.

He grinned then, his eyes remaining sober. "I'll get it, too."

She opened her mouth, but no words emerged. Another topic. She had to get away from the charged conversation and think away from him. Her thoughts and emotions were just too damn jumbled at the moment. "Um, okay. Let's concentrate on the immediate situation. Greg. What are we going to do with him?"

Amusement—that had to be amusement—creased Ryker's cheek as he let her off the hook. "While I think Greg is safe for you, I'm not sure if the kid has enemies. If anybody comes to light, I'm moving him to my apartment, and I'll cover you. Heath and Denver can watch over Greg if necessary."

She reached out and cupped his whiskered jaw, warming to the safer topic. Yet she had to know more about him. "Why did you become a private investigator?"

He moved to her other foot, somehow relaxing her entire body. "The three of us need to find people. Heath wants to find the man who killed his mama, Denver wants to know about where he came from, and I want to find my birth parents. We figured that opening up a detective agency was the way to go."

"Have you had any luck?" she asked, her heart jumping at finally learning the truth.

"No. Not even a little." Ryker sat back, her foot on his thighs. "We discovered on the way that we have a talent for finding lost people, so we've stuck with it. Once in a while we're too late." His voice sobered.

Ah. The girls murdered by the serial killer. Ryker was a guy who'd be haunted forever by that. "I'm sorry, Ryker. Are there any leads on the serial killer case?" she whispered.

"No. Heath is monitoring the FBI, and we're trying to figure out a plan, but right now we have a lot going on." He stopped talking and shoved back to stand up. "I need a shower, and then we'll grab some shut-eye." Within a second, he'd disappeared into the master bath.

Zara watched him go and pressed her hands on her knees, looking around her comfortable bedroom. For some reason, the room always seemed different with Ryker in the house. More exciting and richer. She'd chosen the green bedspread with him in mind, although she'd never admit it. White pillows and furniture kept the room feminine, and the red throw rug on the wood floor added a pop of color.

The room smelled like Ryker—wild man and leather. He'd been there only a short time, and the room had taken on his essence.

So had she.

He'd opened up to her more than ever before, and the idea was both intimidating and exciting. How much more did he have hidden away, and what was it? What was so bad in his past that he wouldn't share it with her? While he had certainly opened up, she knew he hadn't told her everything.

The shower turned on in the bathroom. At the moment, the lost look in his eyes kept nagging at her.

She pushed from the bed, dropping clothing as she moved across the floor. Nudging open the bathroom door, she stopped as steam blasted against her. Ryker looked up from examining in the mirror a dark bruise across his rib cage, buck ass naked. "Zara?"

"What happened?" she breathed, running a finger along the purple mark. Who had hurt him? Anger mixed with her concern, and her hand shook.

"Jay got in a good punch. One." Ryker reached over her shoulder to push the door closed. A veil had dropped over his eyes. He was retreating from their conversation. From their closeness. "What are you doing?"

Steam surrounded them. She paused. A smart girl would go back to the other room and shore up her emotional defenses as he did the same.

Turmoil turned his eyes a deep green, turmoil and something else. What was that? Need. It was need, and he was no longer hiding it. She couldn't turn away. "I thought you might want company in the shower." Her knees wobbled.

His gaze darkened and ran down her nude form. Hunger rolled, heated and strong, through the misty room. "We're not making it to the shower." Hooking her by the waist, he took her down to the plush white rug and rolled until she sat on his hips.

The steam dampened the air, and she ran her hands down his torso. Hard muscle and ripped ridges filled her palms. "I never imagined a man could be so beautiful," she murmured. Strength could be stunning. "Everything about you is pure male."

Evidence of that fact jumped against her inner thighs. He was hard and ready to go that quickly.

Pure male possession crossed his rugged face while hunger for her curved his dangerous lips. "I'm taking more than just your body, Zara." He flattened his palm on her abdomen and dragged his fingertips up her torso to her breasts.

She arched into his rough palms, wetness spilling from her. "Think you can handle that?" she moaned.

"Watch me."

She could only nod as need coiled inside her. Her nipples ached, and deep between her legs, she throbbed.

"I want to be inside you. Now." The commanding tone of his voice licked right through her, and she shivered. The man had a definite bossy side in bed, and she'd be totally lying if she said she didn't like it.

So she lifted up, grasped him at the base, and tried to lower herself onto him. "You're too big." She gasped as her body fought her.

"Now, Zara."

More wetness spilled from her, and he chuckled. Then his hands abandoned her breasts and clamped onto her hips. She stiffened out of instinct.

"Relax your body, baby. Trust me." The words were coaxing, but the tone was all command.

She relaxed and breathed out, her body obeying instantly even as her mind fought to catch up.

He widened his hips, which widened her thighs. She fell forward, stopping herself with her hands on his broad chest. Sinew and muscle filled her palms. Then he slowly, inexorably lowered her inch by inch without giving quarter.

The feeling of being penetrated, of his slow and sure movements, lit her body on fire. She threw back her head and let him control them both, feeling her internal muscles clench and release. The pressure built to almost too much, and she stiffened again, her gaze catching his. "Wait a sec."

He lowered his chin and studied her. Then, apparently reaching a conclusion, "No." He moved her down his length again.

The need to challenge him, to fight his dominance, rose in her along with an impish chuckle, so she found purchase with her knees and tried to lift her butt.

He held her in place but stopped moving. "Zara? You really want me to stop? Or do you wanna play, baby?" His voice was a low rumble that moved through her abdomen with a rush of heat.

If she truly asked him to stop, he would. But what fun would that be? "Oh, I wanna play," she whispered, desire shooting through her nerves. "You want such control? You're gonna have to take it." Yeah, she knew challenging him, especially like this, might be more than she wanted to take on, but as the haunted look completely fled his eyes, it was definitely worth it. "Unless you're not up to it?"

Oops. Too much. Definitely too much.

His fingers flexed on her hips and he yanked her down until her butt hit his thighs. Pleasure edged with pain surged through her, vibrating with raw pleasure. She sucked in air, and her eyes widened. Move. Oh God, he had to move. She wiggled her butt and dug in her nails, trying to lift back up.

He held her still. He grinned and her heart stopped.

Her sex fluttered around him, and heat uncoiled deep inside her. "Ryker," she breathed.

Keeping one hand clamped around her hip, he slid his other down over her abdomen and kept going until his thumb brushed her clit.

Electricity.

She pressed her lips together to keep from whimpering. When she was a little more in control, she breathed out. "Oh, I like the dangerous side of you." Her body was one huge nerve of need as she gave him the truth.

He smiled. "You're far more dangerous than I could ever be. Sexy and smart…and so damn sweet you kill me sometimes."

Those words from him. They gave her power and trust. A shiver wound down her back. She flashed him a smile right as her nails dug into his chest, wanting to push him a little.

He didn't even wince. Instead, he pressed hard on her clit and then rubbed. "Sheath the claws or I will."

She gasped and gyrated against him. "No."

He released her clit and grabbed his belt from his discarded jeans. Her eyes widened. Wait. Oops. Crap. While she tried to draw back, he secured her wrists and quickly bound them behind her back.

"Hey." She struggled against the leather and couldn't release them. A startled laugh, one full of joy and surprise, erupted from her. Heat flared through her so fast she swayed.

The pads of his fingers grazed her hips and moved up to her breasts to tweak both nipples. The small pain bit into her, and she groaned. So much. Way too much. Then his thighs widened more, and she lost any sense of being in control.

She had to fight to remain upright and not fall forward onto him, and in doing so, her internal muscles clenched along his hard length.

His eyes turned molten. "You're stunning, Zara." Keeping her gaze captive, he ran his thumb across his tongue and then reached out to rub her clit, his thumb rough and worn. He scraped across her delicate tissue, caressing and rubbing, giving no mercy. She moved against him, so close but nowhere near enough. Little tremors cascaded inside her, catching on his shaft.

He grinned again. "I could do this every day for the rest of my life."

She chuckled. "It would kill me." She couldn't get her balance enough to lift up and down, having to satisfy herself by gyrating against his hand.

"Then the world would become too dark for any of us."

Sometimes he was so sweet she didn't know what to say. So she remained in place, trusting him with this new level of...them. He was fun in bed even while torturing her so perfectly. Maybe she did trust him completely. When had that happened? "This is different, right?" It wasn't just Ryker...It was them. Vulnerability assailed her for the briefest of moments.

His gaze darkened. "Yeah, baby. This is just you and me...It's better than anything else in the world." He played with her breasts again, his hands rough but his hold nearly gentle.

Her heart thumped hard. Yeah. It was them. No matter what happened, they had this, and it was special.

"What do you want, sweetheart?" He reached around, grazed down, and grasped her buttocks, separating them just enough to give her pause.

Hunger clawed through her. "You. All of you."

"You have me." A quick flick of his wrists, and he unleashed her hands. She barely had time to move them in front of her before he grabbed her waist, flipped them both so she lay on her back, and pulled out only to hammer back in her. Hard.

She arched against him, her breasts brushing his chest. How could anything real feel so good? "Oh God."

He kissed her, his tongue diving in, his mouth stealing every bit of her. Finally, he lifted his head. "Zara. Feel me," he whispered. A muscle twitched in his cut jaw, and determination of the dangerously masculine kind was stamped hard on his features. Tension, dominant and hot, swelled through the steam. Need. She could see that he needed her. Way more than want...and it was a gift.

His cock pulsed inside her, every damn ridge filling her. Oh, she felt him, and not just in her body. He knew it, too.

Her body thrummed to the point of pain, right on the edge. Her heart turned over, so she gave him what they both wanted. She knew what he wanted, what he perhaps needed. Maybe she could make him whole, too. "I feel you, Ryker Jones. All of you," she said softly.

His entire body stilled, and his eyes flared a heated green through the blue. He slid an arm up her back to grasp the nape of her neck in an unrelenting hold. His other hand anchored her hip, and her hands were trapped against his chest.

She. Couldn't. Move.

She gasped, and a fine tremor shook her. So much need.

"That's my girl," he said. Then he started to move, fast and deliberate, increasing in speed until there was nothing but his body inside hers.

She curled her fingers into his skin, completely open to him. He moved her where he wanted her, hammering inside her, unerringly hitting her clit with each hard thrust. A live wire uncoiled inside her, sparking out. She detonated, her body stiffening, raw fire catching her unaware. She cried out his name as the waves took her under.

He pumped harder and then jerked with his own release.

Finally, he dropped his head to the crook of her neck. A lazy swipe of his tongue made her tremble. He lifted up, his expression one of satisfied male. Then he frowned and glanced toward the still-running shower. "I think the hot water is gone."

Humor bubbled up inside her, and she threw back her head and laughed.

Was this what happiness—the real kind—felt like? One last chuckle and she lowered her chin, seeking those bluish green eyes. God, this *was* happiness.

Suddenly, reality and the world crashed in. She couldn't lose him. She couldn't lose this. Not now.

CHAPTER
20

Ryker drove Zara and Greg back to his place first thing in the morning. While they'd have to sleep at her house for now, he wanted them near his offices during the day. After a breakfast of blueberry pancakes, during which he could almost forget the danger stalking them, Ryker desperately tried to concentrate on Greg and how Dr. Madison tied into Ryker's own past.

Denver and Heath worked in their offices while Greg assisted Zara by measuring the apartments upstairs for furniture. After she'd fed him pancake after pancake, the kid had followed her around like a duck that had imprinted. He had even given a little growl when Ryker kissed her on the forehead before heading for his office.

Heath poked his head in, tension in his shoulders. "The FBI has about twenty suspects they're following up on with the Copper Killer case, but I've gone through them all, and I think they're on the wrong track. None of those guys really fit."

Ryker sighed. "Do we have anything?" If they didn't get a move on, the bastard would take another girl within the next week, if not the FBI agent. Gut instinct told him the killer was too smart to fall for the trap.

"Nothing." Frustration marred Heath's forehead. "If we had something, I'd head out, but I have no clue where to go."

"Hey, guys!" Denver called. "Come here."

Ryker pushed from the desk and followed Heath through the main room to Denver's office. "What?" he asked, dropping into a chair while Heath did the same.

"I've been searching for Isobel Madison, and I found a string to pull. My gut says it's a trap, and once we bite, backtracking software will kick in and trace us here." Denver scratched his chin and looked at the computer like it might bite him.

Ryker's stomach ached. Did they really want to find that woman? Logically, he knew they had to, but deep down, he was that scared kid again who just wanted to run.

"We could create software that won't allow the backtrack," Heath said, scowling.

Ryker held up a hand. He needed to be in control to think, and he had to be proactive. "What if we allow her to track us? We could do the same thing to her as we did to Greg. Draw her in. It's probably the only chance we have of getting her." She'd had a lot more years than they had to learn surveillance, subterfuge, and strategy. "Let's fall into her hands." He wanted to puke as he said the last sentence.

Denver's hand folded into a fist on his desk. "I hate this."

"Me too," Ryker said.

"We'd have to use safe house three," Heath said.

Ryker nodded. "If we want her close, it has to be in Cisco." They'd created three safe houses when they bought the current building just in case they needed to move and fast. "We can wire the place, so if anybody shows up, we can be there in ten minutes."

Heath kicked his boots out and crossed his ankles. "If we go forward with this, there's no going back. I don't know where it'll end, but right now we're somewhat safe from the past. She *is* the past, men."

"She's the key," Denver replied softly.

"I'm damn tired of playing defense. Let's take control. Plus, she's the only way to find these missing brothers of Greg's," Ryker said. If his brothers were missing, he'd be out of his damn mind. He had to help that kid find his family.

Heath shook his head. "Speaking of which, if Greg has brothers somewhere, why won't he tell us where?"

"He said their school was blown up, and he has no clue where his brothers were relocated," Ryker reminded him.

"The kid isn't telling us the whole truth," Heath countered.

Ryker nodded. "Would you tell us? I mean, if you were that kid, would you reveal all?"

"Shit no," Heath said slowly. "He trusts like we do: not at all."

"If I couldn't find you guys, I'd be desperate," Ryker said. "He is, and that's why I trust him. He has to find those brothers the same way I'd need to find you guys. That's the only reason he came to us—to anybody—for help: desperation."

Greg appeared suddenly in the door. "I'm not desperate."

Denver typed quickly on the keyboard, waited a minute, and then flipped the monitor around. "Here's the depot in Utah that was blown up." Scorched earth and shattered buildings littered the snowy ground. "How do you expect us to believe you?"

Greg swallowed and stepped inside the room. He paled, and a look way too stark to belong to a kid filled his eyes. "Scan to the north."

Denver reached for the mouse and manipulated the screen beyond the buildings to a wide field. "Yeah?"

"Zoom in to the left."

Denver did so, craning his neck to see around the monitor. "Okay." He frowned. "What's that?"

Greg paled. "That was my grave, man."

Ryker jerked his head back and narrowed his gaze. A grave marker did line the area away from the downed fence. But...he looked closer and then whistled.

"Yeah," Greg said. "It's been dug up."

"So you think your brothers are looking for you?" Heath asked.

Greg shook his head. "No. I set up several places on the Internet that they could find if they were looking, and only they could find those places on the dark web. They haven't looked, so they don't think I'm alive."

"Why the hell would they move your grave, then?" Ryker asked.

"If they left the compound, if they found safety somehow, they'd take me with them." Faith in his brothers colored Greg's words.

Ryker fought a shiver. "True that," he murmured.

"You think kids would've dug up and moved a coffin?" Heath asked.

"If it was you, I would've moved you even when we were kids," Ryker said while Denver nodded, his gaze stark.

Heath pointed to the monitor. "We have an idea to bring Dr. Madison here. To fall into a trap of hers so she has to come calling. What do you think?"

Greg's face lost all color. "Shit no, man. You don't understand." Panic swelled from the kid. "Madison won't come. Soldiers—ones trained beyond what you could even imagine—will storm the entire town."

"We can take care of ourselves," Ryker said, more than a little surprised by the panic. Nothing had seemed to get to this kid. "We won't let anybody hurt you, Greg."

Greg's chin dropped. "Oh man. You have no fucking clue. Jesus." He turned to go, and only Ryker's hand on his arm stopped him. "I have to get out of here. This was a mistake." His voice rose on the last in pure panic.

"Wait a minute—" Ryker started and stood up.

Greg swept out with his leg, catching Ryker in the knee. It buckled, and he went forward. Greg followed up with a cuff to the temple and turned to run.

Pain bloomed in Ryker's head. He grabbed Greg by the leg, pulling him down. Greg fought hard, punching and kicking, using a combination of several martial arts moves as well as street moves. Ryker countered each one, his head ringing, his temper trying to spring free. He kept his moves to defense and held back from harming the boy.

Greg connected with a solid punch to Ryker's mouth.

He growled and gripped the kid's wrists, jerking him up and off his feet to plant him against the wall. "Knock it the fuck off," he growled, his face in Greg's.

Denver leaned against the door frame, and Heath had moved behind them to keep track.

"Where did you learn to fight like that?" Greg hissed, struggling against Ryker's hold.

"Me?" Ryker spit blood off his lip, his chest heaving out. "What about you? Jesus. You been training since diapers?"

Greg stilled. "Yeah."

Ryker blinked and lowered the kid to the ground. Shock slowed his movements. They'd made the boy learn to fight before he'd walked? How fucked up was that? "Listen. We're in this together, whatever it is. Dr. Madison tested all of us, and there had to be a reason. Do you have any idea what it was?"

"No." Greg stuck out his chin.

Interesting and twice as heartbreaking. "You're lying."

"Prove it." Greg shook out of Ryker's hold. "There's no trap for Madison that will capture her. She won't come." He shrugged. "Unless the commander is dead, which is totally unlikely. He runs the military side of their little fiefdom."

Ryker stepped back to give him some room. "All right. Let me get this straight. You and your brothers were raised in a military-type school where they trained you to fight." Only size and strength had allowed Ryker to keep Greg from hurting either one of them. When Greg reached adulthood, he'd be one dangerous motherfucker.

Greg blinked. "I take it you weren't trained?"

"Madison studied only our IQs and conditioning. We were taught for free by a local martial arts expert and then attended a military training camp," Ryker said. For the first time, he wondered if it had indeed been free. Had Madison arranged for them to be conditioned to fight? "We learned a lot on our own through the years as well."

Heath cocked his head. "I wonder why we were trained at all. I mean, this is all so damn confusing. We have to find that woman to get some answers. It's the only way."

"I can't stop you," Greg said. He stepped toward Ryker. "But take some advice. If they come for you, they'll come at your weaknesses. They'll come at what you care about. Cut Zara loose now."

The words spoken by such a young face sent chills down Ryker's back. Anger tried to take hold, and he forced it back, needing to stay calm and in control for Greg. "I can take care of Zara."

Greg wearily shook his head.

"Greg, you have to trust us," Heath said. "We're trained, too. We won't let anybody hurt you or Zara."

"Poor stupid sap," Greg murmured.

"She studied us, too," Denver said, finally chiming in.

Heath nodded. "She might be the key to our pasts and our families. This isn't just about you."

Greg shook his head more wildly. "Don't you get it? You have family right here and now. You guys are brothers, which is all anybody ever needs. Anything else you find out is just gonna hurt in a way you don't even understand. These are not good people. If Madison is involved in your past, then believe me, you do not want to know a damn thing about it." His eyes filled with tears, and he angrily brushed them away. "Live your very good lives and stop looking back."

Agony swelled from the kid along with a strong shimmer of fear.

Ryker tried to calm his system. No matter what happened, he wouldn't let anybody hurt this boy ever again. Right now he needed cooperation to make that happen. "How about we show you the plan to draw in Madison or her soldiers? If soldiers show up, they can lead us back to her. It's really the only way."

Greg dropped his head forward. "You're all gonna end up dead."

"We're tougher than you think." Ryker gently slid a hand along the kid's nape and tugged him to his side. "How about we all work together on this?"

Greg's shoulders slumped. "Fine, but don't ever say I didn't warn you. For now, please distance yourself from Zara. She doesn't have any clue what's out there, and it's your job to keep it like that."

"I know. But she has her own issues going on, and I need to cover her on that side, too," Ryker said.

Greg's head jerked up. "What issues?"

Man, the kid had a crush, didn't he? "I've got it covered, pal." Ryker nudged Greg back into Denver's office. He would try to protect the kid as much as possible. "So here's the plan. We have a safe house across town, and there we can set a trap for Madison or her soldiers or whoever shows up." Grabbing a notepad from the corner, he started to sketch. "Feel free to jump in with ideas."

CHAPTER 21

Zara shifted beneath the covers and tried to find a cool spot for her feet. Ryker put off a lot of heat at night. He lay on his stomach, taking up most of her bed, breathing softly into a pillow.

It felt right, ending their day together.

She swallowed. Her throat ached. Man, she was thirsty. Gingerly, she slid from the bed and drew on her fuzzy pink robe. Chances were Greg was dead asleep, but just in case, she didn't want to freak out the kid in her Minnie Mouse shorts and tank top. She shoved hair away from her face and padded quietly through her bedroom and out into the living room.

Cool air hit her.

Good. She'd have to start sleeping with the window open if Ryker kept staying over. At least if there was a long-term heat outage, she'd be toasty warm every night with him.

If he stayed. The idea gave her warm tingles through her abdomen.

It kind of felt like he did want to stay, and she'd started to wonder if they could make it work. She reached the kitchen and poured herself a glass of water, then quickly drank it down. Better. Much better. She slowly refilled the glass.

The air felt funny. She stilled.

Muscled arms grabbed her from behind.

She stiffened and then struggled. Panic swamped her.

A huge hand, covered in hair, slapped duct tape over her mouth.

She screamed for Ryker beneath it, shooting both elbows back into the guy's gut, panic giving her strength.

Suddenly, the body behind her was ripped away, sending her sprawling into the refrigerator. She fell to the floor. Pain slapped from her hands to her elbows. Two bodies hit and kicked quickly, grunting in anger and pain. One was much slimmer than the other one. "Greg?" She shoved to her feet. The guy he was fighting with wore all black, and something covered his entire head.

Ryker barreled out of the bedroom in a rush of speed.

The front door blew open, and two more men rushed inside, both wearing ski masks and black clothing. Ryker pivoted and attacked both men, tackling them against the wall. Pictures dropped. A gun flew out and spun across the room. Something loud crunched, and one of the men screamed, pain filling the sound.

The guy in the kitchen lifted Greg and threw him. Greg hit the counter, bounced up, and lunged at the attacker right before he could reach Zara.

Zara ripped the tape off her mouth, shoved to her feet, and dove for the gun in the living room. What was going on? Her hands fumbled madly for the weapon.

A foot connected with her chin, and stars flashed behind her eyes. Nausea filled her stomach. God. Tears filled her eyes. Where was the gun? What happened to the gun? She crab-walked across the room, her hands slapping against the floor.

The attacker in the kitchen shoved Greg into cupboards, and pots and pans flew out. Greg kicked up, hitting the guy beneath the chin. The attacker flew back and into the refrigerator.

Zara blinked tears from her eyes. How could this be happening? Her jaw pounded in pain, and dots filled her vision. Ryker fought near the door, taking on two men, punching the first in the jaw. The guy's head snapped back with an audible crack.

The man in the kitchen punched Greg in the gut. The kid doubled over.

Fury flowed through Zara, and she pivoted to help him.

The attacker slammed Greg on the shoulder and took out a gun. Greg dropped to one knee and looked up, pure rage across his young face. His muscles bunched to move, but the attacker cocked the gun and pointed it at his forehead.

"No!" Zara jumped up, grabbed a cast-iron skillet, and swung with all her strength. It hit the guy in the shoulder, and he partially turned toward her.

Greg swept out his leg, hitting the guy in the knee, and he fell.

Zara swung the skillet again at the guy's head. The edge hit mid-temple, and the man's head jerked back, he hit the floor, and bounced. His eyes fluttered shut, and his entire body went limp.

Ryker came flying over the kitchen island, landed hard, and rolled, a gun in his hand. He leaped up, firing into the living room. One guy bellowed in pain, and his buddy grabbed him, yanking him through the door. They ran out into the night.

Zara sucked in air, her head still spinning. She grabbed the counter to keep from going down.

Ryker reached her in seconds. Blood flowed from a cut on his chin, dripping to his bare chest. "You okay?"

She nodded and rubbed her aching jaw. "Yeah. Just got kicked."

He leaned in and studied her jaw. Tension emanated from him, and with the gun in his hand, he looked like the badass vigilante he was.

The screech of tires outside filled the night.

Greg shoved to his feet and kicked the downed man in the kitchen. The guy didn't even groan.

Zara hurried through the mess to the boy and tilted his head back. "Oh, sweetie. You're gonna have a black eye." The poor kid. Her heart lurched and continued its hammering.

"Not my first." Greg smiled through bloodied lips, nudging a pot away from his foot. "You okay?"

"I'm fine." The kid could really fight.

Sadness whipped through her. The poor kid must've had to know how to fight. As did Ryker. Lost, wounded males all but surrounded her. She reached for a paper towel to press to Greg's lip. She looked down at the unconscious man. "He duct-taped my mouth."

Greg gingerly fingered a bruise forming by his cheek. "Was he here for you or me?" He looked at Ryker. "Or you?"

Ryker leaned down and ripped off the face mask. Thick black hair covered the guy's head along with a matching beard. He had a strong jaw that went with his powerhouse of a body. "Anybody recognize this guy?"

Greg peered closer. "Nope."

Zara shook her head. "No." Her knees went weak.

"Whoa." Ryker tugged her against him for a moment. "Take a deep breath, baby."

She did so, and her lungs seized. Shuddering, she burrowed into the warm safety he provided. Then she looked into the living room. A chair lay in pieces next to her shattered lamps. One painting hung haphazardly from a corner, and blood marred the throw rug. The front door remained open with the damaged lock half out of the frame. "Should we call the police?"

Ryker studied the guy on the ground. "Not yet." He crouched and grabbed the duct tape. "Zara? Go pack a bag for a week's stay. Greg? Get your stuff." Her grabbed the guy's arm and started winding the tape around his hairy wrists.

Zara stumbled. "What are you doing?"

Ryker looked up, giving her his full attention.

She took a step back.

Cold intent filled his eyes, which lacked any warmth. Blood dotted his chest, and a couple of purple bruises had begun to form along his muscled arms. Danger cascaded from him along with an untenable tension. "Do as I've said, Zara. Now."

She didn't know him like this. Not at all. Wrapping her arms around herself, she turned and all but ran for the bedroom to pack a bag.

What had she gotten involved in?

* * *

Ryker finished binding the guy's wrists and ankles with the duct tape, and then for good measure, he slapped a piece across the guy's mouth. With that beard and mustache, it'd hurt like hell when pulled off.

Greg returned to the kitchen with his backpack over one shoulder. A lump marred the skin above his left eye. "I told you to cut her loose, man."

Ryker stood. "What if this was about her, not you?"

"Think it was?" Greg asked.

"We're gonna find out. He duct-taped her mouth, which might mean he wanted to take her. Or maybe he just wanted her quiet while he killed you. Or me." Ryker stretched his aching jaw, adrenaline pushing him to hurry it up. He had to cover Zara and now. "Either way, we need to get her out of here."

"Okay."

Ryker studied the kid. "You okay with what's going to happen?"

Greg lifted a dark eyebrow, his lips curving in a smirk. "If you don't have the stomach for it, I do. Give me five minutes with the guy, and he'll tell us everything we want to know and then some."

Great. Ryker ignored the warnings clamoring in his head even as his heart hurt for the kid. Man, he saw himself in Greg—another lost kid just trying to survive and build a family with his brothers—and Ryker would protect him no matter the cost.

What a shit-storm. He had a woman in the other room now frightened of him and probably in more danger than she understood, and he had a boy in front of him who was well versed in torture at only about twelve years old. Plus, the past was breathing down his neck and about to explode again—he just knew it. "We're fucked," he muttered.

Greg scratched his elbow. "Copy that." He stared at the man on the ground. "Though this guy wasn't after me."

Ryker frowned. "How do you know that?"

"Because you and I are both still alive. The commander and Madison wouldn't have sent anybody we could've fought so easily. Sorry."

The kid had a real fear of his commander. "I don't know, Greg. You handled yourself pretty well."

"So did Zara. Did you see her swing the skillet? Went right for the knockout shot to the head." Greg grinned through bruised lips.

Yeah. Ryker's chest swelled. She was one tough woman when necessary. He crouched down and dragged the bound man up and over his shoulder. He let out a groan. The guy weighed a ton. "Here's the plan. I'll get this guy and Zara into the truck while you follow. Try to get the front door as closed as possible."

Greg looked around. "The shades are drawn, so nobody can see the mess."

"We'll come back and clean it up later. Right now we need to get Zara to a secure location and then figure out who this guy is and who he's working for." Ryker turned and kicked a bowl out of his way.

Zara emerged from the bedroom. She'd changed into dark jeans and a blue sweater that matched her eyes. Her skin was so pale as to be luminescent, and her eyes were wide like a doe's. She had a duffel bag over one shoulder, and she didn't quite meet his gaze. "What are you doing with that guy?" she whispered.

"He's coming with us." Ryker headed for the door. "Come on, Zara." He kept a low thread of command in his voice. For now, he needed her strong and quick. The woman could fall apart later, and he'd be there for her. "Move."

She followed him out to the truck in her driveway, wincing when he tossed the bound man into the backseat. Darkness shrouded them, but dawn would be breaking soon, and they needed to be out of sight by then.

Ryker opened the passenger side door and lifted her in. He turned and watched Greg finish setting the front door to rights. It looked okay and not like it had been busted open. Good. The kid hustled down the walk and reached the car. Ryker handed him the gun. "Do you mind sitting in back with this guy?"

"Nope." Greg slid into the backseat and shoved the bound man over to the other side. "Not a problem."

Everything in Ryker wanted to find the mysterious commander and beat the ever livin' shit out of him. No preteen should be okay with holding a gun on a hostage. "Thanks," Ryker said, shutting the door.

He got into the driver's seat and started the engine, quickly pulling out into the street.

Zara sat next to him, her teeth worrying her bottom lip. "I still think we should call the police."

"We still might," Ryker said, keeping just under the speed limit while dialing Denver.

"What?" Denver growled into the phone.

Ryker paused at a stop sign. "I need the boiler room prepared for a guest." He clicked off.

"Boiler room?" Zara asked.

"When we get to my place, I need you to go up to the apartment and wait for me," Ryker said, looking into the backseat. "You too, kid."

Greg didn't answer and kept his gaze level.

Snow fell around them, soft and drifting. Ryker made tracks through town and pulled into the underground garage, where Denver and Heath were already waiting by the boiler room. He pulled Zara his way and helped her out his door. "Upstairs, sweetheart. It you can get some sleep, do it."

She looked at Denver and Heath and then swung around to face him. "This is a bad idea."

He ran a knuckle down the newest bruise on her face. So far, he was doing a piss-poor job of protecting her. The idea that somebody had infiltrated her home and put his hands on her threatened to steal Ryker's self-control. The pressure of possible failure was nothing compared to the reality of the outcome. She couldn't be one more person he'd lost. Thank God Greg had been there. Ryker owed the kid now, for sure. "Go. Now."

She rolled her eyes and turned on her heel, heading for the stairwell.

Ryker opened the back door, and Greg jumped out. "I need you to cover her," Ryker whispered. "Until we figure out if this guy was after her or not, she needs to stay in my apartment."

Greg paused, looked at the door Zara had disappeared through and then back at Ryker. "I can get the guy to talk."

Ryker blanched. "Give me something, kid. I can't live with having you a part of this." It was as honest as he could get with the twelve-year-old.

Greg tucked the gun into the back waistband of his pants. "Fair enough. If you need help, just holler." He headed for the stairs.

Ryker watched him go, his chest actually hurting. Then he reached into the truck and hauled the bound man out by the armpits.

"Holy shit," Heath said, moving forward to grab the guy's knees and lift. "Who the hell?"

"He and two of his buddies broke into Zara's tonight." Ryker pivoted and headed for the boiler room.

Denver opened the heavy metal door, silent as usual.

"Do you think he's one of Sheriff Cobb's men?" A muscle ticked in Heath's jaw, and his gaze hardened on the guy in black. "If so, he's still working with Sylvia—I mean, Isobel Madison."

"Dunno. We're about to find out." Ryker carried the guy inside the cinder-block room and shoved him onto the one metal chair.

Heath cut the duct tape and fastened shackles in the same places. "He's out cold."

Denver shut the door and grabbed a bucket of cold water from the floor. "We can fix that."

CHAPTER 22

Zara finished dishing another waffle onto Greg's plate as he sat on the floor. The kid ate hungrily, seeming completely unaffected by what was probably happening down in the boiler room.

He glanced up. "It's okay. Ryker won't kill the guy."

Zara blinked. "How are you so knowledgeable about this kind of thing?"

Greg pushed his shaggy hair away from his face. "I was trained from day one as a soldier. So were my brothers. This is no big deal."

Yet it was. It truly was. "We're supposed to be the good guys."

Greg lifted an eyebrow. "We are, I think. The good guys have to be able to use bad methods in order to win. You get that, right?"

She shook her head, everything in her wanted to soothe the boy, who was so familiar with violence. Ryker and Greg were cut from the same cloth, without a doubt. "I'm a paralegal, and I chose the law on purpose. We need to follow it."

Greg snorted and shoveled in more waffle. He swallowed the entire chunk. "Your man doesn't care about rules or law right now. A guy broke into your place and put his hands on you." Greg shook his head. "Forget what I said. Maybe Ryker will kill him."

The door opened, and Ryker strode in. Blood marred his torn shirt, and his jeans were wet.

Zara pushed away from the counter. Fine tremors attacked her nervous system. "Well?"

"The guy's name is Jonny Reese, and he's a thug out of Denver." Ryker stretched bruised knuckles. "He and his buddies were hired to kidnap you, Zara."

Pins pricked down her back. She believed in law and the rules. The idea that some thugs would just break into her safe home to take her made her knees weak. She looked at Ryker with new eyes. He didn't believe in law or any rules. Nausea boiled in her stomach, and her breath quickened. "Why would they want me?" She tried to keep the fear out of her voice, but her voice trembled.

Ryker shook his head. "I don't know yet."

The world seemed darker somehow. A shadowed place where guys like Ryker moved freely. If he hadn't been there, it was doubtful she and Greg would've won the fight. He'd saved her. She could've been the person in a boiler room.

Why? Why would anybody want to hurt her? "I don't understand," she whispered, her voice thick with tears.

Ryker's gaze softened on her. "You have my word. Nobody will hurt you, baby."

She nodded and swallowed several times. Ryker would kill to keep her safe, but what about him? What if he sacrificed his life for hers? She couldn't let him do it. "I'm not scared."

His lip twitched. "It's okay to be scared. Means you have a brain."

Oh. Okay. So she wasn't weak. Time to think. She needed to copy how Ryker handled danger and think clearly without the fear. "Who hired that guy?" she asked, her mind spinning.

"Unfortunately, Jonny didn't know that tidbit," Ryker growled. "Only one of the guys was in contact with whoever hired them."

Greg stretched to his feet, carrying his empty plate, shaking his head. "And you let him get away."

"Yep," Ryker snapped.

"What about Jonny?" Zara whispered, her body preparing to flee even while her mind wanted to fight.

Ryker turned and strode toward the bedroom. "Denver is dropping him off at the hospital. He might need stitches." Anger he was failing to mask trailed in his wake, and he disappeared into the bedroom.

Greg threw his paper plate away. "See? Nobody got killed this time."

This time. "If you want more orange juice, it's in the fridge." Zara hustled after Ryker. None of this made any sense. How could it? She swallowed and opened the bedroom door. Clothes littered the floor to the bathroom, and the sound of the shower being turned on filled the morning.

The last time she'd followed Ryker into a bathroom, she'd ended up on her back, moaning his name. Was that only a night ago? So much had happened, she just couldn't grasp a thought. Who would want to kidnap her? It was good that it was okay to be afraid, because she was terrified. She stepped gingerly over his discarded clothing, not sure how much of the wetness was actually Jonny's blood. "Ryker?" she pushed open the bathroom door.

Dark tile and chrome fixtures made up the bathroom with its double vanity and three-sided glass shower stall. A toilet was in a side room. Ryker stood under the spray with steam billowing all around. His head was down, and the water sluiced over his muscled back and down to the tile, spreading over his bird tattoo like it was dancing along the fire.

She hesitated to go inside, and that just pissed her off. "Hey. The guy had no clue why somebody wanted to take me?" The very thought made her stomach hurt. Her nicely routine life, the one from a week ago, seemed far out of reach.

She wasn't sure she could survive in this reality without a safe routine.

Ryker looked up and allowed water to stream over his face. Then he turned away from the spray and grabbed soap off the ledge. "The guy knew only about the job and not where they were supposed to take you." Anger vibrated through the steam.

Her breath quickened, and she kept her distance, leaning back against the door. Ryker in a furious mood didn't bode well, and she wasn't sure how to handle him. *If* she could handle him. "The failed kidnapping has to have something to do with Julie's murder, right?" Finally, her brain was kicking into gear.

His eyes flared a hard bluish green. "That's the most likely scenario. Either the person who killed her thought you saw something that day or maybe they think Julie told you something." Ryker lathered up his hands. "I'm not sure, but I do have a line on Jonny's buddy—the one who hired him for the job. As soon as I get my hands on him, we'll get the name of the guy who hired him."

"More torture," she hissed.

He turned then, his gaze harsh. "I'll do what I have to do, Zara. Nobody is going to get to you. I promise."

She recognized a vow when she heard one. This one made her shiver. There had to be something she could do to figure out this mess and get back to her ordered life. "I want to go into work today. See if I can find out anything about Julie or her case. See what kind of connection I may have to the case." Figure out why somebody had tried to kidnap her.

Ryker nodded. "I agree. We have to act as normal as we can, and I've been hired by your firm, too. I can cover you all day as we read the files." He soaped his chest, and his chin lowered. The anger turned into a smoldering tension…one with a dark promise. "You should probably shower before going into work."

Tingles exploded beneath her skin. Even pissed and way too dangerous, the guy was insatiable. His mood intrigued her when it should warn her. She'd been nearly kidnapped, Ryker had tortured a guy in the boiler room, and now he wanted to have sex? How was any of this her part of reality? "With everything going on right now, I'm just not sure where we stand."

"We stand together. Take off your clothes." He stopped moving beneath the water. Vulnerability flashed across his face for the briefest of seconds.

She paused as realization hit her. The man felt responsible for everyone and everything, now, didn't he? "This isn't your fault."

His jaw hardened. "Three men broke into your house, and one put his hands on you."

She blinked. He was blaming himself? Oh, that wouldn't work. Everything in her wanted to ease his fury and help him find peace. Right or wrong, she wanted to help him. To be the one woman in the world who could. So she dropped her jeans to the floor.

He opened the door for her with a muscled arm after she'd ditched her sweater.

Warmth and the scent of soapy male filled her world.

He drew her under the spray, letting it wash down her back. "So long as we keep working with each other, we'll figure us out." He reached for shampoo to lather through her hair, his big hands caressing her scalp, his gentleness in direct conflict with the turmoil in his eyes.

She closed her eyes and tipped back her head, allowing pleasure to wash down her entire back. "I don't want you to get in trouble because of me." The idea of a man like Ryker ending up behind bars hurt her chest. He was wild and free…and he'd die in containment. "You can't take risks like the one you took tonight." No more torturing people.

He chuckled and rinsed the suds from her hair. "The guy broke the law by hitting your house, so there's no way he'd go to the cops. My detaining him wasn't the risk that you think." He tugged on her hair, and she opened her eyes.

The water had slicked his dark hair back from his face, highlighting the strong angles. "Are you scared?" he asked.

She paused and let the question sink in. "A little." Somebody had entered her house with the intention of kidnapping her. Three men, actually. If Ryker and Greg hadn't been there, she wouldn't have been able to fight all three of them off. "I just don't know what's going to happen next, you know?" On so many fronts.

The safest place for her was with him, yet it was also the most dangerous to her heart.

He nodded, looking imposing and so damn determined through the mist. "Two things. First, there's no need for you to be frightened. You're smart, and you need to be alert, but I'll stand between you and danger every time. You're safe. And second? I'll show you exactly what's going to happen next." He pulled her to him, and his mouth descended on hers.

*　*　*

Ryker kept to Zara's six as she climbed the stairs of her law firm, truly appreciating her lush ass in the black pencil skirt. She wore a frilly pink shirt on top that made him want to unbutton its tiny pearl buttons to get to the beige cotton bra beneath. Although it wasn't as skimpy as some of her bras, there was something hot about it. Maybe because it cupped her full tits perfectly.

Yeah. That was it.

He discreetly adjusted his jeans and tried to force his brain to focus somewhere other than on Zara's nude body. He'd just taken her in the shower, for pete's sake, and he wanted her again right now. Wanted to feel her around him and know she was safe.

Needed to know she was safe.

There was a moment during the fight in her house that he realized if he lost, they'd get her. He'd lose her. Everything in him had rioted and then calmed in a deadly way that now freaked him out a little. There was nothing he wouldn't do to protect her.

He didn't want to return to those cold days when she wasn't brightening the world with a simple smile. God, he was getting maudlin.

She pushed open the wide wooden door and smiled at the receptionist, an older lady with wild gray hair and sharp blue eyes. "Hi, Mrs. Thomson."

Mrs. Thomson pushed green spectacles up her nose. "Morning, Zara. And it's Mr. Jones. Back on a case, are you?"

Ryker nodded. "Yes, ma'am. Brock hired me this weekend."

Mrs. Thomson snapped her gum. "I assume it's the Pentley case. So sad. Such a terrible outcome to a divorce." She shivered.

Ryker took a quick inventory of any possible attack points in the reception area. They should get a couple more bookcases to provide cover. "Have a nice day, Mrs. T."

She winked at him and turned to answer the phone.

Zara tripped ahead of him and regained her balance, winding through desks to reach her office toward the back. "What's your plan, Ryker?"

To bend her over the desk and fuck her hard and make sure danger never came within a mile of her again? Ryker cleared his throat. "I plan to have a quick meeting with Brock and then set up in either an open office or the conference room like last time." In the meanwhile, Heath was checking in on the Copper Killer case, and Denver was tracing Julie's movements for the last two months. "Do you have any contacts at the police department?"

She shook her head. "Not really. Brock usually works on civil cases, not criminal, so we don't have a lot of work with the police. In fact, if this ends up being a criminal case, Brock will pass it off to the criminal litigation department."

"No problem. I think Heath knows a couple of cops, so we'll see what we can find out." Ryker stretched his still-sore knuckles. That Jonny had had a hard jaw. "In fact, if I remember right, Heath may have dated a cop last time we were here." Man, he had to call Heath. The time was definitely ticking down for another victim to be taken, and none of them could face another dead girl. Failure was weighing on them already.

Zara moved around her desk and sat. "Heath dated a police officer when you worked the last case for us?"

Ryker brought himself back to the most immediate problems. "Yeah." An accountant had fled with his client's money, and the firm had represented the client. They'd hired Lost Bastards to track the accountant down, and Ryker had found him in Mexico, having a really good time on a white sandy beach. "I'm pretty sure Heath and a cop named Bernadette got together."

"Okay." Zara opened a manila file, looking ready to get to work and solve all the mysteries in her life. "Have fun with Brock."

CHAPTER
23

Well into the afternoon, Zara straightened her shoulders and walked into the small conference room with her notepad in hand.

Brock glanced up from a stack of papers spread out on the mahogany table.

Jay Pentley looked at her from the head of the table, no expression on his face. Dark circles marred his eyes, and scruff covered his jaw. Even his button-down shirt appeared wrinkled and tired. "What happened to your jaw?" he asked.

"Tripped on my front steps," she said, drawing out a chair to sit.

Brock sat back and gazed from the new bruise on her jaw to the older one right below her eye. He blinked several times, glanced at Jay, and then obviously decided to have a chat with her later. "We're trying to go through the police report from Julie's murder as well as trace her steps."

Jay pushed his chair away from the table. "Excuse me for a minute. Restroom is down the left hall?"

Brock nodded. The second Jay left, Brock quickly texted something on his phone. "What happened to your jaw?" he asked Zara.

"I told you. Nothing." Zara crossed her arms. They engaged in a small staring contest, and heat soon filled her face.

Ryker strode into the room and slipped his phone into his back pocket. "You texted me?"

Brock frowned. "Yes, but now I'm wondering just how long you've been in town, Ryker." He glanced at the bruises on Zara's face, his lips pressing into a white line.

Ryker eyed Zara and then crossed to take the chair opposite the one Jay had vacated. "I arrived in town after the bruise on her cheek but before the one on her jaw," he said without an ounce of discernable sarcasm.

Brock narrowed his gaze. "Did you hit her?"

"Of course not," Zara burst out. "Geez, Brock."

"No." Ryker sat back.

Brock looked from one to the other of them. "If you did hit her, I'm coming after you myself."

Zara snapped her lips shut. While he was coming from a point of sweetness and friendship, the guy was way out of line. He'd made a couple of nice moves on her to go to dinner, but she had to keep her professional and personal lives separate. Then Ryker had entered her life, and she could no longer even think of another man. "Brock. For goodness' sake. Ryker did not hit me."

"Then who did?" Red bloomed in Brock's wide face. He made a strangled sound as he took in Ryker's bruised knuckles. "I'm calling the cops." Reaching for his phone, he held out his other hand when Zara began to protest. "This isn't okay, Zara. The evidence is on his hands as plain as day."

Panic heated her lungs. Things were getting way out of control. "Jay hit me," she blurted out.

Brock stopped mid-dial. "Excuse me?"

"I'm so sorry." Zara clasped her hands together. If Brock called the police, too much could go wrong. "Julie was my friend, and she needed help. Jay beat the heck out of her, but there wasn't any proof, and I just lent her money until she could get a settlement."

Brock studied her and then slowly set his phone down. He put his lawyer face back into place. "Go on."

"Julie stayed at different motels around town, and I took her money and clothes out on Route 27 last week. Jay was there, and they were fighting. He punched her in the face, and I jumped in." Zara rubbed the almost faded bruise along her cheekbone.

Jay strode back into the room, his usual gait lurching. He stopped by his chair and looked around, his body stiffening at the obvious tension. "What?"

"Zara just told me about the altercation and that you're a wife beater," Brock snapped.

"That's slander." Jay retook his seat, his face flushing. "I believe it's also malpractice and a whole shitload of other stuff." He glared at Brock. "Your paralegal shared privileged information with the opposition. I have quite the case against you."

"Did you hit her?" Brock asked, his voice hoarse.

"No. It's her word against mine." Jay put on his mayor expression. "I'm the victim here."

"You're about to be," Ryker said evenly.

Jay paled. "I admit Julie and I got into a scuffle, but she hit me first. Then your employee jumped in, swinging while also violating attorney-client privilege. Everyone had better settle down, or I'm calling another attorney to sue your asses."

Brock pinched the bridge of his nose. "Zara? Did you reveal privileged information?"

"Of course she didn't," Ryker answered for her. "However, the fact that she did see Jay physically abuse Julie is relevant, don't you think? Especially since Julie is now dead."

"I didn't kill Julie," Jay spat, his tone heated. Emotion swirled in his eyes. He drew a shaky hand through his thick hair. "I can't imagine anybody killing Julie."

No. Just beating the snot out of her.

Jay looked at Ryker's hands. "Zara committed malpractice for the firm, violated privilege, and then sent her boyfriend to rough me up at the office."

Brock coughed and swung his head to Ryker, completely losing the professional look. "You did what?" His voice had risen at least two octaves on the last.

Ryker bobbed his head to the side. "I can see how this might upset you, Brock."

"You think so?" Brock shoved back from the table and swung his hands out. "You're all assholes. Jay? We've been friends for decades. Did you really beat your wife?"

"No. There was only that one scuffle," Jay said smoothly. "Things were contentious during the divorce, but before that, and before Julie got all depressed and started self-medicating, we were happy."

Ryker lifted an eyebrow at Zara.

She cleared her throat. "That's not what Julie told me."

"Yeah, but you and Julie just started talking recently. Did she reach out for help at any time before the divorce?" Brock asked.

"No." Zara shook her head. "We lost touch." Guilt hunched her shoulders. Why hadn't she made more time to keep her friendship active? Could Jay be telling the truth? She'd seen people get totally out of control during a divorce, and maybe Julie had been exaggerating. Zara had driven up just as the two had been scuffling by the door, and she had jumped in.

Jay breathed out and tapped his fingers on the table. "Listen. We've all screwed up. I shouldn't have fought with Julie, Zara shouldn't have helped the opposition on a case, and Ryker shouldn't have butted his knuckles in. Let's everybody just forget it and concentrate on finding out who killed Julie."

There was the reasonable guy Zara had dated. She should feel awkward about that, but with all the real-life emergencies happening around her, she couldn't summon up the emotion. Thank goodness she hadn't slept with him. "I agree," she said.

Brock plastered his palm against his forehead. "If you'd like to find another firm to represent you, I can help you choose."

"No. Let's all just move on here together." Jay steepled his hands, looking every bit the politician.

Relief flowed through Zara, although she no doubt would have a chat with Brock later. He could still fire her for putting him and the law firm in such jeopardy. Had she misjudged Jay? There had to have been something decent in him for her to like in the first place, right?

What if Jay was actually telling the truth about Julie? Had she been on drugs?

Ryker leaned back. "Just so we're clear, Mayor. Clean slate as of now. If you ever even remotely lift a hand to a woman, I'm going to snap it off."

Jay cut him a look and then focused on Zara. "You could do better."

Ryker huffed out a breath. "People keep saying that."

Zara bit her lip. A part of her was starting to enjoy Ryker's protectiveness, and she wondered if that was all right. It seemed all right. Perhaps it was time to get back to business. "Where are we on the investigation?"

Brock spun a picture toward her. "I have a friend in the sheriff's office, and I got most of the file. Julie was stabbed fifteen times in the neck and chest. She didn't have a chance."

Nausea rolled through Zara's belly as she looked at the picture. Blood covered Julie's entire body, and even some bones could be seen. God, her poor friend. The fear and pain she must've felt. "Any suspects?" She tried to keep her voice from shaking.

"Right now me," Jay said. "They always look at the husband first."

"I'm tracing all of Julie's credit cards and phone calls from her cell,"

Ryker said. "Should have more information for you by tomorrow noonish." His phone buzzed, and he glanced at the screen. "Zara? A moment, please." Without waiting for an answer, he pushed away from the table and pulled out her chair.

She fumbled and then stood. Her breath heated. She followed him outside the conference room. "What? Is it Greg? Is he okay?" The kid should've come to work with her. Her knees bunched with a desperate need to run and get him.

"The police are at your house," Ryker whispered. "Denver heard the call come in on the scanner."

"The police?" The hallway spun around her. "What I mean, why?"

"Dunno. Our best move is to meet them there and see what's up." He poked his head back inside the conference room. "I need to follow up a lead, and Zara's coming along to assist." He shut the door before Brock could respond. "Let's go."

Zara followed Ryker woodenly through the office, her mind going blank. One of her neighbors must've seen the break-in. What if they'd also seen Ryker kidnap the attacker? What was she going to do? Should they run? Her breath panted out.

They walked outside to the truck and drove in silence through town, both lost in their own thoughts.

"If I tell you to run, then do it," Ryker said quietly.

"Where?" She turned on him in the Hummer. "Where exactly am I supposed to run?"

"My apartment. It's listed under a dummy corporation and can't be traced to Lost Bastards or me. Or anybody else for that matter." He swung into her neighborhood.

"Who are you hiding from?" she whispered.

He glanced at her, his eyes shuttering closed. "It doesn't matter. The past doesn't matter for us, baby. It can't."

Yet that's what seemed to drive him, now, didn't it? "Why won't you level with me, let me into your world?" She needed to know who to fear. Or rather, who to fight.

He sighed. "You are in my world. I promise. The past is just that and only that. Well, except for Greg." Ryker turned toward her, his gaze somber. "Greg wants us to find a woman who knew Denver, Heath, and me as kids. She was a scientist, and she studied us."

"But, well, how?" Zara shook her head. "How does that make any sense?"

"It doesn't. I mean, my mind goes places about it, but everywhere I go seems too bizarre to contemplate." Ryker turned down another snowy road.

She needed to tread lightly, but finally...some answers. "Is this because you're, well, a little different? Did this scientist study you because of that?"

Ryker stiffened and kept his gaze on the road outside. Darkness had already begun to descend. "Different?"

"Yes," she said softly. "Not in a bad way or anything. But you definitely have some gifts not everybody has. Your hearing is unbelievable, as is your strength. And don't get me started on your instincts in finding missing people. Remember when we interviewed the wife of that accountant my firm hired you to find?"

"Yeah." His fingers tightened on the wheel.

"You knew she was lying. Somehow you completely knew, and it wasn't easy to tell. Then you started guessing at facts that there's no way you could've known." Zara had gone over it in her head so many times, she remembered the day clearly. "Maybe you're just good at reading people and can guess well from their reactions, but, Ryker, there's something a little bit more about you."

His nostrils flared as he breathed in. "Okay."

She stopped moving. "Okay?"

"Yeah." He breathed. "I don't understand it, but I've always had a few skills that are out of the norm. The scientist—we think her name is really Isobel Madison. She said that Heath, Denver, and I had high IQs, and she wanted to study us both mentally and physically."

Zara warmed to the subject. "Well, that makes sense, right? A higher IQ might give you a few abilities that have developed more than most people."

"I guess." His frown looked like it hurt his forehead.

"So this woman, whoever she is, studies people with higher IQs. Greg is definitely smart, so it fits. But how did Greg find you?"

"He found us on the web and went through all our files, figuring out that we could find lost people when nobody else could. He wants to find Isobel in order to find his brothers, who were also studied by her." Ryker's upper lip twisted.

Zara leaned back and tipped her head to look up at the ceiling of the truck. "It's an odd coincidence, though. You, Heath, and Denver being at the same orphanage way back when."

"According to Greg, it's no coincidence." Ryker slowed the truck as her house came into view.

Two police cars blocked the driveway, and uniformed cops were beginning to move down the sidewalk. A forensics van was parked half on the street and half on her lawn.

"What in the world?" Zara jumped out of the truck.

"Zara, wait." Ryker pulled to the curb, stopped the engine, and barreled out of the truck in one smooth motion. He reached her and grabbed her arm, halting her on the snow-covered driveway. "Calm. Let me handle this."

Detective Norton came out the front door, took one look at her, and reached for his phone to bark something. Finishing, he stomped down the walkway, his boots scattering snow. "Just canceled a BOLO on you, Ms. Remington."

She faltered. "A BOLO? I don't understand."

The detective paused and scrutinized her. "What happened to your jaw?"

"Ah." She rubbed the bruise along her jawline.

"Mr. Jones? I'd like you to come down to the station to answer a few questions," Detective Norton said, his gaze hard.

Zara sighed. "Ryker didn't hit me." Why did everyone keep suspecting the poor guy?

"Then who did? And while you're at it, please explain what happened here. Your door is busted, and your living room appears as if a large altercation took place." The detective blocked her way to the house.

She sighed. "I got carried away the other night exercising, and frankly, I don't owe you an explanation. Please leave my premises, as you don't have a warrant to search." Yeah, that was right. She thought. Maybe?

The detective slowly lifted his head. "We were called in about a possible kidnapping. There's blood in your kitchen. I could see it through the open doorway, thus I don't need a warrant."

She blinked. So he had probable cause to search? She was a paralegal, not a lawyer, so she wasn't sure. Could she lie to him? Since it wasn't a federal case, she could lie, but would that be hindering an investigation? It wasn't illegal to lie, yet if the lie led to obstruction, then it could become a problem. What the heck should she do?

Two weeks ago the answer would've been clear: Tell the truth to the police. Now? Now she had to protect Ryker and Greg. God, things had changed. The feeling of responsibility weighed down her shoulders, and yet she'd never felt so alive. She had people who mattered to take care of, and she could do it. She would to it. "I cut my hand, so now you can go," she said evenly.

Several techs walked out carrying brown boxes of evidence. Her heart sank. Would they be able to identify the guy Ryker had kidnapped? If they did, would he tell the truth?

Snow swirled down, and she blinked it from her eyelashes. "Who called you, anyway?"

The door to her neighbor's house opened, and Detective Norton nodded toward the porch.

"Grams?" Zara whispered.

Her grandmother gave a happy cry and rushed off the porch, her sensible galoshes scattering wet snow as she ran across the lawn. A bright pink scarf protected her white curls, and a long green coat covered her tiny body. Snow matted against her thick glasses. "Zara." She barreled into Zara's arms for a rose-scented hug.

Zara returned the hug, careful of her Grams's delicate bones, and then leaned back. "I thought your trip ended next week?"

"Yes." Grams waved red nails in the chilly air. "Florence got caught doing the nasty with that retired grocer from Missoula. Well, his wife joined us for the second part of the tour, and things just went to hell. So I came home."

Zara snapped her head in a quick shake and held tight to the one person who'd always loved her. "Florence?"

"Yes. Those hormone pills make her horny." Grams shook her head and looked up at Zara. "Anyway, I came over, saw the mess, and immediately called the cops."

"I'm fine," Zara croaked out. She had to protect this frail woman at all costs.

Grams partially turned and then fluttered her eyelashes. "I do hope you're Ryker."

A smile played around Ryker's full mouth. "I am."

"Yep. I would've bought new undies for you, too." Grams smiled big.

CHAPTER
24

Ryker tried to ignore the elderly woman in the backseat of the truck, but it was difficult, considering her face was right next to his. She perched her hands and head over the seat like a colorful bird. He had no clue how to deal with old ladies.

"You even smell good," she purred.

"Thanks, Mrs. Remington."

"Call me Grams, Ryker. Everybody does."

Grams? He shifted in his seat. What would it be like to have a Grams? Looked like he was about to find out. As a lonely and scared kid, he'd wanted family members to provide warmth. A grandmother was almost too much of a dream. "Please put your seat belt on, Mrs. Grams." If they were in a wreck, her little bones would snap. He had to protect her now, too.

She completely ignored him and turned her head toward Zara. "You never did say who hit you, Zara. I know it wasn't Ryker. His eyes are kind."

"It's a long story, Grams." Zara's voice remained calm with just a threat of hysteria in it. "The bad guy is long gone, I promise."

"Humph. Well, he had better be. That wasn't your blood in the kitchen, was it?"

Zara shook her head, obviously not sure what to say. The tension pouring from her hinted at pure panic.

Grams poked Ryker in the neck with one bony finger. "Did you do that? I mean, leave somebody's blood in the kitchen?"

Ryker cut Zara a look, and she just shrugged. "Yes, I did."

"I see. So somebody broke into your house, Zara, bruised you, and then Ryker made him bleed. For some reason, you two don't want the police to know what happened." Grams pursed her red-lipsticked mouth. "Are you wanted by the law, Ryker?"

"No, ma'am." At least not with his current identity.

Zara sighed. "I kind of broke confidentiality with a client to help Julie, then she was murdered, and we think the guy who did it wants to talk to me for some reason."

Grams gasped. "Julie was murdered? Oh, honey. I'm so sorry. Did her dirtbag husband do it?"

"I'm not sure," Zara said. "If I'd kept in better touch, I might know." Guilt infused her tone.

Grams patted Zara's shoulder. "It takes two to keep a friendship going, and if you ask me, she was the holdout. You asked her to lunch many a time, and she didn't come. Now I wonder why."

"Me too," Zara said.

Ryker turned another corner. Julie might've been busy, or she might've been a battered wife being isolated. Or perhaps...perhaps Julie had been doing drugs.

Grams perched even closer. "The guy who tried to kidnap you— did he think you saw something or knew something about Julie's murder?" Her voice was hushed.

"Maybe. By the time we figured that out, Ryker had already beaten up and kidnapped a guy from my house, so now if we tell the police, he'll get in trouble." Zara hunched her shoulders.

"I see." Grams flopped back into the rear seat. "That is a conundrum." She squinted through her glasses, waiting until Ryker met her gaze in the rearview mirror. "Are you sure you're not wanted by the authorities?"

His stomach rolled over. "I'm not wanted. I promise." The old woman was damn shrewd, wasn't she? He had to stay away from the cops.

"Good." She wiggled her eyebrows. "Though if you are, you should let us know in case we have to help you get out of town."

He bit back a smile. "I appreciate the thought, but I'm fine here in Cisco." At least, he was until Sheriff Cobb got a whiff of his location, and then he'd be screwed again. So he had to keep off the radar. "Where am I taking you, Grams?"

Zara turned and frowned. "Is she safe? I mean, if somebody is after me, do you think she's safe?"

"I do," Ryker said. "But if it'll make you feel better, we can put her up at my place." Greg could move into Denver's spare bedroom. "Though we need to buy some beds if we keep adding people." He had no problem sharing Denver's and Heath's places as well—they were family. That's what normal families did, right? Plus, he had a feeling having a Grams was going to be a lot of fun, and he wanted to share her with his brothers.

"I'd love to stay over," Grams chirped. "Lovely. Just lovely."

Ryker kept one eye on the road while glancing at his phone for an update from Heath, who'd been tailing Jonny after he'd left the hospital. So far all Jonny had done was hit a pharmacy, a fast food joint, and a convenience store, where he'd purchased deodorant, cough drops, and porn.

Ryker kept a close eye on the surrounding block as he pulled into the underground garage and parked the truck. Silence pounded around them, and he turned to his senses, the ones he didn't understand, to make sure no threats were nearby.

Nothing.

He got out of the truck and assisted Grams from the backseat. She tottered for a moment on the concrete and then looked up more than a foot to his face. "Thanks." Her smile flashed dimples.

"You're welcome." He gently turned her toward the stairs, more aware than ever of his odd strength when faced with somebody so breakable.

She stomped snow from her boots as she made for the stairs, reaching for Zara's hand as she neared.

Ryker followed in somewhat of a daze. He now had a woman, an elderly lady, and a kid all coexisting in his apartment. So much for being on his own. For some reason, his heart felt lighter. What would Heath and Den think of the colorful Grams?

Even so, he kept listening for threats, so when they shoved open the door of his apartment, he could only stare. Black leather couches faced a monstrous television, where Greg was playing some high-speed car-chase video game. Modern end tables were scattered around a stark white rug.

He slowly turned to see a kitchen table in the other room. "Greg?"

The kid paused the game and turned. "I bought some shit." He glanced at Grams and instantly turned red. "I mean stuff."

Ryker closed the door behind himself and leaned against it. "How?"

Greg smiled at the women. "Hacked your credit card. Well, the one you're using these days, anyway. Oh, and it cost a lot extra for the super-fast delivery."

Ryker shut his eyes and drew on patience. "Did you get bedroom sh—stuff?"

"Yep."

"Good. This is Grams, and she's taking over the spare bedroom. You can bunk with one of the other guys or just take the couch." Ryker rubbed a hand through his hair.

Greg nodded. "I'll take the couch. It's totally soft and comfortable, man."

Grams clapped her hands together. "I'm starving. How about I make some homemade chili?"

Greg's eyes glowed. Actually glowed.

Ryker looked around the suddenly packed apartment. Packed with people he cared about and needed to protect. His lungs compressed, and responsibility hit him so hard in the chest he almost bent over.

He could do this. He had to do this. The fear that he'd fail had to be banished, because no way could he fail. Not with this, and not with them.

Control. He'd use his wits to keep everyone safe, no matter how brutal he had to become.

Ryker's phone beeped, and he glanced down. The alarm in the safe house had been activated, showing movement. Hell.

Keeping his face placid, and wanting nothing more than to run away for just a few minutes to be alone, he cleared his throat. "I have a work situation." Retreating through the door, he bit back a smile at the panicked look on Zara's face. "I'll be back. Um, everybody stay here." He shut the door before the woman could argue.

Turning, he took the stairs to the garage three at a time while dialing Heath, who answered on the second ring. "Hey," Ryker said. "Where are you? We have a hit on safe house three." Could it be Isobel? Finally, some answers.

"I'm heading back to town and should be there in an hour or so," Heath said. "I put a tracker on Jonny's car, but I'm thinking he's a useless hired thug who isn't going to get us anywhere."

"Yeah, that's my gut feeling, too. I'll get Denver. See you back at the office." Ryker didn't wait for agreement and quickly dialed Den. His voice mail message came on. "Break-in at safe house three, and I'm headed over," Ryker said tersely, hoping Denver got the message soon. He jumped into the truck and sped out of the garage.

The snow was falling faster, accumulating across the slippery roads. He drove for nearly ten minutes, circled the block, and then parked behind a 7-Eleven down the street.

Safe house three was a one-story bungalow in a dismal part of town. The chipped yellow paint and cracked concrete matched the burned out porch light and broken porch swing in the corner. The neighborhood was quiet with everyone inside and out of the cold, dark storm.

He kept low and jogged around to the back, shoving a rickety chain-link gate out of his way. Pine needles marred the freshly falling snow, and some appeared as if the wind had blown them around.

There was no wind. Just snow and cold.

He moved up to the back door and listened. No breathing, no sound. He closed his eyes. Heartbeat—one. Slow and steady. The guy was well trained to be so calm.

So was he.

Taking a moment, he glanced at the screen of his phone. Nothing. Denver hadn't checked in yet.

The smart thing would be to wait for Denver, but the interloper would leave. So Ryker gingerly slid the back door open and slipped inside, pausing to accustom his eyes to the dark. A streetlight out front provided some illumination but not much.

The house had a living room, a kitchen, two bedrooms, and a bathroom along with a basement. He made no sound as he crossed the living room and turned left.

Movement sounded ahead of him, and he pivoted, ducking from a wide roundhouse. He came up with a sharp uppercut, catching himself at the last moment and pulling the punch as much as he could. Even so, his knuckles struck Denver's chin and sent his brother flying backward.

Denver slid to the ground, his head knocking the wall on the way. His black hair was mussed, and a shadow covered his massive jaw.

"Shit, Den." Ryker rushed to help him up. The smell of Scotch hit him first, followed by the smell of blood. "You okay?"

Denver shrugged him off, turned his head, and spit out blood. "Bit my tongue. Thanks for pulling the punch. Didn't realize it was you when I attacked." The words were only slightly slurred, but for Denver, that was seriously drunk.

Ryker smoothed down Denver's wrinkled T-shirt, noting the bloodshot eyes and rigid stance. He took a deep breath, concern swirling through his gut. "What are you doing here?"

Denver jerked his head toward a computer system set up against the far wall. "Decided to do a couple of manual searches to draw Isobel Madison in faster. Am tired of waitin'." He swayed. "Somebody bit at the other end. Should have company by tomorrow."

So much for having time to lay a good trap. "Dude, you are not thinking right now."

"Neither are you," Denver snapped.

Ryker glanced frantically at the computer. "You can't lay traps like that while drunk, and you know it." Had Denver screwed up?

"Since when do you care about rules?" Denver challenged.

Apparently the talk they'd been avoiding was going to happen in the safe house. Ryker nodded. Fine. "Let's hash this out."

"No." Denver brushed past him.

Ryker grabbed his arm, a pit opening in his stomach. "Stop."

Denver yanked free. "Not now, Ryker."

Hell, he really didn't want to do this. But Ryker moved fast and blocked the way into the kitchen, panic threatening to blind him. "Talk to me."

Denver lifted his chin, and his eyes narrowed to a pissed blue flecked with gold. They both stood at about six foot four, maybe five, and a fight between them would be disastrous. "Get the fuck out of my way."

Ryker swallowed and shoved down his rapidly approaching temper. Denver was the peacemaker between them all, and it was unsettling to see him out of that role. Ryker tried to keep his voice calm. "It's time you stopped punishing yourself for leaving her. It's been a year, Denver. Let it go."

Red infused the hard planes of Denver's face. He bunched and swung.

Ryker blocked the punch and shoved hard. Denver slid sideways into the wall. Oh, he was definitely off from the booze. "You're drunk," Ryker snapped.

"Jealous?" Denver countered, regaining his balance.

Ryker winced. He had been in a bottle not too long ago. "Come on, Denver." Ryker's chest ached. There had to be something he could do to ease his brother's pain. "I'll do whatever you want. We can go get Noni right now and bring her here."

Denver moved faster than Ryker could track, grabbing his shirt and shoving him against the wall. "I cared for her, damn it. You don't take a nice woman like that and bring her into our shit-storm of a life. *I* wouldn't do that."

Ryker stilled. "This is about Zara?"

"You're an asshole," Denver spat, shoving him and backing away.

"I know," Ryker muttered, remaining against the wall, his entire body hurting all of a sudden. "I should've let her go, but then I convinced myself she was in trouble and needed my protection." But that was a lie. Even before he knew she was in danger, he'd been playing mind games with himself. "Then somebody actually tried to take her."

"Yeah." Denver ground a fist into his left eye and took several shuddering breaths. "Fuck, I'm sorry, Ryker. Of course you have to provide cover. She's in danger." His head hung, but he faced Ryker. "Sorry."

Ryker knocked his head back on the wall, feeling raw from the look in Denver's eyes. "I kept her even before I knew that. She's in me,

Denver." He hit his chest with a closed fist, needing to confess it all to somebody who'd get it. "In here. I don't want days without her in them." His voice sounded a whole lot more tortured than he wanted, but he didn't hold back with his brother.

Denver closed his eyes and nodded. "I get it. This is my deal, not yours. I'm sorry for dragging you into it."

Ryker frowned as realization slapped him upside the head. "It hurts you to see me with Zara." Why hadn't he thought about that? He was playing house, and he hadn't given one thought to how that would make Denver feel. "I'm sorry."

"Not your fault, man. I made my choice." Denver's broad chest shuddered. "She doesn't even know my real name. Never gave it to her."

Ryker grimaced. "So there's no way she could reach out to you?"

"Figured it was safer and cleaner." Denver's lips peeled back, the booze no doubt giving him freedom of speech for the moment. "We had only a month together. It's been a year, and I still taste her."

"Then she's not going away," Ryker said gently, wondering if he should just go get Noni and bring her to Cisco. The self-hatred in Denver's voice ate him alive. "Maybe you should call her."

Denver snorted. "She may have been a sweetheart, but that girl had a hell of a temper. She surely hates my guts now."

"Not if she loved you." He'd met Noni only once, because the case had been mainly Denver's, but she'd seemed like a gal who would stick. "Of course, you'd have to admit that you initially asked her out as part of a case." Ryker blanched. "They kind of insist on honesty."

"Shit."

Ryker nodded, his chest relaxing as he got back in synch with Denver. "We can come up with an excuse for you to see her."

Denver sighed, and his eyes finally focused. "Right now we have enough on our plates. Let's get Greg to his family, find out who Dr. Madison really was, and save your woman from whatever danger is after her. Oh, and find the Copper Killer."

They did have a lot going on. As if on cue, the computer in the corner dinged. "What?"

Denver glanced toward the screen. "Another bite. They're coming, brother. We need to get ready."

CHAPTER
25

Zara finished up her bowl of chili while Grams and Greg chatted happily about recipes and spicy foods. After a couple of uncomfortable moments when Greg couldn't stop looking at Grams and kept smoothing back his hair like he was heading to church, they'd moved into a mutual love of all things edible.

Ryker had been gone for a couple of hours, and Zara couldn't help but worry. Not only about his safety, but also how quickly the guy had wanted to escape his suddenly full apartment. As a loner, he didn't seem comfortable with houseguests. He'd all but had CONFIRMED BACHELOR stamped across his tough features as he'd run away like a wounded dog. She set her dish in the sink, wandered into the guest room, and noted the queen-sized bed with a dark blue bedspread. The furniture was almost utilitarian and without any warmth. A few throw pillows would warm it up a little.

Sighing, she returned to the living room just as her phone dinged. Hustling for her purse on the counter, she dug it out. "Hello?"

"Zara? It's Brock. I'm at the law office, and there's an issue."

She swallowed. Was Ryker in trouble? "What's up?"

"Detective Norton was just here. Apparently the techs started running prints from the break-in at your house, and your prints came up. They think the prints are yours because there are so many, they have to be."

"That makes sense." She bit her lip.

"Yes. But your prints also matched a bunch found in Julie Pentley's room at Lazy Horse Motel."

Zara stopped breathing.

"Zara?"

"Holy crap, they got those results fast."

Brock snorted. "It's a priority, and they were looking for similarities between the two crime scenes."

So the cops were already suspicious of her. Thank goodness she'd already told Brock everything about Julie. "What do I do?"

Brock paused. "You need to go to the police station and make a statement, and do it now. I told Detective Norton that you'd be right down in order to prevent him from sending uniforms to escort you."

Her stomach lurched. "Okay."

"It gets worse. There's now a conflict between my representing Jay and my representing you, and since I'm already his lawyer on this case…"

She nodded. "I understand. You can't represent us both."

"No. But I'll call in a couple of favors and get you a lawyer from a different firm." More papers rustled.

Her chest warmed. "You're a good guy, Brock. Don't worry about me. I can take care of it." She had a couple of friends who worked at other firms, and she'd call them for recommendations. No way was she meeting with Detective Norton without representation.

"All right. The detective informed our senior partners of the case, so you're suspended for the duration of the investigation." Brock was silent for a minute. "I fought for an hour to make sure it's with pay, so don't worry about that. If you need anything, let me know. I'll help if I can." He clicked off.

She woodenly sat there for a moment.

"Everything okay?" Grams asked, looking up from her chili.

Zara nodded. "Yes. Just some business I need to take care of." She quickly texted Ryker with a brief recap of what had happened. Then she started calling friends and leaving messages for them to call her back. Where was everybody? Geez.

Finally, she went into the master bathroom and freshened up, putting on pink lipstick and brushing her hair before slipping into a pencil skirt and warm sweater. The last thing she wanted was for uniformed police officers to start knocking on doors in her neighborhood looking for her. So she grabbed her coat and headed out to the living room. "I have to go take care of some things."

Greg frowned. "It's after eight at night."

"I know." Brock had promised the police she'd be down that night, and Detective Norton didn't seem like a guy who'd just wait around for long. Zara tried to appear calm. She needed to throw up. "I'll be back in a couple of hours."

A knock sounded on the door, and Heath poked his head in. "Just got a text from some lawyer named Brock? Ryker had given him my number for some reason. Rumor has it you need your own lawyer."

Grams pushed away from the counter. "A lawyer? Why would you need a lawyer? Is this about the break-in at your house?"

Greg turned around on the barstool, his chin lowering. "I can have you out of town and to a safe location within thirty minutes. Somewhere totally off the grid where they'll never find you."

Zara gaped at him. He was twelve years old, for goodness' sake. "Um, thanks, but I think I'll just go make a statement." She hurried forward and kissed her grandmother on the cheek. "Oh. Grams, that's Heath."

Heath nodded.

"Nice to meet you," Grams said, her eyebrows drawing down.

For good measure, Zara pecked a kiss on Greg's cheek. "We'll keep your idea for plan B," she said with a smile.

His ears turned red, and he nodded.

She grabbed her purse and hustled toward Heath. "Don't worry, you two. The police just want a statement from me, and then I'll be home." Hopefully. Were her prints at the murder scene enough probable cause to arrest her?

Heath closed the door behind them. "You can explain everything on the way to the station."

She nodded. Ryker's blood brother had shortish brown hair and stunning greenish brown eyes. He wore faded jeans, motorcycle boots, and a brown leather jacket, looking more like a badass biker than a lawyer. For some reason, that calmed her. "Where is Ryker?"

"On a case." Heath led the way down to the stairs and pushed open the heavy door to the garage before stalking toward a decked-out black muscle car. "She's solid enough she doesn't really need snow tires yet. Hop in, Zara."

Zara opened the door and slid onto black leather seats softer than a peach.

The car started with a loud purr. Heath backed out of his spot. "All right. Tell me everything, and start at the beginning."

She took a deep breath and told her new attorney everything, trying not to notice how concerned his expression was by the time they reached the police station. "What do you think?" she finally asked.

He sighed and looked at her, his gaze beyond serious. "How do you feel about starting over somewhere else?"

* * *

Dr. Isobel Madison followed the crumbs along the Internet to a small Wyoming town called Cisco, her fingers clicking easily across the keyboard in her office. Oh, she kept her signature off her trace, and she made sure nobody knew she was calling.

Interesting that her searches, mainly across the dark web, had brought her back to this rather clear beacon. Even for a carefully laid trap, there was something sloppy about it.

The men she'd created in test tubes, even the ones she hadn't personally raised, had extraordinary intelligence ranges. Not one of them would make a mistake like this one. So that prompted questions: Had one of her creations lost his mind, or was somebody else looking for her?

Interesting.

She quickly texted Todd to come see her. He was training his pseudo Protect army down at the barns. Truly, she couldn't wait to terminate her association with them.

If this beacon led where she hoped, that would happen sooner rather than later.

She clicked over to another screen, this one password protected. Methodically working her way beyond the encryptions, she noted the progress of her newest lab. Excellent. Another couple of weeks, and it'd be operational.

Destiny shone bright and hard before her.

Sheriff Cobb strode into the room.

Isobel sat back behind her glass desk and studied him. Much, much better. She'd reached out to him months ago, and surveillance videos had shown him to be almost portly. The man had let himself go in the years they were apart, and he was only forty-five years old—ten years her junior. Yet now he looked like the mean fighting machine she remembered from years ago. Ripped muscles moved beneath his pressed uniform, and he walked with the angry grace she remembered from their time together. Obviously he'd started working out the moment she'd contacted him. "Thank you for coming. It's time we brought the Lost boys back into the fold."

"I've been trying to find them for years," he countered, his eyes glittering with a primal light as he leaned against a tall file cabinet. "The assholes killed my brother."

She shifted in her seat. While she'd had many lovers through her life, the sheriff had always held an edge that fascinated her. "When my lab is up and running, I'd like to do some tests on you."

"Why?" His gaze dropped to her chest.

"I'd bet my slush fund that you have the warrior gene." As did all of her creations, she was sure.

He frowned. "Isn't that the one psychopaths have?"

"Sometimes." She smiled and stroked his ego, truly intrigued by him. "You're not a psychopath." He was most likely a sociopath, which would work nicely with her plans.

"I like that you like all of me." Vulnerability, rare in him, shone in his eyes. "That you're not turned off by my darker urges."

"I like dark urges," she said, lowering her voice. "You know that."

He shuffled his feet, looking endearing and dangerous all at once. "I'm glad you called me a few months ago. I've missed you."

"I've missed you, too, and appreciate your coming so quickly when I called."

He cocked his head. "I never figured we were quite finished with each other."

She smiled and leaned back to stretch her neck, not missing when his eyes flared. "We aren't, but I need you to keep that between us until I'm finished with Todd and his forces."

The sheriff lifted his chin. "You're sleeping with him."

"No," she lied. "Yet he seems to have a bit of a crush, and I need to use that for the time being. He's such a moron, but he does have a fighting force."

"So when we're done with him, you're fine if I slice open his jugular?"

She smiled. "Of course. I'd appreciate you taking care of me that way. Did he show you to your quarters?"

"You mean, my room?" Elton patted the grooved wooden wall. "This is more like a cushiony lodge than a training facility."

Wasn't that the truth? "The soldiers and I use that term loosely. All bunk down in the barracks, which used to be barns." The only hitch in her plan would be if Todd and the sheriff started fighting over her, especially since Elton would kill Todd, and she really needed Todd's fighting forces. Her own force was at an all-time low since the depot in Utah had been blown up. "I need you to act as if you're here as an advisor to bring the Lost boys back in, and not because of me. Temporarily."

Elton rubbed his hand across his jeans. "Fine, but you're gonna have to earn my cooperation." His tone was gritty and thick with dark promise.

She'd figured. "Yes?"

"My room, midnight." Without another word, he pivoted and disappeared from sight.

Apparently the good sheriff had gained a backbone in the years they'd been separated. She'd be smart not to underestimate him.

Heavy footsteps clomped down the hallway, and Todd came into view. "You texted me?"

The man moved like an elephant. She couldn't help but compare Sheriff Cobb's hard abs and lack of conscience with this soft, silly pretend soldier. Soon she'd be rid of Todd and his bizarre quest to rid the world of science. Even so, she forced a smile. "Yes. I had an alarm go off, and I think I know where a couple of my test subjects are. Cisco, Wyoming."

He smiled, revealing a slight gap between his front teeth. "We'll take them out."

"No." She held up a hand. "First, we need to find them and see who we're dealing with. Many of these boys formed connections with each other when they were young, so if we find one, we should be able to use him to find more. Your mission is one of intelligence gathering."

His face settled into harsh lines. "I'm a soldier."

He wasn't even close. She nodded. "Yes, and part of any mission is to gather intel. Just go to Cisco and stake out the address I sent to your phone. Trust me, darling. This is the right way to get the job done."

"Where were you this morning? When I awoke, you were gone." He sounded petulant.

She'd had to shower him off her from the night before. "I came to work, as usual." Forcing her lips into a flirty smile, she sent him a wink. "You know successful ops stir my desire, Todd. Do a great job on this one, and I'll let you do anything you want to me."

He moved then and leaned over to kiss her on the mouth. His lips were too soft and mushy. "I love you, Isobel."

"Then trust me with this op. I know what I'm doing." She licked along his lips. "I love you, too."

He stepped back, warmth in his eyes. "All right. I'll check in." Turning sharply, he stomped out of the room.

She breathed out and lost her smile. The man was straining against his leash. She couldn't guarantee he wouldn't let emotion overrule logic and try to kill whoever was on the other end of that beacon.

Well. Hopefully it was one of the men she'd created. If not, or if they'd lost their edge, Todd or his men would kill them.

CHAPTER 26

Zara fiddled with her purse strap in the interrogation room of the police station. The heat blasted through, warming the surprisingly cozy area. The oak table appeared well polished, and the chairs were upholstered in thick leather. Pretty landscapes covered the walls, and even the commercial mint green carpet seemed well vacuumed.

Detective Norton sat across from her while Heath kicked back at her side.

"I expected something colder," she said, looking around.

Norton smiled, wrinkling the corners of his deep brown eyes. "This is more of a conference room. The cold concrete block room is down the hallway a bit."

"Oh." Even though the place was nice, she couldn't banish the hard knot in her chest. She glanced at Heath.

Heath nodded. "My client would like to make a statement."

The detective lifted both eyebrows. "All right. Go ahead."

Zara took a deep breath and told the detective about her helping Julie, about being in the motel room the day of the murder, and finally about the break-in at her house, where the intruders got away. She left out the tiny part about Ryker kidnapping one of the intruders and then questioning him.

Norton just looked at her, no expression on his rugged face. For a man in his early forties, he had very few lines fanning out from his eyes. Maybe he didn't smile much.

Heath drummed his fingers on a blank legal pad in front of him. "As you can see, my client may have been in the wrong place at the wrong time, but she hasn't broken any laws. Are we done?"

The detective blinked, not taking his gaze from Zara. "No. We are nowhere near done, counselor, and you know it."

"It's late, Detective. Get to it so I can get my client safely home." Heath kept his voice even, but strength and intelligence clipped his words.

"Ms. Remington, let's chat again about the motel. Your fingerprints were all over the place—from the dressers to the walls to the bed. It appears as if you searched the room. What exactly were you looking for?" the detective asked.

Zara swallowed. "I already told you that Jay Pentley said Julie was on drugs, and since I had been loaning her money for bills that had possibly already been paid, I searched for drugs."

"Did you find any?"

"No." The need to defend her friend rose hard and fast in her.

"I see. Were you looking for anything else?" the detective asked.

Zara shook her head. "No."

Norton rifled through papers. "You say you saw Julie's car in the rear parking lot, but she wasn't there."

"True."

He looked up. "I find it odd that you hid your car in the back lot, making sure nobody saw you."

"My firm was representing Julie's husband in a divorce action. I was breaking firm rules, malpractice rules, and legal ethics." Her face heated. "But Julie was my friend, and she needed help." The idea that Julie was gone still made Zara's chest ache, and the fact that somebody had stabbed the kind woman made her sick. "So I helped her."

"By giving her three thousand dollars a month," the detective said.

"Yes." Zara abandoned the purse strap and clasped her hands together in her lap. Her skin flushed cold, and she felt guilty even though she'd done nothing illegal.

"Hmmm." Norton scratched his head, his lips turning down. "Sounds more like blackmail."

Heath leaned forward. "Be nice, Detective. My client is here of her own free will, trying to assist with your case."

"Right. So blackmail? What did Julie have on you, Zara?" Norton asked, his gaze shrewd.

"Nothing," Zara whispered, her head beginning to pound. How much trouble was she in? Would a jury believe the detective even if he was wrong? Bile rose in her throat, and she cleared it. "We were friends, and I was helping her out."

"Jay Pentley thinks you're still in love with him."

Zara took a second to catch up. "Still? I was never in love with Jay. We went on a few dates, and then I broke it off. He and Julie started dating a few months later."

"You want me to believe that you broke it off with Jay and you were just fine with him dating your friend?" Norton banged his fist on the desk.

Zara jumped. God, she wished Ryker was there with her. "Yes. I mean, I thought Julie could do better, but I wasn't upset about her wanting to date Jay." She fidgeted in her chair. Did Norton really think she had something to do with Julie's death? "Julie was my friend, and while I didn't care much for Jay, I wanted her to be happy. Then when the divorce got so ugly, I wanted to help her, and I did."

"Zara, I want to work with you here." Norton's eyes lightened, and he leaned toward her, his face in earnest lines. "But I can't do that unless you level with me."

"I am," she burst out, trying not to panic completely.

He sighed. "Why didn't you report the break-in at your house?"

She didn't have a good reason that didn't include Ryker distrusting the authorities and wanting to do things himself. Was he wanted by the law? If so, he should've told her. She would've helped him—that she knew. Man, her life had changed.

But Ryker had changed it, and he needed to be completely honest with her. She cared for him so much it scared her. Too much of her life was spinning out of control. Her hands shook, and she felt the walls closing in. Who exactly was Ryker?

She needed to make a decision, so she made it. Ryker was hers, and he was going to remain hers. Whether he liked it or not, they were going for it. Period.

She faced the cop head-on and continued with her story, her loyalty completely secured by Ryker. "I scared the guy off, and since he wore a mask, I couldn't identify him anyway." Heath had advised her to make it one guy instead of three for plausibility.

"And he made it only to your kitchen? Not to any of the bedrooms?"

She thought back. None of the guys had made it to the bedrooms. "Nope. He didn't go beyond the kitchen and living room."

"You figured the intruder had something to do with Julie's death?" the detective asked, scribbling in his notebook.

"No," she lied. "I thought it was random."

"That's a pretty lame excuse for not calling the police." The detective's head snapped up, and his focus fixed on her.

She fidgeted, and a blast of terror shot down her throat. What should she do? "I'm sorry. It all happened so fast, and I wasn't thinking." Her voice rose, and she couldn't control it. Heath had told her to leave both Ryker and Greg out of the story, so it now didn't make any sense, did it? "I didn't break the law, so let's just move on."

"All right." The detective tilted his head. "Tell me about your involvement in the Picalo Club."

She frowned. "The what?"

"The Picalo Club. You know, the private club in town where key switching and threesomes is the norm?" he asked.

Zara glanced sideways at Heath, her mind spinning. "I have no idea what he's talking about."

Norton reached beneath his nearest manila file and drew out a laminated card. "We found this in the dresser of your bedroom."

Zara reached for the ID card. It had her picture on the left, her name below it, and to the side, a symbol for the Picalo Club, which was an intricate *P* surrounded by roses. "I've never seen this before in my life," she said, looking up, her brain fuzzing. "I don't understand."

Heath reached for the card and flipped it over. The back was blank. "What's the Picalo Club, Detective?"

Norton sighed. "It's a sex venue. It's a very exclusive private club where members have parties and meet different people. There are orgy parties, key-swapping parties, BDSM parties—you name it. Your client is a member, as were Julie and Jay."

Zara coughed, her eyes widening in what felt like pure panic. This didn't make any sense. Was that what Julie had been talking about? She and Jay had tried some wild stuff to keep their marriage fresh. Was it the Picalo Club? "I'm not a member," Zara snapped. "I've never even heard of it."

"This card doesn't prove anything. There's no signature," Heath said, tossing it back to the detective.

"Oh, it's kind of the missing puzzle piece." Norton crossed his arms. "Want to know what I think happened, Ms. Remington?"

No. Absolutely not. "Sure." She swallowed back a huge lump in her throat.

"I think you never got over Jay, and when he and Julie invited you to the Picalo Club, you jumped right in." Norton's gaze dropped to the ID card. "Then I think you ended up over your head, possibly with film or pictures, and Julie blackmailed you for drug money."

"That's crazy," Zara whispered, prickles tingling down her back.

"You started to run out of money, and you decided to kill Julie. Or there was a knife, and you lost your temper. I'm not sure." Norton eyed her calmly.

"What about the break-in at her house?" Heath asked.

"What break-in?" Norton smiled then, a quick flash of teeth. "There are no witnesses, and only Ms. Remington was there, apparently. I think she staged it for some reason—possibly to make it look like she's a victim, too?"

"Then why not report it?" Zara asked. The detective couldn't really believe all of this, could he?

"Oh, please. Your grandmother coincidentally finds your door open and calls the cops? You as good as did report it." The detective gathered all of his papers together in a lopsided pile. "Let me help you. Tell me everything, and I'll go to the DA for you, say you cooperated."

Zara flushed hot and then cold. "I didn't kill Julie. I swear."

"Oh, I'm gonna prove you did." The detective planted both hands on the table. "Now. Let's start again. When did you last see Julie Pentley?"

* * *

Ryker paced the offices after he dropped a snoring Denver into bed. He should be down at the police station, but Heath had told him to stay put until the interview had concluded, and Heath was a hell of a lawyer, even if he didn't much like the law.

Greg and Grams were upstairs sleeping, but no way could Ryker get shut-eye before Zara came home. Maybe not even then. The base of his neck tickled, and time was running out.

Whoever had intercepted their little trap would be coming, fast and hard.

Would it be Isobel Madison and her soldiers? He hoped so, but God only knew who else was out there looking for her. Or them. What if Cobb had somehow found them?

He bit back a snarl. The sheriff had taken their childhood away. He wasn't getting close to Zara or her Grams…or to Greg.

Nervous energy rippled through him, and he stalked toward Heath's office. The furniture had finally arrived. Once entering, he let out a low whistle.

Glass, wood, and chrome. It was a combination of Ryker's and Denver's offices with a sprawling black leather chair behind the desk. A wide glass panel had been mounted on one wall with pictures and notes showcasing the Copper Killer murders.

He strode forward and checked out the neat lines. If the killer stayed true to form, he'd take another victim within the week. Heath had been almost obsessed with the case, and only Ryker's personal life was keeping him in town right now. Of course, there wasn't anywhere to go until the psycho took another victim. There wasn't much they could do until something happened.

God, he hated waiting for something to happen.

He scrubbed a hand across his eyes. Going semi-public and setting down roots in Cisco as a private detective agency to catch the killer had been a good, albeit risky, idea until Greg's case had come in. Now being semi-public could be a disaster. They had to get to Dr. Madison before she found them.

At the moment, all he could do was wait with a clock silently clicking down in his head.

His phone buzzed, and he read a text from Heath: INTERVIEW ALMOST OVER. ZARA FUCKED. GET A CONTINGENCY PLAN IN PLACE.

Ah shit.

CHAPTER
27

Zara shivered in the cold as she exited the police station, Heath by her side. Detective Norton had elected not to arrest her quite yet, but he'd implied, rather strongly, that a warrant would be forthcoming. "This is all too weird," she muttered.

Heath nodded just as Ryker's truck pulled up to the curb. He opened the door, and helped Zara inside. "She's in trouble, man. We have to figure this out."

Ryker nodded, a muscle clenching in his jaw. "I'll debrief her, and then we need to talk."

Heath paused. "Safe house three?"

"Yeah, it was Denver. Guy needs help."

Zara frowned, her chest hurting. "What's a safe house three?"

"Later," Ryker said.

Zara frowned. Why were all these bad things happening? Her temper wanted free, and she really needed to kick something. Too bad her gym wasn't open, because they had an awesome set of boxing dummies. "Why don't you guys just go talk now? I could use some alone time."

Ryker cut her a look. "No. You and I will talk, and then I'll meet up with Heath and Denver."

Oh, he didn't get to go all bossy on her now. She moved to get out of the truck, needing space. Definitely space. "Heath? I need a ride home."

Ryker grasped her arm and tugged her across the seat until she was flush against him. "Heath? Shut the door."

Heath shut the door and turned to jog through the storm to his car.

"Damn it, Ryker." Zara struggled against him, fighting not only the man but her entire crazy evening.

He pressed an arm around her waist and drove the truck onto the snowy road. "I know you had a shitty night, and I want to hear all about it. I'm sorry I wasn't there." Easily controlling the truck with one hand, he kept her in place.

That was just it. The world was crumbling around her, and the last thing she wanted at the moment was to take a leap of faith with a guy she still didn't completely know. "I'm staying at my place tonight. Please bring Grams over in the morning, since she's probably already asleep right now."

His hold tightened. "Baby, I'm tryin' real hard to be patient here, because I know it's been rough. But I suggest you lose the fuckin' attitude for a few moments." He turned off the main road and headed away from the center of town, his temper all but swelling from him and engulfing through the truck.

That was it. The barely veiled threat, said in that deep voice, made her completely lose her mind. The world was out of control, and rage boiled through her so quickly she just stopped thinking.

She jerked her elbow back into his rib cage as hard as she could. He grunted, and his hold loosened. Taking advantage, she shoved away from him and scrambled across the seat, putting her back to the door. "Listen, asshole," she hissed, drawing her purse in front of her, "I'm done with the *baby* and the manhandling. I'm not the type of woman you just keep in the dark and then order around. So take me home. To my *home*." Her breath was so heated, she was surprised she didn't spit fire. "We're done. Just buddies from now on." She was so angry, the words spewed out, and she wasn't even sure what they meant.

Ryker pulled the truck over next to an empty lot and cut the engine. Quiet descended suddenly and completely.

Oh shit. She clutched her purse tighter against her chest.

He turned toward her—a dangerous man in a dark truck—and focused those intense eyes on her. "Oh, baby. Now you definitely have my attention." His hoarse voice sounded like he'd swallowed sharp gravel.

Her heart pretty much exploded in her chest, making her ribs ache. Her eyes widened to keep track of him. Now she knew what a deer in a scope felt like. "Ryker, I—"

"That hurt," he said slowly, rubbing his rib cage. "Did you think I wouldn't retaliate?"

She stopped breathing. Her lungs just up and quit. "No, I—"

"You thought wrong." His voice lost that teasing tone he usually had when going all alpha dominant.

Her breath caught and her abdomen tingled.

And he knew. His lip quirked, and his gaze deepened. Tension of a different kind rolled through the space, surrounding her, vibrating against her. "Take back the buddy comment." One hand moved to her nape and fisted in her hair. Erotic tingles spiked across her scalp.

"I won't." Her voice quavered. She couldn't *breathe*.

"Zara, take it back, or I'll make you." He propelled her face toward his, and heated breath brushed her lips.

Oh yeah? He seriously underestimated her. All of a sudden, the fear of the night disappeared. She couldn't be afraid. She needed to escape reality for a moment. Just one. It was time to play. She leaned in and bit his bottom lip. Not hard enough to pierce the skin but with definite intent.

He sucked in air.

Oh God. What the hell was wrong with her? It was like she

couldn't help but challenge him. Even so, she licked her lips with a small hum. Everything inside her responded to this man. Only him.

"I bite back," he whispered.

A quiver took her, and she tightened her thighs against his. With his hold absolute on her, she forgot all about the police station, the break in at her house, and the upcoming warrant for her arrest. There was only Ryker and the passion all but exploding around them. Would this be all the time they had? If so, she was taking it. "Promise, promises," she murmured.

He took her mouth then, all gentleness gone. Hard and fierce, he kissed her, holding her exactly where he wanted her. The kiss moved beyond hungry to carnal, something so damn male bursting free in Ryker. Her body softened in response. He shoved her skirt all the way up to her waist and snapped her panties free, tossing them to the floor.

The wildness—*she* brought that out in him. Power flushed through her along with need. For him, and not just for now. She could ease him, find her place right there.

She gasped, still kissing him back, reaching for the hem of his shirt. He halted her movements by grabbing her lapels and ripping open her shirt, scattering buttons to ping against the windows. He jerked her bra up, revealing her breasts, his mouth still destroying hers.

"So pretty," he growled against her mouth, palming her breast.

She moved against him, sliding her hands up and into his thick hair. Unreal heat flashed through her, followed by a craving for more. For Ryker.

His fingers found her, and she partially lifted up, throwing back her head.

"So wet," he murmured, rubbing against her clit.

The ache intensified, zinging through her abdomen. She whimpered and rubbed against him, her hold tightening in his hair.

He jerked his jeans open and ripped them down his legs, somehow not letting go of her as he did so. Grabbing her hips, he lifted her above him. "Spread your legs, baby."

She widened her thighs, gasping as his hard shaft penetrated her. Slowly, he lowered her until her knees rested against the leather seat again. "Weren't we in this position not too long ago?" She gasped, her insides rioting with pleasure.

He chuckled and kneaded her breasts. "Yes, but look what I can do from this position." He tweaked a nipple.

Jolts of electricity shot through her. "That is nice," she moaned, dropping her forehead to his. "I'm sorry I was so angry with you. The police detective scared me, and I took it out on you."

"I know." He pressed her back and pushed the hair away from her face. "I have a lot to tell you about my night, and I was in a crappy mood, too. But first, take back the buddy comment."

She blew out air. He was unbelievable. "You will never be my buddy," she muttered.

"Was that so hard?" Flattening his hand between her breasts, he gently pushed until her upper back rested against the dashboard, completely opening her to him. Then he tugged her bra straps down her arms along with her shirt, stopping when they reached her elbows and he had effectively immobilized her arms.

The moon shone down, sparkling off the snow outside the truck. Goosebumps rose on her skin.

She blinked. "I'm, ah, feeling a little vulnerable, nearly nude with you still dressed." Giving a quick struggle against the bra and shirt, she gave up when she couldn't get free.

"Trust me like I trust you." He traced up her abdomen to her breasts and back down again, his nails lightly scraping. Then he leaned over and turned the ignition key, starting the truck and the heater.

She moaned as warmth once again spread around her. "You're

trusting me." His dick pulsed inside her, so big and full. She needed him to start moving and fast. Or at least to allow her to start moving against him before her entire body just combusted right then and there in the truck.

"Completely. I can't do anything else—you're for me, Zara." He punctuated his words with tugs on her nipples.

Pain and erotic pleasure rippled through her, and she sucked in her breath. "Ryker," she breathed.

"Yes." His palm flattened across her lower abdomen, and he swept his thumb across her clit.

"Oh," she hissed, pushing against him. Her thighs began to tremble.

He rubbed in small circles until she began to pant, shocks resonating through her. "Zara?"

Her lids half closed. "What?" A little more pressure, and she'd be in heaven.

He paused, his thumb pressed right to her but not moving. "Things are about to get really dicey in both our lives, and we need to be on the same page, so we're sitting here just like this until we reach that page." He tucked his thumb barely inside her, where there wasn't any room, and tugged gently.

Clarity rushed in, and she focused on him, her body exposed, vibrating, and on instant alert. "You have my attention," she whispered, trying not to move.

"Thought I might." Amusement, dark and male, glittered in his gaze. He left his thumb where it rested, against the cock stretching her nearly too much. "I'm not going anywhere. While I understand you have definite issues of being abandoned, based on not only losing your parents but also your mother flitting from man to man, I'm tired of taking the brunt of them. We're doing this, and we're seeing where we can go."

She blinked and tried to draw on the protective walls she'd built. "You only wanted temporary."

"That was before I knew you, and before I was ready to see if I could do this any other way. I'm ready to try." His hand twisted, and his freed thumb scraped her clit again.

She whimpered. Full-on, weak-girl whimpered. Her shoulders struggled, but she still couldn't free her arms or hands. "This isn't fair," she hissed.

"Oh, baby." He caressed her again and played with her breasts with his other hand. "You should know now that I don't play fair. Ever."

Tears of pure, raw need pricked her eyes. "What do you want?" she moaned.

"You." He pinched her nipple, and she bucked against him. "All in, giving us a shot. No more pushing me away or expecting me to run out the door. I ain't easy, I know, but I'll be worth it."

"I already decided to do just that...So there." How could she turn away from such an offer? Ryker was the real package of pure male. No guarantees, but he was asking for a chance. Well, not exactly asking.

"You did?" His voice lowered.

"Yeah." She swallowed, her heart warmed, and she took the jump. "We've danced around enough."

"Tell me more." He soothed her smarting breast.

"No more pushing you away, and I'll give us a real shot. No more second thoughts or doubt...I'm all in." The words came out fast and breathless.

"Good." His chest shuddered as if a weight had been lifted, and he grabbed her hip and reached up her spine to her nape, holding her off the dash. "Hold on, sweetheart." Spreading his legs as much as he could in the half-off jeans, he shoved deeper inside her. He frowned.

"What?" she groaned.

"No leverage." He grinned, appearing almost boyish, even with lust stamped hard across his face.

She bit her lip. "I swear to God, if you don't find leverage, I'm going to kill you. Like really dead."

He nodded and reached forward to yank the bra and shirt off her arms, freeing her. He pulled her thighs to the sides of his hips. "You have leverage."

She grabbed his shoulders and lifted up, using her knees for balance.

"Faster." His hands clamped on her hips, and he lifted her and pulled her back down, setting a rapid rhythm that she fell naturally into. The sound of flesh against flesh filled the quiet night.

Close. She was so close. Tightening her internal muscles, she detonated, crying out his name. The orgasm tore through her, taking everything. She dropped her head to his neck just as he shuddered with his own release. His teeth clamped onto her shoulder and dug in. Finally, blinking away tears, she leaned back. He'd bitten her.

The man did bite back.

CHAPTER
28

Ryker waited until Zara snuggled closer in the bed before tuning his senses into the apartment. Grams slept in the guest room, and Greg was out on the sofa. The kid had stirred when they'd entered but hadn't awakened, so that had to be a good sign. Maybe Greg was settling in and could relax a little.

Family was all around Ryker, needing him, and instead of being terrified, he jumped into the warmth. He could do this.

"Well? You said you wanted to talk," Zara murmured sleepily.

His mouth felt dry. "How about we sleep and then talk in the morning?" he asked. The world had bombarded the woman. She needed to store up her defenses, and he needed to provide cover and make sure she stayed safe. No matter the cost. "Sleep now." He pulled her against him.

Her breathing smoothed out so quickly, he figured he'd made the right decision.

He partially turned and spooned Zara, drawing in her scent of fresh tangerines. He loved that shampoo. He breathed her in and settled. In the morning, he'd tell her everything about his past. If it was going to catch up to him, he needed her prepared.

After one more cursory check of his surroundings, he allowed himself to drop into a light sleep that quickly became deep.

He was sixteen years old, nursing bruised ribs and a possible concussion. Ned Cobb, the proprietor of the boys home, and his brother, the sheriff, had gone at him for hours, using threats and more than a couple of punches, but not once had he broken and told them that Ralph had stolen the food. The kid was too young and too small to take a beating, so Ryker had taken it for him.

Heath had gathered Ralph into their little family the second he'd taken a look at the short kid. Ryker hadn't had the heart to object.

Spring had finally arrived, so the bunkhouse wasn't as cold now. He sat on his bed, surrounded by other beds. Birds chirped outside, and the sun gleamed through the dirty windows. The place had been built by nature-loving rich people who thought they were helping kids who needed a safe place in nature. Dumb-asses.

Heath ran into the room, his jeans torn and bruises across his jaw from a run-in with Ned the previous week. "Shit. They found out it was Ralph." *Heath had turned fifteen the month before, and he'd quickly started sprouting up. Soon he'd be as tall as Ryker. His eyes darkened, and he ran a bruised hand through his dirty brown hair.* "I think they knew from the beginning and just wanted to make you tell."

"Probably." *Ryker pushed to his feet and winced as his ribs protested.* "They're both sick fucks."

"Yeah." *Heath eyed him.* "You okay to walk?"

Ryker stumbled toward the door. "Yeah. My legs are fine. Tell me they don't have Ralph."

Heath shoved the door open to full sunshine. "They've had him for hours, and I just found out. Denver is there, too." *He cleared his throat.* "I just saw Sheriff Cobb go into town, but he's sure to be back soon."

"Fuck." *Ryker held his arm close to his ribs, trying to bracket them.* "We have to get Denver and Ralph out of there."

"We should do it now before the sheriff gets back." *Heath ran around the building and quickly returned with two baseball bats.* "I raided the *elementary school down the way a few weeks back so we'd have these just in case."*

"Nice." Ryker accepted the well-worn but smooth wooden bat and left the aluminum one for Heath. "This is it, then. If we do this, we have to run." He was ready. At some point either the sheriff or Ned was going to swing a belt too hard, and one of them was going to die. It wasn't going to be his blood brothers or him, and now they needed to save the new kid. "Are you ready?"

Heath's jaw tightened. "Yeah. It's time to run."

Ryker nodded. They'd get Denver and the new kid, and they'd head south through the hills. He'd stashed boots and supplies in a gully behind a bunch of bushes, so they'd be all right. The key was getting out of the state as soon as possible, because the sheriff had a long reach. The dickhead.

Ryker led the way around several bunkhouses to the main house, where they slid through the side door and entered the quiet kitchen. He silently moved for the back stairs, his odd senses keeping track of Heath right behind him.

They crept down the wood stairs to the dirt-packed floor and turned into a storage area complete with several freezers and shelves of canned goods.

Ryker's head ached, and his ribs pounded, but he kept going through a narrow hallway to a room at the rear. The room. His gut clenched.

"I'll go first," Heath whispered, his voice shaking.

"No." Ryker was a year older than Heath, so that meant he went first. "Just get Denver and Ralph out of here if Ned grabs me."

"We all get out of here," Heath said, his voice losing the shake. "We've got this."

Ryker reached the wooden door with the white peeling paint. No loud sounds came from within, but he could hear heartbeats. Two of them. He nudged open the door and stepped inside, his grip tightening on the handle of the bat. Then he froze.

Ned leaned over Ralph, pressing on his chest, nearly pounding. The kid lay in the dirt, his eyes open, and with no color in his face.

Denver leaned against the far brick wall, bruises and blood mottling his head, and tears streaming down his face. A metal folding chair was tipped over near him, and blood flowed from a cut in his arm.

Ned stood, his hands shaking. The owner of the boys home was tall and thin with thick blond hair and angry brown eyes. At about thirty years old, he still had pimples, and his teeth always seemed yellow. He spun around and looked at them, his narrow mouth opening and closing. Blood covered his knuckles.

He did like to punch.

Ryker looked down at the dead kid and then up at Ned again.

Ned sucked in air and tugged his button-down shirt into order over his khaki pants. "Denver killed Ralph. You saw him."

Ryker slowly shook his head. "No."

Ned's thin chin went down. "You both saw him. Or maybe you did it? Who do you think my brother will believe, me or you?"

Heath turned so pale he looked like he might pass out.

Ryker swallowed down what tasted like acid. His hands shook. "Denver, get behind me and get out."

Denver took a step forward and then stumbled. Heath hustled for him and shoved a shoulder beneath his arm.

"We're leaving," Ryker said, forcing words through his clogging throat. He didn't know Ralph, but the small dark-haired kid didn't deserve to die like that. Nobody did.

Heath propped Denver against the wall and blocked him, looking toward the dead boy. "We didn't even get to cut his hand, Ryker."

Ryker's eyes filled. "He's still a brother, Heath. I promise."

Heath caught his breath on a sob.

Anger and fear rushed through Ryker so fast he swayed. What if they didn't get out? They were all dead. Terror felt like sharp spikes inside his

skin. "Ned, don't try to stop us and don't come after us. We'll tell everyone
what you've done if you do."

Ned rushed him.

He reacted and swung the bat at the same time Heath rushed forward
and did the same. The bats hit the man in the head, and the sound exploded
through the air.

Ryker shot up in bed, breathing so hard his head spun. His heart
pounded, and his chest compressed. Okay. He was fine. Just fine.
Yeah, he'd failed Ralph, but he could protect everyone in the house
now. He wasn't a scared kid any longer.

Zara rolled over, her eyelids opening. "Bad dream."

He nodded, suddenly freezing. Thunder ripped the sky apart outside, and wind barreled against the window. Hell of a storm. Slowly,
he slid back under the covers.

She rolled right up against him, her hand flattening on his chest.
"Tell me about it."

Part of him wanted to tell her everything, but the other part
wanted her to remain unaware of his past and of the pain they'd endured. She'd hurt for them, and the woman had hurt enough.

Yet he needed her to trust him, and she was so damn strong, she
could handle it. "When Heath, Denver, and I were kids, we lived at a
shitty home for boys where the proprietor liked to hit. He was a prick,
and sometimes I have nightmares." Ryker ran a hand down her hair
and over her sweet back. "Sorry I woke you up."

She caressed his chest. "I'm sorry about the boys home. Did the
proprietor ever get caught?"

"Not really." Ryker kissed the top of her head. "He died in a fire
at the home, so he never really faced justice." In fact, it had been way
too swift. Either his bat or Heath's had hit the guy's temple, and it was
suddenly over. Neither of them had meant to kill Ned, but he'd been

dead before he hit the dirt floor. Denver had been the one to set the place on fire to cover their tracks long enough for them to get away.

They'd been running ever since. He figured the haunting nightmares were karma or penance or whatever.

"I'm so sorry, Ryker," Zara said, leaning up to kiss his chin.

He relaxed into the bed, and his lungs finally released all the air. "I'm okay, sweetheart." For the first time in so long, as he held his woman, he actually believed it. Then at her trust, at her acceptance, he told her everything, his heart pounding so hard it hurt. The entire story of his life, of meeting Heath and then Denver, and finally of that night. "So I swung the bat, and the sound—shit, Zara, the sound—there's nothing else like it. I heard a melon explode once, and that sound was close, but there's a sick *thunk* to a skull caving in that's impossible to describe."

She held him tight, running her hand over him, offering soothing sounds. "That's horrible."

"Yeah." His hands were sweaty, but he felt cold. "We were so scared, and then we had to run. Really run, you know? The sheriff would've caught us and not turned us in." Even now, years later, Ryker shuddered at the revenge Cobb would've sought. The man was sadistic enough to know their weaknesses, and he would've definitely tortured Heath and Denver in front of Ryker. Hell, he'd promised to do it more than once.

Zara kissed his chin. "I'm so sorry, and I'm so glad you were strong enough to survive."

At her acceptance, something tight in his chest eased and loosened. He calmed and told her all about Dr. Madison and Greg's connection to her. To them.

"That's unbelievable," Zara said, anger in her voice. "She experimented on all of you?"

"Yes." Warmth surrounded him as he shared with Zara—as he

gave her everything. "She said once that Heath, Denver, and I were her special projects—just hers—like some type of secret. Like her main job was at the facilities where Greg and other kids were raised, and we were just a detour or something she did for fun. Our lives were her fun." Bewilderment filled him, and he didn't bother to battle it back.

"Damn, that's fucked up," Zara said.

He barked out a surprised laugh. "You've summed it up perfectly." God, he adored her.

"Thank you for trusting me." She settled against him, and they lay that way, just the two of them, for a brief moment in time.

Finally, he tuned into the apartment. It was still dark outside, so it must've been early morning. Ice cracked outside while silence ruled inside. Greg breathed quietly in the living room, and Grams shuffled around her room.

"Your granny is up," Ryker said.

Zara nodded. "I wish we could stay here forever."

"Me too." He sighed. "But we can't."

"I know. Today I want to go to the office and fetch my belongings before anybody gets there."

He paused. "You're not fired. Just on leave."

"I know, but it's embarrassing. Chances are I'll be fired, no matter what. So I'd like to get my things without facing everyone." She sighed. "I'm a coward."

"No, you're not." He ran his fingertips across her waist and over her butt. "I'll take you first thing, and then we need to make escape plans."

"Okay." She licked along his jawline. Her phone buzzed, and she stopped to roll over and read the screen. "My neighbor has my mail for me. Let's stop by there after the office." She rolled back and nipped beneath his chin. "Then maybe we can go back to bed."

Barely evading his quick kiss, she shoved from the bed and stood, stretching.

"Sounds good." He followed her into the shower, where he proceeded to make sure she was very clean. Several times. Being with her felt like he'd always imagined *home* would feel. Until now, the idea of a home had been just a farfetched dream.

But Zara was home to him.

After the shower, he quickly dressed in clean jeans and a T-shirt while she messed with her already perfect face. "Meet you downstairs." Pressing closer for a kiss, he breathed her in. Woman, spice, and sweetness.

Then, to prevent himself from taking her back to bed, he hustled through the apartment and jogged down the stairs to the offices, whistling a Christmas tune. It was the only happy tune he knew.

Tension hit him the second he opened the door from the stairwell.

"God fucking damn it," Heath bellowed.

Ryker stiffened and then hurried to Heath's office, his body going on alert. Heath had thrown a paperweight across the room, and it hung drunkenly from the windowsill. "What?" Ryker asked, just as Denver caught up from his office.

Heath vibrated in place. "The Copper Killer got Agent Jackson. He got through the FBI to Jackson."

Ryker rocked back on his heels. Shock stilled him. He'd been focused on Zara's problems and hadn't figured Jackson was really in danger. How could this happen? "When?"

Denver pivoted and ran back toward the better computer system in his office.

"Late last night," Heath snarled, primal fury in his eyes. "I just intercepted an FBI e-mail about it—they're keeping it quiet for now."

"That's good." Ryker glanced at the window. God, Heath would lose his fucking mind. The guy had made a connection with Jackson and seemed to really like the agent.

Lightning zigzagged outside, and snow pelted down along with freezing rain. "The case just became our number one priority." He'd have to get Zara out of town for now and then go chase the killer and cover his brother's back. "Special Agent Jackson lived in Snowville?" There was an FBI satellite office in the large Washington State town.

"Yes." Heath ripped open a desk drawer and rummaged, yanking out a wad of cash.

Ryker held up a hand, trying to calm him when all he wanted to do was grab a gun and go hunting. "The guy won't be in Snowville any longer."

"Don't care. It's a place to start." Heath strode around the desk, his brown hair ruffled and his eyes pissed.

Denver caught him at the doorway. "Airport and interstate are closed. Storm's a bastard."

Heath paused. "Then we get on computers and the phone." He turned back. "The second something is open, I'm going."

"We're going," Ryker corrected. He glanced at his watch. "Right now I'll take Zara to get her stuff, and then I need a safe house for her and Grams while we go after this guy. We'll put Greg with them."

"I'll get on it," Denver said, his voice and hands steady for the first time in too long.

"Thanks." Now all Ryker had to do was convince Zara to go along with his plan.

CHAPTER
29

Zara smoothed down her jeans and squinted to see through the windshield. Snow piled up so quickly, the wipers barely made a dent. "Maybe we should've waited."

Ryker's hold remained relaxed and sure on the steering wheel. "We need to take care of this before Heath and I head out on the serial killer case."

Zara nodded. How crazy was the entire situation? "Shouldn't you let the FBI handle it?"

"Yeah, because they've handled it well so far." Sarcasm lowered his voice. He shook his head and swerved around a pile of ice. "I need you and Grams to hunker down in a safe house until we get back."

"The police won't like that," she murmured.

"Doesn't matter. You haven't been arrested, and you don't have to stay here. It's time for a little vacation." Ryker came to a stop in her driveway, sliding the last few feet on the snow-covered ice. "We need to hurry, sweetheart."

Zara nodded. "I'll be right back." She slid from the truck and shut the door. Cold instantly snapped against her face, and she ducked her face down under her scarf before turning and jogging through the snow to her neighbor's door. Mrs. Ogleby was always up by early morning, so Zara knocked briskly.

The door opened, and the elderly lady peered out. "Goodness. Come in."

Zara stepped inside, careful to keep her boots on the tile. Ferocious heat slammed into her. "Morning. I came for my mail?"

Mrs. Ogleby nodded and smoothed back her curly white hair. "Were you at your house last night? I could've sworn I saw lights."

Zara paused, and her heart rate picked up. "No. I stayed with a friend."

Mrs. Ogleby leaned to peer past her flimsy red curtains. "Is that your friend, dear? The hot pants in the truck?"

Zara bit her lip. "Yes. Hot Pants is my friend."

"Very nice." Mrs. Ogleby turned and grabbed several envelopes and a small package. "Here you go."

"Thanks." Zara glanced toward the truck. "Are you sure there were lights at my place?"

Mrs. Ogleby nodded vigorously. "Yep."

"Thank you." Zara turned and stepped back outside. Had the men come back to her place? If so, why? What in the world did they want with her? She slipped on the walk and quickly righted herself before plowing through the swirling snow and reaching the truck. She was breathless when she finally jumped in and closed the door.

"You okay?" Ryker asked.

She nodded. "Yeah, but Mrs. O. saw lights on at my place last night. Do you think those guys in black came back?"

Ryker frowned. "I don't know. How about we get you back to my apartment, and then I can come take a look around?"

She shook her head, shoving everything into the glove compartment. She'd go through her bills later. "Let's look around now."

"No." Ryker reversed the truck onto the street, his control firmly back in place. "Sorry, baby. There's too much going on right now, and I need to get you to safety."

She opened her mouth to argue, but he quickly shook his head. What the hell? She could help search her own house, for goodness' sake. "We're going to have to work on this Neanderthal issue you have going on," she muttered.

"Humph." He pulled out onto the main thoroughfare and glared through the windshield. "I think the storm is actually getting worse."

She shivered and flipped the knob to turn up the heat on her seat. "You guys won't be able to fly in this."

A siren blared through the air. Ryker leaned to glance in the rearview mirror. "Damn it."

He slowly pulled the truck to a safe area off the road.

Zara tensed and looked around. The black car behind them wasn't a patrol car, but it had a light in the dash and a siren. Her breath caught, and adrenaline sped through her veins. "You weren't speeding."

"No." Ryker leaned over and opened the glove box, shoving Zara's mail out of the way, to retrieve a stack of papers before sliding his window down.

Men walked up on both sides of the truck.

Her door opened. Ryker grasped her, and tugged her toward him, but a gun suddenly appeared near his ear. He stiffened.

"Zara Remington? You're under arrest for the murder of Julie Pentley." Detective Norton reached in and took her arm. "Please exit the vehicle."

She coughed and let go of Ryker's arm. Panic and shock buzzed through her mind. "I didn't kill Julie," she whispered as the detective assisted her into the cold. He turned her around and quickly snapped cuffs on her wrists. The metal was cold and bit into her skin.

Fury lit Ryker's eyes, but with the gun at his temple, there wasn't much he could do. "Don't say anything until your attorney shows up," he ground out.

Dazed, Zara gulped in air. "I won't."

Norton turned her, almost gently, toward his car. "You have the right to remain silent." As he continued with her rights, she blanked out, her mind spinning.

What now? Her shoulders shook, and her knees weakened.

The detective guided her into the back of his car and shut the door before taking the driver's seat. The officer with the gun then slipped into the other seat.

Silence ruled the car as Norton drove through the blustering storm to the police department. Zara endured being fingerprinted and then sat in a cell for about fifteen minutes before Norton fetched her. She entered a different interrogation room from last time. This one was cold and stark with one of those one-way mirrors she'd seen only on television. From a metal table, Norton pulled out a metal chair for her, facing the mirror.

She swallowed and sat, trying not to shiver.

He took the seat across from her, his brown eyes somber. "We know you did it."

She blinked.

"The only motive I can think of is that you were still in love with the mayor." Norton tapped a manila file on the table. "Or maybe Julie came at you, full of drugs, and you had to defend yourself? If so, tell me. I want to help you, but you need to help me first."

Right. "I didn't kill Julie, and I wasn't present when she died." Zara sat back and crossed her arms, her voice trembling. "I'm not saying another word until my lawyer arrives." She knew the detective's goal was to get her talking about anything and then catch her in some sort of mistake. Since she hadn't killed Julie, she shouldn't be afraid, but she knew better than to speak without Heath present.

"That's your choice." Norton also sat back. "But when your fast-talking attorney gets here, I won't be able to help you."

Like he really wanted to help her.

"Did Julie leave you anything? Any proof that you were her friend, not a jealous rival?" the detective asked.

"I gave her three thousand dollars a month to help her with bills," Zara burst out. "Why do that if it wasn't for friendship?"

The door opened. "Stop talking." Heath strode inside and immediately shrugged out of a snow-covered jacket and placed it on the back of his chair. He wore a black button-down shirt, faded jeans, motorcycle boots, and a pissed-off expression on his handsome face, and his light brown hair was ruffled and sprinkled with snow.

Zara kept herself from edging away from the barely controlled violence rolling off him. He had another case to worry about and shouldn't have to babysit her. "You don't have to stay," she whispered.

Heath ignored her and faced the detective. "This is going to get you sued, Detective."

"I don't think so." Norton waited until Heath sat next to Zara. "We have proof, a lot of it, so your client needs to help herself out here and cooperate."

Heath's upper lip curled. "You have fingerprints at Julie's motel, which makes sense because my client visited Julie there. They were friends." He pushed back from the table. "If that's all, then I want to bail out my client."

Norton shook his head. "That's nowhere near all. We have your client's ID for the Picalo Club, which is related to the blackmail, I believe. Your client was explaining the money to me."

Heath frowned. "Right. Zara lent Julie money because her asshole of a husband wouldn't give her any. There's no crime in that."

"I think Zara bought drugs for poor Julie because Julie was blackmailing her." Norton smiled, full of triumph. "I have a dealer, folks."

Zara's mouth gaped open. "No—"

Heath held up a hand. "Stop talking."

She breathed out.

"You don't have a dealer who will say that, because that never happened. Stop fishing, Detective. It's a waste of time." Heath glanced at a well-used watch on his wrist. "So far, you're just wasting our time and courting a false arrest lawsuit. Maybe harassment." His nostrils flared.

Norton leaned to the side of his chair and reached into a briefcase. "Well, we did find this." He tossed a see-through bag onto the table. It fell with a loud *thunk* and bounced once.

Zara squinted at a knife covered with what looked like crusty blood. "What the hell?" she breathed.

"I'm betting the farm that it's the murder weapon." Norton smiled. "We've tested the blood, and results should be back soon."

"So?" Heath asked.

"So? We executed a search warrant last night on your client's home, and we found the knife hidden in her bedroom closet beneath several boxes of shoes. In fact, the knife was found in a box of those fancy Manwelloo Blonkers, or whatever they're called."

Zara coughed. "That's impossible." Her mind spun, and a pit opened in her stomach.

Heath again held up a hand. "I'd like to see the warrant."

"Of course." Norton opened his file and slid a stack of papers toward Heath.

Heath read quickly. "Who found the knife?"

Norton lifted an eyebrow. "One of the uniforms found it and called me over. We have pictures and everything."

Zara turned toward Heath. "Somebody had to have planted it."

Norton scoffed. "You said your attacker the other night was contained in the kitchen and living room. Nobody entered your bedroom."

Yeah, but she hadn't been home since, so somebody could've easily entered her house. "But—"

Heath leaned forward, and she stopped talking. Time to listen to her lawyer.

"Fingerprints?" Heath asked, peering closely at the knife through the plastic.

"None."

Heath glanced up. "So you're telling me she was smart enough to wipe her prints, but stupid enough to stash the murder weapon in her own box of shoes? Seriously?"

Norton shrugged. "Criminals rarely make sense to me. Maybe she wanted to use it again, or perhaps she gets off on seeing the blood. I don't know or care."

Heath shook his head. "You need more than this."

"Actually, I don't." Norton patted his belly. "But I do have more. Guess what, Ms. Remington? I have a witness who saw you at the motel during the time of the murder. The kid at the front desk wasn't completely asleep when you snuck by right before the time of Julie's death." He pushed back from the desk and stood. "Time for a lineup, lady."

CHAPTER
30

Ryker barely kept his temper in check as he clicked off the call from Heath.

"How bad?" Denver asked from across Ryker's desk.

"Bad. Somebody planted the murder weapon in her house, and she just got picked out of a lineup by the front-desk kid of the motel. Heath is posting her bail now, and they should be here within an hour. We might have to run sooner rather than later." Ryker shot a hand through his hair. "I can't believe this."

"Greg will run in the opposite direction." Denver scratched his scruffy jaw.

"Fuck." Ryker glanced at the ceiling. "No, he won't. I'm more worried he'll try to break into the police station and steal any evidence against her. Or kidnap her and take her to a safe place. The kid adores her." At the moment, Grams was making cookies in an effort to keep Greg close and eating.

Ryker's phone buzzed and he glanced at the screen before frowning. What now? Hell, he didn't have time to talk to the lawyer. "Hi, Brock. I don't have any news on Jay Pentley's case." Except that Zara had been arrested, damn it.

"I'm at the office, and I think I have a lead on Pentley's case. Zara's being set up. Can you drop by?" Brock asked.

Ryker sat up. "What kind of lead? Did you hear about Zara?"

"Yeah, and that's partly why I'm calling. I have some information here, and I need help going through it. It's odd, and, well…" Brock ruffled papers. "There's a pattern here, but I might be just trying to help Zara. I'm not sure."

Ryker stood. "I'll be there in a few minutes." He'd go insane just sitting and waiting for Zara to return and the weather to clear, so he might as well figure things out. He clicked off. "I'll be at the law firm," he told Denver. In fact, they hadn't had a chance to grab Zara's things from her office, so he'd do that for her, too. One less thing for her to worry about. "Call me the second Zara and Heath get back."

"Yep."

"Would you go check on Greg and Grams?" Ryker asked.

"Yep." Denver rubbed his bloodshot eyes and stood, then gracefully strode from the room.

Ryker watched him go, unease settling in his gut. Denver hadn't been right since they'd relocated, and maybe the best thing was to force him back to Alaska to face his past. Something to think about another day, however. Ryker jogged through the office and down to his truck, rushing into the swirling snowstorm and fairly empty streets.

He slid through several intersections before reaching the law firm and parking out front. The snow battled him as he made his way to the main entrance and shoved inside, stomping up the stairs to the office.

Mrs. Thomson smiled at him. "Go on back to the smaller conference room, Ryker. Brock is waiting for you." She peered through her thick glasses. "Tell him to take a break and grab some lunch, would you? That boy worked all through the night and hasn't eaten."

Ryker nodded and hustled past her, down the hallway, and to the small conference room.

Papers littered the table, and piles of them were perched on the chairs. Brock hunched over more papers, mumbling to himself.

Ryker shut the door behind himself. "Dude. You need sleep."

Brock looked up, his eyes twice as bloodshot as Denver's had been. "Somebody is pulling the strings here, and I don't like it. Have a seat."

Ryker's chest compressed. He lifted a bunch of papers off the nearest seat and set them on the floor. "What's going on?"

Brock scrambled through a stack and shoved a piece toward Ryker. "At first, I thought Jay Pentley was somehow involved in his wife's death, but now I think there's somebody else pulling all the strings."

"Why?" Ryker asked, taking the paper.

"Because after the break-in the other night, I put men on Zara's place. We keep a rotating security firm on retainer." Brock looked around and grabbed a coffee cup, frowning into its empty bottom.

Ryker stilled. "You had a detail on her place?"

"Yeah." Brock set the empty cup down and grimaced. "I figured the break-in might have something to do with one of our cases, most likely the Pentley divorce, and I wanted to know what was going on. Plus, if Zara stayed there, I wanted her protected."

The guy really liked her, now, didn't he? "Wait a minute. If there were men watching the house—"

"Exactly. Nobody got in, Ryker. Which means that the knife was planted…"

"During the search." Ryker sat back, his mind reeling. "One of the cops?"

Brock nodded. "Yeah. That's a list of the officers and detectives on the scene. I called in a favor. A couple of them, really, in order to get that list. You have the resources to track the names." His hand shook when he patted the papers in front of him. "These are all my current cases that Zara is working on, and I've been going through them to look for leads on the off chance this isn't related to the Pentley case. Haven't found anything yet."

Shit. Zara was at the police station. Ryker grabbed his phone and quickly texted Heath. The returned text relaxed his lungs. "Zara made bail, and Heath is taking her to my place now." He quickly texted the most recent info and a request to lock down their building for safety.

AFFIRMATIVE was the response.

Good. All right. Ryker narrowed his gaze at the lawyer. "You need food and sleep, Brock. At least food."

Brock grimaced. "A shower wouldn't hurt, either. I'll head home, and you track down those names and see what you find. We'll touch base later today?" He stood and swayed.

Ryker shoved to his feet and tried to calm the nervous energy ripping him in two. "How about I drop you at your place on the way to my office? You're in no condition to drive." While he didn't like the guy's interest in Zara, Brock was trying to help.

Brock rolled his eyes. "I can make it home. The faster you get on that list, the better."

True. Ryker grabbed his jacket and followed Brock through the office, where they checked in with Mrs. Thomson, and then outside into the freezing snow. He headed for his truck and waited until Brock had swung his Jeep around the corner. While the lawyer had said he was fine, he was barely functioning, so there was nothing wrong with following him to make sure he didn't hit a building.

Ryker pulled his truck into the deserted street and followed the Jeep. The lawyer drove slow but steady. Maybe he didn't need a tail.

Ryker watched him for a couple more miles and then decided to turn off. Right as he was about to move, blue and red flashed behind him. He pulled over and tensed until he saw Detective Norton loping up his side of the car. "What now?" Ryker growled.

Norton shoved a gun in his face. "You're under arrest, asshole." He jerked open the door.

"Why?" Ryker kept his hands on the steering wheel.

"Accessory after the fact," Norton said grimly, grabbing his arm.

Damn it all to hell. Ryker allowed the cop to pull him from the car, flip him around, and cuff him. "Based on what facts?"

Norton read him his rights. "Let's get you booked and then we'll have a nice chat in interrogation." He pulled Ryker around and shoved him toward the car.

The detective was trying to mess with their heads, but Ryker didn't have much of a choice unless he wanted a manhunt on his ass. So he trudged through the snow and let Norton shove him into the backseat. His butt hit cold vinyl, and he scooted over. The door slammed.

Norton got inside and slowly pulled the car into the street.

Wait a minute. "Where's your partner, Detective?" Ryker asked.

"Gathering information on you, dickhead," Norton returned evenly, his brown eyes concentrating on him in the rearview mirror. "I know you assisted Ms. Remington, but she's the one I really want for this. Tell me where the package is, and I'll let you out right here."

Package? Ryker felt along the cuffs. Nice and tight. Something wasn't right. "What package?"

"I am so tired of you assholes." Norton turned down a tree-lined street.

Ryker studied the buildings surrounding them, his body settling into attack mode, his mind going clear and ready. "The police station is the other way."

"Yeah. It is." Norton made another turn. "Where's the diary?"

Ryker's analytical side clicked facts into place. Oh, so not good. "What diary?"

"Julie's. She had one, and I know she sent it to Zara. Where the hell is it?"

Julie's mystery man. The detective? Ryker hadn't seen it coming—not even close. "You planted the knife." Ryker tugged on the hand-cuffs, but there was absolutely no give. How had he missed this? He usually read people better. His personal life was fucking with his abilities.

"Yep." Norton shook his head. "I tried to keep you and Zara out of this, but the diary never showed up. You took care of the guys I sent to fetch her, and you've left me few options. I've searched her house several times, so it must be at your place. Right?"

The package that Zara had received. The one in his glove box. "Yep." Ryker calculated the odds of getting loose without getting shot, and they sucked. His body vibrated from a rush of adrenaline. "We picked up a bunch of Zara's mail, and a nice small package was included. She probably hasn't even opened it yet. I think it's on my desk."

"Good." Norton took another turn.

Ryker fought the urge to kick the back of the detective's seat. "Did you mess with the brakes on Zara's car?"

Norton frowned. "Yes. Thought she saw me with Julie, and when I started investigating, I discovered she hadn't."

Anger roared through Ryker so quickly he did kick the back of the seat. "I'm going to fucking rip off your head and reach down to rip out your lungs."

Norton winced. "She was fine, right? God. No offense, but you should probably worry about yourself right now."

Oh, the cop had no clue who he'd just pissed off. "You're a dead man," Ryker spat.

Norton turned right. "If you say so. Where's your office?"

Ryker gave the directions. He'd have backup at the office.

Norton went in the opposite direction.

"What the hell?" Ryker asked.

Norton flashed a smile and grabbed his phone.

* * *

Zara stomped snow from her boots just inside the garage. Arrested. She'd actually been arrested. There would be a trial. "I just don't understand who would plant that knife," she stuttered. Again.

Heath pushed out of his coat. Anger vibrated around him and had since he'd heard that the airport was still closed. "We'll figure it out. I promise."

Zara's phone dinged, and she lifted it to her ear. "Hello?"

"Ms. Remington? This is Detective Norton. Don't say a word and don't let anybody know who I am."

She blinked. "Um, all right." What in the world?

"I have your boyfriend cuffed in the back of my car, and I'm planning to put a bullet in his head unless you do exactly as I say," the detective said slowly and clearly.

Zara stopped breathing. Her lungs hitched. "Wh-what?"

Heath turned around, his gaze intense.

"You heard me. I'll let him go if you get me the package from Julie," Norton said.

Zara's mind scrambled facts into place. "Wait— You were seeing her? *You're* the guy." Shock coated her throat, with fear following. The cop had killed Julie, and now he had Ryker? Oh God, Ryker. She partially bent over to keep from passing out.

"You have twenty minutes to bring the package to me at your house. If you're not here, or if you bring anybody with you, I'll blow a hole in your man's forehead." While Norton sounded calm, a thread of pure panic had lifted his tone.

"Okay," Zara said, her stomach cramping. "I'll be there." She clicked off, looking wildly around.

"What?" Heath asked, appearing big and broad.

Norton had said to come alone and not tell anybody, but that would get Ryker and probably her killed. She was smarter than that, damn it. Heath was probably as well trained as Ryker, and she needed his help. "Detective Norton has Ryker and said he'd shoot him if I don't bring a package to him. He was the guy seeing Julie." The words had burst out of her. If she was going to save Ryker, she definitely needed help. "He said he'd kill Ryker if I told anybody or brought anybody with me."

Heath's face hardened and he was quiet for two seconds, no doubt calming himself the same way Ryker did. "Do you have a package?"

She shook her head, panic swarming through her. "I think there was one in my mail that I picked up this morning, but it's in Ryker's truck. In the glove box."

"Okay." Heath grabbed both her arms. "Take a deep breath and relax. Norton thinks we have something he needs, and he won't hurt Ryker until he gets it. You find a package or envelope around here that's about the same size, and I'll go grab Denver. Okay? Can you do that?"

She nodded.

"Good. I'll be right back." Heath turned on his heel and ran up the stairs.

She sucked in air and scrambled up to Ryker's office, where she found a large padded envelope that kind of looked like the one she remembered. Quickly, she stuffed a book inside just as Heath and Denver ran from one of their offices.

"What's going on?" Denver asked.

Heath quickly brought him up to speed and gave the lowdown on a plan he'd already put together. "I'll take the package to the front door and Denver will come in the back. We'll hit him from different directions."

Zara held up a hand. "No. I have to go in the front. He'll be waiting for me." If he didn't see her, he just might cut his losses and shoot Ryker before running. "If he sees me on the front step, then you two will have time to get into the place. It's the only way. He's a cop and he's trained."

Denver shook his head.

Heath blanched. "If we take you, Ryker is gonna kill us. You're his heart, lady."

Hearing the words from Ryker's brother filled her with warmth. If she was his heart, then she had to save his ass. "I understand, but the best plan is if I'm there."

Heath glanced at Denver. "We don't need you to go, sweetheart. It's better, much better, if you stay here."

"Better for whom?" she asked, already moving toward the garage.

"Ryker," Denver said.

"And us," Heath added, loping into a jog. "If my brothers let my woman confront an armed man who'd already killed one woman, I'd rip their skin from their bodies inch by inch and then use a squirt gun to spray them with saltwater."

Zara looked over her shoulder. "Dude."

Denver snorted and hustled alongside her. "I agree with most of what he said. We can take the house without you."

She shook her head. "Yeah, but he said he'd kill Ryker if I even told anybody else."

"He'll try to kill Ryker anyway," Heath said curtly. "It's better if we go without you."

She shook her head. "Maybe, but with me there, Detective Norton will be distracted just long enough for you guys to get inside. You know that, or we wouldn't all be moving toward the vehicles right now."

Denver sighed. "Ah hell."

"Exactly," Heath said grimly.

Zara said a quick prayer in her head. Ryker had to be all right. He just had to be.

CHAPTER
31

Ryker settled onto the sofa in Zara's living room, his hands still cuffed behind his back. The cushions were way too soft and gave him barely enough leverage to jump up if necessary. Detective Norton was no idiot. "Why did you kill Julie?" Ryker had to get the gun from the bastard before his brothers showed up. No way was Zara stupid enough to come alone, and the second she told his brothers about the detective, they would set a plan into motion. So now Ryker needed to distract the prick. "Detective?"

Norton paced by the front window and moved a filmy curtain aside to look at the raging storm. "She was gonna tell my wife about us and about our time at the Picalo Club."

"You created the fake badge for Zara."

Norton nodded. "Yep." He clearly had no intention of letting them live. He wouldn't be confessing everything otherwise.

"So what if Julie told your wife?"

"So what?" Norton turned around, his eyes hard. "My wife is Margaret Rapperton."

Ryker snorted. "The governor's daughter?"

"Yeah. She would divorce my ass, and her daddy would destroy any hope of my making chief. Ever." Norton shook his head. "Julie and I did drugs together along with a couple of other things I'd rather weren't made public, and that bitch put it all in her diary."

Ryker kept his gaze stoic while adrenaline flowed through his veins. "So you killed her. Just stabbed her until she bled out. A woman you'd been intimate with." The bastard deserved to be skinned alive.

Norton rolled his eyes. "She was a great lay, and on drugs, we were flying. But then she got all clingy. We had too much meth, got in a fight, and before I knew it, she was dead. It wasn't my fault." His gun rested loosely in his hand. "I'd planned to frame her dickhead of a husband for her death, but you and Zara Remington kept getting in the way. This is much better, though."

Ryker gingerly moved to the edge of the sofa.

"If you move another inch, I'm shooting you before she gets here." Norton aimed the gun at Ryker's chest. "Then I'll have some fun with her before I have to shoot her in self-defense. So sad. She got caught up with the wrong guy, and look what happened."

The man was insane. Smart but insane. "I'm not going to waste my breath telling you this will never work." Ryker calculated the distance between them.

"Good."

"But I will tell you that if you somehow do succeed in this, my brothers will rip you apart limb by limb. They won't rest until they've destroyed you."

Norton turned back to the window. "We'll see."

A noise behind the house caught Ryker's attention. Footsteps and breathing. What the hell? Neither Heath nor Denver would make so much noise. The kitchen door opened, and Ryker instantly started coughing, trying to mask the sound.

Norton turned around and studied him.

"Swallowed down wrong tube," Ryker gasped out.

Norton frowned and looked toward the kitchen. "Shit." He strode by the couch toward the kitchen.

Ryker leaped up and slammed his shoulder into the cop's side, throwing them both into a wall. Norton pivoted and punched Ryker in the jaw, smashing him into the arm of the couch.

With an explosive roar, Brock Hurst leaped from the kitchen, a frying pan in his hands.

What was the lawyer doing there? Ryker shouted a warning.

Brock swung just as Norton fired. The explosion ripped through the house. Blood bloomed across Brock's leg, and he fell back, his mouth wide in shock.

Ryker bunched and moved. Norton pivoted and shot again. Pain burst across Ryker's shoulder. He dropped and then jumped up, ramming his head beneath Norton's chin. The cop's head snapped back and hit the wall. Ryker kept going, using his head, knees, and feet, keeping the detective off balance and ignoring the blood flowing from his arm.

Then Norton slammed the gun down on his wounded shoulder. The world went black. Ryker dropped to a knee and shook his head, trying to focus. His vision cleared. He tensed to strike, and Norton rested the barrel of the gun against his forehead.

Fuck.

"Get up," the detective hissed.

Ryker used the coffee table for balance and shoved to his feet. Norton checked him into the sofa, and he bounced, heat flaring through him. "Brock?"

The attorney was leaning against the wall by the kitchen, his face pale, his leg bleeding. He grimaced and pressed on his wound. "I came to help."

A timid knock sounded from the front door.

Ryker angled his head to see who was outside. Zara stood there, pale and being bombarded by the snapping storm. What the hell was she doing there? He stopped breathing.

Norton leaned in. "If anybody moves, I'm shooting the bitch in the head."

Ryker snarled. She wasn't supposed to show up. God. She'd told Heath and Denver about Norton, hadn't she? "You touch her, and I'll make sure you beg for death. Which I won't grant."

Norton moved toward the door, the gun pointed at head height for Zara. He opened the door. "Give me the package."

"Not until I see that Ryker is alive," came Zara's clear voice.

Everything in Ryker settled and stilled. She was in the crosshairs of a gun, and he was handcuffed. He moved to the edge of the sofa, tucking his feet beneath him, preparing to ram the detective so Zara could run. She had better, by God, run.

Norton yanked Zara inside and shut the door, quickly locking it.

She saw him, and her eyes widened. "Ryker. You've been shot." She tried to move for him, but Norton stopped her with a hand on her arm.

"I kill him right now if you're not alone," Norton growled, jerking her up onto her toes.

Ryker readied to attack.

"I'm alone." Zara reached into her jacket and shoved an envelope at Norton, her gaze not leaving Ryker.

Brock coughed, and she stilled, craning her neck to see beyond Ryker. "Brock?"

"Hi, Zara," Brock rasped out.

She paled. "You've been shot, too?"

"This is a mess," Norton agreed, taking the envelope. "I'm afraid you all have to die."

Ryker's head swam, but he focused on the envelope. It wasn't the same as the one in the truck. Zara was bluffing with the psychopath? He jerked his head to the left, and she gave a barely perceptible nod.

Then he struck, his head down.

He smacked into the detective's chest and jerked up, hitting Norton beneath the chin with his head. The cop's head snapped up, and he bellowed, smashing his elbow down on Ryker's wound. Ryker howled and levered his legs up with a series of kicks.

Movement caught his attention from the other room, so he dodged to the side and took Zara down to the ground, covering her with his body.

Cool steel suddenly rested against his temple.

Norton stood above him, his legs splayed. "I guess you die first."

Two additional guns cocked.

Ryker stilled and slowly turned his head. Then he smiled. "There are two guns pointed at you, Detective," he rasped. Heath and Denver aimed at Norton from opposite angles.

Norton looked around, his eyes wild.

The moron might actually go for it. Ryker fell back, twisted, and kicked up, nailing the prick in the groin.

Norton let out a pained "Oof" and leaned over, his face flushing a deep red. "You asshole." He swung the gun toward Ryker.

A shot rang out.

Norton yelled and dropped the gun, holding his bleeding right hand. "What the fuck?"

Ryker looked around. Denver grinned and spun his gun before setting it in his back pocket.

"Nice shot," Ryker breathed, rolling off Zara.

She moved with him, her hands pressing on his wound. Pain lanced through him and he grunted. "Sorry," she murmured, her beautiful face set in concerned lines, tears filling her eyes. "How bad is it?"

He pushed himself up. "What the hell are you doing here?" he ground out.

"Told you he'd be pissed," Heath said.

"Her plan worked." Denver took Norton down to the floor and searched his pockets, grabbing a key and tossing it to Heath, who knelt down and uncuffed Ryker, then threw the cuffs to Denver, who secured them firmly around the detective's wrists.

Ryker bit back a moan. "Brock? You okay?" He tried to see past the coffee table.

Brock grunted as Denver tugged him up and then helped him to the sofa after apparently having tied his belt around Brock's thigh. "I'm good," Brock groaned, settling back into the cushions. Blood covered his pants and hands, but some of the color had returned to his face. "How about you?"

"I think I'm all right." Ryker winced as he tried to pull off his jacket. Zara helped him and then pulled his shirt over his head. Pain exploded in his arm again.

Denver instantly knelt and studied the wound. "Bullet went through," he said, probing the wound.

Agony ripped through Ryker's shoulder, and he jerked away.

Heath looked around. "Zara? Do you have a big bandage around here? We can use that until we're back at headquarters."

Zara nodded and jumped to her feet, hustling into the bathroom.

Ryker took in the entire scene in bemused silence. He would rather avoid the hospital and any records. However, Brock needed a doctor. "Brock? You're solid, man. Thanks for rushing in here."

Brock nodded. "Next time I'll bring more than a frying pan." He coughed out a laugh and then groaned again. "We should probably call the police."

Ryker frowned. "Yeah. Let's get you and the detective here to the hospital, and then you and I will call them." He had to cover for his brothers.

Brock frowned. "Um, why aren't you going to the hospital?"

Ryker paused. "I'm undercover and can't." He yanked a dollar out of his back pocket and tossed it at the lawyer. "You're our lawyer now." That way Brock couldn't say a thing about them.

"Okay," Brock said, his gaze knowing.

Heath assisted Brock up. "I'll stick with you guys since I'm Zara's lawyer, and I've met most of the cops around here anyway. We need somebody to grab the real envelope out of Ryker's truck to give to the police for good old Norton there."

Norton watched the proceedings. "I'm going to kill you all."

Ryker snorted. "You are such a moron." Not for one moment had he doubted that Heath and Denver would come for him. His chest warmed. "Let's start at the beginning. Which of you dumb-asses allowed Zara to put herself in danger?"

"Allow? Did you really just say 'allow'?" Zara emerged from the bathroom, her hands full of bandages. "Boy, are we going to talk."

He met her gaze levelly. "Oh, baby, you've got that right."

CHAPTER
32

Zara's hands shook as she finished drawing one of Ryker's big T-shirts over her head in his master bathroom. He'd been shot. The man had actually been shot. Tears pooled in her eyes again, and she shoved them away. Not once in her life had she felt fear like that. She didn't want to go back to her lonely life without him. Never again.

She rubbed lotion into her hands and moved into the bedroom, where he rested on top of the bed. Shirtless, with a bandage covering his right shoulder and his long legs stretched out in sweats. "Are you sure Greg is contained?" The kid had finished waiting for the weather to change and now wanted to hot-wire the truck to go searching for his brothers on his own.

Ryker nodded. "Yeah. He's bunking at Denver's, who's going through all the computer searches with him to prove we're trying to find Dr. Madison. The airports are still closed, but I'm thinking they'll be open tomorrow, and Heath will head to Snowville on the Copper Killer case."

Good. That was good. "How's the shoulder?" she asked.

"Better." He scratched at the bandage. "Denver stitched me up nicer than a doctor would have."

Zara lifted both eyebrows. "Brock Hurst called from the hospital while you were being stitched together. He gave the diary to the cops

along with a cuffed Detective Norton, and it looks like you and I need
to go give statements tomorrow. Right now Brock is handling everything as my lawyer, and he said the cops seem to be reeling a little bit."

"I'm sure. Norton had it all planned out."

"I guess Mayor Pentley has already held two news conferences and
is using the situation to his advantage," Zara said.

"He's a prick," Ryker agreed.

"Also, Brock said that Julie's autopsy results came back. Her body
shows long-term use of several narcotics." Zara's voice wavered, and
her stomach hurt.

"I'm sorry," Ryker murmured.

"Me too."

He kept his gaze on her, his eyes so damn direct. "Come here, baby.
We need to talk."

That voice. Dark and deep…so intent. She moved toward him, her
bare feet padding on the hard concrete floor. "I can't believe Detective
Norton killed Julie." Finally, now that there were answers, the reality
of her friend's death hit her. "Or that she was doing drugs and playing
with those Picalo people. I honestly had no idea." How could she have
lost touch to such a degree? Guilt swamped her.

Ryker snagged her wrist and tugged her onto the bed. "None of
that was your fault."

"I know." But her friend had been in trouble, and she hadn't even
known. First, Julie had ended up with a guy who hit, and then with
another who did drugs and had killed her. "But still, I had no clue.
Part of me feels terrible for her, and the other part is angry that she
lied to me. That she used me for drug money."

Ryker's gaze softened. "It's okay to feel a lot of different things at
once. The entire situation is painful."

She nodded, knowing he was somebody she could truly trust. "You
got shot." Tears filled her eyes again, her heart aching.

"I'm fine." He pulled her, and she slid forward, kneeling next to him. "We need to leave Denver out of our reports when we talk to the police."

She drew in air. "I figured."

He smoothed hair back from her face. "Denver doesn't exist to them, and I'd like to keep it that way as long as possible." Ryker settled his hand over her shoulder—her entire shoulder. "All right?"

"Do you exist?" She looked up to his knowing gaze.

"I'm right here, aren't I?" He caressed down her arm to take her hand.

Warmth surrounded her palm as his enclosed hers in safety. "You know what I mean."

He nodded. "I do know. I exist, and I'll make a statement to the police about Detective Norton."

She eyed him. "All right."

Smoothly, he grasped her waist and lifted her to sit astride him.

Startled, she pressed both palms to his ripped chest. "Do not tear out those stitches."

"I won't." Determination and desire commingled in his eyes, turning them as intense as the raging sky outside. "Now we need a quick chat about who fights psycho killers and who...does...not."

"You were in danger, so I did what I had to do," she returned, lowering her chin.

"I told you to stay safe, and I don't like repeating myself."

Her lips quirked, and she settled more comfortably across his hard thighs, her knees sinking into the bed. "Neither do I," she said softly, leaning closer and nipping across his lips.

He didn't move a muscle but somehow took over the kiss, going deep and taking control. By the time he let her take in air, her head swam, and her body thrummed.

After almost losing him, she realized how much she wanted to stay with him. "Let's reach a compromise on the other issue. How about neither one of us ever deals with psychotic killers?"

He grinned, his lips moving against hers and providing all sorts of delicious tingles. "While I like that thought, just in case, let's agree that I handle danger and you don't." Before she could protest, he continued, "I'm trained, sweetheart. By everyone from martial arts experts to former soldiers to street fighters…I've trained hard. It's my job, not yours."

If he was in danger and she had a chance to help him, she would. "Ryker, I'm fine. The plan worked."

He threaded his fingers through her hair and twisted. Her head lifted, and erotic pain tingled around her scalp. "You're not listening to me," he rumbled.

"I'm listening but not agreeing," she breathed.

"If anything happened to you, my heart would just be cut out for good." He pulled her to him and kissed her, his tongue sweeping inside her mouth.

His sweet words warmed her heart while his deep kiss heated her a lot farther south. She moaned into his mouth and pushed closer, flattening out atop him like a kitten stretching on a boulder.

He rolled them over, his body bracketing hers, his kiss stealing everything she was and would ever be. She kissed him back, caressing his flanks, careful to stay away from his bandages. Hard ridges and smooth muscle filled her palms, and she marveled at the strength. So much power right beneath her fingertips.

Pushing up, he tugged his shirt over her head. "So pretty," he murmured, kissing along her jawline. "Smooth as silk and twice as fragile."

She arched up into him, her eyes closing, as his lips teased hers again.

With him, everything feminine inside her rushed to the surface—

soft and powerful all at once. She melted beneath his kiss, her body settling with definite welcome. "Ryker. I was so scared you'd be hurt," she whispered.

"Never." He lifted up again and looked at her, his breath hot as he smoothly kicked off his sweats. "Trust me, Zara. I've survived the worst already. But you have to trust me and stay out of danger. Please."

If there was danger, of any kind, she'd fight it with him. "I do trust you." It was all she could give.

His broad hands trembled as he cupped her cheeks with reverent grace. "So much beauty and intelligence," he murmured, almost to himself, sounding thoughtful. He caressed along her jaw and down her neck, pressing against the pulse point rapidly pounding for him.

Her thighs trembled beneath his. He slid one muscled knee up, spreading her legs. Then he leaned over her, his mouth taking her again. A claiming. She could sense it—something different in Ryker, something possessive and hot. He took her mouth. No mercy, no gentleness.

Ryker Jones completely unleashed.

Jolts of pleasure shot through her, and she returned his kiss, raising her knees on either side of his hips. He slowly invaded her, pushing inside, the crest of his cock unrelenting as it stretched her. She gasped against his mouth, her body arching into the hard planes of his.

He gave no quarter, stroking inside her, each push going deeper. Every hitch stoked the fire inside her, pulsing sensitive nerves alive. The primal movements and the raw tension swelling through the room trapped her as surely as his kiss. Only Ryker could bring this to her. She softened beneath him, taking all that he gave and letting him have all of her.

He paused as if sensing her submission. Then, with a deep growl, he started to pound. Deep and full, he filled her, over and over again, his thrusts deliberate and complete.

She broke first, crying out his name, shutting her eyes against sparks of color. She bucked, almost violently, her body wracked with wave upon wave of fierce pleasure. He hammered harder, his breath ragged, and shuddered as he came.

"Ryker," she murmured, her eyelids already closing. She caressed down his back to his butt and smiled. "Mine." With that one last, satisfying word, she drifted into sleep.

* * *

Ryker snuggled Zara against him, making sure the comforter covered her completely. The night's events—all of them—seemed to have exhausted her. She slept so trustingly against him, her dark hair splayed across his arm and the pillow.

So small and perfect…and brave.

Not for one second had she reconsidered walking into danger for him. And he hadn't missed the fact that she'd failed to make the promise to never do it again. If anything happened to the sweet woman, he wouldn't survive.

Making her happy would keep her with him, and it shocked him how much he needed her to stay.

Not once had he considered *forever* with a woman before Zara had started cooking him dinner and making him laugh. Now he couldn't imagine life without her.

For nearly an hour he tried to sleep and then gave up, heading down to the offices. While he wasn't surprised to find Heath poring over files about the serial killer case, he was a little taken aback to see Greg and Denver working with him. "Boys?" he asked.

Heath shrugged. "Kid hacked the system last night and had a

bunch of questions, so what the hell? We apparently can't keep him out."

Greg smiled, looking twelve years old again.

Ryker sighed. "Fine."

Heath nudged Greg in the arm. "Tell him your grand plan, kid."

Pink tinged Greg's cheeks. "I thought I should get a red wig, act like a chick, and draw this guy in."

Ryker barked out a laugh. "Are we that desperate?"

Heath nodded, his jaw looking harder than rock. "Yeah, but first we need to find Special Agent Jackson."

Ryker lost the humor. "Agreed," he murmured.

"The airport has been cleared, and I'm taking the nine a.m. flight to Snowville," Heath said, his duffel already packed behind him.

"I'll go, too," Ryker said.

"No. I'm going to Snowville, Denver and Greg are heading to Utah to investigate where Greg used to live, and you're staying here to cover Zara and figure out your next step," Heath said, his gaze direct.

Ryker blinked. "No."

"Yes," Denver countered.

"We've been talking about it," Heath chimed in. "Even though Zara's cleared in the murder, you guys have decisions to make, and we're giving you that time. Once either of the other cases opens up, we'll need you. Right now take care of your woman. If I had one, I would in a heartbeat."

Ryker rocked back as the thought of how close he'd come to losing her hit him. Hard. Yet the idea of the three brothers going in different directions, and toward danger, didn't sit well. "I appreciate you guys looking out for me."

Heath rolled his eyes. "Just take the reprieve. It's temporary."

Wasn't it always?

CHAPTER
33

Zara finished the spicy scrambled eggs cooked by a very quiet Denver Jones. She had no illusions that Jones was his real last name, just like Ryker's wasn't Jones. When she'd asked, they'd both looked at her blankly.

"Nobody ever told me," Denver had said.

It was the most Zara had heard the quiet computer expert say without being prodded. She smiled at him and then fought a frown as she glanced at Greg. For the first time since she'd met Greg, he refused to eat. Instead, he kept looking at the storm, which had lightened slightly outside.

"We're gonna drive if the airport closes again, right?" he asked the room at large.

"Yes," Heath said, sitting on the sofa next to Ryker, both of them eating eggs.

Denver was in the kitchen, and Grams twittered at his side, offering tips on spices. He seemed to be genuinely enjoying himself, discussing food with her, so Zara let them be.

Zara studied Ryker. He ate slowly, his gaze on Greg, appearing every bit as protective as she knew him to be with her. She burrowed into her warm bathrobe over her long burgundy nightgown. It was a tad old-fashioned, but it was warm, and for some reason, it amused Ryker.

Ryker's phone buzzed, and his head jerked back. He read the screen and gave some odd signal to his brothers.

Heath and Denver launched into motion, both jogging toward the door.

Ryker stood and dropped a kiss on Zara's head before heading for the door too. "We have an alarm on a different case. Make sure he stays here until I come back," he whispered, moving past her and quietly shutting the door.

Greg frowned. "I hate being left here." He walked over to the window and looked down. "This storm has to end."

"It will, sweetie." Grams bustled around the kitchen, cleaning the counters.

Lights flashed outside, and the loud hum of a helicopter pierced the noise of the storm.

Greg frowned. "That's weird." He moved toward the north wall of windows.

Lights flashed at the west windows.

Zara turned her head. "Is that a helicopter? In this storm?"

Greg stilled. His head swung around. "Run!" He leaped for her just as the windows crashed in on both walls.

She screamed and ducked her head from flying glass, reaching for Greg to push behind her. But he moved faster than she could track, shoving her onto the couch and leaping over her to the other side.

What the heck? She bounced off the leather and scrambled to her feet, her head swimming. Greg fought hand-to-hand with a man in all black, kicking the guy right under the chin. A rope hung from the guy's belt and led outside the window.

She swallowed and ran around the couch to help, trying to avoid the glass with her bare feet.

A second man, also in black, stood just inside the northern windows, his hand on a rope connected to his belt. Lights flashed again outside the windows. He held something in his hands, but she couldn't tell what it was.

"Greg," she screamed, running for him.

The guy fighting with Greg punched him hard in the face, and the kid windmilled back, quickly regained his equilibrium, and charged. He tackled the guy, and they crashed to the floor.

The guy by the window rushed forward, and Zara jumped between him and the two fighting on the ground. She planted her feet and then shot a knee up, nailing him in the groin. He grabbed her by the neck and shook.

Pain ripped through her trachea. Her eyes watered, and she struggled, punching and kicking.

Body armor. The fucker was wearing some sort of armor—definitely a bulletproof vest. She twisted her hips and kicked his knee twice. Thick boots protected his ankles, so she kept her aim high.

His hold tightened, and her lungs protested. Her vision swam.

Grams appeared at her side, flying at the man.

He casually turned, grabbed her arm, and threw her into the counter. She hit with a dull thud, fell to the ground, and didn't get back up.

"Grams," Zara squeaked, her knees wobbling. Desperate, she dug her nails into the guy's arm, trying to loosen her neck from his grip.

His eyes were a dark brown with glee filling them. He liked hurting her. She struggled harder while furniture crashed behind her. Was Greg okay?

Finally the guy gave one final squeeze and swung with his free hand. His fist smashed into her cheekbone, and she flew across the room, slamming into the granite counter by Grams and then hitting the hard floor. Pain exploded through her head and her hands, followed by agony in her knee.

Grams groaned and rolled over, opening her eyes.

Zara pushed to her feet, her head still swimming, and turned around.

The first guy held Greg in a headlock while the other guy pushed a needle into the kid's arm. In less than a second, Greg's eyelids fluttered shut, and he went limp.

"Greg," Zara croaked, her voice not working. She took a step forward.

The first man turned and ran for the window, pushed off the sill, and flew into the open side door of the helicopter. It was so unreal as to be hazy.

The guy with Greg hustled forward, all smooth muscle, and reached the window.

"No!" Zara ran for him and reached his back, jumping on. She couldn't let Greg go out that window. They'd never see him again.

The guy roared and pivoted, throwing her back against the couch. He handed Greg to a man actually leaning out of the helicopter. What if they dropped him? They were a story up.

Zara pushed to her feet, her entire face screaming in pain. Greg was safely in the helicopter. Oh God. They'd taken Greg. The guy at the window stepped through almost easily, jumping a couple of feet to the helicopter. The craft rocked when he landed.

Shouts came from outside the apartment followed by running steps. Ryker would get there too late.

Zara grabbed her phone out of her purse on the floor and shoved it down her nightgown, which was tight at the waist and held it in place. Then she bunched her knees. There was only one thing to do. Shutting off her brain, she launched into motion, running full bore for the window. "Phone, Grams," she hissed. She jumped, her feet touched the sill, and she pushed off. At the last second, she turned, so when she hit inside the helicopter, her shoulders and back took the brunt of the pain.

Her head slammed back into metal, and darkness slashed across her vision. Her last thought as unconsciousness took over was a quick prayer that they didn't throw her out of the helicopter.

* * *

"Zara," Ryker roared, clearing the sofa table and couch in one long jump. He reached the window, and strong arms clasped him from behind. He struggled furiously, trying to get out, as the helicopter banked away and up.

"It's too far," Heath said into his ear, his hold stronger than steel but his voice calm. "The helicopter door is closed now. Even if you could make it, which there's no way, you'd just hit the side and drop. You can't save her if you're dead." He waited until Ryker stopped fighting before loosening his hold.

Ryker watched the helicopter glide up and away, his chest burning. He had never seen anything like that. "They got Greg, too," he ground out.

"I know." Heath released him.

Ryker slowly turned around to see Denver helping Grams up. She was pale but steady. "Zara jumped out the window," she whispered.

"Yeah." Ryker would never forget the sight of her leaping into the storm. He'd run upstairs the second they'd heard a helicopter. Make that two of them.

"Fucking brave," Denver said quietly, his eyes beyond tortured. He scouted the west windows and kicked glass out of the way.

Ryker clenched his hands into fists. "How did they find us?"

"Don't know." Heath moved to help Grams to a chair not covered with glass. "My guess is they followed our trap but just watched us before striking." He scrubbed his face. "Until now, of course. The dings from the safe house must have been a diversion so they could grab Greg."

Heat rushed through Ryker. "We'll get him back. Them back."
He said the words as a vow, trying to banish the raw terror eating
at his heart. His gaze caught on Grams's desperate eyes, and it was
like being kicked in the chest. "I promise," he vowed. No way would
he let that sweet elderly lady down—no matter what he had to do or
become.

Denver stood now by the door, his body alert and no doubt tuned
into any more surprises from downstairs. "I'll get on the computer
right now and try to track the helicopters by satellite. We find the lost,
Ryker. It's what we do, and we'll find them." His tone was low and
determined with a new hardness—a deadly edge.

Ryker nodded. Zara and Greg were now beyond lost. "Heath?"

Heath nodded. "Good idea. Try to track the trap we set on safe
house three to see how Dr. Madison traced us." He paused. "I guess I
shouldn't assume Madison is the one who has Greg and Zara?"

"It has to be her," Ryker said, his gaze going back to the snow
blowing through the broken windows. He spied Zara's purse by the
door with the contents all spilled out. He charged over and lifted it
up, quickly rifling through everything.

"What?" Denver asked.

"Her cell phone isn't here." He turned and looked at the window.

Grams coughed. "She said 'phone.' Before she jumped, she pushed
something down her nightgown and said 'phone' to me."

"We can GPS track it," Heath hissed.

"Yes," Ryker said. Smart woman. "She would've known. If she
shoved it in her nightgown, she might've thought it was the only way
to track Greg." Though it had been fucking crazy.

Heath's eyes lit with determination. "They'll search her pockets."

Hopefully it didn't just fall out in the helicopter. Ryker looked
again at the gaping window, somehow wishing to get one more look
at her.

"I'm on it." Denver turned and ran for the stairs.

Ryker hurried over and assisted Grams up. "How about I get you to one of the other apartments that have windows keeping the storm out? You need to rest after that fight."

Grams shook her head. "I want to help." Her voice shook as much as her hands.

Ryker took her gently by the arms, failure making his hands shake too. "I promise I'll get your granddaughter back, and when she gets here, she'll kick my butt for not taking care of you. Please go rest, and then we'll figure out what to do."

Grams nodded and headed toward her bedroom. Ryker waited until she'd shut the door. "We have image and GPS satellite tracking going. Something will break," he said.

Heath frowned. "How are you so calm?"

It was taking everything Ryker had not to rip his apartment apart even more than it already was. "I'm not calm, not really." Heat seared him from within, turning quickly to ice. "If I give in to the panic or the rage, then I can't think. Right now I have to think, and so do you. We have to be smarter than they are, and we have to believe we'll get Zara and Greg home. Any other reality is unacceptable."

"This isn't your fault," Heath said.

At the words, Ryker's breath heated. Fury clenched his hands. He turned and punched the wall as hard as he could. Then again.

Heath grabbed him from behind and yanked him away, struggling hard until Ryker subsided. "There it is. Okay. You let it out, and now you're okay. Now you're in control, and now you can think." His voice remained low and soothing.

Ryker breathed out several times, and his vision cleared. He relaxed, and Heath released him. "Shit. I lost it."

"It's okay to freak out a little." Heath frowned at the battered wall. "Again, not your fault."

"Yeah, it is. Zara and Greg are mine to protect."

Heath leveled him with a look. "They're family, which means they're ours to protect."

Ryker nodded, his throat closing. God, they had to be all right. "We have to find them."

CHAPTER
34

Dr. Isobel Madison crossed her legs and continued typing on the new computer, though all she wanted to do was pace the small office and peer outside like a child awaiting the tooth fairy. But she had work to do, and she'd keep her senses about her. After all this time, Greg really was alive. Her soldiers had discovered him after tracking the men trying to find her.

Truth be told, she'd forgotten all about the preteen. What a marvelous job she'd done with him. And to think that he'd somehow found the Lost boys for her.

She bit back a giggle. Life was very often on her side.

Her work would continue, but the procedure was bogging her down. While she had two men—Todd and Elton—doing her bidding, neither had the connections or drive she required to rebuild the program. The men she'd created and trained would help her. Maybe Elton would be a good partner in that. He was certainly driven.

The incentive for the creations from her past should arrive any moment…in the form of young Greg.

Her door opened, and Sheriff Elton Cobb strode in. "Is the dickhead back yet?" he asked.

Isobel forced a smile. "Not yet, and I've asked you to remain civil. We need Todd and his men a little longer." Then the entire Protect group could fry in a volcano for all she cared.

"Do we?" Elton asked, obviously unimpressed with the self-taught soldiers. "Your four soldiers piloted the helicopters and took the boy. You didn't need the extra Protect morons."

"This time," she said smoothly. "Think of Todd's men as foot soldiers. We need them for strength and numbers right now, but when we restart my program, we may not need them. Or, more likely, we'll just weed out Todd and his big believers, and use the rest as soldiers and guards." That was an admirable plan.

"That's fine, but I need to get back home and to work soon. I'm here because you required help, but at some point you're coming to me," Elton said.

She nodded. "That has always been my plan. After I no longer need Todd or his Protect soldiers."

"If he gets any idea you intend to continue your work, he'll try to kill you," Elton said, his muscular hands planting on the desk.

She stood and moved around the desk to lean against him. "Then I expect you to defend me."

"You know I will," he said, his blue eyes darkening.

"Of course."

"I hope you'll remain with me this time," he said slowly.

She nodded. He did have sadistic qualities she quite enjoyed. She stretched up onto her toes and pressed her mouth against his.

He bit her.

Pain lanced along her lips, but she allowed it. "You're becoming predicable," she murmured.

Wrong thing to say.

He clamped his hands on her arms and yanked her over the desk, turning her and shoving her facedown. A rough hand ripped up her skirt, and after a quick unzipping of his pants, he shoved inside her. "You're lucky you're not wearing underwear," he breathed against her ear.

Pain filled her. She hadn't been anywhere near ready for him. He gripped her shoulders with bruising fingers and hammered inside her, grunting into her neck. Her face rubbed against her stapler, and she tried to push it away with her chin.

He laughed and grabbed the stapler.

Her body seized.

"What in the world could we do with this?" he asked, embedded in her, not moving.

She shivered but knew not to speak.

He ran the cool metal down her back and over her butt. "Ever been stapled?"

She trembled.

He chuckled and slid it around her hip and over her clit. "You're gonna come either now or with staples in you." He pushed the device against her.

She pushed back, twisted, and exploded in an orgasm so hard, tears filled her eyes.

He dropped the stapler, grabbed her hips, and stroked inside her three times, shuddering as he came. Then he pulled out and flipped her around. "You are one sick fuck, you know that?" He leaned down and kissed her lips.

She kissed him back and pulled her clothes back into place. "Look who's talking." Then she leaned back, quite satisfied. The darkness in him drew her, and she should probably spend some time studying that fact. When she had time, of course.

He nipped her lip. "I like that you think you're going to win this."

She tilted her head and studied him. Sometimes she forgot he wasn't just a country sheriff. While he certainly lacked her intelligence, sometimes evil held a brilliance of its own. She'd be a fool to underestimate him. "I was hoping we'd win together."

"Hmm." He leaned down and retrieved the stapler, opening it and sliding the slightly exposed staple along her knuckles and hand. She curled her fingers around the edge of the desk and tried to ignore the scratches. "Every once in a while, I feel like you're playing me," he said.

Of course she was. "Never. Everyone but you." She held perfectly still.

He flattened his palm over the stapler.

She kept his gaze. "I wouldn't."

"Why not?" he whispered. "You love a good bite."

"That's a staple," she said, her voice clipped. "It would leave a mark, and you like me unmarked."

Then he lifted her hand and kissed her unblemished skin "You're perfect, and you know it." He grabbed her waist and lifted her onto the desk, shoving her onto her back. Tugging up her skirt, he dropped, his face right between her legs, beginning to use his mouth against her clit.

As her thighs began to tremble and pleasure filled her, she recalculated her plans. Sheriff Cobb was still useful, and the wild part of him, the side she couldn't quite control, intrigued her enough to make her want to keep him. For a while, anyway.

* * *

Zara slowly came to, noticing her head ached and her butt was cold. She gasped and opened her eyelids, her body flashing awake.

"You're all right," Greg said, sitting about three yards away across a cold room. "Maybe a concussion."

Nausea ballooned in her belly, and she took several deep breaths, looking around. Grungy white cinder blocks made up the walls except where there was a steel door, dirt covered the floor, and one lone light bulb swung from a frayed wire dangling from the ceiling. Both she and Greg sat on dirt, and her housecoat was gone, leaving her in her burgundy nightgown. Although it was formfitting, at least it was long. "Where are we?"

"Dunno." He rubbed his face. "Whatever they gave me knocked me out until just a few minutes ago."

"Have you tried the door?" She pushed to her feet, and her legs wobbled. Slowly, she breathed out. Okay. She shifted her weight. Man, the phone was pressed under her right breast before the gown tightened at the waist. Apparently they hadn't searched her that closely.

"Yep. Locked." Greg eyed her. "Probably well guarded by guys with guns. Maybe sit back down? You look like—"

Dizziness assailed her, and she dropped.

Greg lunged and slid between her head and the wall. Her temple glanced off his chest, and she kept sliding down. He grabbed her by the armpits and settled her gently, pressing her back against the bricks. "Sit for a few minutes," he murmured, crouching next to her. "We really can't do anything at the moment."

Zara looked around the dismal room and repeated, "Where are we?"

Greg shook his head. "I have no idea." His brown eyes sobered. "I'm sorry I got you into this."

She forced a grin and gave up when the bruised tissue in her face protested. "I jumped into the helicopter on my own." Thank God they hadn't just shoved her right back out.

Greg patted her arm. "That was the bravest thing I've ever seen. Why in the world would you jump?"

She blinked. "I couldn't let them take you."

He leaned back, his face losing expression. "You jumped just to save me? I mean, me?" His voice cracked at the end.

She reached out to touch his arm. "Of course. I'd do anything to protect you, sweetie."

His eyes filled. "Okay. Um. All right."

Her heart broke in two, right then and there. "We'll be okay." She leaned over to whisper, just in case. "I have my phone."

He shook his head. "Where?"

"Solar plexus region." In fact, the plastic was rubbing against her skin. "Ryker will be able to track us."

For the first time since she'd awakened, hope filled Greg's eyes. "You're brilliant."

She coughed out a laugh.

A scrape sounded, and the door shoved inward. A man in green camo gestured her out with a long black gun. Tall and broad, he was bald with deep blue eyes—maybe around fifty years old.

She stood in her bare feet and kept Greg behind her. "Who are you?"

"Shut up and move." He gestured with the gun. "I have no problem shooting either one of you."

Fear coated her throat. She swallowed and walked outside. They had been in an outbuilding. Icy trees surrounded them, and snow covered the ground. The wind chilled her right through, and she rubbed her arms. Snow covered her feet and she shivered. Another soldier, the one who'd hit her in the face in the apartment, stood nearby. "Move it," he said.

She glanced down at a boot-stomped trail and headed toward the soldier. "Where are we?" she asked over her shoulder to the bald guy.

"Doesn't matter." He prodded Greg in the back with the gun.

Greg moved silently, keeping close to her. "Just go, Zara. It's too cold out here to make a move."

She slipped in the snow but kept on moving, trying to keep her feet from freezing off. As she rounded a bend, she paused at seeing a sprawling western-style log lodge against the mountains. The word

PROTECT was burned into the wood above a door in an intricate and bold pattern.

In the far distance, maybe about a mile down a snowy road, stood what looked like a huge barn. Men milled around, some shoveling snow, some practicing target shooting.

Greg nudged her toward the lodge, so she continued on, following the guy who'd hit her up some stairs and into a large gathering room with a homey stone fireplace that lay empty and waiting. Greg reached her side and looked around. Closed doors were in the far wall, and wide staircases led both up and down.

Her feet hurt from the icy snow.

The soldier started down the stairs, so Zara followed, allowing the heat from the place to sink into her bones. Her aching feet slid on the wood, and Greg caught her arm to steady her. He was so calm, she had to wonder about his upbringing. Not by one breath had he given away the anger and fear he must be feeling. Maybe the drugs were still in his system.

They reached a landing that opened up into a small conference room. A long hallway, lined with black-and-white photos of different landscapes, headed down another way. Zara followed the soldier down it to a nice wooden door, and he shoved it open.

Tension suddenly spiraled around them, and she knew without looking that Greg had gone on full alert.

A woman sat behind a desk, her black hair in a bun, her blue eyes sizzling. "Greg. It's so good to see you alive, boy. I have to say, I'm having a rather proud moment."

Greg sucked in air, his fear palpable.

Zara slid to the side to stand in front of him, instinctively shielding him.

"Inside," the bald soldier ordered from behind her.

She moved into the room and waited for Greg to do the same. The bald soldier followed them and shut the door, leaning back against it. Two guest chairs, both of a smooth log design, sat before the glass-topped desk. A wide window took up one wall, and diplomas—tons and tons of them—decorated the rest of the walls.

"Sit," the woman said, her lascivious gaze aimed over Zara's shoulder at Greg.

Bile rose in Zara's throat, but she took a chair, careful to walk normally even though she probably had frost bite on her toes. The phone couldn't be seen in her nightgown, probably. She sat and put her hands in her lap.

Greg sat, no expression on his hard face. "Dr. Madison."

Oh no. Zara gaped. "You're the doctor who's done so much damage?"

"No—" Dr. Madison began and then caught the eye of the soldier behind Zara. She cleared her throat. "Yes, but I'm trying to rectify my wrongs. We made mistakes in messing with science, and I'm fixing that. Right, Todd?"

"Yes," the soldier said. "We're destroying all the aberrations, and then your soul will be clean."

"Destroying?" Zara whispered.

Dr. Madison nodded. "I'm afraid we'll have to start with you, Greg."

CHAPTER
35

Ryker hacked into Sheriff Cobb's files at work without a qualm, while Denver tried to track Zara's cell phone and Heath worked on satellite imagery through the storm. They'd moved their computers into the central room to all work around the same table and coordinate their efforts.

"What about the Copper Killer case?" Ryker asked, his shoulder still aching. "Heath, you can go. We'll cover this."

"You're kidding, right?" Heath's head jerked up. "Zara and Greg are family...my first priority. I'll help the FBI out after we're all safe."

Ryker's throat closed, and he nodded. Family. Yeah. He held on to that fact to keep himself from panicking and blowing up the entire building. He'd sent Grams to stay with a friend far away from the offices, just in case another attack was coming. "Dr. Madison won't kill Zara. She won't." He kept the words going in his head like a mantra.

Heath set his tablet down. "Madison won't kill Zara because she'll want to study her and get into her head, figure out what kind of woman you would love. Plus, if Madison's main goal is to recapture all of us, either for herself or for Sheriff Cobb, she must know Zara is great bait for you. Logic dictates that Zara is fine for the time being."

Some of the heat in Ryker's chest cooled. He'd gotten worked up and lost his temper more in the last week than he had in years, and that had to stop. "She wants to study Greg, so he's safe. If he doesn't do something stupid."

Heath rubbed his eyes. "What do you mean?"

"The kid is trained, but he might try to spring Zara, and she isn't trained." Greg could get shot.

Heath nodded. "She would've told Greg about the phone, so he knows we're tracking them. Greg will hold tight."

Ryker tried to calm his racing heart. He'd done a shitty job of protecting them, and he hoped to hell he'd be able to apologize.

"Isn't your fault," Heath said, not looking up from his tablet.

Ryker nodded, his head and heart filled with Zara and Greg. They had to be all right. What if Madison decided she wanted only Greg and not Ryker and his brothers? Would Zara be safe then or unnecessary?

"Stop running scenarios through your mind." Heath looked up again, concern sharpening his voice. "Get back to the computer and get to work."

Ryker gave him a look, then faced his computer to rip through Sheriff Cobb's life to see if Isobel Madison had made appearances after the boys home burned down. He worked for about thirty minutes before taking his notes out to the table. "Cobb has purchased tons of land, in different states, including the thirty acres that used to hold the boys home."

"What about Cobb and Madison?" Heath asked.

Ryker flipped through his notes. "I'm not sure if they ever met up again, but Cobb took several vacations through the years that don't seem like him. Spas and faraway getaways." His phone dinged, and he drew back. "What the fuck?"

Running into his office, he checked the alarm on his computer, looking up just as Heath came into the room. "There's an alert on the safe house. Another one."

Heath's brow furrowed. "Why? I mean, Dr. Madison just took Greg. Why would she infiltrate the house?"

Ryker shook his head. "I don't know. Gut says it isn't her." But who it was, he had no clue. He yanked his gun from a desk drawer and tucked it at his waist. "I'll go check it out." He was already running through the office and almost to the door.

"Stop," Heath bellowed. "You need backup, and you were just shot. Your shoulder has to be burning."

"It's fine." Ryker turned. "You're a million times better on the computer than I am. I need you on the image satellites and Denver on the phone tracking. Somebody has to check out the safe house, just in case, and it's me. Maybe it'll be a lead to Zara." He didn't wait for his brother to argue, launching back into a run.

Within seconds, he'd pulled the truck out of the garage and onto the mostly empty roads, trying to ignore the pain. The freezing snow battered the truck, and visibility sucked, even though it was midday.

He reached the block before the safe house, his heart thrumming, his head clouded with thoughts of Zara in danger. Taking several deep breaths, he parked and then ran through the storm. The cold slammed through him, finally bringing clarity. Good. He needed to be focused.

Even so, as he silently crept into the backyard and into the house, he had trouble concentrating. So he closed his eyes and listened. One heartbeat. Okay. Just one. He could handle the intruder. The beat was calm and steady...and somewhat faint. The person had to be at the other end of the house.

He moved with stealth, crossing the kitchen and entering the living room.

A punch caught him unaware, exploding agony across his jaw. The force threw him across the living room and into a cheap card table, which splintered into pieces. He fell, rolled, and jumped up at the guy, who was supposed to be in the back room.

Had he managed to subdue his heartbeat? Who the hell was he? His attacker was his size, fit, and wearing a ski mask. He moved gracefully, light on his feet and no doubt well trained.

One solid punch to the gut, and the guy grunted, before swinging again for Ryker's head.

Ryker ducked and came up with an uppercut, his damaged shoulder protesting.

The guy's head jerked, and he growled as he moved forward.

"Shit. What's your jaw made of?" Ryker hissed, punching for the gut and nose.

The guy took the hit and kicked out, nailing Ryker in the ribs. Pain lanced through Ryker's torso, and he shoved it down, going for a one-two punch that threw his attacker back into the door frame. It cracked.

The guy shoved off the wood and tackled Ryker, propelling them both over the dingy sofa. They hit the coffee table and smashed onto the dirty carpet, both angling for position.

Ryker clapped his hands on the guy's ears and flipped backward to his feet, then retreated toward the kitchen. The guy rolled and did a similar backflip and instantly angled to the right, his hands in fists. He kept moving, his gaze intense in the dark room, his movements slow but sure.

Hell. The guy could really move.

While Ryker wanted to be fair, and he really wanted to know if he could take this guy, he needed to know where, or rather who, Isobel Madison was. So he reached in his waistband for his gun.

Cold metal instantly rested against the base of his neck.

Fuck.

He stilled and breathed out. Not one slice of sound had given the man in the basement away as he'd climbed the stairs. If Ryker didn't know better, he'd guess the guy was a ghost.

But the gun pressed to his nape belied that theory.

He lowered his hands, waiting for an opening.

The guy behind him didn't give it and, instead, relieved Ryker of his gun. Then he moved back and to the side, his gun still pointed at Ryker, until he was just a yard or so away from his buddy. He wore a similar ski mask as the other guy and stood shoulder to shoulder with him. Solid muscle, and both moved with grace.

Isobel Madison could certainly afford the best—if that's who they were. Or perhaps she'd attracted some dangerous enemies. Just as likely. These guys were trained killers. Maybe Greg hadn't just been hysterical and paranoid.

Ryker wiped blood off his chin. His entire face pounded from the hit. "Where is Isobel Madison?" he asked quietly, trying to make out any of their features in the darkened room.

The guy with the gun glanced at his partner and jerked his head.

The other guy reached behind himself and flipped the light switch. One dingy light in the center of the room lit up.

Ryker blinked and kept them both in his sight. He couldn't make it to the bedroom or the kitchen without being shot. While he could duck below the couch, there wasn't a good move after that point.

Both men stilled. Tension swelled through the room, causing the hair to rise along Ryker's arms.

They didn't move. Just stared at him.

He stared back. "We're at a standstill here. Tell me where Isobel is, and we'll each go our separate ways."

"Who are you?" the guy with the gun whispered.

Ryker frowned. There was something familiar about the voice, but he couldn't place it. "None of your fucking business. Who are you? More important, where is your boss?"

The armed man looked at his gun, looked back up at Ryker, and then slowly lowered the barrel a couple of inches, as if he didn't want to point it at Ryker's chest.

Ryker stiffened and drew to his full height.

"What's your name?" the gunman asked.

Ryker flashed his teeth. "Fred. Fred Johnson. Yours?"

The guy lifted the gun and pointed it, his hand steady. "Try again."

Something, call it instinct, told Ryker that there was no way the guy would shoot him. Why, he had no clue. But his body relaxed. "No. Your name?"

"Shit," the other guy muttered. "Can you believe this?" His voice held a small, very small, thread of uncertainty.

The armed guy shook his head.

Ryker tensed to jump across the couch and tackle the guy with the gun.

"You won't make it," the other guy said casually.

Ryker cut his gaze to him. "He won't shoot me."

"Won't I?" the armed guy asked softly.

"No." Ryker edged back a couple of inches. "I don't know why, but you decided not to shoot me the second the lights came on. Care to explain why?"

Several beats of silence filled the tension-soaked room. "In due time. For now, why don't you tell us why you're searching for Isobel Madison?" the armed guy asked.

"Do you work for her?" Ryker asked.

"Hell no," the other guy said. "No way."

Truth. Definitely the ring of truth. Ryker frowned. "Yet you set up a trap, and when I went looking for her, you followed the string here."

"This is your trap," the armed guy said. "We just were nice enough to enter it upon your kind invitation."

Ryker lifted his head. "You're looking for her, too?"

"Fuck no," the other guy said.

Jesus. "Stop talking in riddles. Either you shoot me or you take off the masks. If you do neither, I'm turning and heading out the door." At this point, he didn't seem to have any other options.

The unarmed guy looked to the armed guy, who shrugged.

"Fine." He shoved the gun into the back of his trousers.

Ryker tensed, prepared to lunge.

"Wait." The guy held out a hand and slowly reached up to rip off his mask while the other guy did the same.

Similar bone structure, angled faces, deep gray eyes. They looked alike. "Who are you?" he snapped.

The armed guy studied him, his gaze intense. "If I had to guess, I'd say we're family. This is Jory, and I'm Matt. Now, who the hell are you?"

* * *

Zara jumped from her seat. "You will not harm this boy."

Dr. Madison waved her back down. "Oh, he's going to die, but just relax yourself. Right now we need him as bait." She flashed extremely white teeth in a parody of a smile.

Greg snarled.

Madison drummed perfect nails on the desk. Her hands were small, dainty even, with a light bandage resting on her left one, below the knuckles. "I can have Todd here torture Miss Zara until you tell me what I want to know." She narrowed her gaze on Zara's face. "Actually, I would like to know how much you can take. My Ryker wouldn't fall for just any woman, and the way you jumped out a window to stay with this kid? Tough. Definitely tough."

Her Ryker? "Lady, you're batshit crazy," Zara muttered.

Madison's smile widened. "That settles the matter, then. I believe I know just the person you should spend time with."

Todd pushed away from the door. "I don't want that sheriff around any of us. He's not right in the head, and he needs to go back home."

Madison looked up and nodded. "I agree, but right now we don't have a choice. He owns this land, and we need it for training." Her gaze lightened. "Plus, he has certain proclivities, and I think he'd enjoy demonstrating those to Zara before he leaves town." She lowered her voice to a husky whisper. "Do you think Ryker will accept you damaged?"

Greg coughed. "Ryker will cut off your head, reach in, and discover firsthand that you don't have a heart if you even think of harming Zara. You think I'm bad? Or my brothers? Ryker is fuckin' crazy, lady."

Madison clapped her hands together once. "How wonderful. You've bonded with Ryker." She frowned. "Let's see. Ryker, Heath, and Denver were thick as could be. I'd wondered. I really did." Her lips twisted. "Very similar to *your* brothers. Remember them?"

"Yes. Are Chance, Kyle, and Wade still alive?" Greg spoke quickly as if he couldn't stop himself, his voice cracking and his entire body going stiff. He held his breath at the last.

Zara reached out and grabbed his hand to give him support and then held her breath, too.

"Of course." Triumph glittered in Madison's eyes.

Zara breathed out. Good. Joy nearly filled her to compete with the fear.

Greg didn't even twitch. "Where are they?"

Oh, you'll see them soon enough," Madison said quietly. "I promise."

Greg sucked in air, and his chin went down. His head tilted to the side, and he stared intently at the doctor. A chill wafted through the room.

"What?" Madison snapped.

"You…you've lost them." Wonder filled Greg's voice. "They got away." He glanced frantically around, his gaze landing on Todd. "Oh shit. This guy wouldn't be here if…if… The commander is gone? You left him?"

Madison paled. "Yes, he's gone."

Greg swallowed and suddenly looked his young age again. "Dead?" His voice quivered.

Madison nodded, sorrow in her eyes. "Yes."

Greg shook his head, his mouth dropping open. "I-I didn't think he could die."

Zara shifted her weight in the chair. She needed to get the upper hand somehow. "Where are Greg's brothers?"

Madison arched one perfectly plucked eyebrow. "I don't know, but they'll come back for Greg here. Like I said: bait."

Greg chuckled, the sound full of joy. "No, they won't. They're gone, really gone." He turned to Zara, his eyes alive fully. "They're free, Zara. Can you believe it? They actually got away."

Madison slammed her hand down on the desk. "You're about to be beaten, young man."

Zara caught her breath. She had to turn the focus away from the boy. "Are you with Todd here or with the sheriff? I mean, we know you and the sheriff bumped uglies years ago, so it has to be still going on, right? Are you seeing them both at the same time?" She kept her voice at a stage whisper.

Madison drew back. "Of course not. Todd and I are together, and we share a glorious vision for the future. Don't we, sweetheart?"

Todd waited a moment to speak. "We better, woman."

Sparks flew from Madison's eyes, but she kept her face in serene lines.

Oh, that bitch had both men fooled, now, didn't she? Zara lowered her chin, keeping her gaze on the scientist. "It doesn't smell right to me. You wouldn't be seeing both men and hiding it, now, would you?" The sharp rap to the back of her head had her crying out. Her skull ached, and her eyes bugged.

"Thank you, Todd," Madison said, sending him a beaming smile.

Greg jumped up and turned to face Todd. "You ever think of touching her again, and I'll take out your still-beating heart and eat it. Believe it or not, it wouldn't be my first heart."

Man, the kid could be tough. But Todd was armed, and from the sound of things, he'd be just fine with shooting Greg. "Please sit back down," Zara whispered.

"That's not necessary," Madison said, rising from her chair. "Take them to different buildings this time." She tilted her head to the side. "Sheriff Cobb and I will meet you, Zara, in yours after suppertime. He likes to inflict pain, and I'm finding myself looking forward to seeing how much you are able to endure."

Zara glared at the woman and shoved down fear. Her knees shook. God, how long would it take Ryker to get to her once he pinged her location?

How much time did she have?

CHAPTER
36

Heat exploded in Ryker's chest, and part of him wanted to run fast and hard in the other direction. "Family?" He stared at them, noting their gray eyes and tightly packed bodies. "You're fucked up."

Jory cut a look at Matt. "Jesus. Where to start?"

Matt had jet black hair and square features. Jory had dark hair and a more angled bone structure. "With his name," Matt said. "I'm not calling you Fred."

"Ryker." Ryker's knees itched, and he really wanted to sit down. "Why are you calling me family?"

Jory blew out air and shook his head. "Dude. I need a beer for this conversation."

Ryker edged toward the door.

"Stop," Matt breathed out. "Get your phone, Jory. I saw you taking pictures during the ski lessons the other day."

Jory grabbed a phone from his back pocket and scrolled through it quickly. He tossed the phone to Ryker. "That's Nate. He's our brother."

Ryker easily caught the phone and stared into a face way too similar to his own. His stomach clenched and rolled. "What the hell?"

"Your eyes aren't gray, so we probably don't share a father." Matt glanced at Jory. "Maybe they share a mother? They'd have to, right?"

Jory rubbed what looked like a damn strong jaw. "That'd be my guess. Dr. Madison liked to experiment with our lives, and I guess it makes sense she'd use genetic material from women to make brothers, too."

"It's like she threw a bunch of sperm in a salad spinner and just went for broke," Matt muttered.

"We should check his back," Jory murmured.

Matt eyed Ryker. "Think so?"

Ryker took a step in the other direction. Sperm salad? "Excuse me?"

Matt strode toward him, maneuvering around broken furniture. "Dr. Madison planted kill chips near our spines in order to control us, and we deactivated them. I doubt you'd still be alive if there's a chip in you, but how about we just make sure?" He reached Ryker and grabbed the bottom of his shirt.

"Hey." Ryker slapped his hands. "Knock it off."

"Don't be a baby." Matt flipped him around and jerked his shirt up.

Jory chuckled. "Get used to it. Unless you're older? How old are you?"

"Thirty-two." Ryker kept still, mainly out of shock, as Matt probed his upper spine.

Matt lowered the shirt. "Then you're the same age as Nate. Maybe you're twins? Fraternal since you have different eye color. You're fine. No kill chip." He turned Ryker around. "We have a lot to talk about." As if he couldn't help himself, he yanked Ryker in for a hard hug and a slap on the back before moving away. "I can't believe we found you."

Ryker eyed Matt, his entire body short-circuiting. "You were looking?"

Matt nodded. "A few months ago we discovered we might have other brothers, and we've been searching since."

"We?" Ryker asked.

Jory grinned. "There are four of us. Matt, me, Shane, and Nate."

"Five now. Don't forget Chance." Matt ran a broad hand through his hair. "He's quite a bit younger, and we found him a while back. Plus, he has other brothers as well. Dr. Madison liked to experiment with family units—so she created them. We'll explain it all over drinks."

Experiments. Ryker leaned back against the wall, needing something solid to hold him up. "This is too much."

"Just wait," Jory muttered. "How about we do this over a beer? Or a bottle of tequila? Just not here in this shithole."

"No. I have a job to do." Ryker ran a hand through his still-wet hair, Zara filling his mind. "I do want to talk to you guys, but I'm only here because I thought you're breaking in would give me information I need right this second. Give me your number and we'll talk when I'm done." Zara and Greg were his priority, and time was ticking away. He tossed the phone back to Jory.

Matt frowned. "What kind of a job?"

Ryker studied him. He didn't have time to bring somebody new in, but the guy seemed to know a lot more about Madison than he did. "Dr. Madison has kidnapped one of my clients as well as my, ah, my woman." The word *girlfriend* seemed wimpy, and even though *woman* seemed a bit much, she held his heart and soul in her hands, so *my woman* was the absolute truth.

Jory drew back. "What? Why?"

"I don't know. Just tell me what you know about Madison, please." He tried to keep the panic out of his voice.

"Okay." Matt launched into motion for the back door. "Let's get out of here. I'll ride with Ryker."

Ryker stopped. "You're not coming with me."

Jory moved around the couch to clap an arm around Ryker's shoulders. "You'll get used to Mattie. He's a little bossy."

Ryker hurried for the door, not having much of a choice. "I don't want your help." Although, the guys could fight.

"Oh, we're not letting you out of our sight now that we've found you," Jory said urgently. "I should apologize now for what complete pains in the ass we're about to be. How do you feel about Montana?"

"The state?" Ryker tripped over his own feet, something he never did.

"Yep." Jory steered him through the back door. "You kind of clumsy?"

"No. Just freaking out." Ryker stomped down the snowy steps. "My guard is down, too."

Jory nodded and gingerly turned Ryker toward the fence.

Ryker pulled free. "Knock it off. I'm not a klutz."

"Uh-huh." Jory gestured Ryker through the rickety gate, where Matt waited on the other side. "The fact that your guard is down, when you surely have excellent instincts, must tell you something, right? You can trust us."

Did Jory have odd instincts like Ryker did? Was it a family thing? "Right. I always trust guys holding a picture of my possible twin. Always."

Jory chuckled. "I knew you'd be funny. I'm usually the funny one, and it'd be nice to pass that baton."

Matt frowned. "You aren't the funny one. Not at all."

"Sure I am." Jory seemed to hand Ryker off to Matt. "You take him. I'll grab the truck and meet you at his place."

"Nobody needs to take me." Ryker blew out cold air and tried to step away from the duo. "I'm not going to ditch you guys, because you have answers I need."

Matt leaned in, his face going hard and losing any semblance of friendliness. "Listen, Ryker. I haven't slept a decent night in four months, since we learned you were out there, by yourself, with a kill order over your head. Now that we've found you, no fucking way are you getting out of our sight until we know you're okay. Now take me to your rig or I'm going to beat the shit out of you, and then you're going to take me to your rig."

So much for brotherly love. Defiance and the need to hit something rose fast and hard in Ryker. It'd be a damn good fight—that was for sure.

Jory shoved him in his uninjured arm and knocked him an inch to the side. "Come on, you two. Stop acting like morons. We have to get to Madison."

Ryker turned on him, his fists clenching. "What? Are you the peacemaker?"

Jory slowly nodded, his gaze solemn. "Yep. Always have been. And you don't want to cross me, brother. When we were sparring in there, I was pulling my punches because we needed you alive for questioning."

Ryker leaned in. "So was I."

Jory grinned. "Good to know you're not a pussy. We need to move now." Even though his voice was congenial, a thread of concern rode through it.

The entire neighborhood spun around Ryker. Was this vertigo? "Fine." He turned and headed down the street to his truck, then suddenly paused. "Wait a minute. Kill order?"

"Yep." Matt caught up to him. "I'll explain as we go. For now, where's your truck? It's cold out here."

Ryker slowly moved back into motion. "Who wants me dead?"

"The good news is, not us, because then you would be." Matt slung an arm over his shoulders. "Welcome to the family, Ryker."

"I don't believe this," Ryker muttered. "I already have two brothers, Heath and Denver."

"Interesting." Matt stiffened but kept up the long stride to the truck. "I wonder if any of us share a mother. It's nice to have three more brothers." He crossed to the passenger side and jumped in. "If you're a brother to one of us, you're a brother to all of us."

Ryker forced himself to keep calm as he moved into the truck and started the engine. His phone buzzed and he read the message from Heath. They'd found Zara. His body electrified. "Hold on, Matt. It's going to be a fast drive back to my place." They'd have to get to the airport quickly.

It was time he and Dr. Madison faced each other again.

* * *

Less than twenty minutes later, Ryker was fully suited up and riding in a borrowed helicopter. He'd quickly introduced Heath and Denver to Matt and Jory, noting belatedly that Denver and Jory had a remarkably similar jawline. Had Dr. Madison created a bunch genetically linked men? It was too creepy to contemplate.

He shook his head to get back to reality. "You guys have a helicopter." He sat back in his seat and tugged down his bulletproof vest. Oh, the vest was his, but the helicopter?

Matt nodded from the pilot's seat. "Yeah. We own a security firm that provides services in other countries, from protection to infiltration. Our headquarters is far away from our homes, and we keep the distance on purpose. We hire a lot of ex-military guys to do the work and pay them well."

Sounded like they made good money. "The business can't be traced back to you?" Ryker asked.

"No," Matt said shortly.

Ryker tamped down on emotion. The helicopter had been loaded with enough weaponry to take out a small country, but he had kept his comfortable Glock and knives instead. Denver sat in the co-pilot's seat while Jory and Heath bracketed Ryker.

Zara had to be all right. Hopefully Greg was sitting tight, but Ryker knew that if the kid found an opening, he'd take it.

"Who are you guys?" Ryker asked bluntly. Sure, they shared features and possibly genetics, but how could he trust these guys when Zara and Greg's lives were on the line?

"We were born in a black-ops pseudo-military organization in Tennessee and trained as soldiers from birth by Dr. Madison and a guy named the commander who's now dead. There were different groups, different brothers, all genetically marked by eye color. We have gray eyes. We blew the place up almost six years ago and got free, but Madison is still looking for us," Matt answered.

Fuck. This was all real. Ryker shook his head as tension rolled from Heath. "I'm getting that we were all Dr. Madison's experiments. But why did you grow up together knowing you were brothers while Denver, Heath, and I just ended up together, not knowing we were engineered or created by the same scientists?"

Matt growled in a low rumble. "The answer is Isobel Madison was studying us all in different environments."

"That is screwed up," Ryker said, eyeing the storm clouds outside the helicopter. "She'd show up periodically at the boys home where we lived, and she'd test us mentally, emotionally, and physically."

"She thinks she owns us," Matt said simply. "She created us, raised us, and wants us back. She's sick, man." He cleared his throat, pulling back on the throttle. "We think Madison has thrown in with a group called Protect, which wants to rid the world of all genetic testing and scientific advancement and kill us all."

"That's the opposite of what she does," Ryker said, frowning and grabbing the side of the craft when Matt banked a hard right.

"Yeah. Our guess is that she's just using them for resources to get to us, and to whatever other creations she has out there. She lost her main resources when we blew them up four months ago," Jory said.

"Sounds like you enjoy blowing things up," Ryker said thoughtfully.

"We try."

Ryker's thoughts rushed through his head. What about Greg? His upbringing sounded similar to these guys. Man, he wanted to trust them. "What about our parents? Do you know them?"

"Our genetic donors are unknown. We all share the DNA of a supersoldier with gray eyes who is dead, and we each have different egg donors, as far as we can tell. Either scientists, hookers, poor people, or just donors. We've never been able to track any of them down, and we gave up a long time ago," Matt said tersely.

"Oh." Ryker rubbed the center of his chest. "I've been looking for them my whole life." What about the odd senses? "Do you have super hearing and strength? Know stuff you shouldn't?" Ryker said, his voice hoarse.

"Yep. Good ole Isobel Madison spliced all sorts of special genes into us when she made us," Matt said. "You're not alone, Ryker, and it's time you leveled with us. What exactly is going on here?"

It was all too surreal, but all that mattered was saving Zara and Greg. Time to trust. "I have a client who wanted to find Madison, and that brought up my childhood, so we set a trap, you got caught in our trap, and here you are."

Matt stilled. "Somebody hired you to find Madison?"

"Yes. We have a business called Lost Bastards Investigative Services, and we find the lost. Have a good track record."

Matt glanced back. "We need to know about your client. Who is it?"

Ryker glanced first at Heath, who nodded, and then at Denver, who shrugged. All right. It was best if they all knew what they were getting into. "A kid named Greg hired us to find Dr. Madison. The kid was nearly desperate."

"Kid?" Matt swung around.

"Watch the sky," Ryker snapped as the helicopter banked.

Matt righted the craft. "Did you say a kid named Greg?" His voice was a little too loud through the helmet comms.

Jory shook his head. "Couldn't be, Mattie. Take a breath. It couldn't be Greg. We dug up his grave, remember?"

Ryker's chest heated. "Um, the kid showed us a disturbed grave in Utah where he was supposed to have been buried. Dr. Madison sent him on a mission, he failed, and she told him he had to get home on his own. It took a while."

Emotion suddenly choked the cab. Matt kept his gaze straight ahead while Jory watched his brother, worry in his deep gray eyes.

"Should we call home?" Jory asked.

Matt shook his head. "No. Not until we get him back and make sure it's him."

Jory nodded.

Heath gave Ryker a concerned look. "I take it you know of Greg?"

Jory glanced at his brother and then breathed out. "Yes. We rescued three boys from Dr. Madison who'd recently lost a brother named Greg. Figures it was another mind fuck by her. Shit. We reburied him on the ranch."

Sounded like another crazy experiment. "We'll get him back," Ryker vowed.

Jory met his eyes and nodded. "Yeah."

Blood or not, Ryker had just met Matt and Jory, and it was a stretch to ask them to put their lives on the line. He cleared his throat. "We can go in and meet you later. You have families at home and shouldn't take this risk."

"You are family, dumb-ass," Matt said, peering out the front window at the raging storm. The helicopter pitched, and he quickly righted it.

Even so, this was dangerous. Ryker turned toward Jory.

Jory held up a hand. "Family is family, and we all go in."

Ryker nodded, his throat closing. Heath gave him a supportive nudge from his other side. Jesus. "Thank you," he said into the comms for everybody.

A series of nods acknowledged everything else he hadn't been able to say.

"What do you know about the Protect group?" Ryker asked.

Matt banked left. "They're a fundamentalist vigilante group, fully armed and dedicated to eradicating the world of all genetic experimentation. They subsist on donations and I suspect illegal methods like drug running and fraud. They've had some training but not anything close to ours."

"The Protect group isn't well trained enough to have taken Greg and Zara." Jory breathed out. "Those guys had to have been former soldiers of the commander, so Dr. Madison has at least a few of them still loyal to her after all these years."

"Even after we shut down Protect and Madison, we'll never be out in the open. Just not going to happen," Matt said. "I know you're trusting us right now, and we're doing the same. We have to start somewhere."

Ryker nodded. "Understood."

"You'd like the property in Montana," Matt said, partially turning his head. "Lots of acreage, trees, water, mountains."

"And security," Jory added. "Some we invented."

Ryker pushed back in his seat, trying to focus on the conversation and not the fact that Zara was in his enemy's hands. "I'm not moving to Montana."

"We'll see," Matt said.

Jory snorted. "Denver and Heath, you guys would like it, too. You'll see."

Ryker cut him a look.

Matt twisted a knob and flew incredibly low. "We're five minutes from landing, and once we're down, it's a three-mile hike to the lodge. If I land any closer, they'll detect us."

"You're assuming the Protect group or Madison doesn't have the technology to track us?" Ryker asked.

"Affirmative," Matt said. "They have numbers and dedication, but they're lacking so far in other areas. Greg could give them an edge in that direction, which is another reason he should still be alive."

The kid had to be alive. Ryker had no option but to trust these men as they began to descend into a snowy clearing in what appeared to be the middle of nowhere. Dusk disappeared and the night pressed in on them. Matt landed the helicopter and shut it down.

Silence suddenly roared in.

Ryker waited until everyone had exited the craft and inserted top of the line comm devices into their ears. "All right. Head out." Both Zara and Greg had to be all right. He'd promised to protect them.

Banishing all emotion, he launched into a run.

CHAPTER
37

Zara struggled against the ropes binding her to a metal chair, but they were tied tight. She was back in the same cinder-block room, and a definite chill pierced the air. The exposed light bulb swung gently back and forth. It was like every torture room she'd ever seen in action movies. A shiver escaped her, and she jerked against the bindings again, wincing as the rope cut into her wrists.

The door opened, and Isobel Madison walked in. She'd donned a thick blue parka and furry brown boots with matching gloves.

"Bitch," Zara muttered, her bare feet freezing.

A man followed Madison, carrying another chair. Tall and broad, midforties, blue eyes and blond hair. He was fit, and an unreadable gleam filled his eyes. Unlike Isobel, he wore only a thick T-shirt over dark jeans. He shut the door and eyed her. "Pretty," he said.

Isobel nodded.

The guy unfolded the chair and placed it in the far corner. Madison hopped almost happily over to sit down, primly crossing her legs and drawing a tablet out of her front coat pocket. She tugged off her gloves and shoved them into her coat. "Zara, this is Sheriff Elton Cobb."

That's what she'd figured. "This is slightly against the law, Sheriff."

He lifted a muscled shoulder. "Eh."

She swallowed and tried to banish the raw terror climbing up her throat. "What do you want?" she asked.

His upper lip twisted. "Oh, so much. But for now, we're gonna talk. Where's Ryker?"

"I assume he's trying to find me right now," she said evenly. If somehow she could get past Cobb and out the door, how was she going to find Greg? Was his outbuilding close by? It seemed like they'd be built close together. Well, hopefully. "How did you find us, anyway?"

The backhand came out of nowhere and threw her head to the side. Agony exploded in her cheek—again. Tears pricked her eyes and she gasped, turning back around.

"I ask the questions," Cobb said calmly, his nostrils flaring.

Oh, the man needed to die.

"Or I do," Isobel said, tapping something on her tablet. She glanced up, her foot bobbing. "How did you meet Ryker?"

Zara frowned. "My firm hired him for a case." Duh. "We hit it off."

"How much of his past has he told you about?" Madison asked.

Zara blinked. "He has a past?"

The next hit came open palmed to the opposite side of her face. She rocked back, and tears filled her eyes. Her face ached from her jaw to her forehead, and her skin kind of itched. "That was so not necessary." She glared up at the sheriff, whose breathing had begun to get heavy.

"Lose the sarcasm," Madison advised.

"That's my strongest characteristic," Zara shot back.

Cobb laughed low. "I like her."

Wonderful. Zara's eye began to twitch.

"Back to my question. How much of Ryker's past do you know?" Madison asked.

"None of it," Zara said wearily. "Just that he, Heath, and Denver grew up together and got out of a bad situation."

Madison tapped on her tablet. "No mention of the murders?"

Zara turned her head to face the woman directly. "What murders?"

Madison focused on her, both eyebrows lifting. "Interesting. I thought the two of you were intimate." She tapped her lips with a finger. "Maybe those three aren't capable of love. I didn't think the Gray brothers were, either, but all four of them found mates." She began to type wildly on the tablet.

Zara watched her work. Risking another hit, she cleared her throat. It'd be interesting to see how Madison spun the truth. "What murders?"

"Oh." Madison waved her free hand. "Ryker murdered a boy at the boys home as well as the home's owner. He always had a devastating temper." She scratched her forehead. "I've been investigating you for days. If you ask me, Ryker killed your friend Julie—not that detective."

Zara snorted. "Why would Ryker do that?"

"He's always eliminated any threats. If your friend was a threat to you—or, more important, to him—he would've taken her out and easily framed somebody. The boy is a genius, you know." Madison coughed. "I mean man. He's definitely a man now."

"Ryker wouldn't kill an innocent woman," Zara said, trying to stretch her back before the muscle spasming along her right side became unbearable.

Sheriff Cobb walked around her and lifted her hair. "I like the color. Is it natural?" he asked.

She blinked. Unease ticked into her. "Yes."

He yanked. "You like it rough? Ryker definitely is a rough guy."

Pain spread along her scalp. "No," she breathed out, trying not to cry. "Not at all."

"Too bad. You will by the time we're done." Cobb yanked again, and her head jerked back. Holding her in place, elongating her neck, he pressed two fingers against the pulse in her throat.

She struggled against him, but she couldn't move.

He counted. "She's scared."

"She should be." Isobel watched dispassionately. "Where did Ryker live before buying the new building in Cisco?"

"I don't know," Zara breathed. Even if she did, no way would she tell the psycho scientist. "He was always on the move and just visited when in town."

"That does sound like him," Madison mused. "Are Heath or Denver seeing anybody?"

"Not that I know of." Zara tried to free her head, and the sheriff laughed. "I just met them."

The sheriff released her, and she lowered her chin, trying to keep from puking. Just how sadistic would Cobb become? She really didn't want to find out. Her stomach cramped, and her legs trembled. "You have to know that Ryker will kill you if you hurt me."

Cobb pinched her upper arm.

"Ow." She instinctively jerked to the side.

"What's their business?" Madison asked. "We saw the offices on the first floor of your building after we tracked Ryker from his safe house, but we didn't get a chance to investigate. What is it?"

Zara lifted a shoulder. "I'm not sure."

Cobb grabbed her neck.

"I'm really not. They invest and do a bunch of stuff on computers," Zara lied. "Ryker doesn't share his work."

"Then what did your firm hire him to do?" Madison asked silkily.

"Something about a case and tracking down missing money," Zara said, stretching the truth. If Madison discovered the true business of finding lost people, she might be able to track their past movements, and that would probably be bad. "Again, I wasn't involved and just met him by the watercooler, so to speak." At this point, Madison was underestimating her enough that she might be able to get away with the lies.

"He doesn't love you," Madison said, setting her tablet on her thighs.

Zara just stared at her.

"I'm sorry, but he's not capable of it. I studied that man from his birth, and I know him better than he knows himself. He's not capable of intimacy. Sure, he'll try to lull you into thinking you have his heart, but really, what do you know about him?" Madison asked, her tone reasonable and knowing. "Where was he born?"

"I don't know," Zara admitted.

"Where is the boy's home?" Madison asked.

Zara eyed the door.

"What's his favorite color, his favorite food, or his favorite movie?" Madison persisted.

Zara calculated the reach in her legs. If she kicked Cobb in the groin, and if he doubled over, could she knee him in the face hard enough to knock him out? It didn't seem likely. The tracking software in her phone had to be working, and Ryker should arrive soon, hopefully. "Where's Greg?" she whispered.

Madison sighed. "Greg is no longer your concern. Has Ryker had any contact with the Gray brothers?"

"Who?" Zara asked.

"Ryker has genetic links to others, and I wondered if those links, ones I trained well, followed his bread crumbs like I did, but apparently not."

The door opened, and the soldier from before came into view. Todd. He eyed Madison and stepped inside, leaning back against the wall with his arms crossed. "What have we discovered?"

Cobb rolled his eyes. "Nothing yet. I don't need you here for this."

Zara glanced at the three. "Isn't this cozy? Do you guys have threesomes or just go one-on-one with the good doctor here when she's in the mood? Does she make you draw straws?"

Todd snarled while Cobb leaned in casually and flicked her lips.

She gasped, and pain radiated through her mouth. Tears tried to prick the back of her eyes again, and she battled them away. That really *hurt*.

"Do you like pain?" Madison asked, her brows drawing down. "A little bit?"

Zara didn't bother to answer the psychopath.

"Continue questioning her," Todd ordered. "It's okay to draw blood and leave scars. It won't matter in the long run."

Zara's lungs seized. Her body was chilled from terror alone, much less the cold.

Cobb crouched down so they were face-to-face. "How are Denver and Heath?"

She eyed him, wanting nothing more than to kick him hard. But she couldn't knock him out, and he'd surely retaliate. She needed to stay conscious to fight when the time came. "I think they're fine," she said. "I've met them only once."

Madison huffed. "That's what I was afraid of. Ryker didn't bother to let you get to know them." She pushed off the chair and headed for the door. "Gentlemen, do what you want with her. She's of no use to me, because she doesn't matter to Ryker." She shoved out into the swirling storm. "See you tomorrow."

The door clanged shut behind her.

Cobb stood and smiled. "Well. I guess we should get started, then."

Todd stopped him with a hand on his arm. "Before you destroy her, I'd like to ask a few questions."

Cobb sighed. "You have an hour, and then I get her the rest of the night."

Pinpricks exploded across Zara's skin. She tried to breathe evenly and not start screaming. She had to get out of there.

Todd nodded. "Fair enough. Be back in an hour."

Cobb opened the door. "I'll just go chat with Isobel. Have fun." He disappeared into the storm.

Todd uncrossed his arms. "Unlike that bastard, I don't find any pleasure in harming women. However, I have no problem doing so to get answers. Let's get started."

CHAPTER 38

Ryker rushed through the storm, impressed with how well Matt and Jory kept up. In fact, neither was breathing heavily. Whatever genetics had gone into them had been superb. For so long he'd wondered how he, Heath, and Denver were beyond the norm, and now he knew. Genetic engineering at its finest.

The men ran beside him, all calm, all focused. Inside, he tried to control himself, but he couldn't get the idea out of his head of Zara in danger. She was soft and sweet, and she had no clue how to deal with the darker side of humanity.

If she'd let him, he'd continue protecting her for the rest of his life.

But at the moment, he had no idea what was happening to her. What if they were torturing her, hurting her? His gut felt too full, and his shoulders shook. Desperation and terror threatened to choke him.

Denver held up a hand, and the group stopped running. He grasped a phone from his pocket and read the screen. Slowly, his chin lowered.

"What?" Ryker asked.

Denver looked at him, his eyes hardening. "My contacts checked in. Sheriff Cobb boarded a plane for this location earlier this week. He's here, Ryker."

The words slammed into Ryker's chest with the force of an anvil. "Here?" he whispered, his voice breaking.

Denver slowly nodded.

Panic gripped him, and he turned to run, only to have Heath intercept him.

"Wait," Heath said. Ryker struggled, and Heath pivoted, putting him against a tree. Snow rained down on them. "Listen. Take a moment and concentrate. Zara is smart, and she knows we'll be coming. She's okay. There hasn't been time for Cobb to get going. Trust me."

True. He had to keep his head, or he wouldn't be of any use to Zara. He took a deep breath. Matt and Jory watched him from near a line of trees while Denver covered his other side. He relaxed, and Heath released him. "I'm okay." God, what Cobb would want to do to her. "We have to hurry though." The bastard liked to swing belts under darkness, and they all remembered his joy in it. Cobb would take great pleasure in breaking the woman who held Ryker's heart. "It's nighttime."

Heath nodded and pushed away.

"Care to share?" Matt asked, jogging closer.

Ryker shook his head.

Heath snarled. "Sheriff Cobb is a sadistic bastard who tortured us as kids. He and Dr. Madison would get it on whenever she visited. He's been, ah, searching for us since we escaped the boys home because of a little fire we may have started."

Ryker glanced at the two men now putting their lives on the line for Zara and Greg. "After we killed the proprietor—another sadistic bastard and the sheriff's brother."

Neither Matt nor Jory blinked. Finally, Matt glanced at the line of trees. "Dr. Madison will want plenty of time to question Zara. We'll have her tonight long before Madison runs out of questions."

Ryker nodded, his mind turning over events, his hands shaking. "Zara doesn't know much that Madison probably isn't already aware of."

Matt paused. "Nothing? She doesn't have anything to share?"

"Not really." Ryker flicked snow out of his eyes.

Matt eyed Jory. "If she doesn't have any information for Madison, then Madison will move on to something or somebody else. We'd better hurry." He turned and shoved between two trees, scattering snow.

Ryker charged after him. He'd just wanted to protect Zara from his past and start anew. The pain of those times didn't need to be a burden on anybody but him. He and Zara had known each other pretty intimately, so there had to be plenty to dissect. His ears rang. "But Madison will want to talk about us, right?"

Matt turned back. "Yes, but what does Zara know?"

Nothing. She'd met Heath and Denver only recently, and he'd given her only a brief glimpse into his odd abilities. "Not enough," Ryker said grimly. "I've tried to protect her from all that."

Jory jogged by his side. "That probably isn't good. How do you know she loves you if she doesn't even know you?"

Ryker cut him a look. "What are you, Dr. Phil?"

Without losing a step, Jory bent and drew a wicked-looking knife from his boot. "I'm just saying if you want to keep a woman, you have to let her know all of you. Even the bad shit." He stopped and held up a hand until everyone halted. "Right through that group of trees is the lodge."

Ryker pivoted to the north. "Jory and Heath, take the front door. Denver and Matt, take the side. I'm going in the back."

Matt leaned in. "I'll go in the back—you and Denver go in the side. There should be less resistance there so you can find Zara. Remember that we've been trained since birth. This is the best plan."

Ryker rolled his shoulder. "I don't like you going in alone."

Matt snorted. "I'll be fine." He paused. "How good is your hearing?"

Heath reached for a gun stuck in the back of his waistband. "We all have abnormally good senses, but Ryker's is over the top. Is that genetic, too?"

"Yep," Matt said. "Make sure you all tune in while we're inside. Could save our asses."

Ryker nodded. "Let's go—infiltrate in exactly one minute." He turned and ducked low, then ran through the trees and zigzagged through the darkness and falling snow until he reached the side entrance.

Denver leaned against the wall next to him. "The security here isn't very good," he whispered.

Maybe the Protect group didn't have the resources they had feared, and perhaps Madison didn't have many soldiers she'd raised. Ryker nodded, counting down in his head for the right moment. "You ready?"

"Affirmative," Denver said, his light eyes cutting through the night. "You sure you're okay after being shot the other day?"

"Fine. Just a scratch," Ryker said, not feeling any pain.

"Good. Zara will be okay."

God, Ryker hoped so.

"So will Greg," Denver added.

"Yeah." Ryker checked his weapon. "Let's go." He pivoted and gingerly tugged the door. Locked. He'd figured. Giving Denver a nod, he slid to the side and covered the area.

Denver removed a small tool set from his back pocket, leaned down, and had the door unlocked within seconds.

Ryker frowned. "That was shockingly easy."

"They're not expecting company." Denver straightened and shoved the tools back into his pocket.

True. Zara had been brilliant hiding the phone down her

nightgown. Ryker waited until Denver opened the door, and then he glided into a mudroom with laundry facilities, his gun at the ready. He waited until Denver had joined him before crossing the room and opening another door to reveal a hallway lined with oil paintings.

The coziness of the place caught him unawares. He moved into the hall, following it to a large gathering room with a huge stone fireplace. He scouted the area and reached stairs leading up and down just as the other men did. Jory and Heath headed up, he and Denver moved down, and Matt stayed central to cover the stairs.

Ryker's heart pounded, and he took several breaths to calm himself and focus. The place was way too quiet. He crept down the stairs and turned right at the bottom. A small conference room sat empty at the side while a hallway containing several doorways extended to the north. He hustled past the large table and reached the first door, nudging it open to an office smelling of cigar smoke and bourbon. Maps covered the far wall with pins stuck in different places.

He moved past the room while Denver stuck his head in, using his phone to take several pictures of the maps.

The next office was utilitarian with a couple of desks and phones.

He stilled and tuned in to the area. Nothing. No heartbeats, breaths, sounds. Where were Zara and Greg? Increasing his speed, he hustled for the next office and pushed open a door. Feminine desk, high-end furniture, and the smell of fancy and too sweet perfume. The scent instantly took him back to his teenaged years. "This is her office." He strode inside and looked around quickly. Papers, files, and maps were organized perfectly on the desk. "You catalog the place and grab what you can," he said, moving past Denver back toward the hallway. "I'll keep looking."

Denver drew up short. "Shit."

Ryker turned toward the computer on the desk, noting a flashing red light. Heat slammed into his abdomen, and he looked up at the ceiling to see two barely discernible boxes. "Motion sensors." He hustled into the hallway and ran for the stairs. "Matt? We're compromised," he whispered into his comm device before heading back and kicking the doors open to the last two offices.

The shouts of men echoed through the building.

He met Denver in the hallway, and they ran up the stairs to join Matt just as three men rushed in the front door. Matt instantly engaged one in hand-to-hand, and his moves were a work of art. The guy he'd been fighting was unconscious on the floor before Ryker could even jump into the fray.

"Holy shit," Denver muttered.

Ryker nodded and leaped forward to take the next guy down.

Matt looked over his shoulder at Denver. "You want this one?" He pointed to a tall soldier circling him.

"Nah. Go ahead." Denver turned toward the back of the building as men shouted from that direction. "I'll go this way."

Heath and Jory rushed in from the area by the mud room, leaped over the fallen guy, and followed Denver toward the sound of running boots in back.

Ryker took a hard punch to the face, and he smiled as he grabbed his attacker around the neck and tossed his ass to the floor. Ryker followed him down, punching his face. Blood sprayed. He leaned in. "I don't want to kill you, so tell me where the woman and kid are."

The guy blinked.

Ryker punched him in the nose, and cartilage cracked. The man screamed in pain.

"Where. Are. They?" Ryker asked. "Last chance or I slice your throat and move on to your buddy."

"One of the outbuildings. I don't know which one. They're spaced fifty yards beyond the trees to the west and east," the guy gasped through blood pouring from his nose.

"Thanks." Ryker punched him in the jaw, and the guy slumped into unconsciousness. Then Ryker stood and nudged the guy onto his side so he didn't choke to death. No reason to kill.

He glanced at Matt, who stood and wiped blood off his lip. "Outbuildings?"

Matt leaned to the side to glance out a window. "Three enemy here, three in kitchen...and it looks like fifteen or so running up the hill." He frowned.

"What?" Ryker asked, quickly frisking the downed men for weapons. Two guns and four knives. He tossed a couple to Matt.

Matt shook his head. "These guys aren't part of Madison's original troops. Not even close." He watched the men outside running through the storm. "Those don't look like it either. All of these guys are Protect soldiers with minimal training." He turned, his gaze hardening. "Let's go find Zara and worry about Madison later."

Ryker's lungs seized. "Side door." He turned and ran for the mudroom, Matt on his heels. They reached the storm. "You go east, and I'll check the western trees," Ryker ordered.

Matt nodded and took off at a run.

Ryker turned, barreling through the snow as gunfire erupted at the front of the lodge. His step hitched, but he kept going. His brothers were trained, and they'd be okay. Zara and Greg needed him now. He ducked his head against the piercing cold, reaching a line of trees and scouting the area for a trail. Fresh snow covered the ground, littered with pine needles, which made it nearly impossible to see footprints, especially in the dark.

So he paused and listened. Wind, firefight in the background, ice cracking on branches. Digging deeper, he filtered all the sounds.

A heartbeat. Wild and fierce, going too fast. To the east. Another one...this one somewhat elevated yet calmer than the first one.

He ducked under swaying branches and ran, following the sound, finding what might be a trail. He was nearly upon the outbuilding when he saw it. The white cinder blocks blended perfectly into the snowstorm.

He ran full bore for the door and kicked it open.

A hard body tackled him, throwing him back into the snow, just as a woman screamed long and loud.

Zara.

CHAPTER
39

Zara screamed and struggled against her bindings as Todd and Ryker rolled in the snow, furiously throwing punches. Reality slammed her in the face, and she quieted. There were more soldiers around. She had to help Ryker and not bring any of them running.

The loud roar of an engine bellowed through the storm.

More troops? She jerked against the ropes, wincing as they cut further into her aching flesh. The chair was metal, so even if she threw herself backward, it wouldn't break, but her arms might.

Ryker punched Todd in the face and jumped up, turning for her. Todd kicked out, nailing Ryker in the ankle, and he stumbled. Todd pushed up and jumped at Ryker with a snarl, throwing them both into the room and right toward her. Zara screamed and ducked her head just as Ryker pivoted to the side and smashed into the cinder blocks, taking the brunt of the impact on his forehead. His head smashed the block with a loud thud.

Zara sucked in air, concentrating on him.

He fell and then instantly bounded up, turning and punching Todd in the neck. Todd grabbed his neck and fell back, his eyes widening. Ryker followed the punch with a kick, and Todd flew out of the room to smash onto the ground and send snow spraying.

"You okay?" Ryker coughed, reaching behind her to slice the ropes with a knife.

"Yeah." The circulation returned to her hands, and she bit her lip to keep from crying out. The blood rushed back into her skin like needles.

Todd hissed and grabbed the door frame. Blood flowed down his head, and his nose was bent toward the side of his face. Slowly, with hate in his eyes, he lifted a gun toward her.

She gasped.

The first shot came from behind her, and she jumped. Blood bloomed from the center of Todd's head, his eyes widened, and he fell directly backward into the snow.

She slowly turned her head to see Ryker setting down a gun. He gently took her face in his hands. "Jesus."

Bruises and blood marred his handsome face while snow and blood coated his shirt and jeans, but he'd never looked better to her. Everything she would ever need was there in his eyes and his gentle touch. Tears filled her eyes, and this time she let them fall. "You came." She'd breathed the words, her chest filling with him. She'd trusted him, and he'd come for her.

He leaned in and kissed her lips, the touch reverent. "Yeah."

Her head jerked. "Did you find Greg?"

"Not yet." Ryker pulled her gently from the chair by the shoulders. "Can you run?"

She nodded and found her balance.

His gaze darkened, and he drew her arms toward him by the elbows. "Holy shit."

She glanced down at her raw and bleeding wrists. "They're fine."

"They are not fine." Fury sizzled across his angled features, and tension swelled, heating the cinder-block room. "Too bad he's already dead." Ryker drew her out of the room and helped her over the dead soldier. "Any clue where Greg is?"

"No." Too many emotions blasted into her, and she averted her gaze from Todd. Apparently Ryker was a good shot. "Thanks for coming to get me," she said through numb lips.

"Always." He drew her from the outbuilding, his solid body between her and any danger. A firefight sounded toward the lodge, and an explosion roared through the night from over the hill, sending fire, light, and debris high into the air. "Fuck. I hope that wasn't our helicopter." Ryker ducked into a run. "Stay right behind me, sweetheart."

She nodded and tried to keep her balance through the thick snow. Her wrists pounded in pain and her face ached as bruises formed, but she kept right behind him, her gaze sweeping the area. They had to find Greg.

Something dark caught her eye. "Ryker." She grabbed his arm and pointed. "There."

He turned and followed a barely there path to another outbuilding made of cinder blocks. He set her to the side of the door and kicked it open. It flung inward and hung awkwardly. Zara hurried after him and looked around the empty room. "He's not here," she whispered. There had to be other buildings. Where the hell was Greg?

A gun cocked behind her, and a barrel pressed against her neck. She stiffened. "Ryker?" she whispered, her voice shaking.

Ryker turned and faced her fully, looking over her shoulder. "Don't shoot her."

"Drop your gun, sweet boy," came a feminine voice. "God, I've missed you, Ryker. Look how grown up and handsome you are." She almost sounded like a proud mother.

Zara shivered as nausea attacked her. "Dr. Madison. Where's Greg?"

Ryker dropped his gun and kicked it over to the right.

"No!" Zara coughed out a sob.

Madison tapped her weapon on Zara's head. "Go toward him and turn around. Both of you get against the back wall. On your knees."

Zara stumbled toward Ryker, feeling that gun trained on her. The second she reached him, he shoved her behind him and backed to the wall. She tried to move to the side, but he pressed her against the hard blocks.

"Well, then. I guess I shoot you," Madison said almost conversationally.

* * *

Ryker faced the woman from his past. "You won't shoot me, and we both know it." He crossed his arms, careful to keep all of Zara out of a bullet's path, just in case. "Where's Greg?"

Isobel Madison smiled, and those deep blue eyes sparkled. "Greg is mine again, and I'm not giving him up. Why don't you and your brothers come with us, shackled of course, and we'll do some tests?"

Do some tests. He remembered those words from that mouth, and he wanted to puke. "Fuck you."

"Oh, the things I could teach you." She kept the gun pointed levelly at his chest—center mass. "Have you missed me, sweet boy?"

He gagged. "No."

"Liar," she whispered, her voice seductive and way beyond creepy. "There are secrets from your past I'd share. Like you're not alone. Not really."

She hadn't seen Matt or Jory, now, had she? "I don't care about secrets, and I've given up the past. How about you just go to hell now?" he said, his voice shaking just enough to piss him off. Had his brothers found Greg? Where was Cobb? He had to get the gun from Madison, but she was right in front of him for the first time, and he needed to ask. "Why me? Why did you leave me in New Orleans as a baby and have me later relocated to North Carolina? Why did you mess with my life at all?"

"Mess with your life? I *gave* you life, boy." Her gaze narrowed.

He rolled his eyes. "It's no coincidence that Heath, Denver, and I ended up at the same place being tested by you. That much I've figured out. So if we're different, and you and I both know we are, I have to think you know why." He went with a false question so as not to give anything away. "Are the three of us really related? Do we share a parent?"

She relaxed. "No. The three of you don't share anything but your creation. That was me and science and brilliance."

Zara made a sound behind him, and he shook his head. "How so?"

Madison's eyes glowed. "Test tubes, experiments, and really good genes. If there are extra abilities in men, and I believe there are, then I created you to have them. Right?"

He didn't answer her.

She settled her stance. "Tit for tat, young man. Right?"

He slowly nodded. "I'm smart, and my reflexes are very quick. Genetics?"

"Yes."

"Test tubes?" he asked slowly.

She smiled. "Yes. So many embryos, and most didn't survive. But you did, as did others. You might have biological brothers out there, but you, Heath, and Denver created your own bond, didn't you?"

If he could keep her talking, then one of his brothers would come up behind her as soon as they discovered this building. How many buildings were getting searched? If she was here, then she wasn't hiding Greg. So Ryker continue to play along, acknowledging that he needed answers. "Who were my biological parents?" He held his breath.

She sniffed. "Doesn't matter. I created you. I'm your parent."

"Biologically," he snapped.

"A soldier was your sperm donor—a truly gifted, brilliant, hard man. He died on a mission." Her lips turned down. "I believe your mother was a lost teenage whore with a shockingly high IQ. After giving birth to you, and taking our money, she was killed by a drug overdose." Madison held up a hand when he opened his mouth. "We did not kill her."

He swallowed. Unfortunately, his ability to discern the truth told him she was being honest. His parents, such that they were, no longer lived.

A part of him wished he could've saved his teenaged mother. Not his failure, but he still hurt for her. His chest ached, but not as badly as he would've expected. His brothers were his family, and that would never change, no matter how many new members they added. "Did my mother have other children?"

"Yes," Madison said. "I also harvested many of her eggs to use with other surrogates. You probably have half-brothers out there."

Zara pressed both her hands against his lower back in a gesture of pure comfort.

"Why are you telling me this?" he asked, his body flushing.

Madison shrugged. "Think about coming with me. I'm rebuilding my business, and you have a lot to offer. I can train you. Think of the advances we could make."

The woman was colder than ice and more calculating than the serial killer they were chasing. "You need to be put down," he muttered. "Your business?"

"Yes. More soldiers, more test tubes, more advances in science. In fact, I'll have a new lab ready in a matter of weeks, and I could use additional genetic material. What do you say?"

"Additional?" he coughed.

She smiled. "I still have some, young man. It's just been stored safely away, and soon I'll have the proper facility."

He shook his head. They'd have to take her out before she created anybody else. For now, he owed his brothers a chance to know their pasts. "What about Heath's and Denver's parents? What's the deal?"

She shook her head and glanced at her wristwatch. "They'll have to come in if they want answers. I've told you enough." She backed away, stepping outside into the snow.

He stepped toward her, and she lifted the barrel of the gun to his face. "Why? After the test tubes, why did you leave me at an orphanage?" he asked. She'd kept the Gray brothers, but she'd set him free. Why? He couldn't ask the entire question, because she didn't know he'd met up with Matt and Jory. "I'd think you'd want to keep your creations close."

She nodded. "All part of the experiment, I'm afraid. I had to see how you three boys—totally unrelated but created with superior genes—would interact and survive. You were *my* project. Just mine. You still are."

A roar of a motor echoed through the trees. Ryker tensed. He needed the bitch off balance and fast. "I killed Todd."

She nodded. "I know, but that's all right. He'd served his purpose, and frankly, his ideals were getting in my way. You did me a favor."

The woman had the heart of a snake. Ryker fought the urge to throw up. "I'm bringing you down, lady. Get ready."

"I'll be in touch, Ryker. This is by no means the end." She took another step back, keeping her aim steady and true.

The roar increased in pitch. Snow sprayed. A snowmobile rushed into sight with Sheriff Cobb on the back.

Hatred, raw and pure, poured through Ryker. He ran forward without thought, wanting to kill more than he wanted his next breath.

Madison fired, and he ducked as bullets pinged over his head. She jumped on the machine, swinging her arm around and continuing to fire.

Cobb gave him a hard look and mouthed the word "Soon" before twisting the throttle. The snowmobile jumped forward, and he drove it through a path between two large pine trees, heading away from the lodge.

Ryker launched into motion. "Stay here," he bellowed at Zara, lowering his head and running behind the snowmobile as fast as the thick snow would allow. He ran hard, branches slapping him, desperation spurring him on. The roar of rotors caught his attention. Sucking in air, he could hear several people behind him, also running fast.

He charged into a clearing just in time to see the door close on a black helicopter. It slowly rose into the air. Madison looked out a back window and gave him a little wave.

Matt burst through trees next to him and halted, breathing heavily.

Madison's eyes widened, and her lips formed the word "Matt." She smiled broadly.

"Fuck," Matt hissed. "Is Greg in there?"

Madison slowly nodded. "I have Greg," she mouthed very clearly. "See you soon." Then she held up a black box.

Ryker squinted. "Is that—"

The world exploded behind them as the lodge blew up with a devastating roar.

Jory ran through trees to the east with Heath and Denver on his heels, all crashing to the ground and rolling. "They got our helicopter, and the lodge just blew. I hot-wired an SUV. We have to go. Now."

Ryker turned just as Zara stumbled through the snow in bare feet toward him. He caught her.

"Greg?" she asked through purple lips.

Rage rushed through him so quickly he swayed. "No."

The helicopter pitched and dropped toward the ground. What the hell? Movement showed through the windows, and the nose dipped down. Greg came into view, fighting furiously with the pilot while hands grabbed him from behind.

Ryker and Matt launched into motion at the same time, running full bore for the landing skids. Ryker jumped on one while Matt caught the other. The helicopter swayed and spun. Ryker's wounded shoulder protested in agony. From the corner of his eye, he saw his other brothers crouching and taking aim. Nobody would fire with Greg in the aircraft.

Screaming came from inside.

The side door opened near Ryker. He pulled himself up...right into the barrel of a gun.

"No!" Greg yelled, shoving Madison to the back and then throwing himself at Ryker.

The kid hit him in the face, and Ryker let go of the door to clamp Greg in a bear hug, protecting him as he fell backward. They landed in the snow with a loud *thunk*.

Gunfire erupted around them, and he scrambled to cover the kid.

Matt landed over to his left and rolled, coming up already firing.

The helicopter banked a hard left and swerved out of the way, quickly rising into the sky. A frustrated scream came from within.

Ryker leaned back. "You okay?" he grunted, shaking snow from his eyes.

Greg, his eyes wide, nodded. "Yeah. You?"

"Yeah." Everything fucking hurt beyond belief, but nothing was broken. Zara skidded in the snow next to him, reaching for his head. "Are you all right? Both of you?" Tears were streaming down her face. "I love you. God, don't do anything like that again."

He smiled. Love. She loved him. Then he passed out cold.

CHAPTER
40

Ryker awoke with a jolt and sat up on a leather sofa. Mini stars detonated behind his eyes, and pain threw nausea into his gut. He groaned.

"You're all right." Zara sat next to him on a coffee table.

He blinked several times and sucked down air. "Where are we?" he croaked. Was there anybody he needed to fight?

"We're safe. A very nice safe house outside of Hot Springs that Heath said you guys own," she murmured, pushing hair back from his face.

He looked around a gathering room complete with plush furniture, smooth wood floors, and a climbing brick fireplace. "Oh yeah. South Dakota. I almost forgot I bought this place." He gingerly tapped a bump on his forehead. "Jesus. How long was I out?"

"Long enough," Matt said, striding in from the outdoors. He shook snow from his coat. "Where's Greg?" he asked Zara.

"Here." Greg loped in from the kitchen. "Hey, Ryker. You're alive."

Ryker nodded. "Somebody catch me up to speed, please."

Matt shoved snow out of his dark hair. "We loaded everyone up in the SUV and drove for about an hour until some of our men picked us up in a helicopter. They flew us here, and now we're waiting for the crew from Montana to show."

Ryker threaded his fingers through Zara's. "You okay, baby?" He should've asked that first thing.

She smiled, her pretty face still bruised but her eyes clear and sparkling. "I'm fine."

"Greg?" Ryker asked.

Greg grinned. "I landed on you, dude. I'm great."

Kids. Ryker studied Matt. "You're fine."

"Yep."

Wait a minute. "Where's—"

Matt kept his gaze. "Your Cisco offices and apartments are busted. Madison and Cobb know where they are, so you have to relocate."

"Madison lost more than half her Protect troops in the little battle we just fought," Ryker said evenly. "We had to have taken out some of her personal soldiers, too."

"Yep, but that doesn't mean she won't keep coming. And she's with Sheriff Cobb, so you have to vacate, brother." Matt eyed the softly falling snow outside. "We're the only ones left here. Our brothers went to move all of your stuff to a different location. Probably Montana."

"No." Ryker stood. "Not Montana. Not now."

Matt's jaw clenched. "We'll talk about it later."

The whir of helicopter rotors broke through the storm.

Greg paled. "They're here. My brothers. Um."

Ryker crossed the room to stand by the kid, taking Zara with him. "I'm taking it you called your brothers."

"Yes," Greg whispered. "Matt called them, and they jumped on another helicopter."

Ryker held him close. "They'll be so happy to see you." He eyed Matt. "What's the plan?"

Matt rubbed his chin. "We told the kids. Couldn't keep it a secret. So as soon as they arrive…"

Greg moved toward the wide patio doors, and Ryker stopped him with a hand on the shoulder. "Reunion happens inside, Greg. Just wait a couple of minutes."

Matt nodded. "I think the place is secure, but I agree. We all stay contained inside while we're here."

"It's my fault," Greg whispered, his gaze wide on the doors.

Ryker frowned. "What's your fault?"

"Failing on the mission. Getting left behind." Greg's voice cracked. "Having them think I'm dead. It's my fault."

"No," Matt said softly. "It was the commander and Dr. Madison's fault. Not yours. Your brothers won't blame you."

The pain radiating from the kid dug deep under Ryker's skin, and he moved closer to provide a shield, just in case.

"They should blame me," Greg said, his lips twisting in fear.

Snow scattered outside, and a helicopter dropped onto the field. A second later, the back door slid open, and a large kid leaped out into the snow and ran straight for the deck.

Greg breathed out heavily.

The door burst open, and the kid stood there, gray eyes, black hair, rigid jaw. His hands were clenched, and his chest heaved. He looked just like Matt. He stared at Greg. "Greg?" he whispered.

"Chance." Tears filled Greg's eyes.

Then they moved. Both kids leaped across furniture, catching each other like two bucks clashing horns. A table lamp smashed to the wood floor, scattering shards of glass.

"You're not dead." Chance laughed even while tears flowed down his hard face. "Shit, man, you're not dead." He hugged his brother. "God. Wade and Kyle." He turned, and two other boys ran into them, knocking them all over the couch onto the coffee table, which crashed down.

There was a flurry of hugs, laughs, and lots of tears, and more broken furniture.

Ryker grinned even as tears pricked the backs of his eyes.

"Should we help them?" Zara asked, her face wet, staring at all the broken glass.

Ryker shook his head. "Not in a million years. Let them break everything."

Two more men loped inside and stood next to Matt. Ryker's breath caught, and he studied them.

"Whoa," Zara whispered. "The second guy could be your twin."

Ryker nodded.

Matt cleared his throat. "Ryker? Meet Shane and Nate."

Nate. Ryker and Nate had very similar bone structure. Did they share genetic material? He moved across the room, taking Zara with him, and held out a hand.

Nate grinned and yanked him in for a hug. These guys sure liked to hug.

Ryker turned and nodded at Shane before peering closer. "Heath has the same birthmark below his left ear," he muttered.

Shane paled. "I need to track him down, then."

The enormity of Dr. Madison's experiments dropped onto Ryker's shoulders, and he steeled himself for a moment. How far had her studies gone?

It took nearly two hours and seven pizzas to calm everyone down and catch everyone up on Greg's life, Ryker's life, and the rest.

Finally, the boys headed for a bunk bed loft upstairs, and Zara excused herself for the master bedroom.

Ryker found himself in front of a crackling fire, bourbon in his hand, facing three men who could relate to his creation and past. "So," he said.

Nate just looked at him. "You sure are good looking."

Matt snorted.

Nate cleared his throat. "Ah, just to catch you up a little since there seems to be no doubt we're genetically linked. I married Dr. Madison's daughter, and she's pregnant."

Ryker's mouth dropped open.

Matt snorted. "Audrey is a sweetheart who's nothing like her mother. She's due in two months."

"You're gonna be an uncle," Nate said with a grin.

Ryker lifted his eyebrows. An uncle? He smiled. "Congratulations."

"Thanks." Nate sipped his glass.

Wow. Ryker tried to make sense of his past. "Heath just checked in. He finished helping in Cisco and then headed out to work on a case. I'm following him after I get Zara settled somewhere."

"Speaking of which—" Matt started.

"No." Ryker took a deep drink. "Not right now."

Nate lifted an eyebrow. "You two fighting already?"

"No," Ryker said, pausing when a figure paused at the bottom of the stairs.

Chance moved into the room, all grace, all young muscle, to reach Ryker. He held out a hand. "I'm Chance. I guess we're all family."

Ryker stood and studied the kid. He had gray eyes and Matt's jawline. What the hell. Ryker drew him in for a hug. "It seems like we all hug."

Chance hugged him back. "You get used to it. Sometimes they get a little girly, but what are you gonna do?" He leaned back. "Thank you for keeping Greg safe."

"He's family." Jesus. Now Ryker sounded like Matt.

Chance snorted. "He's good, too. Just asked if I was gonna give him some space or spoon him to sleep."

Ryker grinned. "Smart-ass."

"Yeah." Chance sobered. "He likes you, and he really likes your lady."

Ryker paused. "We like him, too."

"But he's coming to Montana and not staying with you. Period." Chance's gaze hardened, and he looked exactly like Jory.

Ryker slowly nodded. "Agreed." Based on the security measures he'd just heard about, the Montana ranch was the safest place for the kids, especially since Dr. Madison was still gunning for them.

"Maybe you should relocate there?" Chance said.

"I'm working on that," Matt chimed in.

"Good." Chance turned and headed for the stairs. "I think I'll go spoon the smart-ass." He disappeared.

Jory chuckled. "We may hear more furniture breaking soon."

Matt shrugged. "It's just furniture."

Ryker sat back down and swirled his drink in its glass. "First, I have to tell you that Madison said she has genetic material she's digging up to use in a new lab that's almost ready."

The men around him went still.

He winced. "Thought you should know." They had to stop her.

"We have to take her down," Matt breathed. "Fast."

"Yeah," Ryker said quietly. "Second, right now the kids are our top priority, and I know you agree with me."

Matt's brows drew down. "Sure. What's your point?"

"Madison and Cobb are coming for us as soon as they regroup, and as soon as we catch the serial killer Heath is chasing, I think it's time we went after them." Ryker sat back, calculating the odds. "I'm tired of running. Our company, Lost Bastards Investigative Services, finds lost people, and I want to put all of our resources into finding Cobb and ending this once and for all."

Shane leaned forward from an overstuffed chair, his elbows on his knees. "You can't do that from Montana?"

"No." He shook his head. "There's a chance we'll be discovered and they'll track us. You know that. We can't be located at your ultimate safe house at that time. It's too dangerous for the kids." He took a deep breath. "And your women, one of whom is pregnant." Plus, Denver and Heath still needed to trace their pasts before settling in a safe place. "I'm not saying no forever, but for now, it's too dangerous."

"Where will you be?" Jory asked while the other two remained silent.

"Somewhere safely away from Montana." Ryker finished his drink and stood.

Matt eyed him. "What's your plan with Zara?"

Ryker took a deep breath. "I'll let you know." He turned and headed across the living room toward the master bedroom.

"Good luck, man," Matt said. "She's one hell of a woman, jumping into the helicopter to save Greg like she did. He told us the whole story while you were out cold."

Ryker paused before opening the door. He turned around toward his new family. "I'm glad we found you guys." Without waiting for a response, he turned and opened the door, shutting it quietly behind himself.

Zara sat cross-legged on the bed, her phone by her side. Her long hair cascaded over her shoulder, and her pretty eyes showed intelligence and a softness he wanted to drown in forever. "What a day, huh?"

He grinned. "That's the understatement of the century."

"Yeah." She lifted her chin toward the phone. "Talked to Brock Hurst. He said he's my lawyer now and that charges have been dropped against me. Also, he's in love with a nurse." She smiled.

"He just met the nurse."

She shrugged. "Love happens quickly for some people. I told you he was a good guy."

"Yeah, you did." Ryker stalked across the room and set a knee on the bed. "I'm sorry you were taken."

She plucked at a loose thread on the dark bedspread. Her long black hair sat atop her head with tendrils spilling down, looking so damn feminine his chest hurt. Fresh bruises were scattered across her smooth skin but did nothing to detract from her beauty. Sitting there, so soft, she looked nearly fragile. "I wasn't exactly taken."

He crossed his arms. "I should throttle you for jumping out of a window and into a helicopter."

She grinned. "I had the phone, and I couldn't let them take Greg like that."

Ryker moved toward her. The woman was never going to take the safe route, but perhaps that worked for him. "My life is dangerous, and it's going to become more so before I fix everything. I totally understand if you want to take a break and wait for me to do what I have to do."

She lifted her face. "Which is?"

"Take down Cobb and Dr. Madison." It was the only solution at this point. If he wanted a normal life, if any of his brothers were ever going to have safe lives, it was time to stop running and hiding. "I thought I could keep going forward, but it's time to finish with the past."

"That makes sense," she murmured.

"But here's the whole story: I love you, Zara. Every single inch of you. If you stay with me, it's not gonna be easy, but I'll keep you safe." No matter what, he'd protect her, and he'd let all of his love show in the only way he knew how. "Either way, you and I end up together. That's a vow."

* * *

Zara studied the only man she'd ever love. Strong jaw, muscled body, tumultuous blue-green eyes that showed love. Real love. "If you think

I jumped into a helicopter just to go sit quietly in a corner now, you're crazy." She smiled. "I love you, Ryker Jones. No matter what we have to do, I'm with you the entire time."

He stretched over her, flattening her to the bed. "I'm not sure where we're going next, but we have to leave Cisco."

She nodded and then paused. "What about Grams?"

"Well, I was thinking she might like to relocate to Montana for a little while." Ryker smoothed tendrils away from Zara's face, his touch beyond gentle. "It sounds like the kids have a few grandparents already, and I know she'd be a huge help. In case we need to run again, I'd rather she was already somewhere safe."

"I'll ask her what she wants to do," Zara said, glancing down at his lips. "I'm sure she'd love Montana."

Ryker wandered his lips over hers, sending all sorts of electric jolts through her body. "I'm tired of taking things slow and being so cautious. It's time to jump in with both feet, baby." His breath heated her mouth.

She breathed out and wiggled her butt to get more comfortable, rubbing against his obvious erection. "With both feet?" she asked.

"Marry me."

She blinked. Her rambling rebel had just used forever words. "What?" she whispered.

"Marry me. Take my name, be my wife, promise eternity." He kissed her, long and deep, so much emotion in his touch she felt him deep inside. Finally, he released her mouth. "Well?"

She blinked again. "I never thought to hear those words from you."

"You're the only woman I'd ever say them to," he said, his eyes swimming. "We suddenly have family around, a lot of it, and now at least I know where I came from. The past is gone, and I have a future, and I want it with you. Only you."

Her heart expanded until she could barely breathe. "Ryker."

He grinned. "Well? Marry me." It wasn't even remotely worded as a question.

She looked into those dangerous eyes and saw her future. Her very good, surrounded by family, slightly wild...future. "Yes."

Dear Reader,

My editor (the amazing Michele) and I brainstormed extra content to add to this new book, and we realized that the moment of Zara and Ryker meeting might be an intriguing scene. When DEADLY SILENCE opens, the characters had been dating (kind of) for a couple of months. So I wrote the scene from Zara's point of view. Can you imagine going about your normal day and having motorcycle-riding, hard-bodied, badass Ryker Jones striding into your place of work? It was a fun scene to write, and I hope you like it!

The other additional scene is one we actually deleted from the book because it wasn't necessary for Zara and Ryker's romance. The scene features Heath Jones, Ryker's brother, and FBI special agent Loretta Jackson. They're both working toward a common goal, but they don't trust each other and yet are willing to go beyond that to catch the bad guy. It's a scene where Jackson's sister, Anya, is also introduced to the reader. Anya has a tough past and is struggling to survive, and I think that shows in her small part here. You'll see a lot more of Anya and Heath in *Lethal Lies*, the next book in the Blood Brothers series. The first chapter of their book is also included in the back of this book.

Speaking of the Blood Brothers series, this is a spin-off of the Sin Brothers series, which features those wild Dean brothers. If you liked the Sin Brothers, I think you'll enjoy seeing those boys again—and that evil Dr. Madison is all over this series. The Blood Brothers series stands on its own, however. So even if you didn't read the first series, you'll still be totally caught up on page one with Ryker and Zara.

For more deleted scenes and extra content, definitely

subscribe to my newsletter. There's a huge newsletter logo on the front page of my website where you can click and join. My website is: www.RebeccaZanetti.com. You can also find me on Facebook at: Rebecca Zanetti—Author.

Thanks for reading!
XOXOXO

Rebecca

EXTRA SCENE FOR *DEADLY SILENCE*
WHEN ZARA MET RYKER

Zara Remington organized piles of papers across the mahogany conference table at the law office, humming softly to herself. The song was from a movie she'd watched on Friday night—alone at home in her jammies. As usual.

"Excuse me." The voice, dark and rich, jerked her right out of her thoughts.

She looked toward the doorway, and the spit dried in her mouth. She may have nodded but probably not.

The man—and he was *all* man—smiled, his gaze not leaving her face but somehow seeming to check her out from head to toe. "Sorry to startle you."

She felt her mouth dropping open, all the way, and she hurriedly snapped her lips together. She cleared her throat. "No problem." Hell. Her voice sounded breathy, like she'd been kissing somebody for an hour or three. Not just somebody. The hottie at the door. What in the world was wrong with her?

He blinked and a slow smile lifted his full lips.

Her body shot into overdrive, and she returned the smile. The man stood well over six feet and wore a battered leather jacket and worn jeans over motorcycle boots. His hair was dark, his eyes a mix of blue and green, and his jaw covered with stubble. A dark T-shirt stretched over a tight torso with relaxed muscles beneath. "Can I help you?" she whispered.

His head tilted just a touch, and those sharp eyes softened.

As did her thighs.

"Call me Ryker," he said, his voice a low rumble as he moved to the other side of the table. "I'm supposed to meet Brock here."

Ah. The guy must be the private detective Brock had just hired. Zara was a paralegal who worked often with Brock, one of the junior attorneys. A ruckus sounded behind Ryker, and he partially turned.

Leroy Jarods stomped into the room, his face a mottled red and his hands clenched into fists. "Where the fuck is my attorney?" he spat.

Zara sucked in air and set down the papers. Her heartbeat increased. The disgruntled ex-client hadn't harassed them in nearly two months, and she'd almost forgotten about the guy. "Mr. Jarods, you're not supposed to be within five hundred feet of the law firm." She spoke clearly and edged toward a phone on the back counter.

Leroy snarled. "I want to see that piss-ass dickhead, and I mean right now." He took a step toward her.

Ryker moved suddenly, beyond quickly, and grabbed Leroy by the scruff of the neck. With a whisper of sound, he pivoted and shoved Leroy face first into the wall. "Care to explain, darlin'?" he asked, glancing over his shoulder.

Fast. Fast and dangerous. Zara straightened, more than a little intrigued. "Angry ex-client who's breaking the law right now." Brock had looked at the guy's case and returned his retainer upon learning he was stalking his ex-wife, and Leroy had made threatening phone calls and shown up to harass people at the law firm before they'd obtained a protection order. "I'll call the police."

"No need." A uniformed officer strode into the room. "Your receptionist called us, and we were just down the street." He quickly handcuffed Leroy and jerked him from the room. "We have a situation downtown but will be back to get your statements later."

The tension in the room dissipated as they disappeared.

Ryker turned and grinned again. "Well. I guess we just went through a situation and bonded, right?"

Was he flirting with her? It had been so long, she wasn't sure. "Right. You had it handled too quickly to become a situation." The guy was beyond tough and way too rough.

He lifted a muscled shoulder. "Fair enough. Your name?"

"Zara," she said quietly.

"Zara," he repeated, rolling the sound around on his tongue. "Pretty."

Heat climbed into her cheeks.

"So, Zara. What do you do for fun in this town?" he asked.

Watch television? She'd been thinking about getting a goldfish just for company. "Not much."

"We'll have to change that. Dinner tonight?"

So direct, and, man, was she tempted. "Ah."

"I'm here only for this case, and it'd be nice to see some of the town. Of course, we could always just stay in." The innuendo and promise in his expression weakened her knees.

She took a deep breath. Maybe it was time she had some fun and adventure. The guy would be in town only for a bit, and then he'd be gone. He certainly wasn't the staying kind. But something told her he'd be worth several intense memories. "Dinner sounds nice." What was she thinking? Oh yeah. That body.

Brock strode into the room. "Good. You two have met. You'll be working closely together on this case."

Ryker's smile widened. "Isn't that nice?"

DELETED SCENE
HEATH AND SPECIAL AGENT JACKSON

Heath waited outside the agent's hotel room, taking in the scene and memorizing the layout of the little hotel in the middle of nowhere in northern Utah. The plane ride had taken less than an hour, and after renting a car, he'd arrived easily despite the winter storm.

Snow floated down, and he tracked the vehicles in the wide lot. Three were rentals, two were full of stuff for college dorms, and two had out-of-state plates—probably just passing through. The cold chilled his neck, but he ignored it.

He'd arrived midmorning, so perhaps most people were checking out soon.

Striding across the lot, his boots left prints in the snow. He knocked on the door to room 10.

It opened, and Special Agent Jackson pointed a gun at his head. "I've been watching you scout the place, and I'm thinking you might be into killing redheads," she said, her hand steady and her legs braced.

"You're not a real redhead." He'd purposefully let her see him; otherwise, he wouldn't have hung out in the cold for so long. He leaned slightly to the side. The woman had nice legs. "I like you in yoga pants."

She blinked. "Give me one reason I shouldn't just shoot you right now."

He stuck his hands into his jeans pockets and tried to remain calm.

Why were they wasting time? The killer had probably already found another victim. "You know I'm not the killer. Geez."

"Oh, do I?" she asked, her brown eyes spitting.

"Yep. I was with you when the third victim was taken, and I was with you during the fifth victim's time of death," he said easily, wanting to shake her but knowing better. "Come on, Loretta. You know I want to catch this guy as badly as you do."

"I doubt that." She lowered her gun. "I'm still thinking shooting you is a good idea."

"I get that a lot." He grinned and drew a manila file folder from beneath his leather jacket, knowing instinctively how to gain her cooperation. "How about we trade info? We're good at what we do, and I think we could help you."

She shoved her wild hair back from her face—wild red hair. "The FBI doesn't work with civilians."

"The red is pretty," he mused, "but I liked you better as a brunette. Do you think he'll go for it?"

"We're hoping, but the plan doesn't start until tomorrow in Salt Lake." Loretta stepped back and opened the door wider. "I would like to know how you found me. I'm here under a fake name and even my FBI buddies don't know where."

"I told you. We're good at what we do." He stepped into the room, surprised to find it was a suite. A closed door to the right must lead to the bedroom, and he stood in a nice living area with a log fire crackling. Papers and manila files were scattered all over the sofa and coffee table. "This is nice."

She nodded. "I needed someplace out of the way to think, and I have a detail on my house because of…" She tugged on the red hair.

"You're not his MO," Heath said quietly, oddly glad of that fact. He was angry enough with the killer without actually knowing one of the victims, and there was something sweet, tough, and likable about Special Agent Jackson.

"I know, but I'm visible, and it's a chance we're willing to take." She shut the door behind him and held out a hand. "File."

He handed it over and moved to the sofa to sit, wincing at pictures of the last crime scene spread out on the table.

"Ryker was there, not you," Loretta said. "I wondered why."

Heath took the picture and turned it to see the dead girl's pretty face. His gut twisted. "The guys think I'm getting too close to the case—it's eating at me. They insisted I sit the last one out." How shitty was it that there were so many crime scenes to go around? His fingers clenched. No way would he sit one out again.

"I get that." Loretta flipped through his file, her eyes widening. "Whoa. You traced every second of the three months leading up to Maisey's abduction. We don't have every second."

Heath pushed the picture aside for a list of commonality between the victims. "I figured we could compare it to what you've compiled on the other victims and see what we come up with."

"Okay." Loretta shoved papers onto the floor and dropped into a chair, her voice frustrated. "Although we know how he picks them."

"Yeah." Heath could share her frustration. "He researches law-enforcement-type people and goes after redheads in their lives."

The bedroom door opened. "Loretta, I—"

Heath blinked, and everything in him froze.

A woman stood there hesitantly, bruises across her face and down her neck. She wore an oversize sweatshirt, but he could see bruises on her wrists. "Oh, sorry," she breathed, taking a step back.

Heat roared through Heath so quickly his ears burned. His gaze slashed to Loretta's and he half rose.

She leaned back in the chair, her eyes widening. "Whoa. Easy there, buddy. I didn't hurt her."

Calm. He needed to calm the fuck down. "Who did?" he ground out.

Loretta blinked and narrowed her focus on him, her hand inching slightly toward the gun at her waist. "Sit back down."

"No." He stood and remained on one side of the sofa, turning to the woman. "Who hurt you, darlin'?" His tone came out low and smooth, just like when he'd worked with horses for a brief time.

The woman paused. "Um, Loretta?"

Now that Heath had calmed a little, he could see a resemblance between the women. Same straight nose and fine jawline, but the injured one had crystal-clear green eyes. Puffy and blackened but definitely pure green. And her hair was a natural auburn, a darker red than Loretta's current style.

Loretta smiled. "We're just working, Anya."

"Oh." The woman fluttered her hands together. "Sorry."

"Don't be sorry," Heath said, fighting every urge he had to jump over the sofa and shield her.

Anya backed away and shut the door quietly.

Heath turned on Loretta. "What the fuck?"

The agent stared at him. "Mind your own business."

Heath pointed at the closed door. "If you're not taking care of the guy who did that, then I am. Give me his fuckin' name."

"Two f-words in the span of ten seconds," Loretta drawled, her brown eyes sparking. "You've forgotten the gentlemanly charm, Heath."

He paused. "She's your sister. I can see the resemblance."

"Half-sister." Loretta gestured him back down.

He sat, his blood still racing through his veins. "She has red hair. Real red hair." Good God, the sister was a sitting duck. He started to push again from the sofa. "I'll take her and hide her out. Then you're going undercover with us."

Loretta's mouth gaped. "Heath, I'm an FBI agent, for Christ's sake. Do you really think I can't protect my own sister or run my own op?"

Obviously she hadn't taken care of Anya, but he bit back a scathing response. "What's the plan?"

Loretta sighed. "Marshals are coming in about an hour to take her into custody and squire her somewhere safe. Then my op starts tomorrow in Salt Lake, and hopefully the asshole butcher will make an attempt on me and we can grab the bastard."

Heath's chest settled. If the Marshals were coming, he had to get out of there and now. While he wasn't sure if Cobb had reached out for assistance, he couldn't take the chance. "Tell me you've buried the asshole who hit her."

"I'm still working on that," Loretta drawled, looking at his file.

He shook his head. "I don't get it."

"What?" The agent looked up, her smooth brow crinkling.

"You've purposefully put yourself in the spotlight for the killer. Your sister has red hair, damn it." His voice lowered to a growl at the end.

Loretta scrubbed both hands down her face. "Yeah. I noticed." Her tone lagged...and sounded sad.

Heath frowned. "You didn't know?"

"No." Loretta swung her arms out. "You barely know me, but do I seem like the type of person who'd put a family member in danger?"

"No." He could be fair, and suddenly he felt shame. "I'm sorry."

She nodded. "All right. Let's just say that my upbringing wasn't normal, and I had no clue I had a sister until three days ago, when she saw me on the news. She's only twenty-five—ten years younger than me." She paused. "I'm not talking about this with you."

Heath glanced at his watch. His breath heated. The Marshals would be there soon. "I have only thirty minutes until I have to head back to the airport. We're working on a couple of cases." He took out a business card and flipped it onto the table. "You need to keep in touch about the Salt Lake op." He paused. "And if your sister needs help, let me know."

Loretta shook her head. "Man, you have issues."

"No shit, Loretta." He looked at the files. "Let's see how much you can share in thirty minutes."

Anya Best won't rest until the serial killer who murdered her sister is caught. And she'll do absolutely anything to take him down—even offer herself up as bait to lure him in.

FBI Agent Heath Jones works alone. The last thing he wants is to babysit the beautiful—and infuriating—woman who has inserted herself into *his* investigation, no matter how irresistible he finds her. But it's soon clear that the Copper Killer won't rest until Anya is his prized possession. And Heath will do anything to keep her safe—even risk his own life...

A PREVIEW OF *LETHAL LIES* FOLLOWS.

CHAPTER
1

A flash of red caught Heath's eye as he was about to shut down the computer. He sat back down and squinted at the center monitor on the makeshift desk. Damn it. His instincts humming, he maneuvered the jewelry store camera he'd hacked until the red bloomed into shimmering highlights beneath the weakened sun. Son of a bitch. What the hell was she doing there?

He rapidly tapped keys to scan the street with a multitude of cameras—some he'd hacked and others he'd planted. "Anya," he muttered, shaking his head.

She drew a black wool coat tighter around her slender figure, stopping directly in front of the door to his former, short-lived detective agency. Drawing a card from her pocket, she read it and glanced at the now-scraped-clean window. Her shoulders hunched, and a winter wind lifted her hair.

"Go away, Anya," Heath whispered to the computer monitor, his body tensing.

She frowned and looked around the quiet street before pressing her face to the glass and cupping her eyes.

"It's empty." Heath punched up the camera feed from above the door, which he hadn't wanted to use, just in case others were surveying the area. It'd let out a signal they'd find at some point. But now he had no choice.

She backed away from the window and read the card again.

Heath zoomed in on her face. Delicate bone structure, green eyes, pale skin, and dark red hair. Oh yeah. And a black eye and bruises down her neck. They had faded since he'd last seen her—the only time he'd ever met her—but they were still visible.

Seeing them again pricked his temper just like last time.

A black sedan pulled to the curb, and two men jumped out, spraying snow.

Fuck. He'd known they were still watching the building. Heath reached for a Glock on the desk and tucked it into his waistband. He was three blocks down from the detective agency and could be there in minutes.

If necessary.

He turned up the volume on the camera.

"Can I help you, miss?" The first guy had brown eyes and wavy dark hair. His smile was charming, and he walked like he could handle himself. A jacket covered his large frame, and a slight bulge showed at his waist.

Anya turned and took a step backward. "Um, I'm looking for the detective agency that was here last week." Her voice was low and tentative.

The guy looked at the blank window. "I think they moved."

She nodded, her gaze darting down the street. "The inside is empty."

The other man, a shorter black guy with adult acne, gave her a frown. "Do you know the detectives?"

She shook her head, her eyes wide. "Not really. But I heard they were well trained, and I need a detective."

The first guy smiled again, seeming to relax back against his car while motioning his buddy to cool it. The guy was good. "I've heard excellent things about them, too. Who did you talk to about them?"

Anya frowned as if knowing something wasn't quite right but unsure what. "Who are you?" Her chin lifted.

"Oh, I'm sorry." The guy laughed and dug out a badge holder to flip open. "U.S. Marshal D.J. Smithers. We're trying to find the detectives in connection with a current case."

Anya's eyes widened. "I hadn't known they worked with the FBI. I'm so glad. Do you have any idea where they've gone? Why they've left?"

Fuck. Heath groaned. The badge was a good one, but even through the camera he could see it was fake. Anya's sister was FBI Special Agent Loretta Jackson, and she'd been kidnapped by a serial killer nearly five days ago.

Smithers didn't miss a beat. "No, we don't. In fact, we're concerned about them. It looks like they've gotten caught up in a dangerous case with Colombian drug cartels, and we're concerned for their safety."

Colombian drug Cartels? Seriously? Who the hell was this guy? Heath groaned and fought the urge to palm-smack his own head.

Anya rushed for him, waving the card. "I need to find them as soon as possible. I'll give you my information, and if you find them, please let me know."

Smithers handed over his badge. "Do you remember the name of their agency or any of the detectives?"

Anya glanced at his badge and then handed it back. "Um, no. Sorry about that. I met one of them, but I don't remember his name."

Heath winced. Guess he hadn't been that memorable. Of course, he'd only exchanged pleasantries with her before sitting down with Agent Jackson and exchanging information. Anya was supposed to be in protective custody by now, but with her sister taken, maybe that plan had been scrapped?

Smithers reached into his back pocket for a pen and handed it over with the card. "Write down your name and cell phone number." His tone was perfectly authoritative and polite.

Who was this guy?

Anya nodded and quickly wrote before handing back the card.

Smithers tucked it into his pocket. "We're investigating at the moment but would like to sit down with you later. Where are you staying?"

"At the Two Horse Motel just for the night," Anya said.

Heath gave in to the desire and smacked his hand against his forehead. Of course the woman had no idea she was dealing with trained killers, and one did have a badge, but even so. Though she must be desperate to find her sister.

"Okay," Smithers said. "Can we offer any assistance with your case? We're happy to help."

She faltered. "Maybe. How about we talk about it when we sit down? I'll get my files in order."

"Sounds good. We'll be in touch later today." With a reassuring nod, he moved back toward the car and the two men quickly drove away.

Heath sighed. Why hadn't she mentioned the FBI or her sister missing? Perhaps Anya had sensed something wrong with the guys, since they definitely weren't with any government. Today, anyway. They'd do a background run on Anya and then decide what to do with her—or come up with a plan to nab her. He couldn't take the chance they'd want to question her more about the guy she couldn't remember, considering it was him.

He glanced around the abandoned office he'd been using for a few days to see who came to check out his and his brothers' former business. Surveillance photos and videos lined the table, and he quickly scooped them up. There wasn't anything else for him to do in Cisco, and it was time to get the hell out of town.

After he picked up Anya.

* * *

Anya paced the counter of the car rental facility and tapped her paperwork against her leg. Why the hell was it taking so long? The blond kid behind the counter hummed while he typed happily on a keyboard.

There wasn't time for humming. Those fake Marshals would've noticed her rental car decal, and she had to get rid of the car. She looked through the thick glass doors to the quiet car lot outside. Dark clouds barreled across the sky, and sleet slashed down. So much for the meager sunshine of earlier.

"All righty." The kid shoved glasses up his nose and smiled. "You're all set, and I waived the fuel fee."

"Thank you." She shoved the papers into her purse. Her phone buzzed, and she took it out to read the screen. Another message from her sister's partner, Special Agent Frederick Reese. The guy hadn't stopped calling since she'd headed out on her own the night before. She ignored him again and glanced up at the blond. "When will the airport shuttle arrive?"

The kid's Adam's apple bobbed. "Every hour. So it should be here in about fifteen minutes."

"Thanks." She forced a smile for him and then hurried for the door. "I'll wait by the sign."

"Sure thing." The worker followed her outside and locked the door behind her. "We close at five, and you were our only return today." He gave her a nod and strode around the building, minutes later roaring out of the lot in a lifted Ford with flames down the sides.

She grinned. Not in a million years had she pictured the guy wearing khakis and a button-down in such a flamboyant truck. Clearing her throat, she leaned back against the building, allowing the awning to protect her from the storm.

A heartbeat later, her stomach dropped as a familiar dark sedan pulled into the lot. Her legs tensed to run, but Marshal Smithers waved from the driver's seat.

She faked another smile, trapped in place. Her stomach rolled over.

An engine rumbled in the distance, and a battered Chevy truck careened across the lot, smashing hard into the sedan.

The sedan collided with several cars, and metal crumpled with a loud crunch.

The truck swung around, and the passenger door was thrown open. "Get in," bellowed a low voice.

She blinked at seeing Heath Jones, the detective from Lost Bastards. Her knees wobbled. D.J. Smithers jumped out of the totaled car, a gun in his hand. Her instincts told her she had about two seconds, so she yelped and ran across the snow, leaped through the passenger side of the truck, and slammed the door.

Heath punched the gas, and the truck fishtailed as it roared out of the lot.

Bullets struck the side of the truck with an odd pattering sound.

"Get down." Heath grabbed her neck and shoved her down, sliding down in the seat too but not losing any speed. His hand was rough and his voice tense, but he didn't hurt her.

She blinked, her heart thundering. The glove box slammed open, and a gun dropped onto her knee. She grabbed it and held on tight.

The truck fishtailed around a corner and then several more. Finally, Heath released her neck. "Are you okay?"

She nodded and straightened up on the bench seat. Her ribs hurt from the rapid beating of her heart. "How?" She looked out the back window at an empty and snowy road.

Heath glanced her way. "How what?"

She swallowed and surveyed him. At least six foot four, tightly muscled, definitely strong and fast. Light brown hair waved over his collar, and his greenish brown eyes pierced right through her. While the fake Marshals had been shooting guns, there was no doubt this guy was twice as dangerous. What had she done, jumping into his truck? "Um." She fumbled for the door handle.

"I'm driving too fast for you to jump out." He kept his broad hands on the steering wheel.

She blinked, and her shoulders trembled. "Why are you here?" she breathed.

His frown drew down his dark eyebrows. "Me? Why the hell are you here?"

Okay. So he wasn't happy to see her. "Listen. I was looking through my sister's things and found the Lost Bastards card, and I remembered meeting you the other week, so I thought I'd track you down and see if you were still looking for the Copper Killer." The words burst out of her in a rush. Damn it. She needed to seem in control and calm.

"Oh." His full lips tightened.

"Why were those men shooting at you?" she whispered, her mind reeling.

Heath glanced her way again. "They were shooting at you, darlin'. Chasing you."

She leaned her head back. That was true. "Why?" God. Were they somehow working for her ex? Would he send men with guns to bring her back? "Wait a minute." Her mind ran through likely scenarios. "I first met them at your former offices. They were looking for you, not me."

Heath's upper lip twitched.

She watched, not wanting to be fascinated. Then irritation took over. "You're a jerk."

He shrugged. "You're right. I'm sorry."

God, this was getting too damn confusing, and she was having trouble breathing from the fear of losing the sister she'd just found. "Why are those fake cops chasing you and now me?"

He looked at her again, really looked this time. "How did you know they were fake?"

"I didn't until I took a good look at one of the badges." Plus, her instincts were fairly decent at knowing when a man was lying to her. "There was something not quite right about them."

Admiration glimmered in Heath's stunning eyes for a moment. "Nicely done. So they followed you?"

"I guess." She sighed, warmed by his gaze. "I lied and told them I was staying at a motel, but apparently they didn't believe me. I also gave them a fake name and number." She eyed the snowy trees flashing by outside. "Why are they after you, Heath?"

"So you do remember my name," he murmured.

She frowned. "Sure."

"They're after me because of a different case of your sister's, and you don't have to worry about it." He turned down another road. "Since you were waiting for the shuttle, I'm assuming you have a plane ticket out of here?"

"Yeah. Back to Salt Lake City, where the FBI has a command center looking for Loretta." Just saying her sister's name made her gut ache.

"Okay. I'll drop you off, and you go right through security and get to your gate. The fake cops won't follow you." Heath's phone buzzed, and he glanced at the screen, his body tightening.

"What?" she breathed.

He looked at her, obviously weighing his words. "We have a lead on your sister. I have to go."

Hope exploded in her chest. "Not without me going."

He shook his head. "It's dangerous. I'll check in with you the second I know anything."

She sucked in air and pointed the gun at him. Not once in her life had she even held a gun in her hand much less threatened somebody with one. But she would find her sister, damn it. "I said we're going together."

NEXT IN *NEW YORK TIMES* AND *USA TODAY* BESTSELLING AUTHOR REBECCA ZANETTI'S BLOOD BROTHERS SERIES!

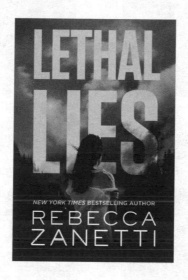

WHEN LOVE BLOOMS UNDER THE WATCHFUL EYE OF A SERIAL KILLER, FBI AGENT HEATH JONES HAS ONLY TWO OPTIONS: SAVE THE WOMAN OF HIS DREAMS OR DIE TRYING.

AVAILABLE IN SPRING 2017!

CHECK OUT *NEW YORK TIMES* BESTSELLING AUTHOR REBECCA ZANETTI'S SEXY SIN BROTHERS SERIES.

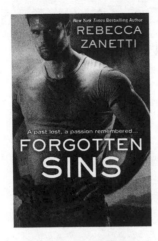

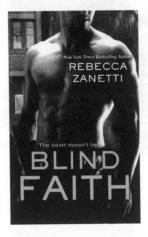

"Top Pick! 4½ stars! Bravo and thanks to Zanetti for providing stellar entertainment!"

—*RT Book Reviews* on *Total Surrender*

"Action packed, thrilling, and heart-stopping romantic suspense at its best."

—Harlequinjunkie.com on *Total Surrender*